Annie Nelles Dumond

Annie Nelles

The Life of a Book Agent - An Autobiography

Annie Nelles Dumond

Annie Nelles
The Life of a Book Agent - An Autobiography

ISBN/EAN: 9783337028428

Printed in Europe, USA, Canada, Australia, Japan

Cover: Foto ©Raphael Reischuk / pixelio.de

More available books at **www.hansebooks.com**

ANNIE NELLES;

OR,

The Life of a Book Agent.

AN AUTOBIOGRAPHY.

———◆———

CINCINNATI:
PUBLISHED BY THE AUTHOR.
1868.

TO THE

BOOK AGENTS OF AMERICA

THIS BOOK IS

RESPECTFULLY DEDICATED.

By THE AUTHOR.

PREFACE.

THERE are several motives which have actuated me in the preparation of the following sketch; among the first of which may be mentioned a sincere desire to serve the public, by warning them against the many errors I have committed. A calm, quiet review of my life, discloses the fact that, in many instances, my conduct has been influenced by passion alone, and that the consequences flowing therefrom have, in every instance, proven to be the most painful. To enable the young and inexperienced to avoid, as far as possible, the rocks and shoals upon which my bark made shipwreck, is one of the objects of this publication.

Another object is, that the world may be informed, so far as is in my power, of the real character of those (many of whom are still living, and will read this work) who have so foully wronged and ill-treated me. I say this in no spirit of revenge—that is a feeling which has long since died out in my bosom—but because I regard it as a matter of duty, not only to myself, but to those with whom they may be hereafter brought in contact. The world is full enough of misery and sorrow, caused by man's treachery and wrong; and if I can in any degree, however small, check this torrent, I shall feel myself abundantly repaid for all the time and labor the effort may cost me.

That the present work contains many errors and inaccuracies of language, is undoubtedly true; but, of one thing the reader may be assured: the main incidents therein described, are actually and literally true. The following pages are a faithful and correct record of the leading incidents of my life, and are freely given to the public for the reasons and motives above indicated. I have confined myself strictly to facts, and have not "extenuated, or aught set down in malice."

One word in relation to the style of the work. If any one should be disposed to charge that it is any degree egotistical, I beg them to remember that that is a difficulty which, to a certain extent, inheres in a work of this character, and which it seems almost impossible to avoid in any autobiography. The writer who gives to the public his own life, must necessarily speak principally of himself; and while this would in no sense condemn the work with the more intelligent and thinking classes, still there are some who will doubtless read the book and find fault with it for this reason, if for no other. To such I offer the explanation above given, and entreat them not to condemn the work until they have tried, and ascertained from their own experience, how difficult it is to write one's own life without speaking of one's self.

With all its faults and errors, and in the humble hope that it will be kindly received and tenderly judged, the work is submitted to a generous and discriminating public, by

THE AUTHOR.

La Porte, Ind., September, 1867.

CONTENTS.

CONTENTS. ix

CHAPTER XIV.

CHAPTER XV.

CHAPTER XVI.

CHAPTER XVII.

CHAPTER XVIII.

CHAPTER XIX.

CHAPTER XX.

CHAPTER XXI.

CHAPTER XXII.

CHAPTER XXIII.

CHAPTER XXIV.

CHAPTER XXV.

CHAPTER XXVI.

CHAPTER XXVII.

ANNIE NELLES;

OR,

THE LIFE OF A BOOK AGENT.

CHAPTER I.

ANOTHER wretched, dreary, rainy day. It really seems as though the god of the weather had a spite against me. For the last week it has rained almost constantly, and I have consequently been unable to prosecute my business with anything like success. Last evening I thought the rain was over, and that we were going to have pleasant weather, but the first sound which caught my ears upon awakening this morning, was the rain beating and dashing against my window. And still the dreary, monotonous patter, patter, of the falling torrents goes on, without the least prospect of cessation. And then the mud in the streets! It is almost unfathomable, and is getting worse every moment. Ugh! it makes me shudder to think of going out to canvass for subscribers to-day. I can not do it.

And yet, what is to become of me if I do not? I can not live unless I work, or unless I do better than I have thus far. I have sold but one book this week, and only made one dollar profit on that. I have to pay six dollars per week for my board, and have nothing to pay with. Ah! poor Book Agents! They have a hard time of it. Certain am I that they earn every cent they get. Here am I without a cent to pay my board, or even post a letter, and no prospect of being able to do anything for—the Lord only knows how long. Were it not for my two precious babes, I should almost give up in despair of ever accomplishing anything.

My weekly board bill is due to-day, and how to meet it I do not know. I pawned my furs for money to pay my last board bill, and now I have nothing that I can spare— Oh! yes, there is my watch—Gussie's watch—but how can I part with that? Dear Gussie! Little did I think when, in happy days long since past, you gave me this precious keepsake, that I should ever be driven to part with it. But I must. Stern necessity knows no law, and there is no help for it. One by one all my little treasures—bright mementos of happier days—have gone to enable me to keep life in my wretched frame, and appease the demands of hunger; and now this last token of affection—this priceless gift, which I thought to keep till my dying day, must go as all the others have done. But it is useless to spend time in vain repining—so, away through rain and mud and storm, for the pawn-broker's.

It is a dismal, gloomy-looking den. Its rough exterior, innocent of paint, and narrow, low entrance, seem to frown ominously at one, and warn me not to seek an entrance. But my wretched fortune drives me to it, and after a moment's hesitation I enter the forbidding portal, while a shudder of agony, at the thought of what I am about to do, involuntarily runs through my frame. Once inside, I am compelled to wait until my eyes become accustomed to the dim light which enters the dingy apartment through windows covered with cobwebs, and begrimed with the dirt of years, before I can venture to transact any business. As my eyes become able to penetrate more distinctly the gloom which pervades the place, I discover a gloomy, heartless-looking old man, in whose soul the last spark of humanity seems to have been long since crushed out by the hard and spirit-blighting avocation he is pursuing. Hesitatingly and timidly I approached the old man, and laid my priceless treasure on the counter before him.

"Sir, what will you loan me on this watch and chain," I said in a choking voice. "I will redeem it in a month. It is a precious keepsake—the gift of a very dear friend—and I would not lose it for ten times its value."

"Madam, I yoost gives you ten dollar. I no like to take him; he not much vort—him not much sale," said the old man, turning over in his hands and carefully examining my treasure.

"Oh! sir, the watch alone is worth fifty dollars, and the chain cost twenty-five but a year ago."

"Vell, madam, such t'ings be not much sale—him be not much vort; me no got much monish to spare, but I gives you twelf dollar. Dat ish more as him ish vort, but I gives you dat."

"Oh! sir, I can not take it. Twelve dollars for a watch and chain worth at least seventy-five!—a treasure with which I would not part for five times that amount. You can certainly give me more than that."

"Vell, madam, I gives you feefsain dollar. Dat ish too much—dat ish much more as him ish vort—but I gives you dat, and not one cent more."

"Sir, I accept your offer. Give me the fifteen dollars and make out my ticket. I will redeem it in a month from this time."

"Was ish de name?"

"S. A. Nelles."

The old man gave me my ticket, handed me fifteen dollars in bank-notes, and thus was the sacrifice completed. Turning from this den of darkness, almost choked with the violence of my emotions at parting with the treasure which was so highly prized on account of the precious memories clustering around it, I again sought my boarding-house. My mind was so much preoccupied with the contemplation of my wretched condition that I scarcely noticed that my feet were soaking wet, until my eyes, falling upon the well-filled show-window of a large shoe store, reminded me that my shoes were full of holes, and utterly unfit to wear in the prosecution of my canvassing during such weather. I hesitated a short time, and then, entering the store, asked for some stout shoes. The accommodating salesman showed me some, and I selected a good pair, for which I paid three dollars, and again set out. Reaching my boarding-house I went at once to my room, and sat down to muse over my situation and prospects.

I was now in possession of twelve dollars—enough to pay my board in my present quarters for two weeks: when that was gone, unless my business improved very much, what would become of me? How could I live on one dollar a week—all that my utmost efforts had been able to earn during the last week? And still the rain continues to pour down; still I sit in forced idleness in my lonely room; and still my mind is dreamily contemplating my present and past, and speculating of the future. The past! ah! the sorrowful past! It is full of grief and bitterness; all marred and scarred over with the baleful effects of passion, and wrong, and treachery, and deceit; and, as I contemplate the fearful picture, my brain almost becomes wild with the dreadful retrospection. Suddenly I started up with convulsive energy. "I can not sit still in idleness,"

I said. "If I do, I will become crazy. I must work, work, or reflection upon the horrible nightmare of the past will deprive me of my reason. I will write the history of my life — will transfer to paper the load which now oppresses my aching brain; and in the employment thus created, will find at least a temporary relief from that still, frightful contemplation which has already driven me to the verge of distraction."

The result of this determination, dear reader, is in the following pages; and if, in perusing them, you should find something to condemn, let me entreat you to judge in charity, and not in hardness of heart. Remember that frail humanity is never perfect—that to err is the common lot of mortals, and that for every error delineated in the following truthful record of my life, my spirit has already atoned a thousand fold in the bitterness of sackcloth and ashes. Suffer, also, the peculiar circumstances in which I was placed during my entire youth, to apologize to some extent for any errors I may have committed. With this brief appeal to the better and more kindly feelings of my auditors, I proceed to the execution of the task I have assigned myself.

CHAPTER II.

I was born on the 7th day of September, in the year
1837, six miles from Atlanta, in the State of Georgia.
My father, whose name was George F. Hamilton, was an
Englishman by birth, and was a grandson of George
Hamilton, of London, a celebrated Freemason, who, in the
year 1737, as Provincial Grand Master, established the
first lodge of that ancient and honorable fraternity at
Geneva, Switzerland. My father was made a Mason in
early life, and in due time attained to the degree of Royal
Arch. I do not know that he ever attained any position
of very great trust or dignity in the fraternity, but there
is abundant proof that he was a faithful and zealous member, and was very warmly attached to the principles of the
Order. I mention his connection with Masonry only to
more fully explain some events of my life which would
otherwise, perhaps, be partially in the dark.

My mother was a Frenchwoman. She was a daughter
of Louis Lacorne, also celebrated in the annals of Freemasonry, and at one time the deputy of the Count of
Clermont, Grand Master of the Grand Lodge of France.

My parents were married in the city of London, England, in the year 1822, and resided there for three years.
I have not been able to learn that their lives were marked
by any events of special importance during this time.
They appear to have lived very quietly and happily together
for the entire period. About the beginning of the year
1825, my father, having been impressed with the growing
greatness of the new world, determined to emigrate thither,
and accordingly, in the summer of that year, he and my

mother came to the United States. Upon their arrival here they settled in Virginia, where they continued to reside until in the year 1831. During their residence there, my oldest brother and sister were born.

In 1830 father purchased the plantation where I was born, near Atlanta, as before stated, and in 1831 removed there. The country was comparatively new at the time, and Atlanta then presented but little the appearance of the flourishing city it has since grown to be. My father and mother continued to live contentedly and happily in their new home until 1840, during which time two children were born to them—my brother next older than myself, and the subject of this sketch. Our family then consisted of six persons—father, mother and four children, George Franklin, Kate, Henry, and myself. We had a valuable plantation, well stocked with slaves, horses, cattle, etc.; a beautiful home in the midst of a lovely grove of cedars, magnolias, and other magnificent shade-trees; while the air was laden with the perfume of flowers, and filled with the music of the feathered songsters who inhabited the wood. A bubbling spring, but a short distance from the house, lent an air of delicious coolness to the landscape. What was there left to desire? But, alas! even in the garden of Eden, pain and sorrow found an entrance and a resting-place, and so it was with our little paradise.

But, before treating of the events which finally led to the entire separation of our family, I must beg the indulgence of my readers while I speak more particularly of myself. My childhood was far from being a happy one. Even in my earliest years it was easy for me to perceive that I was no favorite with my mother, though I would not willingly utter a word against her memory. She was

kind to me, and always strove to do her duty toward me,
but it was very plainly to be seen that her kindness toward me was the result of a sense of duty, and was not
prompted by the powerful overflow of maternal love and
affection which influenced and controlled her conduct toward the elder children of the family, and especially toward my sister. I do not know whether there was anything peculiar in my appearance or deportment which
caused this distinction to be made, but certain it is that
the difference existed, and that its effect was finally to
produce an entire change in my disposition, and doubtless exerted a marked influence upon my entire life. As
a result of this coolness, it may be mentioned that at the
early age of four or five years, I abstained almost entirely
from taking any part in the sports of my brothers and sisters. Even at that early age, I was fond of solitude—
used to steal away by myself to brood over my loneliness,
and to wonder why it was that the love which I daily saw
lavished upon others, and for which my heart so piteously
yearned, was withheld from me. People were accustomed
to say of me, "what a strange child she is," and to express surprise at my serious, old-womanish ways. Ah!
parents, beware how you blight the sunny days of childhood by any seeming indifference toward any of your
offspring. See to it that you chill not the spirit of one
by a more kindly or affectionate demeanor toward another.
You may think that the neglected one has not sufficient
discrimination to perceive the difference, but be assured that
no one is as well able to discern the absence of affection
as an infant child. It may not be apparent to those of
more mature years, or even hardly perceptible to yourself,
but in infancy there is a kind of spirit-communion which
infallibly detects the want of love, and the knowledge of

that want may exercise a most baleful influence upon the entire future of your child. But to return to myself.

With my father the case was quite different. I always appeared to be a favorite of his, and when he was at home, and I could enjoy his society, I was as happy as heart could wish. But this was only a small portion of the time. Business frequently and constantly called him away, and engrossed the greater portion of his attention, and thus my life went on—a dark, gloomy sky, o'ercast with clouds, with only here and there a ray of sunshine breaking through the rift.

In the latter part of 1840 my father's health began to fail, and it soon became apparent that without some relief he would ere long

"Sleep the sleep that knows no waking"

His physician having advised a change of air and scenery, it was decided to go to Philadelphia, where he had a half brother living, in the hope that the bracing air of the North would restore somewhat of vigor to his shattered frame. Accordingly the whole family went thither and took up their abode in a pleasant mansion in the City of Brotherly Love.

Month after month passed away, but brought no relief to the weary and enfeebled frame of the sufferer. Slowly, but surely and steadily, he approached the confines of that land "from whose bourne no traveler returns," and when we had been in Philadelphia about two years, my father one day called me to his bedside, and, laying his hand upon my head, said:

"What will my poor little daughter do when she has lost her papa? who will then love her as papa does now?"

I asked him what he meant by saying I would lose him,

and he told me he was going to live with Jesus, and that if I was a good child and prayed to God, he would let me live with Jesus too. Never while I live can I forget the effect of this simple conversation upon my mind. I had but little idea of what he meant, but his solemn manner produced the most saddening effect upon my childish heart. I had a sort of dim impression that his language imported some great calamity to me, but just what it was, was quite beyond my comprehension. Poor child that I was. I have since learned in the bitterness of unmitigated sorrow the awful portent to me of the journey which my dear father was about undertaking, but then I only regarded it as some earthly journey, and cried to accompany him, saying I wanted to go when papa did.

The next morning father sent for his friend, Captain Charles Lake. When he came, I was sitting on the bed with my father. Father put me in his arms, saying, "Be kind to my little pet when I am gone." Captain Lake promised to be a father to me, and soon afterward the doctor came in with two attorneys, and I was carried from the room. I did not know what was going on, but thought they were going to do something to my papa—was terrified and wanted to get back into the room. I did not see him again that day, and when night came, and my old nurse, aunt Silvia, put me to bed, saying he was sleeping and must not be disturbed to give me my usual good-night kiss, I felt as though my heart was broken, but finally sobbed myself to sleep. My father was already sleeping the sleep of death, but I knew it not.

The next morning I wanted to see papa, and old nurse took me in her arms and carried me into the room. Father lay on a board, covered with a white sheet, and I thought him asleep, and asked old nurse to let me kiss him. She put me down on the floor, and I kissed him, Oh! so gently, for fear of waking him, and then went into mother's room. I found her in tears, and said:

"Mother, what is the matter? What are you crying about?"

"My child," said she, "did you know your father was dead?"

"What do you mean by saying papa is dead? He is asleep. I just saw him, and kissed him very easy, because I did not want to waken him."

"My poor child! your papa will never waken; he will never come back to you any more."

Just then sister Kate came into the room. She was crying bitterly, and I too began to cry. I did not realize or fully understand that my father was gone, never to return; but they were all crying, and my childish heart being filled with terror, I cried in sympathy with them. This morning was the last time I saw my father's remains until the day of the funeral.

How vividly did the incidents of that first funeral I ever witnessed imprint themselves upon my memory! Even the most trifling events of that sad day are as distinctly photographed on my brain as though they occurred but yesterday. Captain Lake took me into the parlor—the room was full of strange people—and there in a coffin, the lid of which was raised, lay all that was left of my dear, dear father. Obedient to the direction of Captain Lake, I pressed my last kiss upon the cold and marble lips of the inanimate form before us, and then the funeral services began. The man of God read, from the eleventh chapter of the gospel according to St. John, that beautiful story of the raising of Lazarus from the grave by our Saviour, and told

us that even so would Christ in the latter day raise our
father from the tomb; and then they sung,

> Hark, from the tombs a doleful sound,
>   Mine ears, attend the cry;
> Ye living men, come view the ground
>   Where you must shortly lie,

I have never heard that beautiful, yet mournful, hymn
sung since that time without feeling a strong inclination to
shed tears. Never do I hear its melody swelling and floating on the air but memory carries me back through the
checkered scenes of my life to that sad, sad day when my
sorrows really commenced. Oh! could I then have foreseen what the next twenty-five years of my life would
bring forth — could I that day have had even the most
transient, fleeting, uncertain glance at what was in store
for me in the future, how gladly would I have been laid to
rest beside the still form in its last, narrow house! But
let us not anticipate.

When we reached the grave, and preparations were made
for depositing in the ground the coffin in which I had just
seen the remains of my father inclosed, then, for the first
time, I began to realize that I was forever separated from
him whom I had so loved. Oh! how my little heart then
throbbed in its agony. Frantically I begged Captain Lake
not to let them put papa in that dark, deep hole, and implored him to take the loved body away with us. The
services were finally concluded by the congregation singing,

> Why do we mourn departing friends,
>   Or shake at death's alarms?
> 'T is but the voice that Jesus sends
>   To call them to his arms.

The grave was filled up, the congregation slowly dispersed,
and I returned with my mother, brothers and sister, and
Captain Lake, to our now lonely home.

Lonely, indeed, was this home to me. All that made it dear to my childish heart was gone. My father, the only one who had ever seemed to love me; the only one who had ever taken any interest in my childish joys or sorrows; the only one to whom I could go with my little griefs or cares, and feel assured of sympathy; the only one toward whom my heart had ever gone out in love; in short, my all, was lying cold and motionless in the graveyard we had just left; never more to listen to my childish tales of grief and sorrow; never more to whisper sweet words of comfort and paternal love, or to gladden and cheer my desolate heart with his presence. He was sleeping the last, long sleep—that sleep which can know no waking until the last great day when the trump of the angel Gabriel shall summon all nations, and the Great King shall come to judge the quick and the dead. Yes, I was alone, and with a heart strangely saddened for one so young—with a spirit crushed, broken and blighted, by the sad scenes through which I had passed, I sought my couch and sobbed myself to sleep.

CHAPTER III.

Six months have passed away since the close of the last chapter—six months have rolled into eternity since my father's death, and we are again at our old home near Atlanta. Oh! how vividly does everything recall to my mind the dear friend I have lost. Every room in the large, old-fashioned, two-story house recalls to my mind some scene of joy and happiness in which he had participated; the porches which surrounded it on all sides were those in which he used to sit, on summer evenings, while he amused and instructed me with many a quaint, and, to my childish nature, interesting story—even the grove, the flowers and birds seemed vocal with memories of my lost parent. What wonder that I wept as I reflected that I should never see him more? For to my young fancy it seemed to me that the entombing of the remains which I had witnessed, was neither more nor less than an eternal separation. I left the house and went to the negro quarters—a row of small, neat, white cabins which gave the place the appearance of a little village—but even these reminded me of my poor, dear, dead papa, and I turned away and wept in the bitterness of my grief. If it be thought strange that a child of six years of age should feel sorrow so acutely, and retain such a vivid recollection of it, it must be borne in mind that the peculiar circumstances of my childhood had given me habits of reflection far beyond my years, and that such reflection had taught me that with the death of my father the sunlight of my young life had gone out.

When my father's will was published, it was found that

he had appointed Captain Lake his executor, and had also nominated him as guardian for the children. He was to have the general superintendence of every thing; was to care for the property and see that the children were properly raised and educated. How well he fulfilled his trust let the sequel show. My father's plantation, the slaves and other property on it, were valued at thirty thousand dollars or thereabouts, and there was, besides, twelve thousand dollars in cash. By the terms of the will, this money was to be put at interest, and the interest applied to the education of the children—the balance of the property was bequeathed to our mother for her natural life, and after her death was to go in equal proportions to the children.

The weeks and months passed away, and nothing was done towards the education of the children, so carefully provided for by my dear father's will. Nineteen months passed away thus, and it began to be whispered about that our Guardian would soon take our father's place in the family and be invested with the entire control of every thing. The children were all very much opposed to mother's marrying him, and I, in particular, was very bitter upon the subject. I had early learned to dislike the man, and I had a sort of intuition that evil would come of this marriage if it was finally consummated. We knew that father had placed the utmost confidence in Captain Lake as an intimate friend, and a brother Mason (how unworthy he was of that high and holy name let this truthful history tell) but still his strange neglect of our interests had led us to distrust him, and it was believed that his only object in marrying our mother was to get more completely the control of the property, the more effectually to carry out his deliberately formed plan of robbing the orphan children of the man and brother who had trusted him with all. The elder children remonstrated with mother on her contemplated marriage, and I declared that I would never call him my father or acknowledge him as such.

But all our remonstrances and our opposition were of no avail. On the 7th day of March in the year 1845, Captain Charles Lake and my mother were married, and he was acknowledged master of the house and invested with the powers which he had so long coveted. The wedding took place on that blackest of all days in the calendar—Friday—and was a very quiet affair. But few guests were present, and thus was accomplished the second great sorrow of my life. Oh! tongue can never tell the vast amount of sorrow, and wretchedness, and suffering, which would have been saved to us all, had mother but heeded the remonstrances of her children, and foregone this marriage. She doubtless thought, in uniting herself with Captain Lake, she was promoting her own welfare and happiness and that of her children; but in after years, when it was too late for repentance, she found, alas! that she had been most sadly deceived. Were one disposed to be superstitious about "black Friday," they could find in this marriage a very strong argument in support of their faith, and could well exclaim: "How appropriate that they should have been married on a Friday."

After the marriage of my mother, matters, so far as the children were concerned, were even worse than before, for whereas, Captain Lake had before given some little attention to them in order to deceive my mother and induce her consent to the marriage, he now totally neglected them, and she very soon found that she had injured, instead of improving, their prospects by marrying again. Studied neglect, then cool indifference, and finally positive dislike, took the place of the slight interest which the Captain had before manifested in us, and but a very short time elapsed ere mother became aware that, in marrying the second time, she had committed the greatest mistake of her life.

Brother Henry's health, meantime, was failing rapidly. His was a delicate frame, a finely organized nervous system; one of those organizations on which pain and sorrow produce their most blighting effects, and which are always selected by disease as their special victims. He had almost worshipped our father in his lifetime, and the intense anguish caused by his death had sensibly affected brother's health, and half produced effects from which he never recovered. Some time before mother's marriage it was feared he was going into a decline, and about the time of the wedding it became apparent from the hectic flush upon my poor brother's cheek, the hollow, hacking cough, the bent form and listless step, that the fell destroyer, consumption, had fastened its fangs upon his delicate frame. This was the disease with which my poor father had died, and Henry had inherited it from him. The seeds had lain undeveloped in his system until the present time, and perhaps, but for the weight of sorrow which pressed upon us all, he might have been spared even for years. But it is one of the characteristics of this fatal disease that its effects are hastened, and its early development promoted, by great emotions of joy or sorrow; and brother Henry was no exception to the general rule. The cloud of sadness and grief which o'ershadowed us all, had, in the most fearful degree, hastened the crisis of the disorder; and now, when summer was filling all the earth with beauty and gladness, he was a confirmed and hopeless invalid. All that care and skill could do to stay the onward march of the destroyer was done, but without avail.   He lingered some time; like our dear father, he clung with sorrowful tenacity to life, but at last the time had come when the fell monster and grim tyrant could no longer be resisted.

Since mother's marriage the summer had waxed and waned; autumn, with its georgeous dyes and gaudy colors, had passed away; another and another round of seasons had rolled away into eternity; and when autumn leaves were again falling, my brother was at rest.   Sadly we laid his mortal remains in the silent tomb, there to rest until the omnipotent voice of Him who has said, "I am the Resurrection and the Life," shall summon him from the dust of the earth to everlasting happiness at the right hand of God.

Upon my already tortured heart this blow fell with crushing force.   After the death of our father, Henry had essayed, so far as was in his power, to supply his place to me.   He had seemed to take much more interest in me than he ever did before.   He had petted and caressed me; called me his dear, his pet; strove by all means in his power to cheer and comfort me, and had succeeded in awakening in my little heart a feeling of love, second only to that which had warmed it toward my poor papa.   Judge then, dear reader, of the bitterness of my anguish as I stood beside his grave, and beheld the clods of the valley piled upon his breast, hiding forever from my earthly vision his much loved form.   What wonder that in the utter desolation of that moment I even dared to murmur against the justice of the decrees of Providence.   It seemed to me that a blighting, withering curse was upon me. Every object upon which I gazed with the eyes of affection was doomed to fade and die before me.

> "'T was ever thus from childhood's hour—
> I've seen my fondest hopes decay;
> I never loved a tree or flower,
> But 't was the first to fade away."
>
> I never nursed a dear gazelle,
> To glad me with its soft black eye,
> But when it learned to love me well,
> And know me, it was sure to die.

But though my beloved brother was gone, I was not yet entirely desolate. I had a darling little half-sister—one of those cherubs which are said to more nearly approximate the angels of heaven than any other created thing upon the face of the earth. At the time of Henry's death she was nearly a year and a half old, having been born about a year after mother's marriage with Captain Lake. She was, I think, the sweetest child of that age I ever saw; so bright, so smart and intelligent, as it were—far beyond her tender age. Oh! how I loved that darling babe. I was never so happy as when I had her in my arms, or was romping with her upon the nursery floor. And the little thing seemed to fully reciprocate all the love and affection which I so warmly and freely lavished upon her. I had named her May, and she, in her childish, lisping voice, always called me Nin. "Many a time and oft" would she come to me, and, putting her little white, soft arms about my neck, would lisp out, "Me 'ove oo, Nin," and then put up her little mouth for the kiss she was sure to receive.

Besides her, there were still little brother Frank and sister Kate. They were, both of them, much older than I, and there was but little in common between us; but still they were my brother and sister—the offspring of a dearly-loved father—and that of itself was a bond of sympathy between us. The affectionate reverence in which we held the memory of that dear, departed parent, would have bound us to-

gether even if there had been no other ties existing between us, and we were further united in a most cordial
dislike of our step-father. Besides, my step-father was
cross and abusive to Frank, and sympathy with him, under
the injustice of which he was often the victim, had drawn
me yet closer to my only remaining brother.

But I was soon to be separated from them—from my
brother and sister, baby May and all. Father had a half-
brother, by the name of Adam Mason, living in New Orleans, whom I had never seen, though I knew his wife,
aunt Kittie. He and father had never been on good terms
with each other, though between our family and aunt
Kittie the most kindly feelings had always existed. She
had visited us on several occasions, and had taken a great
fancy to me—called me *her* girl, said she was going to
take me to live with her—and did all in her power to win
my childish love and affection, in which efforts I must say
she was rather successful. I loved her more than any one
else outside my own family; but when, some two and a
half years after mother's second marriage, she wrote to us,
asking that I might come and live with her, keep her company, and do errands for her, I felt my heart sink within
me at the prospect of leaving the home and friends to
which I was so warmly attached. But my mother thought
it best for me to go; my step-father was unkind and often
cruel, not only to me, but to all the family, and mother
thought that, the pang of separation once past, I would be
happier with my uncle and aunt—removed from the tyrannical treatment of my step-father, and beyond his blighting influence—than I would be at home. Accordingly, it
was decided that my step-father should accompany me to
New Orleans, place me in the care of my uncle and aunt,
and then return to his home. The arrangements were all

made, and at last the day arrived upon which 1 was to bid farewell to home and friends, as it seemed to me, forever.

Ah! how shall I describe that parting? I was to go forth from home and friends; to exchange the society of those from whose companionship I had never been separated, for association with comparative strangers; to leave mother, brother and sisters, and to accept in lieu of the kind and fraternal attention I had received from them, the friendship of relatives of whom I knew next to nothing, and above all, I was to be deprived of that which had been my principal solace and comfort since the death of my brother Henry—the society of my constant playmate, baby May. And to add to the bitterness of my sorrow, in that hour of parting from my little cherub, something whispered me that I should never see her again in this world. Was it a presentiment? What wonder, then, that when this, to me, sad day came, I wept as though my heart would break, or that, long after the journey commenced, I refused to be comforted, and sat in the corner of my seat, sobbing in all the violence of unalloyed and unrestrained grief?

But all things earthly must have an end, and so it was with my journey and my grief. We at length reached the Crescent City, and were received by my uncle and aunt with a degree of kindness which went far towards reconciling me to my lot. After seeing me safely installed in my new home, and transacting some business which he had in the city, my step-father prepared to return home. Although I did not love him, still I hated to see him go, for it seemed like severing the last link that bound me to home and friends. I did not shed any tears at his departure, and yet it must be confessed that my heart swelled a little as I saw him walk away from the house and disappear around the next corner. My uncle and aunt after his departure treated me, if possible, with more kindness than before, and apparently did all in their power to make me happy, and induce me to forget, or at least to remember without regret, the home I had left behind.

In this they were to a very great extent successful. I was then but about ten years old, and at that age, old forms and old impressions are easily effaced from the mind. The bustle and stir of city life, the new faces and new scenes presented to my vision each day of my life; the constant change going on around me, all conspired to wean me from thoughts of home and friends, while the kindness of my uncle and aunt went far toward supplying the place of the protectors I had lost. They were quite aged, and had no children of their own, and upon me they lavished all the affection which would have gone out toward their own offspring had they ever been blest with any. Thus time passed, and I would have been happy could I have had baby May with me. But I longed for her society, and there were times when, even in my happiest moments, thoughts of her would rush across my mind and so stir the fountains of my heart as to cause my feelings to well up in tears which I could not repress.

The autumn leaves were falling when I went to live with aunt Kittie, and when the stern winter months had come and gone, and spring with all her beauties was upon us, my aunt one day received a letter conveying the sad intelligence that both sister Kate and baby May were very ill, the latter with scarlet fever. Upon hearing this news I wanted to go home at once, but aunt Kittie would not consent, saying I would take the fever if I went. I urged and entreated; almost implored, but it was of no avail. I felt sure May wanted to see her old playmate "Nin," but aunt was resolute in her refusal, and of course my will had to yield to her's, and I staid. I have now no doubt that what aunt did was for the best, but at that time it did not seem so to me, and my spirit was strongly inclined to rise up in rebellion against her's. And had it been possible for me to have foreseen what I now know, there is but little doubt that I should have gone, despite aunt's commands to the contrary, or, at least, made the attempt to have done so.

But a few days had passed when another letter was received, and this time it bore the sable seal which tells, even before it is broken, the sad tale of death, and sorrow, and mourning. My darling pet, my poor, dear, little May was no more. How I regretted that it had not been in my power to see her before she died—how bitterly I wept and refused to be comforted, I leave to the imagination of the reader. But this was not the only sad intelligence which this ill-starred letter contained. Sister Kate was not expected to survive—was, indeed, at the point of death, and there was an urgent request that I should be sent home at once.

Of course, there was no delay in obeying this sad summons. Uncle Adam accompanied me, and we hastened to Atlanta by the most expeditious mode of conveyance; but, alas! our speed was too slow for that of the grim monster who was claiming my loved sister. When we reached the old plantation her voice was not raised in kindly greeting to the returned sister; she stretched forth no hand to grasp mine in sisterly welcome; her eyes darted forth no beaming ray of love for the long-absent one; her heart-throbs had ended, and she was cold and motionless in the embrace of death. She had drawn her last breath but ten minutes before our arrival. She died with my name upon her lips—almost her last words being an eager inquiry for

3

my arrival. This intelligence almost stunned me with grief. Why should I be thus tried? It seemed to me that Fate was about to empty her entire quiver of arrows upon my devoted head.

Reader, bear in mind that I was at this time less than twelve years of age—recall the sorrows amid which my young life had thus far been past, and then say was human being ever so chastened before? First, I had followed my loved father to the grave—then came the inexorable summons for him who endeavored to supply the place made vacant in my heart by that first death, my brother Henry—next, the pitiless monster called for my darling little May, and lastly sister Kate was taken away. And to add sting to the poignancy of my anguish, the last two had died in my absence. It was not permitted me to be near them in their dying moments; to receive their last kisses of affection; to receive their latest sighs and final adieus; but, far removed from me they had died, and I could never hope again to listen to the music of their voices until the great day. I was then young, and had not learned to bow in mild submission to the will of "Our Father who art in Heaven;" nor had I learned that great lesson, under all trials, to meekly say, "Thy will be done." What wonder then that I murmured at the dispensations of His providence, or that, in the abandonment of utter despair, I cast myself prostrate upon little May's grave, and prayed that I, too, might die? God forgive me the wickedness of that prayer. I have since learned to bear trials with more of fortitude, and have, I trust, learned to bow with something of submission to whatever chastenings His hand may lay upon me, and in so doing have secured "that peace which passeth all understanding."

The next day a sad procession wended its way to the

graveyard, and there, under the spreading foliage of a mighty oak, beside the low mounds which marked the last resting-places of brother Henry and sister May, a third grave was fashioned, to which, with appropriate ceremonies, we committed the mortal remains of sister Kate; and brother Frank and I were alone—the only survivors of a family of five children. 'Tis true, our mother was still spared to us, but she was so much under the influence of our step-father that she seemed more like a stranger than like a blood relation—much less a mother. And to make our position still more unpleasant, it was evident that our step-father— our guardian—the possessor of all the property which father had left for our benefit, but from which we were destined never to reap any advantage—he who had solemnly pledged to our dying father his honor as a man and a Mason that he would befriend and protect his orphan children, and who was now only seeking to deprive us of our patrimony—he evidently hated us, and desired our absence, no doubt the more effectually to carry out his base purposes toward us.

It is one of the immutable laws of human nature that when we have done, or meditate a wrong toward another, the presence of the one wronged, either in thought or deed, becomes hateful to us. The presence of the person to whom we have done wrong is a sort of standing reproach to the wrong-doer—an ever-present, active and powerful monitor to the conscience which, however calloused and seared with the crime of years, can never be wholly stifled— ever condemning the crime which has been perpetrated, and sleeplessly demanding restitution. Our step-father was no exception to this general law of our nature. Our father had left in his hands a sacred trust to be exercised for the benefit of the orphans ; years had passed away, and not a single step had been taken toward the execution of that trust, but instead he had by his course deprived us entirely of the benefits which our father's legacy was intended to secure—he had wronged, robbed and defrauded us, and as a matter of course our presence was hateful to him. Our sister's funeral was therefore hardly over until he instituted a system of persecution against us with the evident intent to drive us from our home.

It were a useless, unpleasant, and unprofitable task to recount in detail the various means resorted to by him to drive us from that home which of right belonged to us; suffice it to say that he was successful—that our mother was unable, or unwilling, to stem the tide which was setting against us, and that but a short time elapsed after I had seen my sister Kate buried beneath the sod until I was again on my way to the home of my uncle and aunt in the city of New Orleans. But this time I went not alone. My brother Frank—the last survivor beside myself of our once happy circle of brothers and sisters—unable to endure the annoyance and cruelties which were daily meted out to him, accompanied me, and in due time we reached the city, where we were kindly welcomed and tenderly cared for by our uncle and aunt. But we will reserve for another chapter the incidents which attended our sojourn there.

CHAPTER IV.

I MUST ask the reader to imagine that a period of three years has elapsed since the close of the last chapter. Brother Frank and myself are still living at uncle Adam's, and have become so thoroughly domiciled there as to regard it as our home. During all this time our lives had been one constant scene of peace—scarcely a ripple had occurred upon the surface of the stream of time as we quietly glided down its surface toward eternity, and the only strange circumstance I have to record of those three years is the fact that, in all that, time we had not once heard from home. I do not know whether uncle Adam and aunt Kittie had heard from there or not; I suppose they must have done so at some time or other, but if so, they never said anything about it to us. For some time we thought very strange that mother did not write to us, but we finally came to attribute it to indifference toward ourselves, and thus comparatively dismissed the subject from our thoughts. I have since learned to believe that this long silence was brought about by the machinations of Captain Lake, and was part of a deliberately formed plan to harass mother to an untimely grave, and thus get more complete control of the property of which he was steadily and systematically robbing us. God forgive me if I judge him wrongfully; he has grievously wronged me and mine, and yet I would not willingly or knowingly charge him with a single crime of which he is innocent.

About three years from the time of our last arrival in New Orleans, uncle Adam one day brought home with him a gentleman from the neighborhood of our old home ; one who intimately knew all our family.   Of course, the most eager inquiries relative to the family were at once made. Judge of my horror and surprise upon being informed by him that my mother was dead—had been dead then about a year.   Great God! could it be possible that my monster step-father had allowed my mother to pine away and die without informing her only relatives in the United States— her own children—of the sad fact?

"Yes," said my informant, "it is all true.   It is now just about one year since we followed your mother's remains to the tomb."

"And where is my step-father ?" I asked.

"He is still upon the plantation, and is about to give it a new mistress.   The last time I was there he was refitting and refurnishing the place for his bride, and by this time next week they will be married."

"What! did my mother make no disposition of the plantation or other property ?   Did she leave all our patrimony, so carefully provided for us by our father, to that wretched man whose whole efforts since he took charge of us beside our father's dying bed, have been directed toward robbing us ?"

"As to that I can not say.   I never heard of any will after the death of your mother, and only know that matters, so far as the property is concerned, appear to go on just as they did in her lifetime.   He still lives upon and manages the plantation as before."

"Then God help me," I cried; "I am indeed desolate and alone in the world.   No father or mother—not a single one in whose veins runs a drop of my blood, except brother Frank—no home — no means of support—what will become of me ?"

"My child," said he gently, "do not give way to such paroxysms of grief. Remember that God helps those who help themselves, and that He has promised to be the God of the orphan, and the Father of the fatherless. Doubtless some means of support will yet be found for you and your brother."

But, despite his kindly efforts to cheer me, I refused to be comforted. She who had gone, though never treating me with such affection as parents generally evince for their offspring, was still my mother, and I sincerely mourned her loss. And then the future looked very dark to me, for, comparative child that I was, I was still able to realize to some extent our situation. Uncle Adam and aunt Kittie were very old and were poor; we had neither of us ever been taught to work for our living; our education had been so sadly and criminally neglected by our guardian and step-father that we could scarcely ever hope to derive anything from that source; the course of that man assured us plainly that we had nothing to hope from him; and what were we to do? As long as uncle and aunt lived, we could have a home with them, but they were both very feeble, and could not be expected to live for a great length of time, and after their death what was to become of us?

It must be borne in mind that we were but children, and ignorant of law and our own rights, and were without any one to advise or assist us. Uncle Adam did, I think, make some efforts to get at the right in regard to our matters, but my step-father had laid his plans skillfully, and had so hedged himself about with technicalities and the forms of law that it was impossible to reach him except by a long and expensive litigation. This we could not undertake. We were without means, and uncle Adam

was too poor to furnish it to us; and thus villainy was for
the time triumphant, and the orphans robbed of their just
dues.   But, thank God! it will not always be so.   There
is a time coming when all that to us has seemed strange
and unnatural in this life will be set right—when ample
justice will be done—when the secrets of every heart will
be made manifest, and when no amount of ingenuity will
enable the robber of the orphan and the fatherless to escape
the just punishment of his deeds.

After this we continued to live on with uncle and aunt
as before.   They had a fine, large garden, and our principal employment was to cultivate this and dispose of the
vegetables.   From this source, and the milk of our one
cow, we managed to obtain a very comfortable support for
the entire family.   It must be understood that my uncle
had no business, and that he was too old and feeble to do
much at gardening or anything else, and hence the principal support of the family devolved upon my brother and
myself.   He was now about sixteen, and I was about thirteen; our work was not hard, and we managed to get
along very well.

But the seasons passed away—spring had gone—summer had followed in its train, and the gorgeous Southern
autumn had made its appearance, when we found that our
uncle's lamp of life was speedily dying out.   The oil
which had so long and steadily fed the flame was exhausted, and but a short time had elapsed when we laid
him to rest in "the narrow house appointed for all the
living."   Our venerable aunt sincerely mourned for him
by whose side she had so long trod the rough paths of
life, and grief at his loss preyed heavily upon her enfeebled frame.   She became a helpless invalid, and an object of our constant care.   It was a terrible burthen for

two comparative children as we were; but, thank God! we never faltered in the discharge of this painful duty. Looking back through the vista of years to that period, I can not find a single instance in which my conscience reproaches me with any dereliction of duty in the care of my aunt.

But this could not last long. The scene was evidently drawing to a close, and but a few months had passed since the death of uncle Adam before it became painfully evident that she would soon follow him to the silent tomb. At length, one bright spring morning, when all nature was putting on her gayest robes, and the whole earth was brightening with smiles, and joy, and sunshine, we stood by the bedside of our aunt and beheld the Angel of Death slowly o'ershadow her with his dark wing, while her freed spirit took its flight to realms of immortal bliss, there to rejoin his by whose side she had lived and moved so long. With the assistance of kind neighbors we laid her to rest by the side of him who had gone so short a time before, and leaving them to that repose which shall never be broken until the day of the last resurrection, we returned, with bowed heads and stricken hearts, to the lonely cottage which had so long been our home.

We were now alone, and without means, and consequently helpless. We were old enough to know that the future would not take care of itself—that something must be done, but just what that something was to be we could not tell. To increase our distress, we now learned that the place we occupied did not belong to our uncle. He only had a lease of it during his lifetime, and we were now really without a shelter for our heads, although the owner of the cottage kindly consented that we should remain where we were for a short time until we could perfect our plans for the future. Many a long and anxious conversation did we have upon this subject before we were able to arrive at any definite conclusion. Various expedients were suggested, but each was in time found to possess some fatal defect, and one after another they were rejected. Meantime the days were passing away, and something must be done; we could not stay where we were, and our means were about exhausted.

At length, one day my brother came to me with a beaming countenance.

"Now," said he, "I will tell you what we must do. I can get a situation in St. Mary's Parish as a gardener, at fair wages. This will furnish me a living and enable me to help you some, and you must go to Mrs. Armstrong's and assist in her housework."

"But suppose Mrs. Armstrong should not want me ?"

"Oh! but she does. This is no new plan of mine, and I have been to see her, and talked matters all over with her. Her ladyship wants you—I am sure she will be kind to you, and I see nothing else for us to do."

"But consider, Frank, I have scarcely had any experience in doing housework, and I am afraid she will not be satisfied with me. If she should not, and should turn me away, what then is to be done ?"

"She will be satisfied with you. I have talked with her about your experience; know just what she expects and requires, and feel sure you will just suit her."

"But why can we not go to Georgia and compel Captain Lake to take care of us."

"Sister, I would rather beg, or starve among strangers, than to go to that man who has robbed us of our all, and ask charity at his hands. Never will I ask any thing of him. I will die first."

LAYING PLANS FOR THE FUTURE.

"It would be only justice."

"Yes, but until we can demand it as an act of justice I am not willing to go and ask alms of him. This plan of mine, though unpleasant in some respects, will enable us to earn an honest living, and I really see no other course for us at present. Perhaps in the future something better may turn up.

So it was finally settled. He went with me to Mrs. Armstrong's house and introduced me to my new mistress. The house was a fine, large mansion, situated in a pleasant locality, and surrounded with trees; the furniture was handsome, rich and costly, and every thing reminded me of the home in which my earlier years had been passed. But, ah! how different was my situation from what it was there. I thought I was unhappy at home, but there I was a child, and an heiress of the wealth which surrounded me; here I was a servant, laboring and toiling for my daily bread. Mrs. Armstrong was always kind to me, but her kindness could not comfort me, or cause me to forget that I was a mere servant in a house similar to that which should have been my own, had justice been done me. Wherever I went, or whatever I did, this reflection was ever present to me, burning and branding itself into my brain until the thought at last sort of dazed me. I would stand for an hour at a time, motionless as a statue, and when spoken to by any one, would not hear or heed a word that was said. I seemed in a sort of waking dream.

This intense mental excitement at last did its work, and I was prostrated with a brain-fever. I knew nothing at the time, and only learned what followed when, eleven weeks after, I awoke as from a long trance, and found brother Frank sitting by my bedside. I felt weak, and when I attempted to address him, it was with difficulty that I could hear the sound of my own voice.

"Brother, what has happened? Why am I so weak? Why are you here, and how long have you been here?"

"Sister," said he, "it has been eleven weeks since you were taken down with the fever, and I have been with you all the time. You first lost your reason, and the doctor said you would never recover it. Then you became speechless, and have never uttered a word since, and everybody said you would never speak again. I thought, Nin, I was going to lose you, but, thank God! you are better now."

"Eleven weeks! It can not be possible that I have been sick so long."

"Oh! yes, it is true. They all thought you were dead at one time, and you would have been buried long ago if I had consented to give you up. You were as cold as ice, but your cheeks were somewhat flushed, and I could not believe you were dead. But it was only when I held a lookingglass to your lips, and the moisture gathered upon it, that I succeeded in convincing them that you were still living. This is all that saved you from being buried alive. But you are too weak to talk any more at present. You must lie still, and gain strength, and when you are better I will tell you more."

He spoke the truth. Even this conversation had been almost too much for me in my enfeebled state, and, with a sense of inexpressible weariness, I closed my eyes and again slept. When I again awoke, it was mid-day, and brother was not there, but in his place sat one of Mrs. Armstrong's servants. I lay and tried to think, but the the effort was too much for me, in the enfeebled and confused state of my brain, and I gave it up.

I have often since shuddered at the thought of how near

I came to being buried alive, and each time that memory presents this horrid picture, does my mind and heart go out with more of love to that brother whose constancy and fortitude saved me from such a terrible fate. And often, in the silent hours of the night, does my heart well up with gratitude to the Giver of all good, for bestowing upon me such a faithful and trusty friend. But, at that time, I felt that I would almost as soon have died as not. I felt that I was almost alone in the world — a useless, helpless thing, a mere waif upon the stream of time—and had it not been for the love I bore the brother who had so tenderly and constantly watched over me ever since poor Kate's death, I should have wished to join her in that other world to which we are all hastening. But I knew how it would wring his heart if his only sister were to die; I knew he would then have no one to love or care for; and, for his sake, I prayed to God that I might get well.

And God heard my prayer. Slowly, oh! how slowly, but surely and steadily, strength returned to my emaciated frame, and I was at length pronounced out of danger. It was long and weary weeks before I was able to leave my bed, and the weeks had grown into months before they would permit me to go out of doors; but at length it was pronounced safe by the physician, and I was allowed to go into the yard attended by a servant. From this time I gained strength more rapidly; my excursions about the grounds were longer and longer each day, and at last I was pronounced, by the kind old physician who had attended me during the whole of my sickness, to be convalescent.

With the return of my health came an almost irresistible longing to revisit my old home in Georgia. I wanted a change of air and scenery; I wanted to see the dear old place which my father had improved; I wanted to visit and water with my tears the graves of the dear ones in that far-off burying-ground. Brother Frank had gone back to his employer in St. Mary's Parish, and I matured my plans and made my arrangements for going before consulting him, for I felt certain he would oppose me. But my mind was fully made up, and I was resolved to go at all hazards. I did not suppose they wanted to see me there, but they could do no more than turn me out of doors, and then I could go to some of the neighbors. Go I would, and go I did.

When my plans were fully matured and my arrangements made, I then communicated my intentions to my brother. As I had foreseen, he was very much opposed to my going, and vainly used every argument in his power to dissuade me from the undertaking. He spoke of my yet feeble constitution, of the perils and difficulties of the journey, and of every other consideration which his love and solicitude for my welfare could suggest, to induce me to abandon the adventure. To all that he could urge, however, I was deaf, and, in my turn, plied him with arguments to induce him to accompany me, but with equal want of success. Finding all my efforts vain, I at last bid adieu to Frank and the kind friends who had done so much for me during my illness, and set out on my journey alone. In due time, and without any incidents worthy of note, I finally reached Atlanta. In my enfeebled state, however, the journey had been almost too much for me, and when I arrived there I looked like one risen from the dead. I was myself startled at the haggard appearance presented by my own face as I gazed in a mirror, and was weary and worn out to the last degree, but after resting a short time in the city I thought I was strong enough to undertake the journey out to the plantation, and accordingly procured a conveyance and went thither.

When I arrived near the place I decided that I would not go at once to the house—not being certain of my reception—but thought it best to go to the negro quarters and learn what I could of the situation of affairs. Accordingly, I left the conveyance a short distance from the house, clambered over a fence, passed through the orchard, and thus finally, by stealth, gained the cabins of the negroes. How strange it seemed thus to steal my way into that place which should be my own! I felt like a guilty thing, seeking to avoid the gaze of man as I stole into that inclosure and trod upon those broad acres which of right belonged to me, but which I now visited with fear and trembling.

The first one I met was my old nurse, aunt Silvie—the very one of all others I would have chosen should first welcome me to my old home. When she caught sight of me she threw up both hands.

"De Lor' bress you, chile! If dare aint little Missus Annie, or am it her ghost?"

"No, aunt Silvie, I am no ghost, but really and truly your own little mistress Annie."

"Bress you, chile, but you really looks like a ghost, and I most beliebes you is one. De Lor' bress us! here I 'se done been talkin' to a ghost, sho."

"No, aunt Silvie, I am not a ghost, but am really flesh and blood: come and feel of me."

"Den what is de matter? You looks like you had just risen out ob de grabe. Hab you been dead and just come back to life? I 'clar', if I do n't beliebe yer am a ghost. Come here, old man, and see if dis am Miss Annie, shure enough, or am it just her ghost? Bress us! See dem holler eyes."

"I tell you, aunt Silvie, I am no more nor less than your

own child, little Miss Annie.   I have been very sick, and
have but just recovered."

"Recobered!   I do n't see de recober.   You is sick as
you can be.   Jess look at dem thin han's, and dem bony
cheeks, and den say you is recobered.   I like to know
what yer is recobered."

By this time uncle Tom had come up to where we were
sitting.

"Why, de good Lord-a-massy, Miss Annie, dis aint you?
Why, is ye done been dead and berried, and come ter life
again, or w'at de Lord-a-massy does ail yer?"

"Why, uncle Tom, I have been sick, and have just got
well enough to come here and visit the graves of my dear
ones.   Do you think I will be welcome at the mansion?
I think I will get entirely well if I can be at the old house
awhile."

"Bress ye, honey, yer is come her' to be berried wid
der rest ob der family, dat is what yer is."

"No, uncle Tom, I have come to have aunt Silvie nurse
me well again."

"Well, de old Capt'in done heard ye's been berry sick,
and he t'inks ye is dead.   Yer can scare him to death if
yer likes, for we do n't any of us like him—not an inch of
him.   But de missus, she am a good 'oman, and we all
likes her.   She'll take good care ob yer, if yer gets into
her good graces."

"Well, Tom, you go and see Mrs. Lake; tell her I am
here, and if she will give me a welcome, come and let me
know."

"Dat dis chile will do.   Come, old 'oman, make Miss
Annie somet'ing for to eat.   Has yer done forgot yerself?"

While he was gone I had a long talk with aunt Silvie
about my mother, and the cause and circumstances of her

death. After Frank and I went to New Orleans, matters had gone from bad to worse. Captain Lake had treated her with cold cruelty and indifference, until at last her spirit sunk under her trials, and she had gone down to her grave in sorrow. She had never seemed quite herself after the death of May and Kate, and this rendered her less able to endure the ill treatment of her husband. She had finally died—the doctors said of fever, but, the negroes thought, of a broken heart. For more than a week before her death she had been entirely deprived of her speech, and had therefore said nothing about her children in her last moments. About a year after her death, Captain Lake had married a Miss Blackburn, and they now had a son about three months old. She also told me the Captain was now away from home, and that he seemed very much attached to his wife and child.

I was acquainted with the Blackburns before I left the place, and I knew Mary (his wife) to be a good, kind-hearted girl. Though much older than I, she had always been very friendly toward me — had always treated me with the utmost kindness, and I felt sure she would not turn me away from the house, especially as she knew that if I had my rights, that house and plantation, those broad acres with their growing crops, those negroes, cattle, horses and other stock—in fine, all that was there, would be mine. She knew that it had all belonged to my father; that Captain Lake was his executor, and my guardian, and she must have known that he had betrayed his trust and wronged me. I felt that she knew all this, and yet she was my step-father's wife. Still, I could not believe that that relation would obliterate all her sense of justice and morality, and I resolved in my own mind to appeal to her for justice against her husband. The appeal could only

4

be rejected, and could not make my case much worse, and I would risk it.

These reflections passed through my mind very rapidly, and by the time I had arrived at this conclusion I saw Tom returning from his interview with Mrs. Lake. Although I would not really allow myself to doubt the result of that interview, still I could not repress a feeling of anxiety as my messenger drew near. What if he had been unsuccessful, and if, instead of the welcome I had persuaded myself to hope for, he bore an order for my departure from the place? It must be borne in mind that I was yet but partially recovered from my severe fit of sickness, and that both mind and body were reduced to a state of almost childish weakness, and hence my views of everything were sadly distorted and awry. The reader must also remember that I was fasting, for when I was in the city my anxiety to see my home kept me from eating anything, and since I came here, though aunt Silvie had prepared a very nice meal for me, my agitation had been such as to prevent me from partaking of it. My system was, therefore, in a very poor condition to endure the intense anxiety which oppressed me, and my agitation was so great that when I saw Tom coming, and knew that the crisis of my fate was at hand, my feelings overcame me and I sunk to the floor. I only heard aunt Silvie say, " Dere, I tole her she came here to be buried wid de rest ob de family, and now she is done gone a'ready widout seein' de grabes ob her friends." This I heard, and then I sunk into utter oblivion and unconsciousness.

When I again opened my eyes, I was lying in a comfortable bed, in a well-furnished room. A beautiful, sweet face, with goodness beaming from every lineament, was bending over me, and a soft, low voice, which thrilled me with its kindly tones, asked me if I knew her. Yes, indeed, I did know her. It was Mary Blackburn, or Mrs. Charles Lake, as I should rather say. I looked around the room. With what a thrill of satisfaction did I realize the fact that I was in the same room I had occupied when I lived in that house with my mother, now dead and gone. Everything in the room was the same as when I had last seen it. There was the same old-fashioned, high-post bedstead, with its rich crimson canopy; the same wardrobe and bureau stood in the corner of the room; the same chairs were ranged along the wall; the same carpet was on the floor, and all was just the same as memory so faithfully reproduced it to my imagination. Everything, did I say? No, one thing was gone, and I sought in vain for it—it was baby May's crib, with the lovely face of its occupant; and as I looked in vain for them, sad memory reminded me in thunder tones of the many changes which had taken place since I last occupied that room, and it was with the utmost difficulty that my tears could be repressed.

Mrs. Lake waited until I had completed my survey of the room and its furniture, and then, in her sweet, musical voice, replete in every tone with kindness, she said.

"I have had this room arranged for you, as nearly as I could remember, just as you used to have it. Are you pleased with it, or would you prefer to lie in some other room?"

"I thank you most heartily and sincerely for your kindness to me," said I. "I would rather be in my own room than any other"—then recollecting myself, I hastened to add, "or rather, what was once my own room."

"It is yours still, Annie," said she, "it shall be yours just as long as you choose to occupy it. We will do all in our power to make you happy just as long as you see proper to stay with us? And then I have a little playfellow for you — a baby whom you can pet as you used to little May. I know you are passionately fond of children, but now you must not talk any more; you must go to sleep now, and when you are rested I will bring my little pet to you."

"Yes, I will try to be calm, but I must ask one or two questions. Where is Captain Lake? Does he know I am here? And how long have I been here?"

"My dear child, you ask too many questions in one breath. You have been here just two days. The Captain is away from home, was away when you came, and will not be at home for a month to come. But if he were here he would welcome you kindly, and would be glad to see you, I am sure. So be quiet now, and take your rest, and I will go and prepare something for you to eat."

With that she stooped down, and, kissing my pale, hollow cheek, left the room. After she went out, I lay still and tried to compose myself to sleep, but the effort was vain. Busy memory was at work with the past, and would not allow my worn out body to rest. I thought over all the incidents which had transpired since I last occupied that room; the trials and sorrows through which I had passed; the scenes of death I had witnessed; the troop of friends whom I had seen fade and die from around me like autumn leaves: my uncle and aunt, sister Kate and baby May— all, all passed in mental review before me, and I could not but wonder why it was that they were all taken away and I was spared. Doubtless, in the inscrutable mysteries of the providence of God there was some good reason for this; but why I should have been selected from among them all, to endure this great weight of bereavement and sorrow, was far beyond my feeble comprehension. Another subject of contemplation with me, and one from which I experienced a most bitter sense of anguish, was the awful contrast between what my situation was at the present time, and what it was then, and would be now, had not the foulest injustice lent its aid to increase the evils which Providence had seen fit to visit upon me. Then I was in the midst of comparative affluence, ease and comfort—unhappy in some respects, it is true, but still far from miserable; now I was a wretched outcast, without a home, without friends, without means of support, and actually dependent upon the charities of others for a place in which to lay my miserable head, and for the little sustenance necessary to keep life within my enfeebled frame. Then occurred the thought, most horrid of all: what if I should again be sick, as I was at Mrs. Armstrong's? I was in high fever, and, of course, my mind was to some extent disordered, and took but a distorted view of all subjects, and I could not divest myself of the impression that my illness was about to assume the same terrible phase it then did—in which event, without my brother's fraternal care, I should surely die—nay, perchance, be buried alive, as was so near being the case before. The idea of death would not have been, of itself, so very terrible; but with it was connected the thought that my brother would never know of it. It did not occur to me that in case of serious illness those around me would, of course, notify him of the fact; but the dread of being forever lost to him was most insupportable. Then my cogitations assumed another form, and filled me with unspeakable physical terror. What if I should still be ill when Captain Lake returned, and he should be angry with me for coming there, to be a burden to him? His anger would most certainly kill me. Or what if, in his wrath, he should, despite my enfeebled condition, turn me from his house, to live or die as best I might. What would become of me then?

Thus these vagaries chased each other through my brain until it almost went wild, and I am sure I should have become utterly distracted but for the return of Mrs. Lake to the room. She came in with a sweet smile on her lip, and a lovely little babe in her arms, upon which she gazed with all the pride and affection which fills the heart of a young mother for her first-born.

"Here, Annie," said she, "is my baby, my own darling little pet; do n't you think he is a perfect little cherub?"

"He is certainly very beautiful," I said, gazing with delight upon the sweet, innocent face, yet free from the corroding marks of care and sorrow. "You must love him dearly."

"Oh! indeed I do. And you will love him too," she continued, laying the laughing babe upon my arm. "Why, Annie, you look like a young mother with the babe in your arms."

I looked in its angel face. It was almost the exact picture of my darling, lost, little May, at its age. It had the same large, deep-blue eyes, and dimpled chin; the contour of the forehead was the same as her's; the same fat, dimpled chin was her's; the features were all identical with her's, and as my eyes, at a glance, took in all these details, I for a moment half thought my darling had come back to me. But in another instant came the recollection that I had seen her grave and watered it with my tears, and that nothing short of the power of Omnipotence itself could ever restore her to my loving embrace again, and I turned away my head and wept bitterly. I could not help it. The recollection of the happiness I had once enjoyed with her whom it so nearly resembled, and which was forever gone from my grasp, was too much for me, and I sobbed as though my heart would break. Mrs. Lake respected my grief, because she divined its cause, and her heart was one to appreciate such emotions. She waited until the violence of my emotion was passed, and then quietly removing the babe, she gently smoothed my hair and said:

"You must now take your rest, Annie, and when you get stronger you shall have baby again; and I know you will learn to love him almost as much as I do."

And she was right. Day after day my affection for the child and its mother grew in strength, and at length I I learned to look and long for nothing so much as the coming of Mary Lake with her sweet, innocent babe. I was always very fond of children, and especially loved a pretty babe during the days of infancy—this was almost the exact picture of her whom I had once loved more than any other human being — what wonder, then, that my heart should have gone out towards this precious one almost, or quite, as it did toward my own dear sister, sweet little May. Yes, I could love him though, I know he was destined to come between me and my rights. Though fully aware that he would inherit the Hamilton estates—that property which should have been mine—there was no envy in my heart toward him. I did not blame him for the crimes of his ancestor, and I loved him with all the fervor of my nature. Yes, he was the sunlight of my life, during the long and weary days, weeks and months of confinement which followed that relapse. He was my only solace and comfort then.

Wearily the lazy hours dragged themselves away, confined, as I was, a close prisoner to my room. The hours

grew into days; days into weeks, and weeks into months,
and still languid, helpless, I lay, longing once more to behold the outer world, and fretting at the close confinement
I was enduring, but utterly unable to leave my room.
Would I ever be able to go out again? It seemed doubtful, and, even now, I feel that to the kind and affectionate
care of Mary Lake, and the cheering companionship of
her lovely babe, I am indebted, under the Giver of all, for
my restoration to health and strength.

But I must not lose sight of brother Frank during this
long and gloomy illness. I received several letters from
him during the period of my confinement to my room, for
which my heart was full of gratitude to him, and which
were a source of great comfort to me, for he was now my
all. He was still at work in St. Mary's parish, and was
doing very well. He often spoke of coming to see me, but
the urgency of his duty to his employer prevented it. Ah!
how I would have prized a visit from him, but if this
could not be, it was still no little consolation to know that
he thought of me.

The winter had passed away, and it was a bright morning
in spring when I was able to leave the house for the first
time for weeks. With what a sense of exhilaration I
gazed upon all nature, clad in her gayest robes, and in-
haled the soft, balmy air, and listened to the music of the
feathered songsters, as they made the air vocal with their
melody, I leave the reader to imagine. Ask the wretched
prisoner who, after months of weary confinement in his
solitary cell, to which the feeblest rays of the sunlight of
God but seldom penetrate; where the walls reek with
filth and dampness, and the atmosphere is tainted with foul
and noisome smells; where the only living creatures beside
himself are the moles, and rats, and vermin, with which

his gloomy abode is thronged; who has almost felt hope die out within his breast, as day after day passed into eternity, and brought with it no hope of release, is suddenly restored to the blessed sunlight of liberty and freedom, what his feelings are—receive his answer, and you can form some idea of my feelings at my release from the gloomy bondage of pain and weakness which I had endured. I felt that God had bestowed upon me a new lease of life, and my heart was full of thankfulness to Him who had thus far watched over, and protected me all along the journey of life. There had been times when, in my heart of hearts, I had wished that my life might end—that the voyage so full of bitterness and woe as mine had been, might be brought to a close; but with the sense of returning health and strength, after my prolonged illness, came new thoughts, new hopes, and new aspirations. Yes, I would live, and would try to render my life a source of happiness to others, and thereby to myself—would endeavor so to live that when He should see fit to call me I would neither fear death as a monster, nor welcome him as a friend, but would receive him with the calm resignation of the Christian who obeys without reluctance the invitation of his Master to cease from his labors on earth and enter the paradise of eternal rest on high. Who of my readers, upon arising from a long and painful confinement to a sick bed, have not had the same feelings and formed the same resolutions—to be perhaps kept, and perhaps broken.

CHAPTER V.

How grateful to the sense of the patient who has been for weeks, or it may be for months, confined to the bed of sickness, consumed with fever, and racked with pain, is the balmy air of spring, especially in the latitude of central Georgia. It seems to me almost impossible to conceive of anything more delicious, more invigorating, or more health-giving, than the breezes which, during the months of the season aptly termed the youth of the year, come sweeping up from the Atlantic Ocean, retaining in their journey of an hundred miles, that peculiar freshness imparted to them by the salt water, and laden with the perfume of the magnolia, the lilac, and the thousand other fragrant flowers for which central Georgia is so justly celebrated. The system must be, indeed, sadly shattered, which does not attain somewhat of strength and vigor under their kind ministrations.

Thus it was with me. The days wore on, and with each returning sun came additional feelings of vigor and healthfulness. It must be borne in mind, however, that, for the greater part of a year, with but one brief interval, I had been a helpless invalid, my system the seat and prey of disease, my vitals almost consumed by the burning fever which had been my constant attendant, and of course it was to be expected that some time would elapse before a system so reduced and disordered would be restored to its normal condition as regards strength and vigor. My improvement, therefore, though sure and constant, was so slow as at times to excite considerable impatience in my mind. With renewed health had come the desire, ten times intensified, to visit the grave which I had traveled so far to water with my tears, and it may be that my anxiety on this subject, to some extent, retarded my convalescence.

It had been but short time from the day on which I had been first permitted to visit the world out doors and inhale the fresh air, after my long confinement, when I received a shock which, for a time, threatened to reduce me to the condition of an invalid again. It will be remembered that in the first interview between Mrs. Lake and myself, she told me that her husband would not be at home for a month. That month grew into two, before the business which called him from home could be adjusted to his satisfaction: two months lengthened themselves into three, and the business still proving refractory, the whole winter was consumed before it could finally be closed up. Mrs. Lake and I had, therefore, been alone all the winter, and in the enjoyment of unrestrained intercourse with her, I had almost insensibly forgotten my dependent and lonely situation, but it was suddenly recalled most vividly to my recollection.

A letter arrived from Captain Lake, written from a town but a short distance from us, in which he informed his wife he should follow the letter, and would be at home on the next day. My agitation, on being informed of this, by Mrs. Lake, was extreme and very painful, and, for a time threatened to prostrate me again. I could not divest my mind of the reflection that I was but a trespasser on his bounty, and in all probability a most unwelcome guest, though, in justice and equity, my right there was superior to his. Still the power was with him, and my old pet horror returned most vividly to my mind.

"What if he should drive me from the house?" In my present state of health it would be fatal to me. Nay, even an unkind or harsh word, an angry look from him, would, in my enfeebled condition of both mind and body, be attended with the most serious consequences. In vain Mrs. Lake tried to cheer me with the assurance that my fears and apprehensions were utterly groundless—in vain she assured me that the Captain would make me welcome, and treat me with kindness. It was impossible for me to dismiss from my mind the recollections of the dislike, nay, almost hatred, which formerly existed between us, and now that he had the power to still further gratify that hatred, would he not be likely to exercise it? Besides, the memory of the foul wrong he had already done me was ever present to my mind. There we were upon the very scene where that wrong had been perpetrated, and my presence would be a standing reproach and rebuke to him. What so natural as that he should ask to remove this living reproof of his infamy by sending me from the plantation?

These thoughts and apprehensions so worked upon me that I retired to my room and went to bed, feeling almost certain in my own mind that the morrow would again see me a homeless outcast, dependent upon the cold charities of the world, and of comparative strangers, for the poor boon of a shelter, and the food necessary to sustain life. My head ached violently, and, for a time, it seemed to me that I was again about to be attacked with the dreaded fever, so high was my state of mental excitement; but, as night came on my mind became somewhat more composed, and at length I sunk into a dreamy, uneasy slumber.

The next morning I awoke feeling very wretchedly. The excitement of the day before had prostrated my entire nervous system to a very great extent. I had a dull, nervous headache, and a sense of weariness and lassitude oppressed my entire frame to the last degree. I felt so badly that I did not rise from my bed at all, and, to tell the truth, I was not sorry that there was a sufficient excuse for me to retain my own room. I dreaded meeting Captain Lake, and was desirous of avoiding what I was certain would be a sad calamity to me as long as possible, never once reflecting that we must meet sooner or later, and that delay would only injure, instead of improving, my chances. I therefore kept my bed, only engaging aunt Silvie (who had been my constant nurse all through my illness) to tell me when the Captain came, and what he said in relation to me.

But the morning hours dragged slowly by, and no aunt Silvie came. I was feverish with anxiety, and speculated all the forenoon upon the probable result of the coming interview. Fancy still presented to me the most terrible consequences as likely to result from that interview, but having become somewhat accustomed to their contemplation, I no longer dreaded them as I did in the shock caused by the first announcement of the Captain's speedy return. Still I could not divest myself of a considerable degree of uneasiness; and my intense anxiety to have it over with, and know my fate, became almost insupportable as hour after hour passed away, and my faithful messenger came not.

It was almost noon when aunt Silvie came to my room with the intelligence that the Captain had made his appearance. How my heart beat as I listened to the few words in which she imparted this simple information. How I longed, yet dreaded, to inquire what the Captain had said about me, or whether he had been informed of my presence in his house. For some time I hesitated in painful indecision as to whether I should ask her any thing, or wait until my fate chose to reveal itself, but at length my anxiety overmastered every other feeling, and I addressed my sable nurse thus:

"Well, aunt Silvie, does the Captain know I am here, and what does he say about me ?"

"Yes, Miss Annie, he knows ye is here. Missus done told him when he most first in de house."

"What did he say when she told him ? Did he appear to be angry or displeased at my coming ? What did he say ?"

"He did n't say much ob any t'ing. He only say, 'I t'ought she was dead long ago;' and den missus tell him you was berry sick, and came berry near dyin'."

"But what else did he say, Silvie? Tell me all he said."

"Why, Miss Annie, he only said what I 'se done tole you, and nuthin' more."

"Did Mrs. Lake tell him how long I had been here ?"

"Yes, missus she done tole him when you came here, and how you was most dead when you comed, and how she done tuck care ob you, and she did n't tell him I tuck most ob de care ob ye; and den he say, 'My dear, you done ebery t'ing just right;' and den missus she look kinder pleased, and den dey talk about sumfin' else."

"Did he appear to be angry when she told him how long I had been here ?"

"No, Miss Annie, he just say what I 'se done tole you."

"Did he say any thing about brother Frank ?"

"Yes, he ax where he was, and what he was doing; and missus done tole him all about him, den he say he was glad he was doing so well."

"What else did he say, aunt Silvie?"

"He did n't say nothin' else."

"Aunt Silvie, do you think he will send me away, or will he let me stay here, where I have really more right than he has?"

"No, Miss Annie, I does not t'ink he will send you away. Missis would n't let him do so if he done wanted to. I guess he will not say much to you if you do n't say much to him."

At this moment Mrs. Lake came into the room and directed aunt Silvie to go and bring my dinner. As soon as the negress had fairly got out of the room she came close to me and kissing me, said:

"Well, Annie, you have not been up to day. The Captain has come and wishes to see you. Can you get up and come into the drawing-room for a short time? He will make you welcome, just as I told you he would."

"Please, Mrs. Lake, excuse me to-day. My head aches very badly, and I do not feel well and strong enough to meet the Captain to-day. Indeed I am not able to get up."

"Perhaps your headache is caused in part by lying in bed so long, and it may relieve you to get up. Come, Annie, you must come down stairs. The Captain wishes to see you, and besides he has brought home with him a handsome young widower, with whom he says you must get acquainted. Who knows but you may get him for a husband?" said she playfully.

I was but just turned of sixteen, had never been in company any, or seen much of the world, and her remark about the handsome young widower brought the blood to my face. However, I insisted upon being excused, assuring her that my headache was too severe to admit of my rising. My real reason for declining to get up, however, was because I did not feel well enough, or strong enough, to encounter the agitation of meeting the Captain, and besides I knew that I looked like a ghost. Was it a tinge of ordinary female vanity that led me to avoid, if possible, meeting this handsome widower in my present wretched-looking condition? At any rate, I said to myself I could keep my bed, under pretense of illness, until he went away; but to my dismay, Mrs. Lake told me, the next moment, that he was going to stay for several days, and it might be for weeks. Of course, all thought of avoiding him had to be given up, but still I adhered to my resolution not to meet him, or the Captain, that day. Mrs. Lake finally, seeing that it was useless to urge the matter, gave it up, and I was left alone; and right glad was I to be in company of my own thoughts once more.

Though still somewhat in doubt as to the manner in which Captain Lake would treat me, I anticipated much from the kindly feeling which I knew Mrs. Lake had for me, and from her intercession in my behalf, and I felt much more hopeful of my future than had been the case for a long time. Could it be that Providence had meted out to me the full measure of my afflictions, and that the residue of my life was to be passed in comparative comfort? Time alone could tell; but at any rate, after the interview with Mrs. Lake, just referred to, my heart was more at peace than it had been for years. That night I slept soundly, and awoke the next morning very much refreshed, and feeling much stronger than on the day previous.

It was a lovely day, and I dressed myself and went down stairs. I did not see Captain Lake or the widower till tea time, however. I did not get up in time for breakfast, and immediately after the morning meal they went to

the city to transact some business, whence they did not
return until long after the dinner hour was past. I was
in my own room when the bell rang for tea, and upon
going down was greeted by the Captain with a kindness
which was as unexpected as it was pleasant and grateful
to my feelings. His welcome was not merely cordial, it
was really kind and affectionate, and in the grateful surprise of the moment, I for a short time forgot the great
wrong he had done me, and my heart warmed toward him .
in spite of myself. How much of his kindness was produced by my spiritual, almost unearthly, appearance, how
much by some motive he may have had in view, and how
much by genuine sympathy and affection, I leave each
reader to judge for himself in the light of this most truthful
history.

I was next presented to Mr. Giles, "the handsome
young widower," as Mary Lake had called him; but, it
being almost my first introduction to any one, I was so
much embarrassed that I hardly dared look at him, or
even raise my eyes from the floor. Immediately after this
ceremony we took our seats at the tea table, and I then
had an opportunity to observe him more closely. I did
not think him very handsome, nor was he bad looking;
perhaps better looking than the average of mankind. He
was of medium hight and well proportioned, neither too
stout nor too slender, his form was erect and manly; he
had auburn hair, blue eyes, light complection, and his
countenance expressed more than ordinary intelligence.
Altogether he was one to attract a second glance from any
one who was as susceptible to the effect of good looks as
I was. He was an excellent conversationalist, capable of
pleasing almost any society into which he might be
thrown, and his elegant manners, and the delicate little at-

tentions he paid me during the meal, made a very favorable impression upon me.

Before we left the table, Caroline, the nurse, came in with Mrs. Lake's baby. She had taken more than usual pains in attiring him, and the care with which he was dressed, added to his natural loveliness, made him as sweet an appearing child as I ever saw in my life. When baby had been sufficiently admired, caressed, and commented upon to satisfy even as fond and proud a mother as Mary Lake, Mr. Giles went on to speak of his own babe and his other children. He had been married when very young, and had three children, all boys. The youngest was only about six months old, and had been deprived of a mother's care almost from the time of his birth, his mother having died when he was only about a week old. The others were aged, respectively, about two and a half and four years, and all were sadly in need of that care and attention which only a mother could give them.

Thus the evening wore away in pleasant and interesting conversation, interspersed from time to time with music, and when, at its close, I retired to my room, my heart was lighter, and I felt happier than I had for many a long day. It was late, however, before my eyes were closed in sleep. Mr. Giles had been quite attentive to me during the entire evening, and, as these were the first attentions I had ever received from one of the opposite sex, my mind was in a perfect whirl of pleasant excitement. Already, in imagination, I saw myself the wife of Eugene Giles, the mistress of his establishment, and the mother of his boys. He was in comfortable circumstances, so far as worldly property was concerned. I was passionately fond of children, and knew I could love him best; and, altogether, fancy might have presented a much more unpleasant fate to my mental vision. I did not love or dislike him, nor had I any reason to suppose that the vision presented to me would ever be fulfilled, but it must be remembered that I was then ignorant of the world and its ways, and to my simple ideas the attentions which every gentleman naturally pays to a lady, were indicative of love and speedy marriage. Let not the reader blame my simplicity or laugh at my ignorance. I have since learned to appreciate such attentions at their true value.

From this time I date a new era in my life. I had long been accustomed to regard myself as a bark drifting helplessly on the ocean of life, with no one to care for me, or to interest themselves in my fate, no one who cared in the slightest what became of me, without hope, or end, or aim, or inducement to live, and had become careless as to what became of myself. Now all was changed. I felt that I was no longer the helpless child of destiny, but was a woman, with something to live for, some end to accomplish; and though it was not entirely clear to me what my future was to be, still I was not alone in the world, a mere useless atom of creation. That first evening spent with Mr. Giles, in Mrs. Lake's parlor, was to me the birth of a new life. I went to the tea-table that evening a careless, aimless, and helpless child; I went to my room a woman in spirit, thought, and action, with all a woman's hopes, fears and aspirations developed within my heart.

Time passed on, and Captain Lake and his wife continued to treat me with the utmost kindness. No allusion was made to my leaving there, and in a few weeks I came to be regarded, and to regard myself, as a member of the family, and never allowed myself to reflect what would be the end of this season of comfort and contentment, if, indeed, it should ever end but with life. During all this time my health was constantly improving; and restored vigor of body, as well as contentment of mind, with plenty of air and exercise, were fast removing all traces of my late fearful and prolonged illness. The wasted form and haggard countenance, the hollow, lusterless eye, and col orless cheek, and the halting, uncertain step of conva lescence were rapidly being replaced by the rounded form, the bounding step, and bloom and freshness of youth.

Mr. Giles, meantime, had been very constant in his attentions to me. For several days after that first evening, he had remained an inmate of the Lake mansion, during which time he constantly sought my society, and as constantly bestowed upon me the most tender and delicate attentions—attentions which I was only too willing to receive. Did I wish to walk about the grounds? His arm was ever at my service. If I wished to ride out, it was he who ordered the carriage and drove the spirited horses; he was my constant attendant in every scheme of exercise and pleasure, and never wearied in caring for my comfort and happiness. Such attentions won upon my feelings, and I soon learned to look upon him as something more than a friend, and to anticipate the fulfillment of the vision which fancy had presented to me as I lay upon my couch after that first evening.

At length he had concluded certain negotiations, in which he was engaged, for the purchase of a livery stable in Atlanta, and the time had arrived when he must cease to be an inmate of the Lake mansion, and go to the city to take charge of his property, and superintend the business in person. I hated to see him go, for I had become very much attached to him, and though no word had been spoken between us, I felt assured in my heart that he loved me. But there was no help for it, and he went away, and *i*or some time I saw but little of him. He came out occasionally, however, to see us; then his visits grew more and more frequent, until at last I learned to look for him almost every day, and he very seldom disappointed me. He became a constant visitor, and never appeared (as I really never was) so happy as when he was by my side, engaged in animated conversation, or reading to me from some interesting book. He frequently spent nearly the whole day at the plantation, and a marriage between us at an early day came to be a subject of general conversation among the servants, but still he had not spoken.

One beautiful evening, we were, as usual, seated beside each other, on a low bench, in the garden, admiring the beauty of the setting sun. For some time we sat in silence. "The fiery orb" had disappeared from view, twilight was deepening around us, and still neither spoke or moved. With me, memory was busy with the gloomy past, and I could not help contrasting that fact with my present happy condition. Suddenly he caught my hand, and poured forth into my ear the oft-told tale of love, and asked me to be his wife. He told me how lonely he had been since the death of his wife—how his children needed a mother's care—how desolate the world seemed to him, and begged me to cheer his loneliness and brighten all his future by giving him the right to call me his. As for his ability to take care of me, he was in good circumstances, could give me a good home, and had an abundance to maintain me in comfort, and even luxury—would I consent? I was startled, and told him I was too young to marry; that we knew but little of each other, and ought to wait until we were better acquainted; that Captain Lake was my guardian, and I did not know what he would say to our marriage. To this he replied that he had already spoken to the Captain, and had his permission to make me his wife. My other reasons, he met with a lover's arguments, and a lover's impetuosity, and still implored me to accede to his wishes. During this scene, I was trying, as well as I could, under the circumstances, and amid the excitement which I naturally felt, to analyze my feelings toward him. I thought I did not love him as I ought before becoming his wife, yet he was dearer to me than any one else of my acquaintance; his earnestness sort of terrified me, and when he said, "Say, Annie, will you be a mother to my children?" I tried to answer him, but could not—the words choked me, and I remained silent, but did not withdraw my hand from his grasp. He waited a short time for an answer, but I could not speak—and when he said, "Shall I take silence for consent?" I only looked up into his eyes. He was answered; and, clasping me in his arms, he kissed me with all a lover's fire and ardor—the first kiss I had ever received from him.

And thus it was settled that I was to become his wife— to give up my freedom, my individuality, my all, into his keeping. Oh! could some kind angel have lifted, for one moment, the vail which shrouded the dim future, and have shown me the misery, shame, and wretchedness, which were to be the results of that first kiss, methinks I would sooner have leaped into an abyss of living fire, than have suffered his lips to come in contact with mine. But in the inscrutable mysteries of God's providence, the future is wisely hidden from our view, and fortunate is it for us it is so. At the time, my only thought was that I had at last found rest; that the troubles and sorrows which had thus far beset my life were now at an end; that in the future I was to know nothing but peace and quiet, and recur to the past only as some horrid dream or nightmare. How far my imagination was from the reality, let future pages disclose.

From this time I saw more of my lover than ever before. He was with me almost constantly, and was unwearied in his efforts to please me and gratify my every wish. He was exceedingly solicitous to anticipate and supply every desire of my heart, and never seemed so happy as when he was doing something for me, or in some way contributing to my comfort and happiness. Such earnest and unwearied devotion could not fail to produce its effect, and, in time, I learned to love Eugene Giles with all the force of my nature. My disposition was naturally very affectionate and tender. It is a necessity with me to have something to love, and hence, as is the case with all similar natures, when my love is once aroused, it absorbs and overwhelms every other feeling of my soul. Thus it was with my feelings toward my betrothed. I soon grew to be lonely and unhappy in his absence, and to sigh constantly for his return; but when by his side, all thoughts of sorrow were forgotten, and no one, it seemed to me, could be happier than I was.

I also found great pleasure in the society of his children, whom he often brought to see me, frequently leaving them with me the entire day. As has already been stated, I am passionately fond of children, and these were, I think, the sweetest little boys I ever saw in my life. Besides, they were the children of him to whom I had pledged my hand, and whom I loved with all the fervor and intensity of which my soul was capable. What wonder that I should have dearly loved, and should have been so happy in their society?

But time passed, and my lover began to grow impatient to have the day set for our marriage. With the timidity natural to a young girl, I still insisted upon a postponement, and, whenever he broached the subject, managed to put him off in some way, until at length he become too importunate to be resisted, and, with the sanction of Captain Lake, the 7th of September ensuing, being my seventeenth birthday, was fixed for our union. We were to be married at the Episcopal church in Atlanta, and it was arranged that after the wedding we were to go to the city of New York, and other places in the North, and to return in about three months. Meantime our own house was to be fitted up for our occupancy, and immediately upon our return we were to commence housekeeping in Atlanta.

It would no doubt be very interesting to my lady readers—at any rate, men say we have unbounded curiosity in such matters—if I were to describe the bustle and confusion which pervaded the Lake mansion during the few weeks which intervened before my wedding day—the laces, satins, berages, and other goods which were brought into the house to be made up into wedding-dresses, traveling-dresses, and all other kinds of dresses—the small army of dress-makers and seamstresses who were employed in the house to work up all this finery; but the task would be a hopeless one, and I forbear. Brother Frank, too, was to be sent for, for I could not think of being married in his absence, and without his blessing. Captain Lake kindly took charge of this part of the programme, and, accordingly, informed Frank of the entire contemplated arrangement, and in due time received a reply from him, saying he would be present at the wedding, and would then accompany us to New York on his way to California, whither he had determined to emigrate, the California fever being then at its hight.

At length the eventful day arrived, and a lovelier day

never dawned upon this earth, than that upon which I became Mrs. Eugene Giles.   There was not a cloud to be seen in the skies; the air was mild and balmy, and came to us in a gentle breeze laden with the perfume of the gayest flowers of a Southern autumn; the orchards were laden with a bounteous crop of fruit, now ripening in the mellow sunlight; the earth was groaning under the burden of a bounteous crop of corn, cotton, and other products of the sunny fields of the South; and all nature seemed swelling with thankfulness to the Great Giver of all good.   Need I say that my heart partook of the general emotion, shared the great voice of nature, and that I was that day the happiest of all the happy throng I saw around me?

I trembled a little when we stood up before the holy man of God to promise the words which were to bind us together for a lifetime, but it was not with fear or dread. A deep sense of the solemnity of the act we were performing, a vivid appreciation of the immense responsibilities I was assuming, rested upon me, and caused a sort of shuddering agitation lest I should be unable to fully discharge those responsibilities; and when, in answer to the question of the minister, I promised to be a good and faithful wife to him who stood by my side, to love and honor him so long as we both should live, in my heart of hearts I ratified the solemn promise, and uttered a secret vow to my Maker that it should be kept in spirit as well as in letter, and that I would be to my husband all that my obligation implied.   If every girl, who becomes a wife, had as full an appreciation of the solemnity of the step they take in so doing as I had; if they as fully realize, and as religiously observe the obligations imposed by the marriage contract as I did, we should have fewer divorce cases, less

unhappy homes and domestic quarrels, and fewer instances
of husbands abandoning their wives and children for the
false and fleeting charms of licentious dissipation. I, by
no means, excuse men for their derelictions in this respect,
but I most firmly believe that, in many instances, they are
driven to this course of conduct through the fatal mistakes of those who should be their guardian angels in the
hour of temptation, but who, not understanding, or not
regarding the obligations of the marriage contract, drive
them from the homes, where they should find happiness, to
the haunts of dissipation, in search of those enjoyments
which are elsewhere denied to them. To do this it is not
necessary that the wife should be cross, or quarrelsome,
or peevish, though these are, doubtless, very potent agencies for evil. But if she ceases to render home attractive,
and pleasant, and cheerful; if she ceases to practice on the
husband the thousand little arts by which she won the attention of the lover, my word for it, that wife will, when it is
too late, and when her husband has been irreclaimably driven
from her side, realize the full force of the mistake she has
made. It is true there are men so debased by nature and
early education as to be incapable of reformation, but in
a majority of instances the wife has the remedy in her own
hands, and if she fails to apply it, she will, in time, awake
from her lethargy to find herself the most miserable of human beings—a despised, neglected and forsaken wife.

But to return from this digression. The ceremony was
performed, and we returned to the Lake mansion for dinner, after which we were to go to Atlanta, for the purpose
of starting on our wedding tour. It was a gay party
which sat down to dinner that day in Mrs. Lake's dining-
room. The dinner was excellent; every one was in the
very best of humor, and mirth, wit and merriment, were the

order of the day, and each one vied with the others in doing honor to the happy groom and his bride, and to our
hospitable entertainers.   Wine, too, lent its aid to increase
the hilarity, and for a time the demon Care was entirely
banished from our midst.   But the dinner was at last
ended, the old family carriage was at the door, trunks
were packed and loaded upon the clumsy-looking old ve-
hicle, adieus were hastily spoken, kisses and promises to
write were exchanged, and we entered the carriage and
were rolled away in the direction of Atlanta.

CHAPTER VI.

OUR journey to New York, though devoid of any incidents worthy of note, was to me very tedious and tiresome. My husband was unremitting in his attention to my comfort, and did all he possibly could to relieve the tediousness of travel. But I was unaccustomed to journeying, and it was a very great relief to me when we at last found ourselves in the city of New York. We took rooms at the St. Nicholas Hotel, and retired very early, but I was too weary to sleep, and for a long time after my husband had yielded to the influence of the drowsy god, I lay awake and contrasted my present situation with what it was a year and a half ago. Then I was a kitchen servant in the family of a Southern aristocrat; now I was the honored wife of a man of sufficient wealth to maintain me in ease and luxury, and who had already shown that his disposition was entirely commensurate with his ability to provide everything necessary for my comfort. Was I not a happy woman ? Loved, petted and caressed, as I was, by one whom I thought the perfection of earthly nobility; loving him with all the affection with which my soul was capable; possessed of the means to gratify every rational wish; what more had I to desire ?

But there was one thing for which I would willingly have bartered all I possessed. It will be remembered that my father had provided, by his will, for the proper education of all his children; but, through the fraud and dishonesty of our guardian, the benefit of this provision had been withheld from us. It must be observed that at the

South we had not the benefit of the Northern system of free schools, by which every one, however poor, is enabled to obtain a sufficient education for all the ordinary purposes of life; and the kind old uncle with whom my youthful days had been spent, was too poor to afford me any advantages in this respect. Hence I had grown up with scarcely any education at all, and I now felt the deprivation more keenly than I ever had before. I had never ventured to tell Mr. Giles of my deplorable ignorance; though frequently intending to do so, a sense of shame had always kept me quiet, and I had waited for "a more convenient season," ever dreading the loss of his respect, and consequently of his affection, when he should learn how ignorant I was. But I knew, of course, he must find it out some time; and to have been able to avoid this discovery I would have given anything save only his love. But the discovery was even nearer than I thought.

To such an extent had my education been neglected that, though I could read a little, I could not write a single word, not even my own name. Frank could write a little, so that it could be read by any one accustomed to reading writing; but I did not know the form of the first letter. Judge, then, of my dismay when, the next morning after our arrival in New York, my husband came to me with pen, ink, and paper, and said:

"Come, little wife; let me see what a sweet, pretty letter you can write to Captain and Mrs. Lake, just to inform them of our safe arrival here, and how we feel."

"My dear husband," said I, "I do not feel able to write to-day. I have a very severe headache, and wish you would write for me."

Heaven forgive my duplicity. I was still afraid to tell

him I could not write; but my brother, who happened to be in the room, came to my assistance.   Said he:

"Allow me to speak for my sister.   Eugene, do you know anything of Annie's past life, or of our history?"

"Nothing, except what I have learned from Captain Lake.   I have never asked Annie, or any one else, any questions."

"And what has Captain Lake told you?"

"He has told me that he was your step-father; that you have both lived with an aged uncle and aunt since infancy; and that, since their death, Annie had been living in his family."

"Was that all he told you?"

"That was about all."

"Well," said he, rising, and speaking excitedly; "he forgot to tell you the most important part.   He forgot to tell you that every dollar he calls his; every dollar he is worth; the plantation that he lives upon; the servants who till his lands; even the carriage which bore us to Atlanta: all were our father's.   That, by the terms of our father's will, he was appointed our guardian; that he married our mother; that he cheated us out of our property, and drove us from home.   Even the money which our father's will provided for our education was, by this man, appropriated to his own use, and we were left to grow up in ignorance.   Your wife, my sister, to-day can not write her own name; but it is not her fault that such is the case."

"But it seems almost incredible to me.   I have regarded the Captain as an honorable man.   Is this all true that you have been telling me?"

"It is gospel truth, every word of it.   For that I pledge my sacred word and honor."

"How was it about your living with your uncle?"

"That is true. When our guardian, by his cruelty and abuse, drove us from home, having no other place to go, we went to live with an aged uncle in New Orleans, who was too poor to send us to school, and Captain Lake did nothing for us; and thus we grew up without any education."

"Frank," said my husband, "I thank you for telling me all this. It has opened my eyes to some things I could never before fully comprehend; but now I see it all."

Judge of my feelings while this conversation was going on. I reclined upon a lounge, my face covered with my hands, and trembled for the result of this exposition. I had, to a certain extent, deceived my husband, and I wondered if he would love me less on account of that deception. But I had not long to wait. He came over to the lounge where I lay, gently drew my hands from my face, and, stooping down, kissed my cheek —

"My poor Annie," said he; "how you have been wronged. Why did you not tell me before?"

"Oh! Genie, I was afraid to tell you. I was afraid of losing your love if you knew how ignorant I was."

"You should have had more confidence in your husband. Of course, I could not love you less for that which was your misfortune, and not in any sense your fault."

"I should have told you some time, but I did not want you to know it now."

"Well, my Annie, never mind it now. I will educate you myself, will teach you to read, and will set you copies and teach you to write; and the world will never know of your situation at this time. And, Frank," said he, turning to my brother, "if you will give up going to the gold regions I will send you to school, and you shall have a good education, after which you shall study a profession. What say you?"

"You are very kind, indeed, but I do not feel willing to alter my plans. I have been all my life dependent upon some one else, and now there is a chance of making myself independent, and I do not feel like neglecting it."

"But, consider, Frank, how much better it will be for you to stay at home, and, after obtaining a good education, you will then have an opportunity of rising to distinction in some honorable profession; while, if you go to California, your education will probably never be any better than it now is. Besides, think of the dangers and hardships you must encounter in that wild region—all of which will be avoided by the plan I propose. Think well of what I say, before you decide to reject my offer."

"I thank you most heartily for your kind offer, but my mind is made up. I should like to have a good education, but I can not give up the chance of becoming independent. As for the dangers and hardships of which you speak, they do not dishearten me in the least, but rather confirm me in my determination. I am firmly resolved to go."

Argument and entreaty were utterly unavailing to move him, or to shake the resolution he had formed; and, although Eugene used all the art he was master of to induce him to stay, and although I seconded the efforts of my husband with all the eloquence of affection, we found it impossible to change his determination. Go he would, and go he did.

When we finally gave up all hopes of inducing him to forego the journey he had planned, we set ourselves earnestly to enjoying the few days we could yet spend in his society. We visited every place of note in the city, and saw and admired all the works of art which abound in such profusion there. But while we were thus enjoying ourselves, we did not neglect the very important duty of furnishing brother with everything which could conduce to his comfort or safety on his journey. I superintended in person the preparation of his outfit, and, by the aid of some very valuable hints received from an old hunter of the far West, who was to be his companion on the perilous trip, my brother was at length provided with everything which care, ingenuity and affection could suggest to render his journey pleasant.

From New York we went to Boston, and visited the numerous historic sites with which that region abounds. We went to Lexington, and stood upon the green which was moistened by the life-blood of the first martyrs of the Revolution; we visited the classic grounds of Bunker Hill, and gazed with admiration upon the majestic shaft which commemorates the sturdy resistance made by the untrained militia of the colonies to the veterans of England; we climbed the frowning hights of Dorchester, and stood upon the place occupied by the artillery of Washington, and which finally compelled General Howe to evacuate the city; and paid our respects to every spot which the incidents of those times have made dear to the American heart; after which we began to talk about returning to our home in Georgia.

But before returning, I had a duty to perform. My dear father was lying in the graveyard at Philadelphia, far removed from all his friends, and I had reason to suppose his grave was in a sadly neglected condition. To visit that sacred tomb, and see that it was properly cared for, was my duty; and, accordingly, we proceeded by steamer from Boston to Philadelphia, and once more I stood beside that

6

sacred shrine of a daughter's affections. I found my worst anticipations fully realized. The resting-place of my father's remains was overgrown with grass and weeds, and the slab of wood which was his only monument, was so defaced by time that it was with difficulty we could determine by the inscription thereon that we really stood beside his grave. I was shocked to find it in such a condition, and at once went to work to remove these traces of neglect. Before we left the city the ground was cleared of weeds, and beautifully planted with evergreens and roses, while a tall and stately column of marble appropriately commemorated the virtues of my father and the undying affection of his children.

And there I parted with my only brother. The time had come when he must proceed to New York to join the party with which he was going to California, while my destiny lay in the opposite direction. Beside the grave of our departed father we held our parting interview, exchanged our kindly wishes for each other's future welfare, and renewed our pledge of never-ending affection, after which he wended his way to the steamer in which he had taken passage for New York, while I returned to our rooms at the hotel. This parting with the last member of my family was painful in the last degree, for I felt that I should never see him again. A journey to California was then something more than the mere pleasure trip it has since become, and it seemed to me that the parting was forever. Still, it was not like former times when I had parted with him. I was no longer alone in the world, but was blessed with a kind and indulgent husband, who would spare no pains to render my lot a happy one.

The next day we bid adieu to the city of Brothely Love, and turned our course toward the city of Atlanta, which was to be our future home. Our journey thither was unattended with any incidents worthy of note, and we finally reached the Lake mansion on the fourteenth day of February, after an absence of five months, which had been, to me, productive of more real happiness than had ever fallen to my lot in the same space of time. Each day of our absence had been productive of some new scene of pleasure, while the kind and delicate attentions of my husband had left me nothing to desire. I really thought that I, who had so long been the plaything of fortune, had at last reached the haven of rest, and that my future life was to be as pleasant as the past had been miserable. Poor, blind mortal that I was. I could not discern in the horizon the gathering storm which was to make my future life a desert indeed, and by the side of which the past was to be as calm as a May morning. But let us not anticipate.

Our reception at the Lake mansion was more than cordial—it was kindness itself. Captain Lake and his lovely wife met us at the gate, and greeted us in the most affectionate manner, the children shouted their welcome at the tops of their little voices, while the negroes, clad in their holiday attire, and displaying broad rows of ivory, stood at a respectful distance and indulged in the heartiest expressions of delight at the return of the wanderers. Aunt Silvie, however, was not satisfied with this formal display of welcome. Scarcely had Mrs. Lake imprinted her kiss of welcome on my lips, when my old nurse rushed from the group of servants, clasped me in her arms, and covered me with kisses, calling me her child, her darling, and invoking an endless torrent of blessing on my head. I was not a little moved at this evidence of affection on the part of my old nurse. But it was not at all surprising.

My acquaintance with these simple children of nature has taught me that they are more devoted in their attachments, and more intense in their affections, than the more refined, but more cold-blooded white race. And this demonstration of aunt Silvie's was but the natural outburst of her affection for one whom she had reared through the tender years of infancy as her own child.

We passed a very pleasant evening in the society of our friends, during which it was arranged that we should remain with them as their guests for a few weeks, until our house in the city could be prepared for our reception, when we would go to housekeeping by ourselves. And thus passed the evening of our return from our wedding tour.

CHAPTER VII.

THERE are times in all our lives when the hours seem to pass on leaden wings; when our impatience to reach some ardently-desired event so far outstrips even the marvelous speed of Time, as to cause us to wonder that it should move so slowly, and to seek, but in vain, for expedients to hasten its flight.   Witness the lover, as he watches the sun declining in the heavens, and giving place to the "queenly orb of night" which is to light him to the presence of his mistress; or that mistress, as she awaits, in the accustomed trysting place, the coming of him who is dearer to her than life itself, and in whose absence the hours seem heavy indeed.   Who has not experienced this feeling of impatience at some time or other, and not once only, but on numerous occasions?

Such were my feelings during the four or five weeks which followed our return from the North.   It had been settled that we should remain at the Lake mansion while our house in the city was undergoing some necessary repairs, and being refitted and refurnished, when we were to go to housekeeping.   My impatience to become the mistress of my own establishment was so great that it seemed to me the necessary preparations would never be completed. Almost daily I was in the city, watching the workmen with childish impatience, fretting at what seemed to me their frightfully slow progress, and foolishly but vainly wishing that I could do something to hasten the work.   My anxiety was so intense as to reach almost fever heat, and each night I retired to rest, almost worn out with impatience and excitement. I really believe that if this state of mental emotion had continued much longer I should have succumbed to it, and been really sick; but all things earthly must have an end, and so it was with the preparation of our house. At length it was decided that everything was ready, and we were to take possession of the house on the following day; and that night I was perfectly wild with childish excitement and eager anticipation, and the next morning I could scarcely wait for breakfast before starting for our new home.

In the fitting up and furnishing of our house I found fresh proofs of the kindness of my husband's disposition, and of the depth and sincerity of his love for me. He had superintended everything—I was so much of a child, and so much excited, that I was incapable of rendering much assistance—and everything was arranged in the most convenient, comfortable, and even luxurious manner. Beside the magnificent and luxurious style in which the house was finished, Eugene had purchased, from Captain Lake, my old servants—Tom, Silvie, and Caroline—solely because he knew that it would afford me satisfaction to have them around me. Could any one have done more to gratify my every wish than he had done?

I shall never forget the first meal I got in our own house. The Empress of the Russias could not be prouder than I was as I sat at the head of the table, opposite my husband, poured his tea for him, and duly assumed the throne as mistress of my own household. I strongly suspect that my housekeeping, at that time, was not of the very first order— it would be strange if it were, considering the circumstances of my past history; but, nevertheless, I was the mistress of our own elegant mansion; and, as busy memory compared and contrasted the present with the past, my heart filled with gratitude toward him who called me by the name of wife, and who had wrought so great a change in my apparent destiny. Need it be added that my love for him was, if possible, intensified by these reflections, and that I felt as though the devotion of an entire life would be but a small return for all his kindness?

Our children, too (for I now called them ours), were a constant source of delight to me. Willie was now five years old; Frankie was past three, and Eddie was about fourteen months; and I do not think I ever saw more quiet or better dispositioned children than they were. But my especial pet and favorite was Eddie. He was then just in, what is to me, the most interesting period of childhood— was just beginning to lisp "papa" and "mamma," and learning to walk. Many an hour did I spend in training and guiding his timid, halting, staggering footsteps, and the exercise endeared him to me almost beyond description. He was a most lovely child: he had large, blue eyes, light, curly hair, and as fair and clear a complexion as I ever saw. In training and developing his infantile mind and person, I found ample employment of the most pleasing and interesting character. Ah! how happy I was during these days.

One year and four months passed away after our marriage, and I had another object to which my affection was directed. On the first day of January, I presented my husband with a most precious New Year's gift; a fine, lovely, healthy daughter. She was the very image of her father, and, it seemed to me, was the handsomest child I ever beheld. Doubtless all young mothers think the same of their first-born, but be that as it may, my cup of happiness was now full, and I could think of nothing more to desire or wish for in this world. My husband was all kindness,

and was, in my eyes, perfection itself. My home was one
of the most comfortable and luxurious that the imagination could conceive, and I was the proud mother of the
loveliest child upon which the sun ever shone. Was not
my lot a happy one?

But, alas! how true it is that earth's highest pleasures
are but ephemeral in their existence, and that the sweetest
joys are shortest in their stay. It is the common lot of
mankind, that at the moment when we are elevated to the
highest pinnacle of happiness, we are nearest the brink
of the awful abyss of misery and black despair; and my
experience has been no exception to this general rule of
our fallen humanity. In a few short months I was to be
prostrated from my throne of happiness into a gulf of misery
more terrible than any that in my checkered life I had
been called to endure.

The first terrible blow, was the loss of my precious little wild flower. The angel, whose company I had fondly
hoped to keep during the residue of my pilgrimage below,
was too bright for earth, and was summoned by the Father
to her home in the skies, leaving my heart desolate.
Upon the breezes of April, the angel of Death spread his
wing, and summoned my cherub to join the bright throng
above, and the showers of May brought their wealth of
flowers and strewed them upon the grave of our darling.
Her life was brief, but it was not bitter; she was spared
the sufferings and trials which must inevitably have attended her more mature years; and though my heart was
wrung with anguish as I listened to the dull sound of the
clods falling upon her little coffin, I can now look up to
heaven and say, "Thy will be done." My subsequent
misfortunes and sorrows have taught my heart a lesson of
resignation which I did not then feel.

Upon my husband the loss of our child seemed to fall, if possible, with more crushing weight than it did upon myself. It is not usual for the father to experience the same degree of love and affection for his offspring as the mother—it does not seem so much a part of him as of the mother, who has given a portion of her very life to bring it into existence, and his heart does not, therefore, go out toward the child with the same intense yearning as that of the mother. A father may give to his children all the love of which he is capable, but as compared with the intense, selfish devotion of a mother toward her young, it is, in general, but feeble. But in the case of our Mary, who was so early taken away from us, I was surprised to find that my husband felt her loss even more keenly than I did. It hardly seemed possible that my grief could have been excelled; but while my sorrow was as a tempest to my soul, his was as a perfect tornado; and I think it was partially owing to the intensity of his grief that my husband was led into the commission of acts, soon to be recorded, which gave fresh poignancy to the anguish we already endured.

What a grevious mistake it is—what a sin against God and humanity—what worse than folly, when he whose soul is borne down by the weight of sorrow, turns for consolation, to the ephemeral and blighting excitement of dissipation; to the forgetfulness of intoxication, the enchantment of the gaming table, and the forced and senseless mirth of bachanalian revelries. No man ever did, or ever will, secure immunity from sorrow by resorting to such agencies as these. The poor wretch who resorts to these means to get rid of his burden of sorrow, may succeed, for the moment, in diverting his mind from its contemplation, but the relief is only temporary, and when reason is restored, and the mind returns to the contemplation of its grief, its pangs are but intensified by the very means used to arrest them; for to the former sorrow is superadded the recollection of grevious wrong committed to get rid of it. Nor is the effort to obtain even temporary relief at all times successful. Numerous instances are recorded of parties who have resorted to dissipation to drown sorrow, and who, in the hight of a debauch—perhaps in the midst of some bachanalian song, or obscene jest—have suddenly been arrested, and the words frozen upon their lips by the vivid recollection of their great sorrow. Better, a thousand times better, endure with submissive meekness the most painfully afflictive dispensations of our Father's providence, and thus rob them, in great part, of their sting, than to endeavor to drive away their memory by means, which, in the end, will only increase their power in a tenfold degree. But to this philosophy, and this reasoning, my husband, like thousands of others, was a stranger, and he fell into the, alas! too frequent, but ever delusive and unsuccessful attempt, to drive away his sorrow by dissipation.

It was but a short time after the funeral of our little girl until I began to perceive he was becoming irregular in his habits. Before that sad event he never staid from home later than until about ten o'clock at night; now I often sat, and watched and waited for him until midnight, one o'clock, two, and even as late as three o'clock. Many and many a time have I thus watched for him for long hours after the children were asleep, almost vainly striving to crush back the tears which would well up from my burdened heart to my eyes, but which I sternly repressed in order to prevent him, when he should come, from knowing how I had been weeping. Vain were all my efforts to divine, satisfactorily to my own mind, the reason for this change in him; but still I forebore to complain, and always greeted him with a smile, a kiss, and all the demonstrations of affection which had marked our happiest days. And still matters went on, from bad to worse; he still became more and more irregular in his hours, and I began to detect, in his breath, the scent of the noxious fumes of alcoholic drinks.

Oh! the misery of those nights of watching no human tongue can tell. Night after night, when the children were in bed and fast asleep, and the servants had all retired to rest, have I, the only waking being about the house, sat, and alone watched for my wayward husband, frequently prolonging my vigils until the coming day would gild the eastern skies, and still no Eugene would come. Often, after passing the entire night in watching, have I gone down alone to my cheerless breakfast, my eyes red and swollen with weeping and wakefulness, while my heart throbbed with an anguish which none can know, save those who have endured the same fearful trial. Have you, my lady reader, ever endured such trials as these? If not, may God, in his mercy, spare you this great agony.

Never shall I forget the first time he came home in a state of intoxication. It was long past the midnight; the moon, which was at its full, was shining brightly, and made it almost as light as day, and the stillness and serenity of the air seemed enough to hush every display of human passion. I was sitting by the window, gazing out upon the brilliancy of the landscape, which shone like silver in the radiant light of the moon, when suddenly, borne to my ears upon the breeze of the night, came a succession of sounds which almost caused my blood to

curdle, and my hair to stand erect with horror. I do not
think that ever in my life have I heard such frightful
oaths, and such shocking, blasphemous obscenity as disturbed the quiet of that lovely night. As soon as I
recovered a little from the first shock of horror, I opened
the window, and, bending eagerly out, endeavored to ascertain the source from whence proceeded the frightful
sounds.

A gang of half a dozen drunken men were approaching the house, and in their midst, almost utterly helpless
from the extent of his intoxication, and supported by two
of his companions, who were not quite so far gone as himself, was the well-known form of my husband. From
him and his boon companions had proceeded the sounds
which had so thrilled my soul with terror. As I took in,
at a glance, the situation, and the fell import of the scene
before me forced itself upon my comprehension, I uttered
a cry as though a dagger had pierced my heart, and rushing to the door, opened it just in time to receive the helpless form of my husband from his supporters. Once
inside the door, and missing their support, he fell at full
length upon the hall floor, where he lay, utterly helpless
and unable to rise. It was a task requiring all my
strength to get him into the room, undress him and put
him to bed, but it was at length accomplished, and I
seated myself at the window to pass the remainder of the
night, for sleep I could not. My heart was too full of
sadness and sorrow to take any rest. Had any one told
me, a short year before, that my husband would become a
common drunkard, I should have scouted the idea as an
absurdity, but now there was no avoiding it. The proof
was there before me, and how I shuddered as I contemplated what the future might have in store for me. Al-

ready, in fancy, I saw myself pointed and sneered at as the wife of a drunkard and an outcast, while the children, who were as dear to me as though they had been my own, were devoted to a life of wretchedness and shame. The agony that I endured, as these thoughts passed through my mind, during the remaining hours of that night, can never be told.

Similar scenes to these were of frequent occurrence from this time forward, until at last they became so common as to be rather the rule than the exception. A majority of the nights my husband came home more or less intoxicated, while not unfrequently he was so far gone as to require assistance in getting home. During all this time he was not unkind or abusive to me—never spoke angrily or harshly to me, but was practising upon me a species of cruelty, far more dreadful than any personal violence could be.

I soon discovered that he was burdened with some terrible secret which constantly weighed down his spirits, but which he refused to share with me. When sober, there was an air of sadness about him which I at first attributed to remorse for the debaucheries in which he was constantly participating; but though that doubtless contributed somewhat to his moroseness, it was not long till I made up my mind, from some words which he carelessly let fall, that there was even something more than this pressing upon his spirits. No sooner did I arrive at this conclusion than, with fear and trembling, I set to work to find out what it was. True, I dreaded the discovery, but still I felt that it was necessary to know the worst, and anything was better than the suspense I was enduring. Accordingly, one evening when, at my earnest solicitation, he consented to stay at home with me, I broached the subject.

"My dear husband," said I, "I am certain you have some great trouble on your mind, and that it is that which leads to all our recent sorrows. Is it not so?"

"Why, Annie, why do you ask such questions? What if my business does vex and annoy me a little, is that any reason why you should borrow any trouble about it?"

"But I am certain it is not your business. There is something beside business weighing upon your mind. I have seen it in your eye, averted whenever I tried to look you in the face; in your moody, restless air; in your half-suppressed sighs, and in a thousand other little circumstances which none but a wife would observe. Eugené, I am your wife, and have sworn to love and honor you, to share your joys and sorrows — why should you conceal anything from me? If you are in trouble, tell me, and let me share it with you. Will you not, dear Genie?"

"Oh! Annie, do not urge me. If I have troubles, I must bear them alone. They are not for you to share."

"Not for me to share! Who should share your troubles, if not your own true and loving wife? Tell me, my husband, what it is that so oppresses you, and my woman's wit shall find some way to relieve you of your distress."

"Annie, it would kill you to know it, and beside it is entirely beyond your power to afford any relief. Why then should I trouble you with it? No, the troubles which oppress me I have brought upon myself, and I will bear them alone. No one, much less you, my precious wife, must suffer for my own faults."

"But this suspense is worse, and far more painful to me, than any knowledge could be. If you have erred, tell me all about it—be assured of my foregiveness beforehand, but do not conceal anything from me. Come, my husband, tell me all, and not only relieve my suspense, but let us devise means to get rid of the trouble which has destroyed and is destroying all our happiness. Tell me, my husband, tell me all."

But all my efforts and entreaties were vain. To all I could say he would only answer that it would kill me, and that he must suffer alone, and I retired to rest that night with a heavier heart than I had known for a long time. It was impossible for me to divest myself of the impression that some terrible calamity was impending over us, and what it was I could not divine. I mused over it for a long time after my husband was asleep, but could arrive at no conclusion satisfactory to myself, and was finally forced to give it up entirely. How much better it would have been for all parties, had my husband then yielded to my entreaties, and imparted his trouble to me, let the sequel show. Oh! husbands, think not to save your wives from sorrow by endeavoring to conceal from them the troubles which oppress you. In many instances their quick wit, sharpened by affection, will devise means of avoiding the evil where to you there seems no chance of escape, while concealment only leads them to imagine the worst, and thus produces far more pain to them than a knowledge of all the facts would. Beside, it is their duty, and their right, to know and share all your sorrows and all your troubles; and, my word for it, to the true wife the path of duty is always the path of pleasure. What though that path be rough and thorny, still she treads it not only with satisfaction, but with joy, and finds her reward in promoting the happiness of him to whom she has given her purest love. As you value that love, pain not her gentle spirit by striving to conceal from her that which it is her right and her duty, as well as desire, to know.

Some weeks passed away after this conversation, and my

husband grew no better. His evenings were nearly all spent away from home, and not unfrequently he would be gone the entire night, and when he came home, instead of being the strong man of vigorous intellect that he was when I first knew him, he would be a mere infant in strength, and but little more than a driveling idiot. Such are the effects of alcoholic drinks, and such they are known to be by every one. Why is it that men, made in the image and likeness of their Creator, will persist in the use of that terrible poison, which reduces them below the level of the brute, and only fits them for the companionship of the lost spirits of the bottomless pit, and qualifies them for the commission of any crime?

One night my husband was, as usual, away from home, and I was sitting alone in my room, waiting and watching for his coming; for, during all this time, I never once failed to sit up and wait for him to come. I felt it my duty to do so; and, beside, I thought if there was any hope of reclaiming him, it would be accomplished in that way, and no other. As I sat there, worn and weary with my constant vigils, suddenly the door-bell was rung with a violence which caused me to start from my chair, with the impression that something terrible had happened. I was sure it was not my husband, for he had a latch-key, and could come in at his pleasure, and my first thought was that he was dead, or had met with some terrible accident; and, while I stood trembling with alarm, and undecided what to do, again the terrible summons pealed through the house, if possible, with more violence than before. I did not dare to go to the door, but called Tom and Silvie, and directed them to see who was there, and what they wanted at this time of the night. Aunt Silvie got up and opened the door, and found a basket sitting on the step, but no person was to be seen, nor was there any clue as to how it came there. Tom went out into the grounds, and made the most diligent search about the yard and buildings, but could find no traces of any one.

The basket was brought into the house, and when opened we found it to contain a little girl, apparently aged three or four weeks. The child was well dressed, and, at the bottom of the basket, was a note, well written, but in a hand entirely unknown to me. It ran thus:

Mrs. Giles—Take this little one and take care of her. Whatever of wrong her mother may have committed, she at least is innocent, and should not suffer for the wrong of others. Some day you will know all about her parentage, but not now. Her name is Carrie, and she will take the place of the little one you have lost. As you value your happiness and peace of mind, take good care of her.

It was without signature, and I could not imagine who was its author, or why it should have been sent to me. I knew not what to think or what to do. How I wished for the presence of my husband, that he might advise me in this emergency. How could I take care of it? I already had three children; my health was becoming delicate on account of the conduct of my husband; and it seemed impossible for me to add this foundling and its care to my already heavy burdens. And yet, the thought of sending it away was in the last degree abhorrent to me. What should be done?

I was recalled from these musings by the child beginning to cry. It was evidently hungry, and I told aunt Silvie, who had been standing silently by all this time, to get some milk and feed it. She started as if from a sort of trance, and turned to obey me, muttering as she went something, of which I only heard, "a pretty little of

7

fish," "bet it's massa's young 'un," and something else which I could not catch. This gave a new direction to my thoughts, by disclosing to me the suspicions which were floating through her mind. Could it be that my husband was false to me, and that this child was the fruit of his guilty intrigues? Oh! no; it could not be. He had always been so kind and affectionate to me that it was not possible he was deceiving me in this manner. With these reflections, I tried to dismiss the subject from my thoughts; but still my suspicions had been aroused, and I could not cease to think of old Silvie's muttered words. After the child's hunger had been appeased, I took it in my arms, and, for the first time, went to bed without my husband; but though the infant sunk into a sound slumber, and did not wake during the entire night, my thoughts, fears and suspicions would not allow me to sleep. With the first faint streak of dawn, I arose and resumed my watching.

About six o'clock Eugene came home, and, to my surprise, he was entirely sober. I at once showed him the little foundling, handed him the note, and stood by to watch him while he read it. I thought, if he was guilty, as aunt Silvie thought, it would be impossible for him to conceal it; but the closest scrutiny of his features failed to reveal anything to confirm those suspicions. He was evidently as much surprised at the circumstance as I had been, and, in my own mind, I was convinced he knew nothing of the paternity of the child, and at once acquitted him of the wrong of which he had been suspected.

We then discussed the disposition to be made of the child. He proposed sending it away some where; but, now that I was convinced of his innocence, I would not consent to this, and insisted upon adopting her as our own. To this he finally consented, and it was so decided—he saying, that since we had concluded to keep it, he was glad it was a girl, as we already had three boys, and none of the other sex. We therefore bestowed upon her the same care and attention which we gave our own, and, in time, she grew to be sufficiently sweet and interesting to more than repay us for all our trouble. But still the secret of her birth was wrapped in profound mystery, and caused me many an hour of anxious thought. It is true, my husband was no longer suspected of any wrong in connection with it; but my inability to fathom the mystery was a source of constant uneasiness to me. It did not then occur to me that he might be guilty after all, and that his surprise was but simulated to convince me of his innocence. I did not then know him as well as I have since learned to do.

I tried by all means in my power to stimulate the interest of my husband in the new accession to our household, hoping that it would have some influence to wean him from the evil ways into which he had fallen, and, for a few days, flattered myself with the hope that my efforts were going to prove successful. For some days after the advent of the little foundling, he spent his evenings at home; but just as I began to flatter myself that he was reclaimed, he suddenly relapsed, and was, in a very short time, just as bad as ever. Again were repeated the scenes of lonely nights, of weary watching, of helpless intoxication, and beastly debauchery, amid which my time had been passed almost constantly since the death of our little girl; and again I drank to its dregs the cup of bitterness ever presented to the lips of a neglected wife. But this could not last always, and finally the end came.

One evening, a few weeks after the events I have just related, my husband came home very early—about seven

o'clock, I think it was—and was evidently very much depressed in spirit.   He came in without a word, and, taking
his seat, sat for some time without speaking.   At length
the silence grew irksome to me, and I went up to him,
and, putting my arm around his neck, said:

"Eugene, you must tell me what is the matter with
you.   For a long time you have not been yourself, nor
have you confided to me any part of your troubles.   I
have borne it until my heart is well nigh breaking, and
now I feel that I can not stand it any longer.   Do tell me,
I implore you, what it is that troubles you."

He made no reply, but laid his head upon my breast and
wept like a child.   I said nothing, but let his head rest
upon my bosom until his grief had somewhat subsided.
Indeed, I was too much alarmed and astounded to say any
thing.   I had never seen any man, and much less him,
moved as he was by my simple question, and knew not
what to say or do.   When his sobs had somewhat subsided, I kissed his brow, and again urged him, by all the
endearing words at my command, to impart his grief to
me.   Without looking up, he said:

"Annie, I can not tell you all.   I am ashamed to confess
it all to myself, much less to you.   Oh! if you knew all
that I have done, the depths to which I have descended,
you would fly from me and never see me again."

"Eugene, you wrong me.   I can forgive anything for
your sake—can endure anything except this concealment; so tell me the worst, and see how bravely I can
bear it."

"Oh! Annie, you are so kind, so affectionate, and so
dear to me, that I would gladly spare you this trial if I
could.   But I can not conceal it any longer.   Annie, I
have been gambling for a long time, and am a ruined man.

At first I was successful, and became infatuated with the love of play, and, when fortune turned against me, I kept on, in the hope of retrieving my position; and so it has gone on, until I have lost all and my wife and children will soon be homeless. This house, furniture, servants, my livery-stable and all, will not pay my debts, and I may even have to go to jail. What will become of you and the babies?"

I was struck speechless by this revelation. In all my imaginings as to the cause of his irregularities, it had never occurred to me that this might be the case. The worst that had suggested itself to my mind was, that he had been unfortunate in business, and was compelled to sacrifice his property; and had this been so, had he lost every dollar he was worth, but lost it honorably, I could have borne it all without a murmur. Oh! yes, I could have endured the very lowest depths of poverty with him, without complaint, had he been reduced to those depths without dishonor on his part, and simply by the frowns of fortune; but to know that he had brought it all upon himself and us by the contemptible, soul-blighting, and God-dishonoring vice of gambling, so completely overwhelmed me with astonishment and horror that, for a time, I was incapable of uttering a single word, or, indeed, scarcely comprehending it.

How any man, gifted with sense and reason, can so far debase himself as to engage in the pernicious vice of gambling—that pursuit in which all the better and finer feelings of human nature are swallowed up in the fierce and unholy excitement of the gaming-table, and in which the demon Avarice takes entire possession of a man, to the exclusion of everything noble or praiseworthy; that pursuit which is the fruitful parent of intemperance, licentiousness, and every other vice to which frail humanity is subject; that pursuit which almost inevitably accompanies and leads to theft, highway robbery, and even murder; which, in short, transforms men into demons—is beyond my power to comprehend. Had I a son, I would a thousand times rather see him inclosed in his coffin, than to see him seated at the gaming-table: the first would only be the death of the mortal body, while the last would be neither more nor less than the eternal death of an immortal soul. Oh! young man, just starting upon the troublous voyage of life, shun the soul-killing excitement of the gaming-table as you would the bite of an adder. The moment in which you yield to its seductive influences, that moment you may abandon all hope for the future, and "Lost" will be the epitaph you write upon your own tombstone. But to return to my story.

As I have said, I was incapable of uttering a word, but sat stunned and speechless by the terrible revelation just made. After the silence had continued some time, my husband raised his head and looked timidly in my face. He started at the expression he saw there.

"Why, Annie," said he, "how pale you look, and so dreadful. Do not look with that fixed and stony stare. Reproach me; curse me, if you will — I deserve it all — but do not look so terribly upon me."

"Oh! Eugene," I said, bursting into tears, "why have you done this? Tell me all about it."

"Annie, I have nothing to tell, nothing to say in excuse for myself. You know that, in my business, I am constantly thrown in company with what are called 'fast men;' and that it is my disposition to be gay and lively. Well, at first — they began on me a long time ago — they used to say: 'Come, Eugene; go with us to ——'s;' but I would refuse, telling them I must go home to my wife and babies; 'my wife will sit up until I come.' 'Well, Eugene,' they would say, 'go and get a drink with us first.' Thus urged, I would yield. One drink would be taken; then another and another, until I would forget all about wife and children. But it was a long time before they could get me to take a card. At last, one night, after I had been drinking pretty freely, it was proposed that we should have a quiet game of cards for fun. To this I consented, and we began to play. Finally, my partner proposed a bet of five dollars on a hand he then held. I refused to have any part in it; but he and another man bet, and my partner won. They then laughed at me for being so fearful of a paltry bet; and thus, by ridicule and entreaty, and by plying me with liquor, they at last got me to betting. For some time I won almost constantly, and then I began to lose. Maddened by my losses, and by the liquid poison in my system, and muddling my brain, I kept on until at last I awoke to find myself a ruined man. That, Annie, is the whole story."

It was the old, old story. It was but a repetition of the arts by which those fiends insatiate—those sharks, who prey upon the follies and weaknesses of their fellowmen, only to rob them of wealth, honor, and all that makes life desirable—always ensnare their victims. If there is one being upon the face of the earth who is more to be despised than another, surely that being is the professional gambler; if one sinner deserves a higher meed of punishment than any other, it is that creature who, wearing the form but lacking the soul of a man, makes the weak points of those with whom he is thrown in contact his special study, only that he may the more certainly rob them of all the jewels which a kind and beneficent Creator has bestowed upon them; and, if it were possible that one portion of the eternal burning should be hotter than another, surely those demons would, by the justice of the Almighty, be consigned to that hotter portion.

I could not reproach my husband; I loved him too well for that; and, beside, I felt that he was more to be pitied than blamed. Possessed of a gay and lively disposition, generous to a fault, and fond of society, he was just the man to be selected by these sharpers as the victim of their devilish arts; and he must have been possessed of more than human virtue had he been able to resist the many wiles and temptations with which they studiously surrounded him: and yet, I could not repress the reflection, that had he confided in me, at the time I first appealed to him, I might have saved him. But that was now all past. He had tried to conceal it from me as long as he was able; had retained the secret in his own breast until concealment was no longer possible; until he must give up his stables, his horses, carriages; his fine residence and furniture and servants; and now, the only question was, "What was to be done?" An examination of his affairs showed that, after giving up everything he had in the world, he would still fall short nearly a thousand dollars of paying his indebtedness, and womanlike, I began to cast about to see what I could do to help him.

I had some fine jewelry and a valuable watch—presents from Eugene in our brighter and happier days. I could raise two or three thousand dollars on them, but what would this amount to in the payment of the enormous debt hanging over my husband? It would be but as a drop in the bucket; but, still, every dollar would help, and though it ground my heart into the very dust to think of parting with these precious mementoes of his love, stern necessity knows no law, and I decided that they must go. But what could be done to save us a home from the general wreck? I could ask Captain Lake to aid us in this emergency; but though he had money enough, which of right belonged to me, to pay off all Eugene's debts, I very much doubted if he would do any thing, for he was a close, miserly man, who never gave a cent for charity or any other noble and generous purpose. But what else could be done? Our home would be sold the next day, and we would be without even a shelter for our heads, and I must try what I could do.

Accordingly I went to Captain Lake, and told him all about Eugene's temptation and fall, and my plans and hopes for the future, and besought him to aid me to save my servants and furniture, and to my agreeable surprise he agreed to do so. I blessed him from the bottom of my heart, hastened home and told my husband we could save our furniture, and keep our home; for if the house was sold I would sell my diamonds and raise money enough to pay the rent of it for a year, and this would give him a chance to turn around and begin business anew. I told him of my interview with Captain Lake, and what he had promised, and informed him of my plans for the future. He wept tears of joy and gratitude, not unmingled with sorrow, at the sacrifices I was making on his account, and solemnly promised me, upon his bended knees, that he would reform, and would apply himself once more to business, and try to redeem our property. He implored my forgiveness for the sorrow he had given me, and faithfully promised that he would never practice such concealment with me again.

Of course, I gave him my entire forgiveness, but could not refrain from telling him how much better I thought it would have been for both of us, had he placed in me the confidence which every husband should feel toward a true and loving wife. He assented to all that I said upon this point, and over and over again called me his guardian angel, and promised never to have any secrets from me again. But even at the time of registering this solemn promise, he bore within his breast a fearful secret which was one day to destroy all my confidence in him, and more completely blight my happiness than anything else could have done.

The day of sale came, and with it an immense crowd; some attracted by a desire to speculate out of our misfortunes, and others by that insatiable and inexplicable feeling of curiosity which always prompts envious mortals to gaze upon the fallen grandeur of others. I could not stay at home, and see all those articles which were so dear to me hawked about by an unfeeling mob, who knew not their sacredness, and accordingly went to Captain Lake's. On my way out I passed Captain Lake going into the city. He merely smiled, and said, "all is well," in response to my eager salutation. My heart was heavy with grief, but it is impossible to portray the feeling of comfort and consolation which those simple words imparted to me. I felt that it was indeed well, and went on my way with a lighter heart than before. The bidding upon some articles was quite spirited, but Captain Lake bought all the furniture, and the three servants, had the bill of sale made out in my name, and handed it over to me saying, "Here, Annie, is a father's gift to his daughter." I felt as if I could have fallen down and kissed his feet for very joy, and my heart was full of gratitude for his kindness, in this my hour of trouble. I concluded Captain Lake was not, after all, so bad a man as I had always thought him, and my heart smote me, as I remembered the bitterness which had once filled my heart toward him.

In the evening, after the sale was over, and the crowd had gone away, I went home, and soon after reaching there, a gentleman called who gave his name as Mortimore. I at once recognized the name as that of a man notorious throughout the city for being a great gambler, and scrutinized his countenance closely. It was cold, impassive, hard and brutal, just what the countenance of a gambler should be, and, though his manners were elegant, his voice and speech exactly tallied with his countenance. My husband was not in when he came, and without any preliminaries he told me that the house belonged to him; that he had bought it that day at the sale, and he would like to have us move out immediately, as he had use for it. This information was imparted in a hard measured tone, which was plainly intended to intimate that the matter would admit of no debate.

"But, sir, what use do you intend to make of it? Do you intend to occupy it yourself?"

"No; I shall rent it."

"But we can not move to-night, and, beside, this furniture and the servants are all here, and must be taken care of."

"The gentleman who bought the niggers and furniture will no doubt take them away immediately; and as I can get eleven hundred dollars a year for the house, I want to rent it at once, and you must move. Of course, you have no money to pay rent with."

"Is eleven hundred dollars a year your price for the house?"

"It is."

"I will take it for a year."

"You, madam!"

"Yes, sir; I will take it. You can call day after to-morrow morning and get your money for a year's rent."

"You will pay me eleven hundred dollars day after to-morrow?"

"I have said so."

"But what will you do for furniture?"

"Know, sir, that this furniture and these servants are mine. The gentleman who bought them is my father, and he bought them for me."

"Madam, I beg your pardon. Did I understand you to say that this furniture was yours, and that you would pay me eleven hundred dollars, day after to-morrow, for the house?"

"I said so, sir. Can we have the house?"

"Certainly, madam—certainly."

"Will you now do me the favor to go?"

He at once complied with my request, and bowed himself out, quite crestfallen, and much more respectful in his manner than when he came to order us to vacate at once. Soon after his departure my husband came in, and when I told him what had taken place, his indignation knew no bounds. He was for following the brute, and inflicting summary chastisement upon him for his impudence. He had no kindly feeling toward the author of all our misfortunes, and this last insult caused the cup of his wrath to boil over. But I restrained him, and finally soothed him into a promise to take no notice whatever of his brutality.

The next day I sold my jewelry, my watch and chain, and all my silverware, and we found that, after paying the year's rent, we could raise about two thousand dollars for my husband to begin anew with. He thought that, by going into the business of buying and selling horses, he could do well, and, in time, regain something like our old position. This would necessarily take him from home a great deal, and I dreaded his removal from my influence, fearing he would relapse into his old habits again; but there seemed no other chance to do anything, and I yielded a reluctant consent.

Mortimore came the next morning for his rent, but his manner was altogether different from what it had been when he was there before. Eugene would not see him at all, fearing he would be so much exasperated at the sight of him as to be unable to restrain himself; but I paid him his money, and took from him a receipt in full for one year's rent of the house that had been ours alone before the baneful shadow of his presence fell across my poor Eugene's pathway. My heart was full almost to bursting as these reflections rushed across my mind; but, in the midst of all, I rejoiced that I had been able to save even so much from the general wreck.

After making the necessary arrangements, my husband set out on a trading trip, intending to be gone about six weeks; and he solemnly renewed to me, at parting, his promise that he would not touch either cards or liquor. And I have every reason to believe that, during that trip at least, he faithfully kept his promise.

CHAPTER VIII.

It had been about six weeks since my husband started away, and the time of his expected return was at hand. My anxiety to see him was intense; for, despite my confidence in his promises, I could not repress a feeling of uneasiness lest he should be met by temptation too strong for him to overcome. I knew that he was not fully weaned from the excitement of his former evil associations, and dreaded the effect of his meeting once more the society into which I supposed he would be thrown.

As for myself I had got along finely during his absence. I had hired Tom and Caroline out, retaining only aunt Silvie at home; and, with the wages which they earned, and the little money I had when Eugene went away, had lived very comfortably, and had managed to save a little something. Caroline was the nurse, and, as I had never been accustomed to having the care of the children myself, it went rather awkwardly at first to do without her, but I could do it, and would do that or anything else, to economize our slender resources, and enable my husband to get another start in the world.

At length Eugene came. And as soon as I saw him I was satisfied he had been true to his promise. His eyes and countenance were clear, and bore no traces of dissipation, and he met my gaze without flinching. He seemed to read my anxiety in my countenance, and laughing a little, quiet, good-natured sort of laugh, he said:

"Annie, dismiss your fears and doubts. I have most faithfully kept my promise, and have broken company forever with those vile habits which caused our ruin."

What words of joy to me. Although I had never really doubted him, still it was, before that time, impossible to rid myself of some slight traces of fear, not for the uprightness of his intentions — oh! no, I never even suspected that—but I trembled for his strength. I knew he had once been tempted and had fallen, and I trembled at the bare thought of his being thus fearfully tried again. But now I felt that temptation was powerless against him. He was clad in impenetrable armor, and could laugh to scorn the fiercest shafts of the enemy.

He had met with the most extraordinary good fortune during this trip, and had, during the short space of less than two months, almost doubled the money with which he started out. He had purchased and sold one drove of horses, upon which alone he had cleared nearly one thousand dollars, and every adventure in which he had engaged had been in the highest degree successful. Of course he could not always expect to meet with such success; doubtless he would sometimes lose on some of his bargains, but the happy results of this trip elated us in the highest degree, and we at once set about forming our plans for obtaining another home. Our rent was paid for a year where we were, and, of course, we would remain there until that expired. He would continue his trading speculations during that time, and, if attended with any degree of success, he would be able, at the end of the year, to purchase a home of our own, and thus save the enormous rent we were now compelled to pay. Thus we looked at the future; thus in roseate colors it presented itself to us, and we were as happy that night as two human beings could well be—happier, I doubt not, than if we had never known the chastening fires of adversity.

And our fine-laid plans were carried into effect. During the entire year my husband spent but little time at home, applying himself with the utmost assiduity to the calling he had marked out for himself, and though never again, during the entire year, did he have such extraordinary good fortune as upon that first trip—though he even lost money on some of his investments—still he was slowly, but steadily increasing the sum at his banker's which was finally to buy us a home. I, too, did what I could to aid him, continued to practice every species of economy of which I was mistress, and the result was, that at the end of the year, we found ourselves in possession of sufficient means to buy a very comfortable house, though, by no means, equal to the one we were quitting. But we left it without regret. If our new home was less stately and magnificent than the old one—if I had not as fine jewelry and as costly plate as before—still the home was our own, and, best of all, my husband was saved. Was I not once more a happy woman?

But fate was not done persecuting us, nor were our misfortunes yet ended. Scarcely had we got settled in our new home, when our little Carrie was prostrated by a most violent attack of fever, and for three weeks she lay at death's door. Eugene was from home when she was taken ill, and it was a long time before I could get any message to him, not knowing his whereabouts, and I really feared she would die before he came home. We had learned to love her as one of our own, and the idea of her dying in his absence was inexpressibly painful to me. The thought of losing her under any circumstances was the most acute torture; but, when to this was added the dread of her dying without her adopted father seeing her, the agony was almost insupportable.

But, thank God, I was spared this trial. I succeeded

in learning where my husband was, and at once sent a special messenger for him. Of course he dropped all business at once, and hastened home by the most expeditious conveyance, and but a few days elapsed after his arrival until the old physician, who had given her the most unremitting care and attention, announced to us that the crisis of her disease was passed, and that her life would be saved. Never was a sentence uttered which conveyed more joy to a human heart than that did to mine. During her long illness I either sat by her little crib, or held her in my arms almost the whole time, and to know that my watching and care had not been in vain, and that she would be saved to us, filled my heart with thankfulness. Of course she was not out of danger yet, and it was a long time before she was well again; but the worst was now over, and together we lifted up our voices in thanksgiving to Him who had kindly given us the life of our little one, even after almost all hope seemed lost.

But another of our little family was to pass through the same ordeal. Scarcely had the crisis of Carrie's illness passed when Frankie was smitten down by the same disease. The attack, though less protracted than Carrie's case, was more violent; and, for ten days, his moans of anguish and cries of pain thrilled in my ears, and transfixed every nerve of my frame with the most acute agony. But he, too, through the mercy of God, and the skill of our venerable physician, was saved to us; and, again, we wept tears of joy and thankfulness, as we bent over our little lamb, snatched, as it were, from the very jaws of death.

But these afflictions had sadly deranged our affairs. We not only had heavy medical bills to pay, but the constant watching had so worn me out that we were com-

8

pelled to summon Caroline home, and we thus lost the aid of the wages she was earning, while our expenses at home were perceptibly increased. Beside, Eugene had entirely neglected his business in the care of the children, and through the incapacity, or rascality, of an agent whom he had left in charge of his stock when he came home, he not only entirely lost several horses, but the others, for want of care and attention, so much depreciated in value that he lost nearly a thousand dollars upon the stock he had on hand. This amount, which would once have appeared so trifling to us, at this time made a very serious hole in our limited finances, and rendered still further economy and care necessary in the management of our affairs.

About this time, also, I received a letter from the far away land of California, which caused my heart to beat with the most anxious fears, for though it bore the Sacramento post-mark it was written in a strange hand, and my first thought was that my brother, the only member of my father's family under the broad canopy of heaven, was dead. I felt sick at heart, and for a time hesitated to open it, dreading the confirmation of my worst fears, but when I finally mustered courage enough to open the seal, it was not quite so bad as I had thought, though still bad enough. Frank was not dead though very sick, and among almost entire strangers, his only acquaintance there being the friend and comrade who had written the letter to me at his request. The writer stated that Frank was very much disheartened, and was under the impression that he would never be any better, but that his bones would be laid to rest in that far off land.

The reader may imagine, but words will hardly express the pain with which this intelligence thrilled my heart.

My brother Frank — my last surviving blood relation, the brother to whom I had been wont to look for direction and assistance in every trouble — was lying dangerously ill in a distant country, among strangers—doubtless deprived of every comfort, and even of the nursing and attention which his condition demanded, and I was powerless to do anything to aid him. I would have given anything to be with him, but many thousand miles of wild and sterile land separated us; and even had it been possible for me to get to him, the situation of my own family would have precluded me from making the attempt. I looked at the date of the letter—it was nearly three months since it had been written—and who could tell whether my poor brother's gloomy anticipations had been realized during that time? Yes; I felt that it must be so. His depression of spirits, it seemed to me, must have exercised a serious influence upon his disease; and I felt assured that his career must have ended, far from home and friends, and that his last resting-place was in some wild, gloomy dell, unmarked by any memento which would aid me in any way to identify it, should I ever wish to visit and water it with my tears. Ah! how sad was this reflection to my already sorely-tried spirit.

For the next three weeks I was infinitely miserable. Fancy was constantly presenting to my mental vision the most vivid pictures of the imaginary death-scene of my brother; and even in my dreams I heard his voice calling upon me for that assistance and comfort which I was utterly powerless to render. But, at the end of that time came a letter which turned all my mourning into joy, and my weeping into songs of praise and thanksgiving. My brother, instead of dying, as he anticipated, and as his friend thought he certainly would, had finally recovered, and would start home as soon as he could close up his business, which would be in about three or four weeks from the date of the letter.

According to this, he must be on his way home, and would no doubt soon be here. Oh! with what joy I received this intelligence, and how earnestly did I look forward to the time of our anticipated meeting. Time seemed to me to move all too slow, and it was with the utmost impatience that I watched for his arrival. When it is remembered, by the reader, that it was almost five years since I had parted with him, beside the grave of our father, in the city of Philadelphia, it will not be thought strange that my anxiety for his coming was almost insupportable. My husband used to rally me, good-naturedly, of course, upon my impatience, and to say that he should be jealous if I persisted in such demonstration of evident affection for "this foreigner," as he styled him; and I would retort that, if he became at all disagreeable, I should forsake him entirely for the "foreigner."

At last he came, and the reader need not be told that his greeting was the warmest that it was in my power to bestow, for words will hardly express my joy at again meeting him. But how he was changed in the five years since our adieus were spoken beside our father's tomb. Then his appearance was that of a smooth-faced and rather delicate-appearing youth: now he was a man—tall, robust and stalwart, his face bronzed, and his muscles hardened by toil and exposure, while a heavy, dark beard and mustache entirely concealed the lower part of his face, and gave him a sort of brigandish look, so different from his former gentle and almost effeminate appearance that, had I not been expecting his arrival, I should certainly never have recognized him. But, how he had improved! His robust, manly frame, and fine muscular development, now challenged my admiration, as his kindness to me in former days had won my affection; and I was now as proud of my brother as it was possible for a sister to be; while, upon his part, his affection for me seemed to be stronger and more enduring than ever. But we were not permitted long to enjoy the happiness of our reunion. Events were already at work which were to sever forever the ties that had bound us so closely to each other during the whole of our lives.

My brother returned from California in the month of December, 1860. The election of Abraham Lincoln as President of the United States had just taken place, and the events of that fall and winter are fresh in the minds of my readers. The entire South was full of feverish excitement. State after State was adopting the ordinance of secession; the air was vocal with the sounds of military preparation; and the universal topic of conversation was, independence and war to the knife against the so-called Abolition encroachments.

I am about to enter into no apology for the rebellion which so long convulsed our land and drenched it in fraternal gore; which has clothed every house in mourning, and inflicted wounds which can not be healed until this generation shall have passed away. On the contrary, impartial history will record our late civil war as the most egregious folly, if not the most gigantic crime, of the world's annals. Abjuring at once all obligation to that Government which had so long fostered them, and under which they had become opulent and powerful, the Southern States plunged into a ferocious and bloody warfare, for the purpose of protecting certain species of property against the fancied designs of men who were supposed to be hostile to its further continuance; and the result has been just what might have been anticipated by any one not maddened by the excitement which ruled the entire South at this time. The property in defense of which they took up arms, has been swept away entirely and forever; their land has been impoverished to the extent of millions of dollars; and every Southern heart is compelled to bear the burden of mourning for relatives slain and maimed in a cause upon which the blessing of heaven never rested.

That there were many good men whose hearts disapproved of the part they were acting, and who saw no just cause for rebellion in the then existing condition of affairs; but who were forced into the revolt, against their will, by the force of popular opinion, by the wily arts of unscrupulous demagogues, and by the mischievous doctrines of "States' Rights" which had been so long inculcated by leading Southern politicians, is no doubt true; and for such men I have no words of condemnation. While their folly is to be most bitterly deplored—not only for the sake of general humanity, but, also, in view of the fearful consequences which have followed their delusion—still must they be acquitted of the terrible criminality which attends their leaders. But for these last, for those who imposed upon them that delusion — those who molded and formed that public opinion by which they were precipitated into the rebellion—the blood of a million of slaughtered victims, and the tears of countless widows and orphans, cry aloud for vengeance. And so sure as there is a just God who shall hereafter reward every man according to his works, so sure will these men have a fearful account to render hereafter.

My brother was one of those men who, by the arts of those leaders, was duped into giving his support to this movement. Born and bred in the South, thoroughly imbued with the pernicious doctrine of State sovereignty, ignorant of the arts of wily and scheming politicians, reading only those publications which depicted in the most glowing terms the dangerous doctrines and designs of the abolitionists, generous and manly to a fault, and glowing with a hatred of oppression and resentment, for real or fancied injury, what wonder that, viewing the matter from the standpoint to which he had been educated, he earnestly espoused the cause of his native section, threatened, as he supposed her to be, with almost entire destruction by the fanatics of the North? In vain I reasoned with and entreated him not to engage in the struggle at all—to at least remain neutral—his reply was that his honor was at stake, and that his conscience would not suffer him to remain an idle spectator of the contest, in which it might be the life of his country was the stake. In vain my husband seconded my arguments and entreaties with all the means at his command—we were powerless to move him, and each day saw him a more and more ardent advocate of the independence of the South. Captain Lake, who had embraced with the utmost ardor the cause of the South, used all his influence with Frank against us, and his doctrines harmonizing entirely with Frank's inclinations, made him a most powerful antagonist.

At length came the actual commencement of hostilities, the attack upon Fort Sumpter, and the entire nation, both North and South, was convulsed as by a mighty electric shock. As the news flashed from place to place along the wires, business of every kind was suspended, and everything gave way to the work of raising troops for the struggle then inaugurated. The city of Atlanta was no exception to the general rule. The stores were generally closed, eager and excited crowds thronged the streets; the

stirring notes of fife and drum were heard at all hours of
the day and night; at every street corner excited and elo-
quent speakers harangued equally excited crowds, urging
them to rush to arms in support of their threatened and
endangered liberties; the listeners testified their approba-
tion by constant and wild cheering, and the enlistment of
men proceeded with almost marvelous rapidity.   Young
and old, rich and poor, all classes vied in their efforts to
secure a place in the ranks of the army, and none who
applied were turned away.   Could they, at that time, have
foreseen the results of the mad excitement of that hour,
could they have had the slightest glimpse of the horrid
events of the coming four years, how many would have
recoiled, shuddering, from the act they were now so eager
to do.

Among the earliest to enroll himself was Captain Lake,
though already over fifty years of age.   He was lustily
cheered by the unthinking mob, who saw him sign his
name to what eventually proved his death-warrant, and
was rewarded for his "patriotism," by being elected com-
mander of the company of which he was a member.   He
at once proceeded to organize his command, was duly
commissioned a Captain, and entered the service of the
Confederacy in that capacity.

The next day my brother, whom I had not seen since
the beginning of the fierce excitement, came home and
told me that he, too, had enlisted and had been chosen
First Lieutenant of his company.   I wept bitter tears at
this intelligence, but the deed was done, and it was too
late to undo the evil, nor would I then urge him to forsake his plighted faith.   Although my heart disapproved
the cause, still I could not but admire the manhood which
led him to this step, and having once taken it, I felt that

he would be dishonored were he to retract, but the contemplation of the future had no charms for me. He tried to comfort me by telling me that there would be no war, that the North would not fight, and that all they had to do was to make a display of force, and in six weeks their ends would be obtained, and they would all be at home again. But all he could say to me did not divest my mind of the impression that I should never see him again. Was this a presentiment? He then tried to induce my husband to go into the army with him, using all the arguments his imagination could suggest in favor of this course, and making the most extravagant promises of future good if he would consent to do so. But his arguments and entreaties were alike unavailing, and Eugene continued firm in his refusal.

But a few days were allowed the newly raised troops in which to prepare for leaving their homes, many of them, alas! never to return. Captain Lake, before his departure, perhaps realizing how foully he had wronged me, and willing to make what amends he could, made a sort of will, devising fifty thousand dollars to me in the event of his death. My brother too, having been eminently successful in California, made the most generous provision for me in case of his death. He had brought home some eighty thousand dollars, and he gave the strongest proof of his fraternal affection by devising the whole of this vast sum for my benefit. Had I been able, gentle reader, to secure the benefit of this munificent provision for my future, this story had most likely never been written, for many of the vicissitudes of my life had then never taken place.

Within a day or two after these dispositions were made my brother came to bid me good-bye. He was clad in

the uniform of his command, and though at sight of it my
tears flowed afresh, still I could not but feel a natural
pride in the erect and manly carriage which distinguished
him, and the grace with which he bore himself in his new
position.   But the adieus were soon spoken, and in a few
minutes I had again parted with my only living relative,
and this time it really was, what I had often before imagined, a parting forever on this side of eternity.

CHAPTER IX.

TIME in its ever ceaseless flight passed away—the days lengthened into weeks, and the weeks grew into months, and instead of the war being ended in six weeks, as its advocates prophesied, it was evident to the most casual observer, that it was but just begun. The North had displayed a spirit entirely unexpected by the leaders of the secession movement. The unanimity of the people of that section in springing to arms was most astonishing, and, if possible, excelled the ardor of the Southerners. Bloodshed there had been, too, notwithstanding the predictions of the champions of rebellion to the contrary. The bloody battle of Bull Run had been fought, and, though resulting in a victory over the National forces, had carried grief and mourning to many a Southern home, and had clothed in the habiliments of woe many a fair daughter of that sunny clime. My brother participated in that battle, and for a long time after tidings of the conflict came, how earnestly did I look for some intelligence from him, for I trembled lest his name, too, should be found among the long list of the slain.

But at last I received intelligence from him. His regiment had been engaged and had suffered severely; his captain had been killed, and the command of the company having in consequence devolved upon him, he had discharged the duties of his trust in such a manner as to win the favorable notice of his colonel. He had been recommended for promotion, and had no doubt he would be commissioned captain in place of him who had fallen.

How proud I was to have this intelligence of him; for though I regarded him as the victim of a dreadful delusion, still was he not my brother, and should I not glory in his bravery and manhood, even though displayed in a bad cause?   Accompanying this letter was a list of the killed and wounded of our acquaintances, which I waded through, shuddering as I came to each familiar name, until, when the end was at last reached, I felt sick at heart.   Uninformed and ignorant as I was of all that pertains to war, I could see that this was but a beginning, and trembled as the question forced itself upon me, what would be the end, and how long it would be before the name of my brother would be included in some such horrid list as the one before me.   I felt an almost assured conviction that he would fall sooner or later, and this thought was ever present, poisoning all my joys, and investing my solitary hours with a bitterness almost insupportable,

Meantime, the war went on.   The North was making the most strenuous exertions to raise and equip an army sufficient to bear down all opposition, and corresponding exertions had to be made by the Southern States to bring into the field an army sufficient to cope with the National force.   The Southern people found that the war was not the mere play-spell they had anticipated, and the force of popular opinion was no longer sufficient to raise such armies as the exigency demanded.   In order, therefore, to give new force to that popular opinion, the President of the Confederacy, about this time, issued his famous proclamation, warning all persons who were not willing to take up arms in defense of their country, to seek a more congenial home in the North.

This despotic order struck my husband, as it did thousands of others, with the utmost consternation.   Up to this time, we had endeavored, by keeping perfectly quiet and attending strictly to our own affairs, to avoid offending the sense of the community in which we lived. But now the time had come when this would no longer suffice. He must either go into the army and fight for a cause in which he had no heart, or we must dispose of what little property we had, at such sacrifice as we might, and make the best of our way north of Mason and Dixon's line. The first was not to be thought of, and the second was, therefore, the only alternative left us. And thus it was that the Southern people began to reap the sad fruits of the rebellion into which they had so madly and unnecessarily plunged.

We were, at this time, in comfortable circumstances, though far from being rich, and we could ill-afford to make the sacrifice requisite to comply with this cruel order. But neither time nor opportunity was afforded for remonstrance or hesitation. The order was imperative, and close upon its heels followed a most rigorous and merciless conscription, which was to sweep into the military service of the Confederacy every man who had not complied with the other dread alternative by banishment. How wretchedly were these poor people deluded and imposed upon by their designing leaders. Taking up arms to escape from the pretended tyranny of the Government of the United States, they now found themselves subjects of a despotism as much more terrific and intolerable than that from which they were fleeing, as is the Government of Turkey more absolute than the constitutional monarchy of England. But these reflections did not help our situation in the least.

Accordingly, my husband set to work to dispose of what property we had on hand, preparatory to our emigra-

tion from the land of our nativity.   In this matter he met
with no little diffiulty.   The very fact that he was selling
off his property to go North, at once stamped him as a
"disloyal abolitionist;" and, in the opinion of those with
whom he attempted to trade, at once absolved them from
all obligations of honor or honesty toward him.   More
than this; he was met with gibes and covert sneers from
those who regarded him as less patriotic than themselves,
and was, on several occasions, met with positive insult by
parties to whom he applied to make sales of property.
He soon found that it was impossible to sell except at enormous sacrifices; but the emergency admitted of no dis-
cussion, and, accordingly, he disposed of all our property
for about two-thirds of its real value, and we set out for
Memphis, Tennessee, as the most convenient point of
egress from the now hated Confederacy.

During this time I had received several letters from my
brother.   He was enthusiastic over the cause in which he
was engaged, and, at all times, expressed the utmost confidence in its complete and speedy triumph.   Although I
could not believe that such would be the case, nor wish
well to an enterprise which, in my heart of hearts, I con-
demned, still these letters were a source of constant gratification to me.   They assured me, from time to time, of
the welfare of a dearly beloved brother, and my heart
overflowed with gratitude to that God who had thus far
mercifully and kindly protected and preserved him amid
the perils of camp-life, and the dangers of the battle-
field.   He had been promoted two or three times, and at
the time we left Atlanta for Memphis, he occupied the
position of lieutenant-colonel in the same regiment in
which he had gone out as a mere subaltern.   How my
heart throbbed with a sister's pride as I contemplated

those evidences of appreciation of his merit, let those who have thus watched the upward and onward course of a loved brother judge. But to return to ourselves and our journey northward.

My husband had, of course, taken the precaution to procure passes for us from the military authorities at Atlanta; but, notwithstanding this, we were frequently stopped by conscript officers, ourselves and our passes closely scrutinized, our baggage searched, time and again, for articles contraband of war; and, not content with annoying us by all legal means in their power, these petty tyrants, in more instances than one, added insult to injury, by stigmatizing my husband as a traitor and a coward "for leaving his country in her hour of danger." Poor fools! They could not realize that we were fleeing to our country for protection from the persecutions, annoyances and dangers of an illegal and unholy despotism, backed and supported by as fierce and brutal a mob as ever thronged the streets of Paris.

In one instance, I thought our journey was to be summarily arrested. Justly incensed at the overbearing and insolent manner of a petty official, who had stopped us to overhaul our baggage, and losing his accustomed control of himself, my husband expressed his opinion of the contemptible little tyrant before us, in language more forcible than polite. This he chose to construe into disloyalty to the "great government" of which he was the representative, and Eugene was at once seized by a file of soldiers and thrown into prison. They allowed me no communication with him, and, for a short time, I was utterly at a loss what to do; but, after hesitating a time, decided to go to General ———, who was in command there, and endeavor to procure his release. The general listened

kindly and courteously, to my story, and after asking me
a few questions, gave me an order for his immediate release.   Armed with this missive I flew to the prison, and
in a short time we were again on our journey.   I shall
always retain a most grateful remembrance of General
——, for his kindness to me under these trying circumstances.

In due time we arrived at Memphis, which was then in
possession of the Confederate forces, but which was invested by the land and naval forces of the Union, within
a day or two after our arrival.   And there I first witnessed the actual horrors of war.   It was in Memphis
that I first heard the sound of hostile guns, the scream-
ing of shot and shell, the bursting of bombs, and all the
horrid sounds which accompany the destruction of human
life on the field of battle.   Here, too, I first saw wounded
men, and my brain turned with horror as I beheld the
mangled and bleeding forms of those who had once been
stout, healthy, and vigorous men; and as their piteous
moans smote upon my ears I shuddered, in every fiber of
my frame, and hastened to convey myself beyond sight
and hearing of these sickening objects.

Of course, under the present state of affairs, it was impossible for us to get any further North, and we remained
in Memphis until the surrender of that place to the national
forces, when we procured passes and transportation for
Cincinnati, where we arrived without farther incident.
And now, for the first time since the promulgation of the
order before referred to, we could feel that we were free.
Once more I could lie down to rest at night and feel assured that my husband would not, before morning, be torn
from my arms by merciless conscript officers, and hurried
into the army which was using all its energies for the de-

struction of the Government which now sheltered us beneath its protecting wings.

Our stay in Cincinnati was of short duration. We were among strangers, and Eugene did not readily find any avenue of business open to him, and we could not live without doing something. Having heard there was a good opening at London, Canada West, Eugene decided that the best thing we could do was to go there; and, accordingly, we went there, after having staid in Cincinnati but about three weeks. Our journey to that place was unattended with any incidents worthy of record, or in any degree interesting to my readers. I may remark, however, that, on our journey through Ohio, I was forcibly struck with the vast superiority of the country over anything I had ever seen in the South, in point of improvement and advancement of every kind. Large, well-cultivated farms bounded the prospect on every hand; while the comfortable, and often elegant, residences of their owners gave the very highest evidence of thrift and prosperity. Every little town, too, boasted its manufacturing establishments; all of which were now stimulated to the highest degree of activity by the demand for supplies of all kinds for the use of the army. I was immeasurably astonished at the little derangement produced here by the war, as compared with the Southern States. Here business of all kinds was flowing in its accustomed channels, with, perhaps, greater briskness than before the war; while there, everything was almost at a stand-still, and a sense of uneasiness and distrust seemed to pervade the entire community. I wondered, then, at this difference, but have since ceased to feel any surprise at it.

Upon reaching our destination my husband went at once into business, and, for a time, prospered finely. Money

was plenty, and, as Eugene was a good financier, we were
soon on the fair road to comfort, if not to wealth. But the
climate was so much colder than we had been accustomed
to, that we were far from contented. Born and reared beneath the sunny skies of the South, we were illy prepared
to endure the rigors of a Canada winter, and decided to
return to the United States; and we were strengthened in
our determination by the fact that Willie, who had always
been rather delicate, was attacked with a severe cough,
which we—whether justly or otherwise, I know not—attributed to the cold and damp climate of that locality.
Accordingly, my husband, in the fall of 1862, disposed of
what property we had there, and we returned to Cincinnati.

I ought to remark here that, while in Canada, I received
letters from my brother—the first intelligence I had had
from him directly since we left Atlanta, and the last I was
ever destined to receive. Henceforth the fate of war separated us as completely from each other, and as entirely
destroyed our communication with each other, as was afterward done by his death, which occurred in front of Atlanta, during the campaign of 1864. At this time, however, he was well, and was still on the high road to prefer-
ment. He had been several times promoted since I had
heard from him, and was now gracing the position of a
brigadier-general. He was as ardent in the cause of
Southern independence as ever, and was still just as confident of ultimate success as when he marched from Atlanta in the comparatively humble position of a first lieutenant; at least, so he stated in his letters. But I fancied
that I detected in his language a sort of undercurrent of
despondency which induced me to think that, perhaps,
after all, he was not as hopeful as he tried to induce me
to believe.

But, be that as it might, I could not but feel proud of the record of gallantry he was making for himself. How much better pleased I should have been had this record been made in behalf of the Government, instead of against it, may easily be imagined; but still we are constrained to admire bravery wherever we see it, even though it be in a bad cause. How natural, then, was it that I should be proud of the evidences of merit displayed by my only brother, and should rejoice with all my heart to hear of these successive promotions. But, alas! how short-lived are the honors and pleasures of this life. Two years later, my poor brother was buried by strange hands, in an unknown grave, while no friend or sister near him, in his last hour, listened to his dying words, or wiped the death-damps from his pale brow as he breathed forth his parting sigh.

CHAPTER X.

I HAVE said that we returned to Cincinnati in the fall of 1862. This time my husband was more fortunate in getting into business than when we were here before; an opening was soon found, and we took rooms at the Spencer House. My health was so poor, by reason of the excitement we had undergone for some time, and I was so much worn out by the constant changes and journeyings of the last year, that I did not feel equal to the task of undertaking the management of a house; and hence our determination to board for a time, until I should become somewhat improved in vigor.

For the next few weeks we were very happy. My husband had entirely quit drinking, and spent all his evenings at home with me; my children were in good health, and were four of the sweetest little cherubs to be found anywhere; they gave me very little care or trouble. Save some anxiety on my brother's account, my mind knew not a single burden. The children had forgotten all about their mother, and did not seem to know that I was not their maternal parent, and, on my own part, I loved them as if they had been my own. My husband was as kind and considerate to me as it was possible for any one to be; my every want was supplied, and I almost forgot that I had ever been unhappy.

But, alas! my happiness was not to last long. A blow from a new and unexpected quarter was impending over me, and was destined soon to shatter into atoms forever the frail fabric of bliss which now surrounded me; to cast me down from the pinnacle of happiness, upon which I then rested, into the very lowest depths of an abyss of misery and wretchedness so profound that I shudder when I think of it. The time for the revelation of that fatal secret of my husband's, to which allusion has already been made, was fast approaching, and yet I suspected it not. Like Damocles at the festival, when the sword was suspended by a single hair over his head, I reveled in the enjoyment of the bliss presented to me, all unsuspicious of danger, and never dreaming that my happiness could be brought to an end. Then, how terrible the shock when it did come, and with what crushing force the blow fell upon my suddenly-blighted spirit, let the reader imagine; for any words of mine are utterly incapable of describing.

Early one evening I was alone in our sitting-room. The children were all in bed, and my husband had not yet come in, though I was momentarily expecting him. There came a gentle tap at the door, and one of the boys employed about the house came in with a card, which he handed me, with a polite bow. I looked at the card—the name was a strange one to me—it was Mrs. Martha H. Mason, a name I had never heard before, nor could I imagine who she could be, or what should induce her to call upon me. To my look of surprised inquiry, the boy answered that the lady who gave him the card wished to see me in the parlor. In an instant I was struck with an undefinable dread of some approaching evil, but what it was I could not for a moment imagine. Who could she be, and why had she come to seek me? Her summons certainly boded me no good, and I felt sure some deep calamity was in store for me, but what it was I could not divine. I grew weak, and felt myself turn pale as these thoughts, in an instant, flashed through my mind; but I retained sufficient strength and control of myself to tell the boy I would be down in a few moments, when he bowed and withdrew.

After he was gone I sunk back into my seat and tried to collect my somewhat scattered thoughts. I ran over, in my mind, all the names with which I was acquainted and could call to mind, and all I remembered to have heard my husband mention, but could not think who Martha H. Mason was. What would I not have given at that moment for my husband's presence and counsel, and at first I thought of waiting until he came in, before according the desired interview. But no; that would not do. Perhaps it was something which affected his honor, in which case it were better for both that I should know the whole truth before seeing him. I did not for a moment imagine. that it was anything which would prove him to be guilty of actual crime against the laws of God and man; and the conclusion at which my mind finally arrived was, that it was Carrie's mother, and that she had come to reclaim her child. But let the cause of her coming be what it might, or whoever she might be, I must see her and know the worst.

Accordingly, after making some slight changes in my dress, I went down into the parlor. There sat a lady, dressed in deep mourning; and the first glance at her pale, sweet face told me I had never seen her before. Her age was not far from thirty, as near as I could judge; and, despite the evident marks of care and suffering which her countenance displayed, she was surpassingly beautiful. She rose, as I entered the parlor, and timidly approached me. In a low, and finely-modulated voice, she asked:

"Are you Mrs. Eugene Giles?"

"I am," I answered. What do you wish with me?"

"Are you Mr. Giles' first wife; or was he married before?"

"I am his second wife. His first wife died some six years, or more, since. We were married in about seven months from the time of her death."

"Had he any children by his first wife?"

"He had three; all boys. But may I inquire why you ask all these questions?"

"I will tell you soon. May I ask the names of these boys?"

"The eldest one's name is Willie—he is fourteen years old. The second is Frankie, aged eleven years; and the youngest is Eddie, aged about nine. Do you know Mr. Giles, or why are you so particular in your inquiries about him and his family?"

At this question her entire manner changed, and she answered, almost fiercely:

"Do I know him? Yes; far better than you do. Look at this!" and she handed me an ambrotype-case. I opened it, and found it to contain two likenesses—a young man and young woman. In an instant I recognized them: the young man was my husband, and the young woman was the lady before me. Who was she, and what could it all mean? As I asked her these questions she handed me a written paper and bade me read it. My husband had not kept up the lessons he began with me, and it was with some difficulty that I could read it; but I made out that it was a certificate of the marriage of Eugene Giles Mason and Martha Hart. As the fearful import of this document thrilled through my brain, I was nearly wild with anguish. Could it be that this woman was his lawful wife, the mother of his children? Oh! no. Eugene could not be such a villain. Perhaps she was his wife's sister; and there was so much resemblance between them that I had mistaken the likeness for her's. I turned to her to ask an explanation. She was weeping silently but bitterly.

"Who are you," said I, "and what is all this to me? What have I, the wife of Eugene Giles, to do with the marriage of Eugene Mason and Martha Hart?"

"The man who now calls himself Eugene Giles," said she, speaking slowly and bitterly, "is no other than Eugene Giles Mason, and I am Martha Hart Mason, his lawful wife, the mother of the three boys whose names you have just given me. Is this nothing to you?"

Had a two-edged sword at that moment pierced my heart, I could not have suffered half the agony I endured as she pronounced these fatal words.

"This can not, can not be," I cried, in my anguish. "Eugene would never be so base. Beside, he told me his first wife was dead. Oh! take back those cruel words."

"It is all true that I have told you," said she. "I have other proofs of the truth of my statements. Will you look at them?"

Alas! there was no need. I felt that her words were true, and that Eugene was not my husband; and the thought of my situation, in an instant, flashed upon me.

"If all that you have been telling me is true—if Eugene is not my husband—if you are his wife, my God, what am I?" I cried out, and sunk to the floor.

I had not fainted, for I could hear and see everything that was said or done in the room, and my mind seemed imbued with unnatural activity, but the suddenness and violence of the shock had deprived me of all physical vitality, and I was powerless to rise from the floor. I could not move or speak. The last words I had uttered

"IF YOU ARE HIS WIFE, WHAT AM I?"

were ringing in my brain. If she was his wife, what was I? I was only his mistress, and had been such for these many long years. Could it be so? Was it possible that my husband's real name was Mason, and that he was the base and unprincipled villain that her words would indicate? Oh! no; it could not be. Eugene would never, never, never have wronged me thus. There must be some terrible mistake here. His wife was surely dead, and our marriage was lawful. This woman was some base adventuress who had, by some means, possessed herself of his marriage certificate, and was now using it for some purpose of her own. Or, more likely, it was some one else's marriage certificate, which she was trying to fasten upon my husband. But, then, those likenesses—what could they mean? But I could not, would not believe Eugene was so base. Were he here, he could explain all.

While these thoughts ran riot through my brain, I lay helpless and motionless on the floor, and the woman who had been the cause of all this misery, sat staring at me with her great, black eyes, until they seemed to burn and sear into my brain. I could not remove my eyes from her face, nor could I speak. I had never been so completely prostrated and unnerved as I was by this terrible revelation, and did not care whether I ever moved or spoke again. At length she arose and came to my side. She knelt down by me and spoke substantially as follows, while she rested her hand kindly upon my head:

"Poor child; I do not blame you in the least for this terrible affair. No; you are innocent, and have been the victim of the most grievous wrong, as well as myself. My husband left me when I was confined with my fifth child, little Eddie. He stole my babe, only a week old, and my two little boys, and left me with two little girls. He has

now been gone for more than eight years, and, during all
that long and weary time, I have been traveling in search
of him.   I have roamed from place to place, throughout
the whole of the United States, with no other object but
to find my darling babes.   No doubt the heartless monster
thought I was dead when he married you.   He naturally
thought that the loss of my children, in my enfeebled condition, would be too much for me, and that the shock would
kill me.   But, thank God, I have disappointed him.   I
have been wonderfully spared and preserved, and high
heaven has kindly answered my prayer and guided me to
him—and once more I shall possess my darling children,
once more I shall press them to the lonely heart which
for years has mourned and sighed for them.   But I pity
rather than blame you.   You have been most grievously
wronged as well as myself, and I would not harm a hair
of your head: all I ask is the possession of my babes, and
vengeance upon the heartless wretch who has deceived
and betrayed us both.   Where are my precious darlings ?
I long to see them and clasp them to my heart once
more."

·She pronounced these last words with a vehemence and
energy which indicated the depth of her feeling upon this
subject.   I strove to reply to her eager question, but my
tongue refused to obey the mandates of my will, and I remained silent.   She gazed at me a moment, then sprung
to her feet and rung the bell with the utmost violence,
and then turned to raise me and place me on the sofa.
She had barely accomplished her task when the proprietor of the house made his appearance, and, in an eager
and excited manner, she demanded to be shown to Mr.
Giles' room.   Probably he did not observe me lying on
the sofa, or he would have known there was something

wrong; but he proceeded at once to comply with her demand, and they left the room.

I strove to rise and follow them, but I was completely paralyzed by the horrid events of the last hour, and my limbs totally refused to obey my volition. I then tried to speak, to call out and attract their attention, but was powerless even to move my tongue. I would have given anything to have witnessed the meeting between her and Giles, and to have heard him defend himself against her accusation, for I still half believed there was some terrible misunderstanding, and that he could explain it all satisfactorily. Although I was satisfied she had once been his wife, my faith in him was so strong that I believed he would be able to explain away the horrible tale she had unfolded to me. And now, for the first time, occurred to me the thought that they might have been divorced, and Eugene might still be innocent of any wrong. But, then, why should he have told me she was dead?

These thoughts all passed through my brain, and then came the reflection that it mattered very little to me whether her story was true or false. I felt that I should never recover from the horrible paralysis into which these astounding revelations had thrown me. I knew that, in the sight of God, I was innocent of any wrong; and if I was to die, what matter whether my association with Giles was legal or not? Immorality, on my part, I knew there was none; and as long as my soul was pure and uncontaminated, what mattered it that I had sustained toward him a station not sanctioned by the laws of God or man? I knew that I was innocent in the sight of high heaven, and I could well afford that the scorn of those who thought themselves better than I, should be visited upon my memory after my spirit had taken its everlasting flight to the bosom of my heavenly Maker.

For a long time I lay alone in the room. No one came, and I was utterly unable to help myself in any way, or to give any alarm or make my wants known. It seemed to me an age—I suppose it was about half an hour, but it seemed much longer—before any one made their appearance, and then Giles came into the room. He came and knelt by my side, clasped me in his arms, and called me all the pet names which had been so dear to me in our happier days, and implored me to forgive him; told me that he loved me better than his own life, and could not give me up, and begged me to speak to him again. I tried to speak, but the terrible paralysis still held my tongue, and I was unable to utter a word. Meanwhile he continued his demonstrations of affection, and the most passionate entreaties for just one word to assure him of my forgiveness. He did not deny that he had wronged me beyond redress, or that the woman was his lawful wife; he did not dispute the truth of her horrible revelation; but he urged his unbounded and uncontrollable love for me, in extenuation of his folly and his guilt. And all this time I lay unable to move or speak.

Eugene finally observed my situation, and, starting suddenly to his feet, he hastily left the room. He was gone but a few moments, when he came in, as hastily as he had gone out, accompanied by a physician, whose name was Wood. He brought the doctor to my side, and, in the most frantic manner, implored him to save me if within his power.

The doctor took hold of my arm, felt my pulse, placed his hand upon my forehead for a moment, then put his ear down to my heartbeat, and, without speaking a word, took a lancet from his pocket and struck it into my arm. The blood did not start readily, and he held hartshorn to my nostrils for a short time, which had the effect of starting the crimson current in a steady, vigorous stream. The flow of blood loosened my paralyzed tongue, and, in a low voice (for my strength was all gone), I asked the doctor to leave the room. I wanted to talk with Eugene, and hear from his own lips the confirmation or denial of the awful revelation which had had such a terrible effect upon me. But the man of physic replied that my situation was extremely critical, that my life was in serious danger, and that he could not leave until I was better. However, he asked no questions as to the cause of my sudden and violent illness. Doubtless his science revealed to him the fact that some tremendous excitement was the moving cause; but he said nothing in relation to his suspicions, whatever they may have been, but steadily and carefully he attended to his business until my arm was bandaged, when he took his leave—having first left some remedies to calm my terrible nervous excitement and reinvigorate my feeble frame.

As soon as we were once more alone, Eugene, at my request, came and sat down by my side.

"Eugene," said I, "as you value your soul and your eternal happiness, tell me the whole truth relative to this sad, sad affair. Is this woman your wife?"

"Yes, Annie," he replied, "she is my wife—the mother of my three boys."

How the light of hope went out in my bosom as I listened to this confession, uttered in a low tone of voice, and with half-averted head. Up to this time I had hoped, notwithstanding the solemn asseverations of the woman, that he would deny it, and that I would be spared the shame and mortification which were now my lot. My faith in him had whispered that either her tale was a fabrication, or she was the victim of some dreadful hallucination. But when he answered me as he did, this last lingering ray of hope faded out, and, with a deep groan, I sunk back upon my pillow, from which, in my excitement, I had half risen to propound my eager inquiry.

"Oh! Eugene," said I, "how could you treat me as you have? Why should you have done me this grievous wrong?"

"God is my witness," he replied, "that when I married you I thought she was dead. Believe me, Annie, for He knows I speak the truth when I say that the thought of wrong toward you never entered my mind."

"But I am not your wife, and we must part."

"No, Annie, you are not my wife, but I love you as I ever have since I first saw you, and I can not part from you. I will never give you up."

"You must not talk so to me. If we have ignorantly done evil during all these years, let us not continue it now that we know the wrong. Henceforth we will be nothing to each other."

"Oh! Annie, say not so. You are the only woman I ever loved, and I can not live without you. Mine you must be forever."

"What! would you give up your children for me?"

"Yes, every thing I have in the world. I will give up children, wife, property—every thing but you—you I can not."

"Oh! Eugene, how can you talk of giving up those lovely children? It will almost break my heart to part with them, and they are not mine. How then, can you talk so?"

"Annie, I love you enough to give up everything for you. I never knew happiness until I met you, and if you leave me I can never know happiness again. I can be happy with you, but with that woman, never."

"Where is she?" I asked.

"She is up in our room with the children. They were afraid of her, and she was trying to conciliate them by telling them she was their mother, and endeavoring to persuade them to go and live with her. But they would not believe her. They told her their 'ma was down in the parlor—that she had gone there to see a lady who called for her. But she will succeed in convincing them—they will go with her, and she may have them if she will only go away and let us alone."

"Eugene, you must not talk so," I replied as firmly as I could, although it cost me a terrible effort, "we were happy in each other's society because we supposed we were innocent, and without innocence there can be no real happiness. Let us not, then, forever destroy our happiness and stain our souls with the guilt of doing wrong with our eyes open."

But all I could say was of no avail. He still insisted that he could not and would not part with me; and, at length, worn out with conflicting emotions, and with the terrible excitement of the scenes through which I had passed, I ceased to contend any longer. He continued to talk for some time after I had become silent, when thinking, perhaps, that I needed rest, he, too, subsided into silence and allowed me to indulge my own sad thoughts.

And sad and gloomy indeed they were. Notwithstanding the awful strain which had just been imposed upon my mental faculties, my mind was comparatively clear, and my first thought was for Carrie. What would become of her? For the reader will readily conceive that, though I had ceased to contend with Eugene about the matter, I had no idea of remaining with him after the dreadful expose that had taken place. I only ceased to contend with him because it was useless to do so, and because he refused to be convinced of the sin that lay in the course he advocated. What, then, would become of Carrie? Should I take her with me, or leave her to the tender mercies of that dreadful woman? This, it seemed to me, I could not do. It is true, she was no relation to me, but she was a lovely child, and I loved her almost as my own. Ah! yes, my own. How I thanked the God of high Heaven, then, that he had seen fit to take my own little girl to Himself in the bright days of infancy, before her pure spirit had been blighted and sullied by contact with this sinful world. Let not the reader shudder, or think me inhuman, that this thought found a lodgment in my breast. Nothing but my overwhelming love for my offspring gave birth to the idea. What would have been her fate had she lived to adult age?

Of illegitimate birth—born to an heritage of shame and disgrace—a mark for the finger of scorn and contumely—who can ever guess to what depths of sin, and degradation, and shame, the dark cloud which would have rested upon her during the whole of her life might have driven her? Yes, it was far better for her as it was; and in pure singleness of heart, and actuated by naught but the most exalted love for her, I blessed God that she had died upon the very threshhold of life.

Then my thoughts turned to my own future, and, look which way I would, nothing was presented but black misery, shame and despair. Who, and what was I? The mistress of a married man; and for long years I had been living in a state of adultery with him. True I was innocent of any intentional wrong, but, nevertheless, the black and damning fact stared me in the face, and would not down at my bidding. And what had I to hope or anticipate? Alone, aye, doubly alone in the wide world—my brother Frank, my only living relative, far away and, perhaps, wounded or dying on some battle-field, perhaps already dead—no one to care or provide for me, and utterly unfitted by my education to earn a livelihood—with the dark stain of the past resting upon me and clouding my fair name—what wonder that I groaned in spirit, and even questioned the goodness of the Almighty in his dispensations toward me? What wonder that my bowed and crushed heart cried out in bitterest anguish, "My burden is greater than I can bear? Oh! Thou Eternal God, what have I done that I should be so much afflicted above all the children of men? Why is my pathway strewn only with thorns, and why dost Thou utterly withdraw thy face from me?" And then, anon, my spirit became more calm, and I fervently prayed for strength and grace to conquer and overcome all ills that beset me. Ah! how I shudder even to this day as memory recalls the events of that terrible night.

At length I became more calm, and with returning strength came the desire to go to some other room, where I would be less exposed to observation than in the public parlor of the hotel. Accordingly Eugene called for another room, and obtained the key of one adjoining the parlor, and with his assistance I got into it and lay down on the bed. He urged me to undress, but I would not, for I had formed the resolution to leave the house that very night, and in my feeble condition I did not want the trouble of dressing. I had also determined to take Carrie

10

with me, and, accordingly, as soon as I was comfortably disposed on the bed, I asked him to bring her to me. He went to our room and brought her, and informed me that the other children were all asleep, and their mother lying down with them. They had evidently became reconciled to her, and the fact of their making up with her so quickly caused me a secret pang, though I knew it was really nothing to me, and that their happiness would be promoted thereby. I then asked Eugene to go and bring my trunks, and all mine and Carrie's things, into this room. I think this request aroused some suspicion in his bosom, for he hesitated a little, and asked me what I meant, and what I was going to do; but if so, I quieted his apprehensions by telling him, in an indifferent manner that I did not want them in the room with that woman, and that I only wanted them where I could get at them conveniently without meeting her.

Accordingly he ordered the trunks brought down, and closely following them came "that woman." Doubtless she thought we were intending to slip away from her, and this idea aroused the virago in her bosom.

"What are you about?" said she. "You need not think to give me the slip now. I have spent too much time hunting you, and now that I have got hold of you, I intend to keep you. I am not done with you yet."

"I have no idea of slipping away from you," replied Eugene. "But this lady is very sick, and wants her things in her own room, And, beside, she is not in a condition to be agitated by such violence just now."

"You are very careful of her just now, would it not be just as well for you to have some care of me?"

"But I assure you she is indeed very ill. You can see for yourself."

"If she is so very ill, you can get some one to stay with her. But, as for yourself, you had better come up stairs with your wife."

How that last word grated on my ear, emphasized as she emphasized it. And yet it was true. She was his wife, and I was only his mistress. His place was with her, and not with me, and I wanted him to go. And, aside from the question of right and wrong, I had other reasons for wishing him to leave me alone and go to her room with her. In the first place, his absence was necessary in order that I might carry out the plan I had formed of taking my departure from the house that very night. Beside, I knew that a prolongation of this interview would only result in exciting me to such a degree as to wholly prostrate me again, and the little strength I had was barely sufficient for my contemplated flight. Accordingly I seconded her demand with my entreaties, and urged him for the sake of peace, and for the sake of my health, if not of my life, to go with her. After some urging he went and brought some matches, and under pretense of placing them within my reach, came to the bedside, snatched a kiss before I knew what he intended, and whispering me that he would be back as soon as she went to sleep, left the room. She was waiting for him just outside the door, and I heard them ascend the stairs together.

Then I knew it was time for me to act, for I was certain he would be back before long, and any delay might be fatal to my plans. As soon as the echo of their footsteps, therefore, had died away at the head of the stairs I rung the bell, and when the messenger came, ordered him to send the proprietor of the hotel to me. The landlord came in a few minutes, and I briefly told him the whole shameful story—how I had married Giles (or Mason) long

years ago, and had lived with him ever since, believing
him to be my lawful husband; how this woman had came
and claimed to be his lawful wife; how he had admitted
the justice and correctness of her claim, and that she
was really and truly his wife; and of my resolution to
leave at once, and then begged his assistance in my endeavor. I told him I could not stay to see them again,
and asked him to get a carriage and send me away at
once. He used all his persuasive powers to induce me to
stay where I was until I was better—told me over and
over again that it would kill me, if I went out that night—
but it was all in vain. Indeed, the suggestion of death
was the very poorest argument he could have used, for so
intensely bitter had been my lot in life thus far that I
would as soon have died as not.

When he found I was unalterably resolved to go that
night, he professed his readiness to help me, and asked
me where I intended to go. I had not selected any place,
and, after hesitating a moment, replied that it did not
matter where I went—anywhere in the country—until I
was better, and could seek a home in some other part of
the country. He then informed me that he had a sister
living on a farm but six miles from the city, who he was
sure would make me welcome and treat me kindly, and
would give me such care as my situation demanded. He
assured me that I would be comfortably situated, and offered to get a carriage and take me there himself. I
thanked him from the bottom of my heart, for his kind
and generous offer, and he went out to call a carriage.

But a few minutes elapsed since his departure, and
there was a gentle tap at my door. A moment more and
it was opened, and the landlord's wife came in. She was
about forty years of age, of gentle and ladylike manners

and disposition, while goodness and kindness beamed from every lineament of her face, and furnished an unerring index to the noble qualities of her heart. She approached my bedside, laid her hand gently and caressingly upon my forehead, and, with a world of kindness in her tone, said:

"My husband tells me you are going away to-night. Is there anything I can do to assist you?"

"Oh! Mrs. ——," replied I, quite overcome with her kindness, "God will reward you for your kindness to a poor, unfortunate stranger—I never can."

"There, my dear child," said she, gently, "don't say anything about that, but just tell me what I can do for you. I know all about it, and I were less than human to withhold offers of assistance under such circumstances."

"You may dress Carrie, if you please; and should any reverse ever befall you, or you be in need of assistance, may God deal mercifully with you, even as you and your husband do with me at this time."

She made no reply; but, as she dressed the little girl, I could see, by the quivering lip and moistened eye, that I had a friend indeed in her—one upon whom I might rely with the most implicit confidence under all circumstances.

By the time Carrie was dressed, and I had, with the assistance of my kind friend, put on my wrappings, her husband came in to tell me that the carriage was ready; and, as he saw the evident indications of emotion, he began to rally us on our tender heartedness; but, while he did so, there was a tremor in his voice and a moistness in his eye, which told me that he, too, had a heart to feel for the sorrows of others, and that contact with the world had not deadened all the finer sensibilities of his nature.

His wife took Carrie in her arms, I leaned upon Mr. ——'s arm, and we proceeded to the carriage. When I had been assisted in, she kissed Carrie and placed her by my side, and then holding my hand in hers, said, in a tremulous voice:

"If you want any assistance, at any time, do not hesitate to come to me, and be assured that your petitions will never be in vain."

I tried to reply, but could not. My emotions, at such unexpected kindness, quite overcame me; and, after trying, in vain, to give utterance to the deep thankfulness of my heart, I leaned back in the carriage and burst into tears. Her husband, without a word, sprang into the carriage, beside me, and we rolled away toward the house of his sister, where we arrived about two o'clock in the morning. Of course, the family were all asleep at the time, but he called his sister up, introduced me, and briefly explained the cause of our untimely visit.

She welcomed me with a degree of warmth and kindness which showed that my painful fortune had touched a tender chord in her heart, and that nature had bestowed upon her the same noble soul which animated the breast of her brother and his wife, and at once set about making arrangements for my comfort.

Upon seeing me comfortably installed in my new home, Mr. —— took his leave and returned to the city. I have never seen him or his angel-wife since, but should these lines come under their observation, let them be assured that my heart still cherishes a lively sense of gratitude to them for their kindness in that dark hour of my life, and that, daily and nightly, my prayers are offered up to heaven for its choicest blessings to rest, in rich profusion, upon them. And, though their reward may not be of this earth, at the great day, when all shall stand before the bar of God, then shall the righteous Judge say unto them: "Inasmuch as ye did it unto one of the least of these," and "Come ye blessed of my Father."

CHAPTER XI.

MRS. KING, the lady at whose house I was now staying, was a middle-aged woman, in whose countenance a genial, sunny disposition, and an abundant stock of all the better and nobler feelings of human nature, were plainly revealed. Utterly devoid of all affectation or absurd display, calm and self-possessed, and having an unusual amount of strong, practical common sense, she was just the right guardian for me in my present lonely and bewildering situation. For, to tell the truth, the terrible incidents of the last few hours had so shattered my nerves that, for the time being, I was almost incapable of thinking intelligibly upon any subject, or of devising anything for the future.

As soon as her brother had taken his departure, she led me into a room adjoining the one in which she had received us, and told me that was to be my room so long as I chose to occupy it. I looked around the room, and every thing bore the most ample testimony to her character, as the neat, orderly, and unpretentious housekeeper she was. The furniture was all plain—much of it was old-fashioned—but everything was scrupulously clean and in the best of order. There was a rag-carpet on the floor; in one corner of the room stood a comfortable-looking bed, covered with a clean and marvelously white counterpane; an old-fashioned but neat and comfortable-looking sofa occupied one side of the room; there were two or three chairs, a small table, and a washstand; while on another side of the room was a small fire-place, in which a bright and cheerful-looking fire had already been started by my kind hostess. She drew the sofa in front of the fire, brought a pillow, and told me to lie down. She then left me, saying she would return in a few minutes with something to refresh me after my ride. In vain I assured her I did not need anything—that I did not wish her to take any trouble: she replied that I must take something, and went away.

She was gone but a short time, and came back with a tray, upon which was a pot of strong tea, cups, sugar and cream, nice white bread and fresh butter. These she placed upon the table, and laughingly told me to eat my supper and go to bed like a good child. I thanked her kindly, and replied that I had had my supper, but would drink some tea before retiring. She then told me to lie and take my rest in the morning—that she did not have breakfast early, and would rap on my door when it was time for me to get up; then she bid me good-night, and left the room.

After she had gone, I drank a cup of tea, undressed Carrie and put her to bed, and then sat down before the fire to try to think and devise some plan for the future. Oh! how dark and dismal my lot, both present and future, seemed, as I sat there and mused upon it during the still hours of that night. Here I was, an entire stranger; eight dollars, which I had in my purse, constituted my entire fortune; I had myself and Carrie to care for, and I could think of nothing at which I could make a comfortable support, and raise and educate her as I wished to. It was true, I was under no legal obligation to provide for her: she was no relation to me; but I loved her as if she were my own; she did not know but that I was her mother; and the thought of casting her upon the cold charities of the world was not to be endured for a moment. But what could I do?

Once the tempter whispered me to apply to Mason for her support. Notwithstanding his resolute denial, I felt

confident she was his child; and surely it would be but justice that he should be charged with the burden of her main-
tenance, rather than myself.   But the suggestion was no
sooner made than it was rejected.   No; I had deliberately
fled from him, and had taken measures to conceal my
whereabouts; and not for worlds would I now let him know
where I was: because this would defeat the very object of
my concealment from him.   But why not send Carrie back
to him?   Because I could not make up my mind to part
with her in my desolation.   She was the only living being
around whom the tendrils of my affection could entwine
themselves for support; and, were she taken away, then,
indeed, "my house were left unto me desolate."   No; keep
her with me I would; and she should never know but she
whom she called "mother" was of her own flesh and blood.
Yes, she should stay with me, and my trust in God was
strong that he would find some way of escape from my
present embarrassing situation.

Thus I sat by the fire and mused the remainder of that
eventful night, and it was not until daylight was dawning
in the east that the chilliness of the atmosphere (my fire
had long since burned low in the grate, though I noticed
it not) admonished me that I should retire to bed to keep
myself from suffering.   I undressed and got into bed beside my little darling, and, worn out by feebleness and the
exciting events of the night, I sunk at last into a sound
and refreshing slumber.

When I awoke it was late, for the sun was high in the
heavens, and was brightly shining into my room through a
slight opening in the curtains.   Everything around me
looked strange, and for a moment I could not realize where
I was. ˙ But soon the recollection of the horrid events of
the past night rushed across my mind, and, with a groan

of anguish, I sunk back upon my pillow and closed my eyes as if to shut out the hated vision. But vain, vain were my efforts. The dread past was branded and burnt into my brain in characters of living fire, and there was no escape from the horrid torture of its contemplation, and again I groaned aloud in my agony. Poor Carrie was awake and was frightened at the violence of my emotion, and, in piteous tones, asked me what was the matter. The sound of her gentle, bird-like voice recalled me to myself; I turned over toward her, and, after caressing her for a few moments, looked at my watch. Judge of my surprise to find that it was a few minutes after ten o'clock!

I immediately arose and proceeded to dress myself and Carrie, when we went into the next room. Mrs. King was sitting there alone, engaged in knitting. She looked up, with a pleasant smile, as we came in, and said kindly:

"Good morning. I hope you have rested well."

"If late hours are any evidence, I certainly have. But why did you not call me as you said you would?"

"I did tap once on your door about eight o'clock, but you seemed to be sleeping so soundly that I thought it a pity to disturb you. I knew it was late when you went to bed, and thought the rest would do you more good than anything else. So I kept your breakfast warm, and just left you alone. Will you have it now?"

"Yes, I thank you. It was, indeed, late when I went to bed, for I did not lie down until daylight was appearing in the east. But I am sorry to put you to so much trouble."

"Say nothing about that. Poor child! what is my trouble compared with yours?"

"But I brought my trouble upon myself, innocently, it is true, and it is not right for me to cause you trouble."

"My Master tells us to bear each others' burdens, and, although I fall far short of obeying His commands, at all times, I can not avoid so plain a requirement of duty as this."

This little conversation, during which she had been engaged in placing our breakfast on the table, gave me a new insight into the character of my kind hostess. I now understood the secret of the calm contentment which ever rested upon her features, and the genial sunshine which ever pervaded her presence. She was an humble, consistent follower of the meek and lowly Jesus, and her simple, Christain faith imparted to her character a calm and elevated refinement which I have never seen excelled. Surely there is a crown of glory laid up for her at the right hand of her heavenly Master, which Christ, the righteous Judge, shall give to her in that day.

My heart was too full for reply, and, without a word, we took our seats at the table, but my emotions choked me, and I could scarcely eat the food she placed before me. But Carrie, poor child, had nothing to pre-occupy her mind; she did not realize or know the situation in which we were placed, and she eat heartily, prattling away meanwhile in all the merry light-heartedness of childhood. How I envied her freedom from care and sorrow, and almost wished that I, too, were a child again.

Surely, childhood is the happiest portion of life; it can not be otherwise. In infancy, we know nothing of the deceit and sinfulness of the world; the spirit has not been blighted by contact with the rough scenes of adversity, which invariably accompany more mature years; the world seems but a vast storehouse of pleasure, instead of the scene of strife and conflict, which later experience demonstrates it to be; and life seems one long day of sunshine, instead of a succession of tempests, which too often break and blight the spirit of man as he reels before the unequal conflict. It is true that childhood has its griefs, and its little sorrows, but their memory is soon swept away by the torrent of happiness which speedily follows, and all is bright again. Happy, thrice happy, days of childhood! Would that ye were mine again. But vain is the wish. Ye are gone never to return, and I, a lone wanderer amid the children of men, am left to breast the storms of maturer life as best I may. God give me his grace to sustain me in the dreadful conflict, lest I succumb in the unequal strife.

After breakfast was over I took Carrie on my lap and talked to her. I felt certain that Mason would do all in his power to regain possession of us, and proceeded to give her such instruction as it seemed to me would prevent her childish prattle from betraying the place of our concealment. I told her she must never ask for her papa or her little brothers; that they were all dead, and she would never see them again, and that if any one asked her about them, she must say they were dead. The poor child did not understand the import of my language—she knew not what I meant when I told her "they were dead"—she knew, however, there was something wrong, and my solemn looks, and impressive tone and manner, awed her into submission to all my requirements. She promised compliance with my wishes, and I have every reason to believe she kept her promise, notwithstanding her tender years at the time of making it.

As I had anticipated, Mason made great efforts to discover our whereabouts. I had been at Mrs. King's but two or three days, when there appeared in the columns of the "Commercial," and other papers of the city, a notice, calling for information of a lady and child, giving a perfect description of Carrie and myself. This was inserted for three or four days in succession, when, it having evidently failed to elicit any information, it was discontinued, and another, offering a "liberal reward," for tidings of the fugitives, appeared in its place. Mrs. King called my attention to this notice, and said, laughingly, that she thought she had better answer it and get the "liberal reward." But I felt no uneasiness, notwithstanding Mason's evidently earnest attempts to ascertain my whereabouts. We very seldom saw any company, and I had too much confidence in the only persons who were in possession of my secret, to have any fears of their betraying me. These advertisements, therefore, gave me no alarm whatever, and I remained quiet, fully believing that Mr. ———— would let me know when it was safe for me to leave my place of concealment.

And my confidence was not misplaced in the least. For some time, advertisements of various kinds continued to appear in the journals of the city, all pointing to me, and directed to the object of my discovery, but after a time they ceased, and the pursuit appeared to be abandoned. Doubtless Mason would have found me, had I sought a hiding-place in some distant part of the country, but the fact that I had taken refuge so close to him— under his very nose as it were—seems never to have occurred to him, and his efforts were all directed too far away. A day or two after the advertisements ceased to be in the papers, my kind friend, Mr. ————, sent word to me that Mason had gone to New York with his wife, and that all fear of detection was over, for the present at least. Now I felt free again, for though I had never had any fears that either Mr. ———— or Mrs. King would betray me, still I thought that I was not perfectly safe so

long as he continued the search for me. I knew that he
had money, and I was well aware of the wonderful power of
gold in stimulating the efforts of detectives. And I had
every reason to believe that he would spare neither time nor
money in his efforts to find me. And there is ample evidence that he did employ a large number of special agents,
not only in Cincinnati, but in other cities, to discover my
hiding-place.

Now, however, the search was ended, and the question
arose what was I to do? It was very evident that I could
not stay in my present quarters—something must be done
to support myself and my child—and what could it be?
I knew something about painting in water-colors, and
could paint on glass, but it would take time and means to
get up a class of pupils, and, beside, I had no great confidence in my ability to earn a living in this way. And,
even if successful, how was I to support Carrie and myself while I was getting a class and obtaining the practice
necessary to enable me to teach properly, for I had paid
no attention to painting for a long time, and was sadly out
of practice. I had no money, having paid Mrs. King what
little I had when I came there, and my way seemed beset
with difficulties on every hand. But something I must do.

I mentioned my difficulties to Mrs. King, and she
proposed that I should stay with her, while her brother
would get me a class, and that, in the meantime, I could
get material from the city, and attend to my practice
until I was able to take charge of the class. To this
kind proposition, I objected that I had already burdened
her brother and herself sufficiently, and that I was unwilling to tax their kindness any further. It was finally settled that I should leave Carrie with her while I went to
the city and found some employment at which I could

earn my own support while making the necessary preparations to take my class. I dreaded parting from my child, even for the short time which it was supposed would elapse before I could reclaim her; but there seemed no alternative, and I bade her good-bye and went to the city. The result of my efforts to get employment will be found in the next chapter.

CHAPTER XII.

UPON leaving Mrs. King's house I went to the city, and at once made my way to the Spencer House, but what a disappointment awaited me there. The kind friends who had formerly kept the place, and from whose countenance I had anticipated so much, were no longer there. Mrs. ——'s health had been getting delicate for some time, and they had finally rented the house and gone on a journey for her benefit, having left the city that very morning. It will be borne in mind that nearly a week had elapsed since Mr. —— had sent me the intelligence of Mason's departure, and in that time their arrangements had been completed, and they had gone away. What was I to do? I was alone in a great city, without money, and without a single friend to whom I could apply for even the miserable boon of a crust of bread and a night's lodging.

I rested for a short time, and then set out in search of something I could do. By dint of persistent inquiry I at last found a stopping-place, in the family of a Mr. Jennings, on Main Street, near Seventh. They gave me no regular employment, but consented that I should remain there, and work for my board, until something better should turn up. Poor as this arrangement was, it still furnished me with food and shelter until I could do better. For this I was duly thankful, and entered upon my new avocation with zest and gratitude, while, in the meantime, I spared no pains to find some more lucrative employment. But days passed, and no opening presented itself—every avenue of honorable support seemed closed to me, and despair was fast settling down upon my mind. But temporary relief was at hand, and that, too, from a quarter of which I had nót dreamed.

One day, as I was returning from market, whither I had been for Mrs. Jennings, I met a gentleman who was about passing me without notice, but who suddenly stopped, and exclaimed:

"My God! Mrs. Giles, is that you?"

I recognized him in a moment. He was an old neighbor of mine in my happier days, and I returned his greeting as warmly as it was given.

"Where do you live, and where is Giles?" he asked, when our first greeting was over.

I told him where I lived and how I lived; that I knew nothing of Giles; and that, if he would call on me that evening, I would explain everything to him. He promised to do so, and we shook hands and parted, he going down the street and I returning to what was my home.

In the evening he came, and I told him all that had happened since we had seen each other, and with which the reader is already acquainted. He seemed much moved at the story of my misfortunes, and, when I told him of my projects for the future, and that if I could only get to Captain Lake I was sure he would let me have the means to carry my plan into execution, he at once offered to loan me the money to go to Atlanta. He had left there before the war broke out (it was now ended), and he had not been back since, and did not know whether Captain Lake was there or not, but he would let me have the money to go and see. I accepted his offer with thankfulness, and the next day saw me on my way to my once pleasant home.

But I was doomed to the bitterest disappointment I had

experienced since discovering the perfidy of Mason. I do not refer to the horrible devastation which had been wrought by the cruel hand of war in and around Atlanta; this is matter of history, and I was, in some measure, prepared for it—but Captain Lake was not there, nor were my efforts to obtain any intelligence of him successful. It was a long time before I could even find any of my former acquaintances. All had gone, and their places had been filled by others, and at the home of my childhood I was in a land of strangers. At length I succeeded in finding an old man who had known me in better days, and from him I learned that Captain Lake was somewhere in the North, but he could not tell me where. The Captain had been so severely wounded that his life had been despaired of, and he had been compelled to leave the army; and, at the close of the war, finding his property destroyed, in a great measure, and himself nearly a bankrupt, he had made his way north in hopes of repairing his shattered fortunes to some extent.

This was all he could tell me; and sad intelligence it was to me. What was I to do next? My hopes of getting assistance from that quarter had failed, and there I was without any means of supporting myself, or even of scarcely paying my way back to Cincinnati, whither I must go. My child was there, and I must go to her at all hazards. Beside, in the disordered state of things at Atlanta, it was preposterous for me to think of trying to earn a living there.

The difficulties which stared me in the face might well have appalled a stouter heart than mine, but I met them bravely and, thank God! have been to a considerable extent able to overcome them.

Through the kindness and with the aid of the old man

above mentioned, I succeeded in obtaining from a merchant in Atlanta the loan of some money to pay my fare back to Cincinnati, where I proposed to start anew in my search for fortune. Upon arriving in the city, my first duty was to pay a visit to Carrie, and the reader may rest assured that I never performed a duty more willingly in my life. I had not seen her for more than a month, and when it is remembered that this was the first time I had ever been separated from her, the reader will have no difficulty in believing that it was with emotions of no little joy that I clasped her to my heart once more.

I found both her and her kind guardian in the best of health, and was greeted by both with a kindness which told the esteem in which I was held. After spending a day there, I went back to the city, took up my quarters at a boarding-house at No. 208 Fifth street, and at once set about refreshing my knowledge of painting and seeking for pupils. I also took the necessary steps to secure proper rooms in which to receive my class, if I should be so fortunate as to get one.

My success equaled my most sanguine expectations. In about ten days I had a class of some twelve pupils, and had so assiduously practiced my art, that I felt competent to take charge of them. I had also secured very comfortable rooms at No. 115 Elm street, and had decided to keep house there, thinking it would cost me less than to board, while my duties to my pupils would leave me plenty of time to do my own house-work.

For a time I got on swimmingly. The interest of my pupils in their lessons seemed to increase from day to day, and as they progressed under my instructions they took pains to speak of my school to their acquaintances—others applied for admission to my school, and in a short time I had all the scholars which my rooms would accommodate. I even began to think of taking my little girl from Mrs. King, and taking charge of her myself—something I had not yet done for the reason that my finances were not in such condition as to enable me to pay for her board in the city, as it would cost much more than to keep her at her present location.

But I had only lived in my present quarters about three weeks—had only got fairly started with my school when the owner of the house came to me and told me he was about selling it, and that I must look for rooms elsewhere. Of course there was no help for it, and so, dismissing my school for a time, I set out on the weary quest of another stopping place. My search was long and tedious; but why inflict the annoyances of "house-hunting" upon my readers? Suffice it to say that I finally succeeded in getting rooms for barely two months—nothing would induce the owner to rent them longer—at No. 10 Harrison street. And to tell the truth, I did not wish to stay there very long, for I had to pay a most exorbitant rent, and my finances were not sufficient to stand the heavy drain for very long.

When my time there was up, I again found temporary quarters in four rooms—I had to take all or none—on the third floor of a house on Sixth street. But financial considerations induced me to make my stay there as brief as possible, and in a short time I removed from this location to a small cottage at No. 38 Barr street, where I remained as long as I staid in Cincinnati. During all this time I had had a good class in painting, and my receipts had been considerably in advance of my expenditures. I was in fact doing very well.

But from some cause which I have never been able to

explain to my own satisfaction, my business began to decline. The pupils who composed my first classes had obtained all the knowledge I was capable of imparting to
them, and no others appeared to take their places. Becoming convinced that my day of usefulness and pecuniary success in Cincinnati was past, I made up my mind
to sell off my furniture, remove to Detroit, and try my luck
there; and at once proceeded to carry my determination
into effect. Accordingly I converted what few household
goods I had into money, and with this in my pocket went
to Mrs. King's to get Carrie, preparatory to my journey to
the city of Detroit.

I found Mrs. King almost unwilling to let Carrie go
away. She had no children of her own, and she had become so much attached to "the little darling," that she
hardly knew how to part with her. She conceded my
right to take her, but, at the same time, made the most
liberal offers if I would only consent to let her keep my
child. She had an abundance of property, and if I would
only let Carrie stay with her, it should all be her's at Mrs.
King's death. Perhaps it would have been better for Carrie if I had consented to let her stay, but she was all I
had to love in the wide, wide world, and I felt that it
would be the next thing to taking my life to part with her.
Accordingly I declined her munificent offers, and took Carrie away, loaded with presents, and, I am convinced, sincerely mourned by her who had so long acted a mother's
part toward her. Before we left, she exacted from me a
promise, that if at any time, Carrie became a burden to me,
and I found it necessary to part with her, she should have
her. This promise I gave the more readily because I felt
sure that the condition upon which it was based would
never arise. And, thank God! it never has arisen. I

have been steeped almost to the lips in poverty's depths—
I have seen the time that I hardly knew where my next
meal was to come from—I have been driven to pawn my
wearing apparel, my jewelry, and even (as has been seen)
the keepsakes of dear and valued friends, in order to purchase the means of appeasing my hunger, but amid it all,
the time has never come when I was willing to part with
that child.   And though she is no relation to me, though
no ties of consanguinity bind us together, though there is
no bond between us, save that arising from the care I had
bestowed upon her in the helpless days of infancy, the
time will never come, so long as I am able to earn the
merest pittance of food for myself or her, in which I shall
be willing to have her care and training transferred to
other hands than my own.   I may, of course, consent that
temporarily she shall be placed in the care of another, as
a school-teacher or the like, but further than this I never
will while I have life and reason left.

My journey to Detroit was attended with no incidents
worthy of notice in these pages.   There was the usual
amount of annoyance and weariness attending railroad
travel, and with which all my readers are familiar; there
was the usual amount of uproar and confusion at the various stations; there was the usual annoyance from porters, hackmen, omnibus drivers, etc., which is to be met
with in all the principal cities of the United States, to the
disgrace of human nature in general, and of municipal
officers in particular.   But we managed to live through it
all, and, in due time, found ourselves in the city of Detroit.

I had no very well defined plans in coming to this place.
So far from designing to pursue the avocation which had
afforded me such a comfortable subsistence in Cincinnati,

I had become disgusted with it as a means of livelihood, and was firmly resolved to resort to it only in case all other means failed to produce the desired results. I was therefore totally at sea as to the future, and could do nothing but stop at a hotel until something should turn up, or, until I could decide upon my future course of action.

The prospect looked cheerless enough. There I was, in the midst of a large city, amid the moving myriads of whose population I was not aware that I knew a single soul, with but little means in my possession, and entirely at a loss which way to turn for succor and relief. But my confidence in Providence, or my lucky star, was unabated; I felt sure that some means of relief would be presented to me; and I retired to my room at the hotel, and slept as soundly as though the future had been to me a cheerful day of summer sunshine, instead of the dark and gloomy cloud which it really was.

CHAPTER XIII.

THE next morning after my arrival in Detroit, I took an inventory of my means, with a view of determining upon some mode of support for Carrie and myself. Upon one thing I was decided—that I would not again resort to teaching if I could find anything else to do. Not that teaching was in itself so very disagreeable to me—many things are more unpleasant; but it was very confining, and the confinement was telling upon my health. Indeed, this was one reason why I was so willing to give it up and leave Cincinnati.

I found myself in possession of something over five hundred dollars—enough I thought to enable me to furnish a house, and open a small boarding establishment, at which I was confident I could make my own and Carrie's living. The next thing was to secure a house, and I at once set out in quest of one, leaving Carrie in charge of one of the girls at the hotel. My search was long and tiresome, but was at last successful. I found a very neat cottage of six rooms, which was vacant, and which I secured, paying three months rent in advance, and then at once set about furnishing it. My furniture was comfortable, though plain, but everything was high, and when my house was furnished, and a supply of provisions bought, my five hundred dollars had been reduced to an alarmingly small amount. Still I had had several applications for board, and I felt confident of success in my, to me, new enterprise.

A day or two after opening my house, I met on the street with one whom I little expected to see there, and who, on his part, was equally surprised at the meeting. It was none other than Captain Lake. He had been living in the city for some time, but had no idea that I was so near him, though he had made considerable effort to find me. The last trace he had of me, he had obtained from Giles (or Mason), who had been to him in search of me, and had told him all the circumstances of our parting, avowing, at the same time, his determination to find me, and live with me again. The Captain had been very uneasy about this, and was very much relieved when I assured him that under no circumstances would I consent to any such arrangement—that I was not his wife, and nothing should induce me to become his mistress again.

I then inquired about himself and family. His family were well, but he was suffering severely from a wound he had received while in the army, and which it was thought would cause his death. I may remark here that this wound did finally end his life. He had lost a great share of his property during the war, but had saved enough to afford himself and family a rather moderate support. And it was from him at this time that I learned what I have before stated; that my brother had fallen during the campaign against Atlanta. Although I had not heard anything of him for a long time, I had hoped until this moment that he had come out of the terrible conflict unharmed, but this hope was now suddenly dashed to earth, and with what terrible force the blow fell upon my heart can only be imagined by those who, like me, have been called to mourn the loss of a dear and only brother. And poignancy was added to my sorrow by the reflection that he had fallen in what I could not but consider an unjust and unholy cause. But it was vain to mourn. He was gone, and I was alone in the wide world.

Captain Lake told me where they were living, invited me to come there, and offered me a home in his family, saying I should want for nothing so long as I refused to hold any communication with Giles. I thanked him for his kind offer, but told him what arrangements I had made for obtaining my support, and that I preferred not to be dependent upon any one—assured him that I had every prospect of succeeding in my undertaking, and said that in case of failure it would be time enough to tax his generosity for my support. He seemed very much pleased at the energy I had displayed, and assured me that if at any time I found it necessary to call upon him for assistance it would be most cheerfully rendered. He, however, advised me to drop the name of Giles and take my maiden name, which I told him I had already done, and now called myself Mrs. Hamilton. He then bid me good evening, and left me, saying that Mrs. Lake would come and see me the next day, and I must return her visit.

In accordance with his promise, Mrs. Lake came to see me on the morrow. She seemed pleased to see me, as I certainly was her; but she was, oh! so changed. In the few years since I had seen her she seemed to have lived half a lifetime—her once smooth and lovely brow was now deformed with incipient wrinkles; her blooming complexion had faded; and her hair, in various places, was streaked with gray. It could not be that age had wrought so much of change in her, and I could not avoid the conviction that her married life had not been very happy. Nevertheless, she possessed the same degree of humor and gayety as of old—it might be subdued a trifle by the years which had passed over her head—and we passed a very pleasant day together. When she went home,

I accompanied her, and spent the night at their house,
returning early the next morning; for I had advertised
in the Free Press for boarders, and I anticipated applications for my unoccupied rooms during the day.

And my anticipations were not disappointed. Before
nightfall my rooms were all engaged, and I had been
compelled to refuse two or three applicants. My success
had more than equaled my expectations. In less than a
week from the time of opening my house I had filled it
with as agreeable a family of boarders as I ever met in my
life. Two of them, a Mr. and Mrs. Hopkins, were especial favorites of mine, particularly the lady. I do not
think I ever knew a more charming woman than she was,
while her husband was just my ideal of a gentleman. My
situation was very pleasant, and, for a time, things went
on to my entire satisfaction. As I have said, I called
myself Mrs. Hamilton, and I gave my boarders to understand that I was a widow, and that Carrie was my daughter. I had considerable trouble to school her into this
little deception; and my heart smote me not a little as I
trained her to utter the falsehood which was to shield my
own reputation and hers. She would insist that her
father's name was Giles, and would persist in asking for
him and for her little brothers. It was a long time before
I could educate her to the point at which I felt it safe to
allow her to talk alone with others; but at length I succeeded, and the lie was fastened upon her pure, young
spirit. Was it a sin to teach her thus to deceive? Answer
me, ye casuists, who shudder with horror at the thought
of the least concealment of the truth in others, how many
of you, under the same circumstances, would have done
otherwise than I did?

But, though everything was going so pleasantly upon

the surface, there was one matter which gave me no little secret uneasiness. I dreaded lest Mason might succeed in the determination he had expressed to Captain Lake— might succeed in discovering my whereabouts, which, it was very apparent to me, would be immediately and everlastingly fatal to all my prospects of success; and my anxiety was not in the least dissipated when Captain Lake told me he had reason to suspect that Mason was in the city, and was still engaged in the prosecution of his search. I did not know what to do. I hardly dared to go out for fear of meeting him; and the probable consequences of such a meeting were the burden of my dreams by night. One thing which caused this secret dread to weigh heavier upon my spirits, was the fact that I had no one to whom I could confide my burden. I had but one living friend to whom I could have unfolded the tale, and he was in San Francisco, California. Sometimes I though of writing to him about the matter, but I could not broach the subject without giving him the whole history of my past life, and I dreaded to see it in writing: so I kept my burden to myself, and struggled on.

But the burden, together with my constant confinement, was fast wearing me out. I grew pale and thin; I was flushed and feverish at night, and my whole system was enervated and unstrung to a most alarming degree. At length I yielded to the solicitations of my friends, and applied to a physician of eminence and standing for relief. He pronounced my case consumption, and gravely assured me that there was no relief for me; that I must die ere long, and that all that could be done was to smooth my passage to the tomb.

Although I was satisfied he was in error as to what ailed me, still I thought it quite likely he was right about my

early decease, and this reflection but increased my uneasiness.   For, when I was dead, what would become of Carrie?   Who would care for the little bud which was just
developing into the perfect flower?   As this inquiry, in all
its dreadful vividness, presented itself to my mind, I again
thought of writing to my friend in California, and asking
him to take care of my child when I was gone; but how
could I tell him of her without telling him all my history?
And again I shrunk from the dreadful exposition.   My
courage was not then equal to the task I am now pursuing.
Wronged as I felt that I had already been by fate and the
world, I had not yet sustained enough of injury at their
hands to rouse me to the pitch of desperate courage which
would enable me to lay bare for the inspection of mankind
all the miseries and sorrows which had been my lot since
my advent upon the stage of existence—to relate, as
guides and warnings to the young, the many and fatal
mistakes of my career.   And, above all, I shrunk from acquainting him with my condition, feeling assured (so
devoid was I of confidence in any of the human family)
that if the truth, with which the reader is already familiar,
were unfolded to him, he would at once and forever blot
my name from the list of his friends, and he—almost the
the last tie which bound me to the mass of humanity—
be lost to me; and from this fate I shrunk with the most
painful apprehension.   I am now well assured that in
this I judged him wrongfully, and that the revelation, so
far from alienating him from me, would but have bound
his spirit more closely to mine; but it is the province of
misery to render us suspicious of all around us, and at
this time I was intensely miserable.

And now was about to occur an event which was destined to work an entire change in my life—an event whose

consequences were to endure as long as my life shall last, and which was destined to sink me to still lower depths of misery and wretchedness than any I had yet tasted, although, even at that time, it seemed to me I had already drained the bitter cup of sorrow to its very dregs.

I was going to market one evening with my basket on my arm, and, as I walked along, was musing upon the wretchedness which had attended my every step in life, and wondering why I had thus been made the target at which fate delighted to launch her sharpest and bitterest arrows, when, accidentally raising my eyes, I beheld a sight which for a moment caused my heart to stand still, and almost froze the blood in my veins. Crossing the street just in front of me was Eugene Giles Mason—he from whose face I had been so carefully hiding for the last two or three years, and than whose presence I could conceive of nothing more dreadful. Fortunate for me it was that his eyes were bent upon the ground, and that he was looking neither to the right nor the left: had his eyes been cast in my direction he could not have failed to see and recognize me, and I shudder even to this day when I reflect upon what might have been the consequences of such a discovery. I stood still, hardly daring to draw my breath until he had passed out of sight, when I turned and fled homeward as rapidly as my trembling limbs could carry me.

Arriving at my own house, I sat down and tried to devise a plan to meet the emergency, but for some time my mind was incapable of anything like clear or connected action. The one great and terrible fact that the destroyer of my peace and happiness was in the city, doubtless in search of me, loomed up before my mental vision in fearful proportions, and for a time obscured everything else.

It is true, I had heard of him from time to time, still engaged in the prosecution of his search for me; but I had escaped so long, that I had come to regard his discovery of me as of so little probability, as to give me little or no uneasiness. But he was here in the city—I had seen him with my own eyes—and now the chase seemed so near up as to fill me with the most fearful apprehensions, and to deprive me for the time of all power of rational reflection.

At length, however, the fever of excitement having passed away, I set myself to calmly consider what was best for me to do. One thing was evident—I could not remain where I was, nor did I deem it safe even to stay in the city where he was stopping. Of course, he had photographs of me, and, by the aid of these and the assistance of the police, he would doubtless soon be able to find me, no matter how much care I might use in concealing the place of my abode, or how obscure the station I might assume. I at once, therefore, determined to sell out what property I had, in the most secret manner possible, no matter at what sacrifice, and leave Detroit. But whither should I go? This was a question of no little difficulty with me; but, after debating it some time in my own mind, I decided upon Chicago, believing that he would be less likely to seek me in that direction than in any other.

It may seem strange that I did not consult Captain Lake and his wife before deciding a matter of so much importance as an entire change in my mode of life, as well as location; but I must confess that my hasty and capricious temper, which has been the bane of my life, had put it out of my power to do so. I will explain. The reader is familiar with the means by which Captain Lake had succeeded in possessing himself of the property which should have been of right mine. One day when his wife was visiting me, smarting under a sense of my wrongs, I had unjustly and ungratefully (for had she not nursed me back to life from the very door of death's gloomy pavilion ?) accused her of being a party to her husband's wrong—an accusation which she resented with proper spirit; and the result had been an entire cessation of intercourse between us. Oh! how often and bitterly have I repented my injustice and ingratitude; but what availed my repentance? I never saw her again—she died when I was far away, without my ears being gladdened by the sound of her whispered pardon; and yet I know that her pure spirit has long since forgiven the great wrong I then heaped upon her.

No sooner had I determined upon my course of action, than I hastened to carry it into effect. I sold out my furniture, gave up the lease of my house, found a good place for Carrie (for I did not wish to take her with me until I became settled), wrote a note to Captain Lake, telling him my reasons for leaving, but not where I had gone; and, with the little means realized from the sacrifice of my property, set out to commence life anew in the Garden City of the great West, without a single plan of my future course in earning a livelihood.

12

CHAPTER XIV.

In due time I arrived at Chicago, and stopped at the
Massasoit House, at the corner of Dearborn and Randolph
streets, where, however, I remained but one night. My
means were by far too limited to allow me to remain there,
or anywhere else, in idleness, and my first care was to
find some cheap but respectable boarding-house, conveniently located for carrying on the occupation I had determined to adopt, for a time at least—that of a plain seamstress.

I succeeded in finding a very comfortable room, and
reasonably good fare, at the house of a Mr. ——, near the
corner of Lake and Halstead streets, for which I paid, in
advance, the sum of seven dollars per week. In view of
the fact that I had less than three hundred dollars in my
possession, a part of which it was absolutely necessary
for me to lay out in clothing, the price seemed to me very
high ; but, nevertheless, it was the best I could do, and I
comforted myself with the reflection that I could earn at
least this amount each week with my needle. Poor fool
that I was ?   I did not then know that sewing-women do
not *live* by their work—that they sew and *starve*, while
wealthy manufacturers reap the reward of their toil.   Nor
did I know that, before I could get any work, the most fearful inroads would be made upon the little pittance I had
brought from Detroit.

As soon as I had secured my room and adjusted my
furniture (and scanty enough it was, let me assure you,) to
my satisfaction, I set out in search of employment, for I

realized the fact that I could not live in idleness and pay seven dollars a-week for my board. And, even if I had been able, I could never have ventured to sit down without employment of some sort to divert my mind from the contemplation of the gloomy past, and the fearful apprehension of the future. The dread of discovery by Mason had received a new impetus from the momentary view I had had of him in the streets of Detroit, and this fear, together with the contemplation of the past, would have driven me wild had I remained idle. So, with as stout and brave a heart as I could conjure up, but feeling, nevertheless, a little like "a cat in a strange garret," I went forth. And the history of my adventures in search of the employment I sought—the rebuffs and refusals with which I met on every hand—the covert sneers and almost open insults with which my applications were frequently answered—the heart-sickness with which, as refusal after refusal were meted out to me, I pursued my self-imposed task—all these, if written out in full, would make a volume much larger than the one, dear reader, now before you. But my heart would fail me were I to undertake to write them out, and yours would weary in reading them, and for both our sakes I forbear. A few instances must suffice to illustrate the treatment I encountered.

One of the first places at which I called was a large retail clothing store, but a short distance from my boarding place. I omit the name and location of the house for the reason that I have not enough good-will toward them to care about advertising for them free of charge.

As I entered the door, a spruce, dapper-looking little clerk came forward, bowing and scraping; but when he came near enough to see, from my dress, that I was not one of the *ton*, but simply a working girl, his excessive politeness vanished in a moment, his back stiffened, and his manners became almost freezing in their cold formality.

"Good morning, ma'am, anything wanting ?"

"Yes, sir," said I, a little haughtily, for I felt somewhat piqued at his manner; "is the proprietor in ?"

"I don't know whether he is or not. Did you want anything in particular ?" said my dapper friend.

"Yes, sir; I wish to see him."

"Jem," calling out to a boy who was lounging in the back part of the store, "won't you see if Mr. —— is in ? Here's a person wants to see him."

"Jem" departed on his errand, while the gentlemanly (?) clerk stood watching me as though he suspected I intended to steal something. After a time he came leisurely forward, and, in a drawling tone, informed me that Mr. —— would see me. Following him into the counting-room, I found myself in the presence of a fat, pompous old gentleman, of about fifty years of age, somewhat bald-headed, and wearing enormous gold spectacles.

"Good morning, madam," said he, very pompously; "did you wish to see me ?"

"Yes, sir. I am in search of employment. Have you any plain sewing that you wish done ?"

"Well, yes," he replied slowly, scanning me closely through his spectacles; "we have a good deal of sewing to do; have you ever sewed much ?"

"Considerably," I replied.

"Of course, you have references; let me look at them."

This was a poser. I had, as the reader is aware, but just arrived in Chicago, and knew not a single soul there, and where was I to look for references ? For a short time I stood silent and undecided what to say or do ? At last I managed to falter out that I had but just come to Chicago, was a stranger, etc., but was suddenly interrupted by my pompous friend with—

"Well, madam, if you can not give us good references, we can not give you work. We never employ any whom we do not know, without the best of references. "Jem," calling the boy who had conducted me thither, "show this lady to the door," and, waving his hand with a lordly air, he dismissed me without further ceremony.

This was the result of my first effort, and it was far from reassuring to the shrinking spirit with which I had set out. For a time my heart was full, and I was almost tempted to return to my lodgings and make no further attempts that day at obtaining employment. But, remembering that my financial status would admit of no sickly sentimentality, or shrinking, because of a single rebuff, I once more set out. After visiting several places without meeting with any success, I at last found myself face to face with a little bullet-headed, hard-featured wretch, who, when I made my errand known, replied briskly:

"Oh! yes. We have lots of work to do. What do you prefer, pants or plain shirts?"

"What prices do you pay for each?"

"One shilling and sixpence for pants, such as we would want you to make, and two shillings for shirts. How many will you have?"

"What prices did you say, sir?" said I chokingly, for the idea of trying to earn seven dollars at such rates as these filled me with dismay.

"Eighteen pence for pants and two shillings for shirts."

"But how do you expect me to make a living at those prices?"

"That is not our look-out, madam," he replied heartlessly; "those are our prices, and if you do not wish to work for them you can go elsewhere. We can get plenty of hands to sew for that. What say you? Time is precious," said he, pulling out and glancing at a large and showy-looking gold watch, filched, no doubt, from the toil of sewing girls to whom he had paid the magnificent prices he had just offered me.

"Say!" I replied indignantly, "I say that I will sooner starve without work than starve at such prices as you offer."

"Just as you please, ma'am; it is none of our business, you know," replied he, coolly, and I went out from his presence, feeling that the only difference between him and the Southern slave-driver was, that this man, born and reared in the North, was much the worse of the two. They both believed that capital should own labor, but while the Southerner would make slaves of his inferiors, and would furnish them enough to eat and wear, such as it was, this Northerner would subject to the most galling bondage his kinsmen and equals, and would deny them the miserable pittance sufficient to keep them from starvation and nakedness.

But why weary my readers with detailed accounts of my efforts to procure employment, at prices which would enable me to keep the gaunt wolf of starvation from my door; the wearisome search, day after day, until my heart was almost ready to sink with the weight of despair; the cold, heartless, sneering rebuffs and repulses which everywhere met me, until it seemed to me that my brain must go wild, and I sink into the abyss of shame and degradation which I saw around me on every hand, engulphing thousands of those whose lots were cast in the same mold with mine? Suffice it to say that I still struggled on, vainly hoping against hope, working at such employment as I could get, even at starvation prices, until at last my strength failed in the unequal strife, and I was prostrated upon a bed of sickness, from which, but for the sake of my helpless Carrie, I should have prayed that I might never rise.

How I lived through that long night of sickness, among strangers, and with no loving friend near me to bathe my fevered brow or cool my parched lips, or even to administer the remedies which the physician prescribed for me from time to time, I hardly know. It is true, my landlady was kind to me, and gave me all the attention which her own household and other duties would permit; but she had her own family and boarders to care for, and she could spare but little of her time for me. Long time I lingered at death's door, but at last my constitution triumphed, and I began slowly to mend, and at length was able to rise and walk about my room. I even tried to do some work, but when I bent my eyes upon my sewing, my brain whirled and I almost fainted from sheer weakness, and when my physician called to pay me his customary visit, he found me with a very considerable increase of fever.

He at once forbade, most peremptorily, any farther attempts at work, and, instead, ordered me to take exercise in walking, extending, however, my promenades no farther than I could do without incurring too much fatigue. At first my strolls were very short — not more than half a block—but my strenth gradually increased under this treatment, and in a short time I was able to walk half an hour without any great weariness. Oh! how I longed to get strong and able to renew my struggle with the world. And, indeed, stern necessity demanded it; for during my long illness my little treasury had entirely dwindled away, and I had even been compelled to part with some portions

of my scanty wardrobe to supply the necessities occasioned
by sickness.   My board, too, was considerably in arrears,
and though my landlady was very kind, and never alluded to
the matter, this gave me no little uneasiness, and doubtless
contributed materially to retard my restoration to strength.
But relief was at hand, and that, too, from a source of
which I did not dream.

One day, as I was taking my accustomed walk, I turned
a corner and found myself face to face with my step-father,
Captain Charles Lake.   I was so filled with hysterical
joy at seeing him that, for the moment, I was incapable
of speech or action.   .Nor was his surprise at the meeting
less than my own, although less visible effect was produced
upon him.   Coming close up to me he extended his hand,
and said:

"Annie, my child, is this indeed you?"

"Yes," I replied, bursting into tears of joy, for I saw
at once exemption from the miseries which had so sorely
weighed me down; "I am, indeed, your wretched, unhappy
daughter."

"Where are you living?" he continued kindly.   "You
look as though you had been sick."

"Indeed I have.   I have been sick both in body and
mind.   But, come home with me, and I will tell you all
that has happened since I left Detroit.

Drawing my arm within his own, the Captain accompanied me home, where I acquainted him with all that
had transpired, and with which the reader is already familiar.   He seemed much moved at the recital of my
sufferings, and at its close, said:

"Poor child! you have had a hard time, but it is now
all past.   You must go home with me, and Mary shall
nurse you back to health and happiness again.   I shall

be ready to leave the city to-morrow, and in the mean time you must get ready to go with me."

But at this, the recollection of the injustice I had done her flashed across my mind and suffused my face with a crimson glow, and I at once replied that I could not think of going there.

"Why not?" he asked, in some astonishment.

And then I told him that I had done Mary a great wrong, and that in no event could I go there to be a dependent upon her bounty. In vain he urged me to go, or at least to reveal to him fully the reasons which so powerfully deterred me. I was well aware that I had done her a gross injustice, and no amount of persuasion could ever have induced me to open to him the subject of that injustice. When he found that I was not to be shaken, he said:

"Well, I will not insist further. You will at least allow me to make provision to avoid in the future such suffering as you have been subjected to since coming here."

To this I consented, of course; and, seating himself at the table, he drew up an agreement binding himself to pay me seventy-five dollars per month, and a letter of credit authorizing me to draw upon his bankers at Detroit for the same, which he delivered to me, then called my landlady and discharged my indebtedness to her in full, after which he bid me an affectionate farewell, and I never saw him more. He, like the rest of my friends, has passed away, but the memory of this deed of kindness will never be effaced from my recollection. It has almost entirely obliterated from my mind the memory of the great wrong which he undeniably did to me in my childhood, and I fully forgive him all.

When my step-father had gone, I sat down and began

to consider what was best for me to do. I did not intend to leave Chicago, for I must live some where, and I was just as effectually concealed from the pursuit of Mason there as any where, and that concealment was now the prime consideration. I finally decided to try keeping house, believing that it would be less expensive than boarding, and that I would feel much more independent than I now did.

Accordingly, I set out in search of rooms to rent, but for some time I was as unsuccessful as in pursuit of employment. But, after some days spent in search, I was fortunate enough to find some rooms to let on the second floor of a house at No. 51 West Lake street. There were four rooms — more than I wanted, and the rent consequently higher than I wished to pay; but this was the only opportunity presented, and I decided to take them, thinking perhaps I could rent one or two of them, or, failing in that, could take one or two boarders, and so reduce my expenses within something like reasonable limits. I drew my first draft on Detroit, paid my rent for a month in advance, and on the eighteenth day of November, 1865, took possession of my rooms, and advertised for boarders.

I had become acquainted with a young lady by the name of Rosa ———, a seamstress, and a very lively, intelligent girl, of good principles, and a very agreeable companion. As soon as she knew I was taking boarders, she came to apply for a place with me, and was my first boarder. Two young gentlemen, who were employed in a store, immediately below us, applied, and were received as day boarders; others also made application, and, in a short time, I had all the boarders that my rooms would enable me to accommodate, and, for a time, I got along very well indeed. But my unlucky star was still in the ascendant, and it was in this boarding-house that I found some acquaintances who were doomed to exert a most baneful influence upon my future life.

The first was a man by the name of Alvord. He was a constable, and was doing some business for a boarder, who had some difficulty with a former employer about a balance of wages due him.   He called several times to see him on this business, much to my disgust, for I believed he was a bad man, and took no pains to conceal my dislike of him. This aroused his ill-feeling toward me, and when, at a future period, an opportunity was presented him of wiping out the old score, he did not hesitate to repay me with interest.

It was here, too, that I formed the acquaintance of him whose name I now bear—a man who, with the exception, perhaps, of Mason, has caused me more suffering than any other one with whom my checkered life has brought me in contact.   But I reserve for another chapter an account of the incidents attending our introduction and subsequent acquaintance and marriage.

CHAPTER XV.

ONE evening, a few moments before tea-time, a gentleman called, in answer to an advertisement which I had sent to one of the Chicago papers. He was very polite in his manners, and of genteel appearance, and introduced himself as Mr. Frank C. Nelles. I was favorably impressed with him at first sight, though, of course, not the slightest thought of love at that time entered my mind. I only looked upon him as a very pleasant, good-natured and sensible fellow, though he appeared very quiet, and rather inclined to be reserved, as he really was. Little did I then foresee, or even anticipate in the least degree, the sorrow and misery to me, of which that man was to be the author.

He staid and spent the evening with us, and a very pleasant evening we had. There were Miss Rose and another lady boarder, three young gentlemen, Mr. Nelles and myself. All were in good spirits, and the hours flew by unheeded until eleven o'clock struck, when the party separated. I invited Mr. Nelles to call again, and he accepted the invitation with thanks.

From this time he was a frequent visitor at my house, and was always gladly welcomed. I had made inquiries about him, and learned that he bore a good character, and was considered very respectable in the community in which he lived—that he occupied a responsible position in the employ of the street railroad company, and was supposed by his steadiness and prompt attention to duty, to be accumulating some property, while he was constantly rising in the estimation and confidence of his employers. The evidence as to his character was certainly satisfactory in the highest degree, and he was soon established on the footing of a warm and valued friend at the house. For a long time his visits, though frequent, were general, and excited no remark—that is, no one of the ladies seemed to be the special object of his visit, or to receive more attention from him than another, nor did he ever inquire for one more than another.

He had always been inclined to reticence concerning himself and his circumstances, but I had learned from him that he was a widower, and was still keeping house in the same place where he had lived with his former wife. When he told me this, I asked him jestingly if he kept bachelor's hall, and told him Rosa and I were coming around to see where and how he lived. He replied, in the same light, trifling style, that nothing would afford him more pleasure; that he did not live alone, but had a housekeeper, but that she did very poorly, and we would not find the house a very attractive one. But while we thus jested, I had no idea of ever carrying out my senseless proposition—it was only made in a spirit of playful badinage, and with no idea of its ever being thought of again.

I was therefore not a little surprised when, some days after the conversation, Rosa proposed that we should carry out our promise, and visit Mr. Nelles at his home. I asked her if she supposed I was in earnest when the proposition was made, to which she replied that she did not know whether I was in earnest or not; that she was, and that she had determined to go that very afternoon, and that she would have no excuse, but I must go with her. I asked her if she thought it was exactly proper for us to visit a gentleman at his lodgings, to which she answered that it was altogether different from that; that we were not going to visit a gentleman at his lodgings, but at his house, presided over, as he had informed us, by a lady who was his housekeeper, and that there would be no impropriety in our doing so; that go she would, and go with her I must. I advanced numerous other objections but without avail; she overruled them all, and insisted so strongly that I was finally silenced, if not convinced, and against my better judgment consented to accompany her. Beside, if the truth must be confessed, I felt a little anxiety to follow the matter out to the end, and see what was to be seen; and, accordingly, after dinner we equipped ourselves for walking and set out. It must be admitted to the reader, though we did not at the time mention it to each other, that we both had some secret misgivings as to the course we were pursuing, but we were both animated by the spirit of fun and adventure, and were resolved to follow it out to the end. I omitted to mention in the proper place, that Nelles had told us he had three children by his first wife, only one of whom, however, lived with him.

Well, we went to the house where he had informed us he lived. We found a store in the front part of the house, went to the rear, which appeared to be finished as a dwelling-house, and knocked at the door, but received no answer. The only sign of life was a little dog inside, barking most furiously at what he evidently deemed an attempted intrusion upon the premises which he had been left to guard. We then went to the place where Mr. Nelles worked, and were there told that he had just gone to the house. Again we returned to the house, and still finding nobody there, we went to the store in front, and inquired if there was a man by the name of Nelles living in that neighborhood, and were informed that he lived in the rear of that building. We then inquired how many there were in his family. They replied they did not know, but that, when he rented the house, he mentioned, inci-dentally, that he was going to occupy it with his wife.

By the time we had finished our inquiries, Mr. Nelles came up, and we at once accosted him, asking about his own health and that of his wife, telling him we heard she had just gone down in town, etc. There was a lady just crossing the street in front of the store, and he called our attention to her, telling us there she came; and, as soon as she unlocked the house, he would go in with us and give us an introduction to her. We accordingly went in with him, and were introduced to the lady, but not as Mrs. Nelles; he called her Miss Carney, and informed us she was his housekeeper.

We staid some time, and had a very pleasant visit, for Miss Carney could be very interesting and pleasant when she chose; and that afternoon she seemed to take special pains to make herself agreeable. She was then in good humor, and did all in her power to entertain us in the most lady-like manner. I afterward knew, to my sorrow, how differently she could act toward one whom she regarded as an enemy, as will more fully appear in the sequel of my story.

At length I decided it was time for us to go, and said as much to Rosa, to which she assented, and we rose to take our departure. Miss Carney protested against our going, and urged us, very earnestly, to stay to tea; but we refused, and were soon on our way home. Mr. Nelles accompanied us; and, when we reached home, he went in, took tea, and afterward spent the evening with us. This

was, to me, a fatal evening, for it was the one upon which
I gave up to Frank C. Nelles my freedom, my individuality, and upon which I once more agreed to take upon myself the fearful duties and responsibilities of married life.
It was upon this evening that I entered into a contract
of marriage which was to fill to overflowing my cup of
misery.

I had now been acquainted with Frank C. Nelles for
several months, and had seen nothing to indicate that he
was the monster he afterward turned out to be—nay, now,
I will confess that his kind and genial disposition, his (as
I supposed) steady character and correct habits, had
awakened feelings in my bosom which I supposed would
never exist there again, and I already regarded him with
more of favor than I usually bestowed upon my friends.
I will not admit that I really loved him at this time, but I
thought very kindly of him; and though he never said
anything, or indicated any marked preference for me, yet
I knew, by some sort of intuition—by that instinctive
feeling that pervades a woman's bosom—that he thought
more of me than he did of either of the other ladies at
the house. He had never called to see me more than
any one else; he had never inquired particularly for me;
he had never specially sought my society at the house,
and yet I knew, in some indefinable way, that I was
dearer to him than either of the others.

I was not, therefore, very much surprised when, seizing
a favorable opportunity, he asked me to be his wife. He
recalled the circumstances of our acquaintance; told how
lonely he had felt since the death of his first wife; how
his home needed the watchful care of one whose interests were identified with his; how he had watched and
studied my character; how he thought we could be happy

together, and begged me to take pity on his loneliness and make him blessed by becoming his wife.

I said I was not surprised, but, to some extent, I was; for, though I felt very confident such a proposition would some time be made, still it was unexpected at this time, and my answer was not ready. I therefore pleaded surprise, and begged time to consider of the matter before giving him a decided answer to a question of such tremendous importance. He acceded to this, and we parted for the night. I did not tell Rosa, with whom I slept, of the proposition which had been made to me, but chose to keep it within my own breast until I had finally decided upon it, although there remained, in my own mind, but little doubt that it would be finally accepted. But I had once accepted such a proposition in haste, and the result had been the most unmitigated woe, and I was now determined to deliberate well before acting; and yet all my deliberation was in vain, as subsequent events will show.

Nelles was to come, at the end of a week, for his final answer. I was alone in the world; for Captain Lake had taken Carrie and sent her to a sister of his in New Orleans, who was rich and would raise her like a lady, and I had nothing to care for except two little canary birds. Why not marry him, and end all my troubles for this life at once? Beside, it was not my nature to be alone in the world; I was so constituted that I must have somebody to love; some one toward whom the love of my heart would go out like a mighty, rushing torrent, and why not him? I was sure I loved him more than I loved Giles (or Mason) when I married him, and surely I had seen some happy days in my married life (for so I persisted in calling it) with him before my peace was all destroyed by the evidence of his unworthiness; and I

13

thought it was reasonably certain that the same cause for unhappiness did not exist in the case of Mr. Nelles.

But then, on the other hand, I had thought I would never marry again; my past experience had not favorably impressed me with the joys of married life, and I hesitated before entering into that state again. Beside, if I married Nelles or any one else, the seventy-five dollars which Captain Lake had kindly settled upon me, monthly, would end, and would the sacrifice pay me.

But why recount all my cogitations upon this point. Such reflections ever have but one end, and hence the reader will not be surprised to learn that when Mr. Nelles came for his final answer, I laid my hand in his, and promised him that, God being my helper, I would be to him a true and faithful wife so long as we both should live. And to this day, I call high Heaven to witness that I kept faithfully that vow until his tyranny and brutality drove me from home and placed it out of my power to keep it any longer.

There was one thing in connection with our engagement in which my conscience does not acquit me of all blame, and that was in relation to the dark and gloomy scenes in my past life and history. I did not impart them to him. It may be possible that, had I done so, it would have spared us both some trouble in the future, but I could not bring myself to speak of it. My life had been such a gloomy, barren one; there was so little to commend, and so much that was a source of shame and self-reproach to me, that when I would speak of it, I was silent from very shame, and my tongue clove to the roof of my mouth, and I postponed it from time to time, thinking I would reveal the sad history to him after we were married, would disclose to him the reasons which had induced me to keep silent, and would rely upon his kindness and mercy to forgive the deception I was practicing upon him. And here was committed one of the worst errors of my life. Far better for me had the revelation been made before our engagement was consummated, and trusted to his affection for me to overcome the effects of such a sad recital as mine, than to leave him to learn it in an exaggerated and distorted form from another source, while to the intrinsic evil of the story, would be added, in his mind, the reflection that I had deceived him. The fullest and freest confidence should be maintained between affianced lovers at all times; just as full and complete as that which should exist between husband and wife. Nay, I insist that wedded love will tolerate even more concealment, than will simply plighted faith; because, while the first is prone to create the most unbounded confidence, the last is proverbial for its suspicion and its jealousy. How important, then, is it that in no case any concealments be suffered to exist during the engagement, if we would avoid misery and woe during the wedded life which is to ensue. But I did not then practice upon this principle, and to this cause may be attributed no small portion of my subsequent sorrow.

I have not told the reader anything about the family of my betrothed, and will now turn for a short time to them. His father had been dead some time, but he had a mother and several brothers living at Waukegan, of whom he had frequently spoken, but none of whom I had ever seen. He also had two married sisters living in Chicago, one of whom I had seen at the time we plighted our faith to each other, but the other I had not. The first one lived on Milwaukee avenue, and Frank and I had spent one evening there; the other I had not met. I liked this one very well. Frank had three children, the youngest of whom ·

he told me, much to my surprise, was thirteen years old, while the others were old enough to care for themselves. He was older than I had supposed, being, at this time, more than forty years of age, though he did not really appear to be more than thirty-five at the most.

Soon after our betrothal, Frank invited me to go with him to spend the evening at the house of Mrs. Spalding, the other sister of whom I have before spoken, saying:

"You know she will soon be your sister, and it is not becoming to have a sister whom you do not know."

I accordingly went with him to visit her. We passed rather a pleasant evening, though it must be confessed I did not like her as well as I did her sister. There was something in her manners, impossible to be described, but which was very displeasing to me. It was not pride, or ill-nature, nor could I say what it was; but there was that sort of instinctive dislike which we sometimes feel toward a person, and for which we are unable to account, even to ourselves.

> "I do not like you, Dr. Fell;
> The reason why, I can not tell;
> But this I know full well,
> I do not like you, Dr. Fell."

And yet she was a good, kind-hearted woman, and when I afterward had occasion to test her goodness of heart and disposition, I found that I could rely upon her with the confident assurance that she would not disappoint me.

When the evening was ended, and we started away, Mrs. Spalding urged me very earnestly to come and see her again, saying, in a voice and manner which convinced me that she knew of the relationship between Frank and myself, "that we must get to be very good friends indeed." This was the only allusion that was, at any time during the evening, made to our engagement. Frank accompained me to the foot of the stairs leading to my own home, and there bid me good night, promising to call and see me the next evening. The next evening came, but he did not. I was sadly disappointed at even this trifling affair, and really felt as if he had slighted me, merely because he for once failed to keep his promise to meet me, and, could I have seen him then, do n't know what I might have said to him. He had already become dearer to me than I thought, and I was jealous of even any appearance of neglect.

The next evening he came, and, ah! how swiftly the hours flew by in his society. We were both so happy that we took no note of passing time, and when he looked at his watch and declared that it was almost twelve o'clock, words could hardly express our mutual surprise. It did not really seem to me that it could be more than nine, and it was only when I consulted my own watch, and found that the small hours were indeed approaching, that I could be convinced that his time was not too fast.

"Well," said he, " the last car is gone, and I shall have to walk home. But never mind, the time will soon come when we will not part at all."

After this he spent nearly all his evenings with me, and the scene just detailed was often repeated. How happy we were. But during all this time I could not help feeling a sort of vague uneasiness, a dim, indefinable dread of the future, and I trembled inwardly lest our happiness should pass away forever. It may be that it was because I had seen so much of sorrow, and so little genuine, unalloyed happiness in my past life, that I felt so insecure in this. And of a truth, my past experience had been such as to render me suspicious and distrustful to a degree. How often had I seen myself raised to the highest pitch of happiness, only to be in the next moment, as it were, precipitated from my pinnacle of joy to the very lowest depths of the abyss of misery and pain. And is it strange that I should have trembled in view of the possibility of a repetition of my past sad experience? And hence it was that my jealous love was ever suggesting doubts as to the future. Would he always love me as now? Would he ever enjoy, as now, the evenings spent in my society; or would that love of his, which now seemed so ardent, in time wither and fade away, and I be left alone, a miserable and neglected wife? And then my own deep love, and my confidence in him, would whisper that it could not be; that his affection was true, even as my own; that our devotion to each other could never know any change, and that, hand in hand, we would travel adown the vale of life together, and our destinies be separated only by the dark rolling stream of death. Could I have imagined what less than a twelvemonth would bring forth, how gladly would I have laid down and died ere linking my fate with that of him whom I now so fondly loved.

As our wedding-day approached I began to make preparations for its celebration. I advertised my rooms "to let," and my furniture "for sale," and in a short time had an application from a newly-married couple, and sold out to them. They desired to take immediate possession, and I agreed to allow them to do so, they boarding me until the wedding-day. When married, Frank and I were going to Waukegan, to visit his mother and brothers there, after which we were to return to Chicago and go to keeping house, living, for the present at least, in the same house he now occupied. This was our programme, but, like all other programmes of merely human beings, it was liable to fail in some particulars. And in this particular case it was not to be fulfilled, at least until after intense sorrow and trouble to one of the parties concerned.

But I will close this chapter here, and in my next, give some account of the events preceding my marriage, and immediately following it—events which gave me a new insight into the character of Frank C. Nelles, and led me, even at that early day, to almost regret the step which had bound me to him, and placed me in his power.

CHAPTER XVI.

TIME had rolled away until but few days intervened between us and the day which was to witness our marriage, when suddenly Mr. Nelles discontinued his visits. Up to this time he had been in the habit of calling on me almost every day, and I could imagine no reason for the sudden change. At first I thought nothing of it, but when three or four days passed away and he came not, I began to feel uneasy, for it was something which had never occurred since our engagement. Accordingly I sent him a note asking him to call and see me at a particular time therein mentioned.

He came, but oh! how changed he was. He was no longer the same man. No kiss of welcome passed between us as had been our wont, but briefly and coldly he saluted me, and, without noticing the chair I offered him, he remained standing, and apparently waited for me to address him, which I did in a quivering voice, for my heart was full.

"Frank," said I, "for heaven's sake, what is the matter?"

"Do you know Charles Alvord?" he asked.

"Yes," said I; "what of him?" for I knew him to be a man who was capable of anything, and my heart misgave me as soon as he pronounced that name.

Nelles then went on to tell me that Alvord had been to him and told him he understood he was going to marry me, and he felt it his duty to warn him against me; that I was a bad, wicked woman, and was only trying to marry him for some base design; that if he married me he would be sorry for it, and that he had better break off with me while there was yet time.

As I heard these cruel words, I sunk upon the sofa utterly overcome by the violence of my emotions. What had I ever done to this man, that he should attempt to destroy me in this manner? I had never harmed him or said aught against him in any way, and why he should seek to injure me was past my comprehension. It could be for no other reason than because of his purely base and devilish spirit—that spirit which would lead him to trample a poor, unfortunate woman under his feet, and degrade her all in his power, instead of trying to lift her to her feet and aid her in an attempted reformation. Yes, such was his character, and he had only followed out his own base instincts when he tried to injure me with Frank. I did not pretend to be perfect by any means, nay, I had, as the reader is already aware, committed some most grievous errors, but I was not a wicked woman at heart, and my errors and follies had been repented of a thousand times. I ought, perhaps, to have told Frank all about my past life before this time, but the reader knows why I had not, and surely this fault was not entirely past forgiveness.

These reflections passed through my mind as I lay upon the sofa, but I could not answer him a word, and it was only when he asked me, after a long period of silence, what I had to say to these charges, that I found language to answer him. I then told him the truth with regard to the past, with which the reader is already acquainted, gave him my reasons for not telling him before, and wound up by saying that we had better not marry, and that I did not wish to marry him unless we could live happily together. As I said this, he turned on his heel, and saying,

"Good night, if that is your answer," he started to leave the room.

But I could not let him go thus. To part in this way would kill me, for I loved him more than my own life, and I could not have felt worse had he plunged a knife in my bosom. I told him that, notwithstanding the past, if he would trust me, he would find me a true wife; that I would endure suffering, starvation, and even death in the midst of poverty, before I would prove false to him; that I would not marry him to make him miserable, but if he would only give me his love, I could and would endure anything in the world. To this appeal he only responded "Good night," left the room, and closed the door behind him.

Once outside the door, however, he seemed to relent, and I listened in vain for the sound of his footsteps descending the stairs. It would, perhaps, have been better for both if he had gone, but he did not. I lay and listened some time, and then arose, went to the door and opened it. He was standing on the threshhold, and as I opened the door he stepped inside, took my hand in his, and led me to the sofa, where, seating me, he placed himself by my side.

"Forgive me," said he; "I was wrong and hasty just now. But forgive and forget; and let us be married as though nothing unpleasant had ever occurred between us."

"I forgive you freely," said I; "but answer me one thing. If we are married, now that you know all the sad past, will you ever throw it up to me, or taunt me with my errors of by-gone days? Promise me that you will not do this, let what may arise."

His answer to this request I can never forget. It is engraved on my heart in characters of living fire. It was:

"Annie, if you were the worst woman in the city, and I married you, I would never cast up anything to you. Nay, more; if I married you under such circumstances, I would live with you, and treat you kindly, so long as you were a true and faithful wife to me after our marriage."

We were married in a few days after this conversation. God is my witness, that in word, thought and deed, I was a true and faithful wife to him; and how he redeemed the solemn promise just recorded, let the future tell. May God forgive him, as I do, for the black and soul-killing perjury of which he has been guilty in this respect.

Our wedding was set for the sixth day of February, 1866. We were to be married, at two o'clock in the afternoon, at the Baptist church, corner of Morgan and Monroe Streets, by Rev. Edgar J. Goodspeed, pastor of that church. I was just trying on my wedding-dress, before breakfast, in the morning, when there was a rap at the door at the head of the stairs. Mrs. Singer, the lady with whom I boarded, opened the door. There stood a girl, who inquired for Mrs. Mason. Supposing it to be one whom my dress-maker had sent on an errand, I stepped forward, when she handed me a letter, and immediately turned and disappeared down stairs. I called after her, but she went on without paying any heed to me.

I hardly knew what to make of this; but, without wasting any time in vain conjectures, at once opened the letter. It was a sheet of foolscap paper; all four of the pages were written full, in a strange hand, and I could not imagine who should be writing to me, or why. But I had not read far, until I understood what the writer was driving at; for it was filled with such vile and disgusting language as is seldom used by a woman. I can not give any portion of its contents; they were unsuitable for publication: suffice it to say it was written by Angeline Carney, Mr. Nelles' housekeeper, and, if true, revealed a state of depravity, on his part, almost too shocking to be believed.

I knew not what to do or think. If the charges contained in this letter were true, he was not the man to whom I could entrust my honor and happiness; if they were not true, he ought to have a chance to explain them away. True, I did not believe them; but still every word might possibly be true: and, if so, I ought to know it before it was too late. I had no one to whom I could confide the matter, and, hence, no one to advise me how to act. But it was near nine o'clock of our wedding-day, and something must be done, and that quickly. I hastily put on my bonnet and shawl, took a street car, and was soon at Mr. Nelles' place of business. Arrived there, I was told he had gone to the house, and at once sent a man there to tell him to meet me on the next corner, where I would wait until he came up; for I was resolved I would not marry him until that matter was explained to my satisfaction.

I had not long to wait. My messenger had barely reached the house, when I saw him and Nelles coming out of the yard. Frank came up to where I was standing, and, in a voice of some concern, asked what was the matter. I replied by placing the scurrilous letter in his hands, and asking him to explain what it all meant. He read it through, without a word; and, then, handing it back to me, said Angeline was angry because he was going to get married, and thus throw her out of a place; that she had a violent temper, and would do anything she could to accomplish her ends. As for the scandalous letter: he said, most emphatically, that there was not a word of truth in it; that it was only a part of her programme to break up the marriage, and urged me to pay no attention to it whatever. He further told me, that she would be sent away that very day, and that he had employed a German girl to clean up the house and take charge of it till our return from our trip to Waukegan; after which, he observed, it would be in my care.

His explanation did not fully satisfy me, and I said as much to him and expressed my determination to go to the house, see her, and learn from her own lips what they were to each other. I told him we could never be married until this matter was cleared up to my entire satisfaction.

He thereupon called a young man from the house, introduced him to me as his son Wallace, and referred me to him for the truth of what he had said. I showed him the letter, and asked him if he knew anything of it. He replied, after looking it over, that Angeline Carney, his father's housekeeper, had written it and had told him about it after she had sent it, and gave the same explanation of the motives which had prompted it as his father had already given. He also added that Angeline was very angry, and would be sorry for what she had done as soon as she had time to reflect a little. But all this was not satisfactory to me, and I expressed a determination to go to the house, and see her about it, and hear what she had to say, and accordingly started in that direction. Mr. Nelles went with me, and Wallace went on before to tell her we were coming.

When we reached the house, I went at once into the bed room. Miss Carney sat there crying as if her heart would break. I asked her at once why she had written

me such a letter as that, and she replied that she had done
it because she was angry, and wanted to break up the
match.   She did not say it was not true, but only left that
to be inferred by saying she had written it because she
wanted to make trouble, and break up the marriage if
possible.

I decided in my own mind that, dearly as I loved Nelles,
I would not dare to trust my happiness in his keeping,
and walked out of the house intending to go home and
have nothing more to do with him.   A street car was just
passing, I signalized it to stop, and at once got on
board.   I was not aware that Nelles had followed me,
until I turned around to take my seat, when I found he
was with me.   He begged me to get off and go with him
where he could talk it all over with me, which he could
not of course do on the car.   For some time I refused,
and only yielded when I became afraid that his earnestness would attract the attention of the other passengers to
our quarrel, or whatever it might be called.

Accordingly we got off the car, and went to an oyster
saloon where we had a long talk.   He protested his entire
innocence of all the charges contained in the letter, and
strove to induce me to say that they would make no difference in my mind, and that I would marry him.   But
this I would not do, for though I almost believed his protestations I wanted time and opportunity to think the
matter over alone.   I did not want to act hastily, and
hence evaded giving him a direct answer.   He finally
ceased his persuasions, we left the saloon, and walked
down the street until a car came along, when I took that,
and was soon at my home.

I had been there but a few minutes when a half-brother
of Nelles, by the name of Emsley Sunderlin, and his son,

Daniel Nelles, came to see me. They had been informed by Frank and Wallace of the rupture, and came to induce me to change my determination and go on with the marriage. They asseverated his entire innocence of the charges, and urged me to pay no attention to them, assuring me I should have no further trouble on her account, and begged me not to allow that bad woman to break up the marriage by her mean and spiteful jealousy. They told me that Frank was taking it very hard, and had sent them to talk to me about it in the hope of persuading me to accede to his wishes.

I replied that I was fearful we should never be happy in each other's society, and that I believed it would be as well for both of us if we never married. But even while I uttered these words my heart was wrung with anguish, for I really loved Frank, and the idea of giving him up was very painful to me. But they still pleaded with me, urged and entreated me to reconsider my determination, and at length I yielded, almost against my better judgment, and told them they might inform Frank that I would be ready at the time appointed. I asked no further pledges or protestations from him, for I thought that if the promises he had already made, together with those he would make before the man of God, would not restrain him, no others would, and it were worse than useless to demand them at his hands. I did not feel entirely justified in the step I was about to take, but I loved him, and thought he loved me, and I trusted to that love to avoid any difficulties in the future. I have since learned that, however powerful a motive love may be, it will not avail to procure peace and happiness unless sanctioned and controlled by high moral principle.

Two o'clock was near at hand, and still I was not fully

decided in my own mind as to my duty in the premises.
I fancied that duty said, "remain single," while inclination quite as strongly demanded that I should go on with
the wedding.   And thus I remained in the most painful
suspense, and even delaying my dressing on this account
until the clock was close upon the stroke of two, when I
suddenly made up my mind to go through with it at all
hazards, hastened to complete my remaining preparations,
and, just as the clock struck two, gave Frank Nelles my
hand to be led to the carriage in which we were going to
the church.   He handed me in, sprang in after me, and
we rolled away to the church, where, in the presence of a
very few friends, whom we had invited to witness the ceremony, the man of God pronounced the words which
bound us together forever.   Forever, did I say ?   This was
a mistake.   It was said to be forever, but we shall soon
see how, in a few short weeks, I was, by the tyranny and
brutality of the man, who, this day, promised to love,
honor, and cherish me until death, driven from my home to
become a wanderer among strangers, and seek a preca-
rious existence by my own exertions.

After our marriage, we went to Mrs. Marshall's for dinner, had a very pleasant time, and then, at four o'clock,
took the cars for Waukegan, where we were to remain
over night at the house of his mother, then visit two days
among his other relations there, and return to the city the
next day.   Emsley Sunderlin accompanied us, and just
before we reached Waukegan, he proposed to play a joke
upon his mother and the guests whom we knew she had
invited to greet us.   Accordingly, when we reached our
destination, he offered me his arm to conduct me to the
house.   I accepted it, and when we got in he introduced
me to the assembled guests as his wife, Frank in the mean-

time remaining in the background. Everybody was taken by surprise. The old lady had invited them to meet her son and his bride, and they had understood that it was Frank who was coming with a newly-made wife; judge then of their astonishment when one so much younger than Frank, but still a son of the old lady, claimed the honors which they supposed were due to Mr. Nelles. Nevertheless we were greeted with the same warmth which they were prepared to extend to Mr. Nelles and his bride, and many were the congratulations and kindly wishes showered upon us, all of which Mr. Sunderlin received with as much gravity and unction as though he were really entitled to them.

When supper was announced, Emsley, who had never quitted my side for a moment, in order to keep up the deception, offered me his arm and conducted me to the table. We sat side by side at the head of the well-filled board, and "many a time and oft" the health of the bride and groom was pledged by the joyous guests, Sunderlin very coolly appropriating these honors to himself, while Frank sat near the foot of the table, coolly and quietly enjoying the joke which was being perpetrated.

The company were not undeceived until the close of the festivities, late at night, when they were immeasurably astonished at seeing Frank and myself retire to a room together. They at once appreciated the fact that they had been the victims of a huge "sell," and proceeded to inflict summary vengeance upon the offenders. I will not detail all the means resorted to to punish us for the joke we had played upon them; let the reader draw upon his imagination, or his recollection, for the wildest pranks which usually attend weddings in the rural districts, and then double everything he can imagine, and he will have some idea of

14

the events attending our first night's stay in Waukegan.
In vain Frank's mother tried to control them, and induce
them to let us alone; with protestations of vengeance for
the deception we had practiced upon them, they continued
to invade the privacy of our chamber all night long, and
we never closed our eyes for a moment during the entire
night.

We were to have returned to Chicago on Friday, but,
the evening before, Mr. Nelles received a telegram from
that place, which, he informed me, was from his son, Daniel, and made it necessary for him to return at once to the
city. I tried to induce him to tell me the nature of the
dispatch, or let me see it, but he declined to do either, saying it only pertained to some business matters of no special
importance, and that I would know all about it in time.
I asked him when he would go to the city, and he replied
he should go that night, but I must stay in Waukegan, at
his mother's, until he sent for me, which he said would be
very soon. I could not understand the reason for this
secresy, and did not like it; but felt sure some trouble was
brewing. I could form no idea what it was, but my fears
led me to imagine something very horrible; and, after my
husband left, I walked the floor, constantly, until Daniel
Nelles came in. His train arrived about eleven o'clock,
and he, at once, came to his grandmother's, where I was.

I was glad to see him, for I knew his father had arrived
in Chicago before he started out, and I felt in hopes he
had brought a message to me to return to Chicago with
him the next morning. But in this I was disappointed—
he told me his father wished me to stay in Waukegan a
few days longer, and would send for me soon. I tried to
induce him to tell me something about the difficulty which
took him away so suddenly; but he protested that he

could not explain any thing; that he had been advised to send the dispatch, but that he really knew nothing about the trouble, save that it was something about the possession of the house.

Finding that I could learn nothing from him, I gave it up, and retired to rest, with my mother-in-law. She was a dear old lady, one whom I esteemed from the first moment I ever saw her; and, as I came to know her better, I loved her as though she had been my own mother. When she found that my nervous excitement would not allow me to sleep, she began to talk to me; and, as she was a sincere and pious Christian woman, her conversation, naturally enough, flowed into that channel. She asked me if I was a member of any church, and gently expressed her regret when she was informed that I was not. She spoke of Frank's being a member of the church; but said she thought he had almost ceased to comply with the outward and visible forms of religion; expressed much sorrow thereat, and thanked me, kindly and heartily, when I told her that, though not a church-member, I liked to see such things, and would use all my influence to induce Frank to attend church and resume family worship. In such soothing conversation as this, the night passed away, until, my nervousness being somewhat relieved, I at last sunk into slumber.

When I awoke in the morning, however, I was as anxious as ever; and, as the day wore on, I could think of nothing but the strange air of mystery which attended Frank's departure. I was continually wondering what could be the matter which so imperatively called him home; but which I, his lawful wife, must not know, and I finally determined to be put off no longer. Accordingly, I sent a letter down, by Daniel, to his father, telling him I was coming home the next day; that I could not stay away any longer, and asking him to meet me at the depot in Chicago. This letter brought no answer, but still I thought, of course, he would meet me as requested.

The next day I went down to Chicago, and as we rolled slowly into the depot, I looked around on every side for my husband, but he was nowhere to be seen. How bitter was my disappointment. Although I knew he did not approve of my coming, still no thought of his refusing to meet me had ever crossed my mind, and now, to be treated with such apparent neglect, seemed the very hight of cruelty to me, and the tears gushed into my eyes at the thought. I hesitated for some time what I should do. I had never been installed mistress of his house, and did not feel like going there. Beside, who could tell what difficulty might be caused if I went there, not only unexpected and unannounced, but in direct opposition to what I knew and understood to be his wish; and finally I decided that I would go to my old home, and stay there till he came for me. Accordingly I walked over there, it being but a short distance from the depot.

I had been there but a short time when he came for me, and asked me to go home with him. And then, for the first time, I knew what had summoned him home so unexpectedly, and also why he had not met me at the depot, according to my request of the day before.

It seems that Mr. Nelles' housekeeper, who had been sent away from her position on the day of our marriage, being highly incensed at the loss of her place, had gone to Mr. Alvord, and, under his advice, she had returned to the house, expelled the German girl who was left in charge, and, taking possession of the place again, had avowed her determination to remain there, at least until

the arrival of Mr. Nelles. The faithful girl, whose rights
were thus invaded, had gone to Daniel for redress, and
he at once telegraphed his father to come down and settle
the dispute. Mr. Nelles came down at once, and found
her in absolute possession of the house. She avowed
her determination to maintain her possession against
all comers whomsoever. He first tried to make a treaty
of peace with her, but without effect—all his overtures
were scornfully rejected. He then resorted to expostula-
tion, then to entreaty, and finally to threats, telling her
he would give her in charge of the police if she persisted
in her extraordinary and outrageous conduct; but to this
she was equally indifferent. In this way had passed the
entire day, and finally he had gone, that very morning
(the day of my arrival), to carry his threat into execution.
In this way he had succeeded in getting possession of the
house; but in what a condition! While he was gone
for a policeman, she seemed to have tried to dismantle
the fortress which she could no longer hold; or, in other
words, she appeared to have used all the means in her
power to render the house as nearly uninhabitable as
possible. The carpets were torn up, the window-curtains
taken down, and over the floor were scattered fragments
of broken dishes and furniture. These matters had de-
layed him until it was too late to meet me at the train,
according to my request.

By the time he had finished this recital we had arrived
at the house, and such a sight as it was, I never saw before, and hope never to see again. Scattered over the floor
were fragments of crockery, glassware, mirrors, and every
thing that would break; while strips of carpet, fragments
of broken furniture, shreds of curtains, and everything that
one could think of, lay in profusion all around. I was

heart-sick, but it was no time to mourn, and, with the assistance of our faithful German girl, we set vigorously to work to repair damages as far as possible, and in course of time rendered the place quite habitable.

CHAPTER XVII.

Behold me, once more, dear reader, installed as mis‑ tress of a home which I could call my own, and the wife of a man whom I loved and was willing to do anything in my power to render happy. I would endure any cross, privation, or trial without a murmur for his sake, and would only ask, in return, the inestimable boon of his love and confidence. The light of his countenance, and the kindly affection which I knew my conduct merited, was all that was needed to render me perfectly happy; but, alas! there were causes at work which were destined to undermine the castle of peace which my hopes had erected, reduce it to a wreck, and my life to a barren waste of wretchedness and black despair. Let me, in the present chapter, unfold some of these causes to the reader.

During my residence in Chicago I had been so unfortunate as to incur the hatred of certain vicious and unprincipled persons, whose names it is now unnecessary to mention. Two in particular—a man and a woman— had, without any cause, come to regard me with the most untiring and fiend-like malice, and were ready to resort to any means, however base or unprincipled, to accomplish my utter ruin. They began their efforts to separate myself and my husband before we had been married a week, and prosecuted their object with a zeal worthy of a better cause, and with what degree of success, will, in due time, be apparent to the reader.

Their first step was to write letters to all our friends,

in which they denounced me as a prostitute, and applied
to me every base epithet which their unprincipled and
debased natures could suggest. Not content with this,
they attempted to give greater publicity to their vile slan-
ders, by causing them to be published in the Chicago Pic-
ayune, a vile and obscene little sheet, which, in spite of
the efforts of the police for its suppression, was published
in some obscure, out-of-the-way garret, whence it dissemin-
ated its poisonous filth upon the air of Chicago. Could
my life be other than miserable under this state of
affairs? To know that my name was bandied about the
saloons and brothels of Chicago, and was the common
topic of conversation with the brutish and degraded
beings who congregate in such places, seemed to me
more than I could bear.

And to make matters worse, I saw day by day that my
husband was being affected in his love toward me by these
scurrilous and constant attacks. He grew distant, reserved, and cold, his former demonstrations of affection
ceased almost entirely, and he was constantly telling me
something that he had heard said of me, and when I proposed to go and see his informants, and trace to their
foundations the vile reports which they were constantly cir-
culating, he would not consent that I should do so. Then I
wished to have them arrested, and thus compel them to desist from their infamous attacks by the terrors of the law,
but to this he would not consent, and so matters went
from bad to worse until my life was wretched indeed, and
in my inmost soul I regretted that I had ever married
again.

As I now look back to those days of misery, and scan
my conduct with the most scrutinizing care, I am unable
to recall a single instance in which I failed in my duty to-

ward my husband, or, in word, thought, or deed, violated the promise made at the altar before God and man, to "love, honor, and obey." I did not, during all this time, give him an unkind word, or even a look; it mattered not though my very heart-strings were quivering with pain, I always met him with a kiss and smile when he returned from his labor, and at parting the same seal of affection was always exchanged between us. Again, I felt that, as my husband was by no means wealthy, it was my duty to do all I could to help him along in the world, and hence, when he proposed that we should take some of the hands employed in the railroad shops to board, I at once assented to it, although really not able to do the work for our own family, to say nothing of adding the cookery of four or five men to my already heavy burdens. And thus,day by day I toiled on, though often almost fainting with weariness from over-exertion, vainly hoping against hope, that by patience, kindness, and the most unselfish devotion, I would be able to reclaim the love and affection which I saw gradually slipping away from me, as I feared, forever.

Other means, also, I resorted to to accomplish the one great object of my life. The reader will remember that my husband was a member of the church, and that I had promised his mother that I would try to recall him to a discharge of his duties as a follower of the meek and lowly Jesus. Accordingly, the first night that we passed in our new home, I brought the Bible, and, laying it on his knee, asked him to read a chapter, and have prayers before we retired. He looked at me in some surprise, and inquired if I was a member of the church, adding that he had understood that I was not. To this I replied that I was not, but that I desired to become a Christian, and by the blessing of God, and his assistance, hoped, ere long,

to realize the accomplishment of my desire.   He made no
further remark, but opening the Word of God, read a
chapter, and then we knelt together and offered up our petitions to the throne of Divine grace.   And each evening,
before our retirement for the night, this scene was repeated
for some time, and each evening I induced him to go on
in the path of duty, hoping, by the power of God's grace,
to attract his heart more closely to mine.   At times, I
would, at his request, read the Word of God while he listened, after which we would unite in prayer.

I also endeavored to induce him to attend church with
me, believing that by so doing I could win him more
closely to my side and away from the associations which
were poisoning his mind against me, and, for a time, I was
successful in this.   For several Sabbaths he accompanied
me to church, and on such occasions he invariably treated
me with more kindness and consideration after our return
than he did before going.   But the effect was only temporary.   And there was a time coming in which I was to be
deprived of even this partial influence over him, and when
my efforts in this direction were to become of no avail.

While I was thus trying to discharge every duty toward
my husband, my bitterest enemies were as assiduously
working to destroy me forever.   There is something in-
comprehensible in the determined, relentless hostility of
these miserable beings to one who had never done them
any wrong whatever.   It is easy to conceive why one,
who deems himself injured by another, should, at the moment, and in the heat of passion, strive to avenge his real
or supposed injuries, but how one can thus, through a long
period of time, continue a course of unfounded and un-
merited persecution, is utterly unaccountable to me.   It
must be remembered that theirs was not the work of an

hour or a day; for weeks, and even months, they labored unremittingly in the pursuit of their unholy scheme, until their diabolical perseverance was at last crowned with the most complete success.

Such effect had the persistent attacks of my enemies upon my husband, that, in time, he came to apparently avoid my society as much as possible. He no longer spent his evenings at home with me—no longer we knelt in in prayer before the throne of grace—no longer we wended our way together to the house of God to listen to the teachings of his Word; we no longer visited in company any place of amusement, or went out together at all. Solitary and alone, with the light of my husband's love withdrawn from me, with my path hedged about with bitterest thorns, I groped my way along in darkness, only wondering what the end would be, and how soon it would come.

But it was not upon my husband alone that these attacks had their effect to my injury, though the loss of his love was the severest blow which could befall me. The friends and acquaintances I had made, one after another, turned aside their heads and refused to recognize me, or to speak to me when we met; no one visited me, or returned my calls, and, in a short time, I was as completely ostracised from society as if banished to a desolate island in the midst of the Pacific Ocean.

God pity and help the unfortunate wretch upon whom, whether guilty or innocent, society once sets the seal of its condemnation, for there is no help for him or her short of the wisdom and power of Omniscience itself. There is no more unjust, arbitrary or tyrannical ruler upon the face of the earth than this same society. It has no toleration for errors, and admits no repentance in its wretched victims. Let any one, and especially a woman, commit a single error, and attempt afterward to repent of that error, and retrieve their standing and position—will society aid them in the slightest degree ?   Will the friendly hand be stretched forth to aid them, and lead them into brighter paths of peace and happiness; or will the kindly glance of sympathy, and the genial smile of encouragement, cheer them on in the reformation they have attempted ? Will society whisper to the penitent, sin-sick soul, " Come, I will lead, and assist you, by pathways strewn with thorn-less flowers, into a purer, brighter and holier atmosphere, where strength and vigor shall be restored to you; where you shall breathe airs which are never deadly, and gather fruit which holds no lurking poison; where innocence and joy abound forever more, and where the sins of the past shall be remembered no more forever ?"   No; it rises with a whip of scorpions, drives the poor victim from the door, and, with contumely, scorn and reproach, pursues him to the very brink of the grave; and, not content even with having hunted the poor wretch to the tomb, it pur-sues him beyond, and loads his memory with execration and reproach.

And thus it is that society renders almost impossible the reform of one who has once gone astray.   Our Savior was not ashamed, when on earth, to take by the hand the penitent sinner, and, with kindly words and approving smiles, lift him up once more to the position he occupied before his fall; but society, composed of men and women who profess to be His disciples and followers, gathers its robes around it with a sort of Pharisaic pride, and saying, "I am more holy than thou," shuts the door in his face, and drives him back to the darkness from whence he would fain emerge.   Out upon such foul hypocrisy and hollow pretense as this.   Is it any wonder that there are so many outcasts in the world when their reform is thus made impossible? And will not that thing called society have a fearful account of wrong and outrage to settle in the day of the final adjustment of all things? How many souls that might otherwise have been saved, have been driven to eternal perdition by the course to which I have alluded? Who can contemplate the fearful record without shuddering? But to return to the story of my trials.

During all this time I had no suspicion that my husband was not true to me. I knew he had many sins to answer for, but this one I never laid to his charge, and I could endure almost anything so long as I believed him true to me, as I was to him. But I was soon to be undeceived, and to find myself that most miserable of all beings, a neglected and forsaken wife.

I was one day mending a coat which he usually wore about his work, and which he had this day left home for this purpose. As I turned it over, a letter fell from one of the pockets to the floor. I picked it up, and something in the superscription attracted my attention at once, and I immediately opened it, and there found my worst suspicions more than confirmed. The letter was from a woman whom I already knew for one of my worst enemies. She spoke very disrespectfully of me—called me that "thing" he had married—assured him of her undying love—told him she could not give him up, and appointed a meeting with him, that very night, in the ladies' sitting-room at the railroad office.

How my blood boiled within me as I read these damning proofs of his treachery and deceit. What should I do? As I sat thus, with the evidence of his falsehood in my hands, I was for a time almost incapable of thinking rationally upon any subject. My first idea was to retain the letter

until he came home, then show it to him and charge him
with his guilt; but upon reflection, my charity for him suggested that perhaps this letter was written only for the
purpose of being seen by me, as a part of her system of
persecution, and that he might, after all, be innocent.
But, then, why should it be in his pocket? Why should he
have preserved it so carefully? Nevertheless I decided to
wait until I had more complete proof of his guilt, and accordingly returned the letter to his pocket, and when he
came home made no allusion to the matter.

But when he went out that night, I hastily threw on a
bonnet and shawl and followed him at a distance sufficient
to avoid his observation. He went directly to the place
of meeting. The woman was in waiting for him, and they
went away together, I following them at a safe distance,
until they finally disappeared within the door of a low saloon, of the very worst class in the city.

From this time forward I watched his movements with
the closest and most careful scrutiny. Many a time have
I searched his pockets and found letters from this abandoned woman, in which she would speak of prior meetings
with him, and make appointments for the future; and I
invariably observed that he went out whenever the time
came to fulfill these appointments. During this time, too,
I was making inquiries among those who might be supposed to know something about these matters, and was
told that Frank C. Nelles, my husband, was a constant
visitor of this woman. And yet, when I had accumulated
proofs to satisfy myself a thousand times of his guilt, and
charged him with it, he had the effrontery and the hardihood to deny it all. And when I told him what I had
seen with my own eyes, he flew in a rage, repeated his asseverations of innocence, swore that I had never seen

anything of the kind, and actually had the temerity to call upon his Maker to witness that the whole thing was a fabrication, or the offspring of a disordered brain!

Great God! is there no punishment for such terrible falsehood and blasphemy? Here was this man whom I knew—not suspected, but *knew*—to be guilty of the worst crimes which a husband can commit against a wife, and yet he dared to call high Heaven to witness, what? That what I had seen with my own eyes was not so; that my sense of sight had deceived me; that I was in the wrong, instead of being the victim of the most outrageous and grievous indignity which could ever be offered to a true, faithful and confiding woman. And was there no remedy for all this? What could I do? I was helpless, powerless in his hands. The crimes which had already been perpetrated against me, and to which I was now satisfied he was a party, had put it out of my power to do anything to support myself in Chicago, and what to do I did not know. I had no means to go elsewhere, and I could see no way of escape from the horrors of my position. The only thing I could see was to stay and suffer on until death should kindly relieve me from my sufferings. To such a state of despair had I been reduced by the course of persecution and suffering to which I had been subjected.

But there is a point at which we pluck courage and energy, even from black despair, and that point was fast approaching in my case. I had endured, it seemed to me, almost everything that a woman could endure, and yet there was one more indignity and insult to be offered to me—one that was beyond even my capacity for endurance, and which, at last, resulted in our final separation.

One day my husband came home, and appeared to be in a great rage; though it was very unusual for him to

be abusive, angry, and violent toward me. On this occasion he seemed much more so than usual, and led me to
think at once something terrible was going to happen.
But I was wholly unprepared for the terrible accusation
he was about to bring against me. What it was need not
be told; suffice it to say, it exceeded in horror and studied
insult anything which I had before been called upon to
endure at his hands. I was thunder-struck! Not only
did I know that the accusation was wholly false and unfounded, but that he, too, must know it to be so, and yet
I was fully aware that denial would avail me nothing.
The accusation had evidently been made for a purpose,
and to deny it would serve nothing toward defeating that
purpose, and yet how could I rest under such a terrible
charge, and take no steps to disprove it?

We were then expecting his mother to visit us the next
day. She was in the city, at the house of Mrs. Spalding,
and had sent us word that she would most likely come to
our house on the day following, and stay several days
with us. I decided to tell her all my troubles, including
this last insult, and ask her advice; for though she was
his mother, I had sufficient confidence in her to believe
that she would judge impartially between us. But disappointment awaited me. The morrow came; but, though
I waited and watched anxiously for her coming, she did
not make her appearance, but remained at Mrs. Spalding's.

When Frank had gone I threw myself upon a lounge,
and calmly and deliberately reviewed my situation. In the
name of Heaven, what was I to do? My husband evidently wished to be rid of me; the falsehoods which had
been put in circulation about me had blasted my reputation, and ruined all my hopes; I could see no way of sup-

porting myself, and could not stay where I was—what was then left for me but death? Yes; death would end the struggle forever, and would be a welcome relief from miseries which, it seemed to me, there was no other way of avoiding. And then the tempter whispered me, "There is that vial of laudanum in the cupboard; it will afford speedy, sure, and painless relief from the miseries you are now enduring.

There is a certain class of philosophers who maintain that the life of a human being belongs to himself, and that whenever, from any cause, it becomes a burden to him, he is fully justified—nay, that it is a praiseworthy act, and commendable in the sight of God and man—in ending it by his own hands. I thank Heaven that I am not, and never have been, a subscriber to any such doctrine. Life is the immediate gift of God to man, bestowed upon us for wise and beneficent purposes, and not to be ended until the same will which bestowed the gift sees proper to recall it, and we have no more right to endeavor to thwart His will in this particular than in any other. It was just as apparent to my mind then, as it is now, that I was committing a most heinous sin in thus conspiring against my own life; but, yet the misery I endured was such as to render me willing to take any consequences which might follow this last desperate effort to end it, and I went about my preparations for suicide as coolly and deliberately as I ever did anything in my life.

I first sat down and wrote a letter to my husband, telling him that my life, by his persecution and neglect, had been rendered a burden to me; that anything was preferable to the life I was leading, and that I had determined to end my existence and my sorrows together. I also informed him of my former marriage, and how my husband had

15

proved to be a married man; and begged his forgiveness
for any wrong or injury I might have unintentionally done
him.   I told him I had loved him with all my heart, and
had been a true and faithful wife to him; that he had not
appreciated me and my devotion to him; that I was
satisfied he hated me and wanted to be rid of me, and
that I would die to free him.   This letter I sealed and
directed to him, and placed it on the table, where he
would be most likely to find it; then I took the vial of
laudanum in my hand, and raised it to my lips.   Then
the thought of what I was about to do caused me to hesitate, and, for a moment, my heart failed me, but it was only
for a moment.   Gathering new courage, I once more
raised the vial to my mouth, and drank off its deadly
contents; then calmly undressed myself and went to bed,
waiting for the poison to accomplish its destined work.
But the end was not yet.

It was about eight o'clock when I took the poison.
There was an over-dose of it, and it was not until I
had been very sick, and had thrown up a portion, that it
seemed likely to produce the effect I desired.   Ah! the
horror of that deathly sickness, when death stared me in
the face, and when his coming was eagerly and earnestly
desired, no one can ever know.   Not for a single moment
did I repent the course I had taken, and my greatest
anxiety was lest not enough of the drug would be
retained in my system to accomplish the object for which
it had been taken.   But, at last, my sickness partially
ceased; I felt a delicious languor stealing over my body
and pervading every fiber of my frame, and I sunk into
dreamless unconsciousness.   The last thing I remember,
before the period of unconsciousness which followed, was
the clock striking ten.   Frank had not come, at that

time; I was alone, and the world, with all its sorrows, its cares and griefs, as well as its joys and brightness, was fast fading from my vision.

I have no means of knowing what time Frank came home that night. When consciousness was restored to me, which was not until almost morning, he was sitting by my bedside, with the doctor through whose instrumentality my restoration had been effected, and my scheme, for the present, defeated. I had, then, no thanks for the kindness which had prompted them to save my miserable life, but wished they had allowed me to die, and inwardly vowed to renew the attempt at another time and under more favorable circumstances. Since then, dear reader, I have learned to value life; and I thank God, that He, in His mercy, interposed that night to save the life which was then deemed so worthless; and under Him, most heartily do I thank the doctors (there were two of them), by whose exertions my mad attempt upon my own life was defeated.

As soon as I was restored to consciousness one of the physicians left. The other remained until some time after daylight, administering to me such remedies as my situation demanded; when, having seen that my condition was no longer dangerous, he, too, took his leave, promising to come back during the course of the day.

He came again in the afternoon, and found me much better, but still very weak and sick from the effects of the terrible dose I had taken. From this time Nelles seemed to actually hate me, whereas he had before only slighted and neglected me. Now his whole feeling seemed turned into hatred toward me, and language would scarcely suffice to recount the various means of which he made use to display that hate. He did not resort to actual violence, from very shame perhaps, but treated me as a hired servant, and not as his equal, and the woman he had sworn to love, honor and cherish, in sickness as well as in health, until we should be parted by death. There was a cool, calculating, cruel coldness in his manner toward me, an effort to degrade me in my own estimation, and to make me feel that I was his inferior, which was really demoniac.

And as soon as my health was somewhat restored, he proceeded deliberately to make arrangements for our complete and final separation. He first gave up all our rooms on the ground floor, and moved up stairs, into three small rooms, which could only be reached by a stairway passing through a hall belonging to the lower floor of the house. I protested against this arrangement as inconvenient and unnecessary, but it mattered not to him. He deigned to hold no consultation with me, or to make any explanation of his designs or intentions—it was sufficient that he wished it. At this time no idea of immediate separation had occurred to me. I felt sure it would come ere long. If he had not demanded it I should, for to live with him after what had passed was simply impossible, but my health was still too feeble for me to think of leaving him. But when the new arrangements were completed to his satisfaction, he coolly told me he was not going to keep me any longer; that he had been discharged from the employment of the railroad company, and that I must now look out for myself, and asked where I intended to go to! I made no remonstrance and offered no protest; first, because the programme was not at all objectionable to me, and, secondly, because I was convinced of its utter uselessness. I merely asked him for some money, which he refused to give me, saying he had none for me, then put on my bonnet and shawl, went to an employment office, and, on applying for a situation, succeeded in getting one to do general housework for a family in Niles, Michigan. I was to go that very afternoon to enter upon my new sphere of duty.

When I had completed my agreement and settled all the terms, I went back to the house and told my husband of my arrangements for my future support. I was to do kitchen-work, in a large family, for two dollars per week. He made not the slightest objection to my going out to work as a kitchen girl, nor do I suppose he would have objected to anything else which took me out of his way. No, he was entirely willing that his bride of a few weeks standing should go out to the most menial servitude to subsist herself, so he was only left free to follow the baser passions of his nature, relieved from even the trifling restraint which my presence imposed.

And this was the man who had vowed to protect me from the cold and chilling blasts of fate in this world. This was the man who had once professed to love me, and whom I had promised to love, honor and obey—the man with whom I had expected to walk, hand in hand, all adown the vale of life, our pathway all strewn with the flowers of love, and our lives crowned with peace and happiness. How bright had been my anticipations of happiness before marriage—how sad and gloomy the reality to which I had been subjected. Then I supposed that I had found a haven of rest from all the ills and cares of life— I found in reality that so far from being a haven of rest, it was the most troubled and tempestuous sea of sorrow upon which my frail bark had as yet been set afloat. How gladly then I hailed any arrangement, however unpleasant or disagreeable it might be, so it only involved my release from the horrid bondage under which I was suffering. But my arrangements were not yet complete. The train which it was necessary for me to take to reach my destination would go at five o'clock, and I had not a cent of money to pay my fare. I spoke to Nelles about this, and asked him for some money. He replied that he would bring me some in time for me to leave, turned on his heel and left the house.

I felt confident he would keep this promise, despite the habitual falsehoods in which he was accustomed to deal with me, because I felt sure his desire to be rid of me would prompt him to truthfulness, knowing that it was impossible for me to go without money. But the day gradually wore away, and he came not. The time for my departure was drawing near, and still he had not made his appearance. My trunk was packed, and all my arrangements were complete for starting; but still no money to pay my fare had been received, and now the conviction forced itself upon my mind that he intended to do nothing for me. As this opinion gained strength in my mind I began to cast about me to see how I could raise the means necessary to accomplish my object. It would cost me something to go to the scene of my new engagement, and I did not wish to land there, among entire strangers, with no money; for, in case anything was to happen—myself and my employer should not agree, or sickness should intervene—what would become of me?

I was always fond of pets, and had a large cage of very fine canary birds; but they were the only objects upon which I could now lavish my affection, and I did not like the idea of parting with them. I looked around. The house was well supplied with furniture, bedding, dishes, and the like, toward procuring which my labor had contributed as much, at least, as his; and I greatly feared that, as soon as I was out of the way, they would be taken possession of by others whose claim was not so good as mine. Why should I not take some of the most valuable of the articles, and make them conduce to my support? Surely, morally, there could be no wrong in my taking them. Before proceeding, however, to pack them up, I saw Wallace Nelles, and sent him in search of his father, to tell him I must have money to start upon the trip which was to take me out of his way forever.

Wallace went away, and was gone a long time. I waited as long as I dared, and then went to work to packing up, in a box, the articles upon which I designed to raise the means for the prosecution of my journey. I took two comforts, all the sheets and pillows in the house, all the best dishes, and some other articles, and packed them in a box; and my only regret, when I looked around me, was that so much had to be left. About the time my packing was finished, Wallace came back, and said he could not find my husband, and immediately went away again.

Meantime, however, an express wagon had come for my baggage; the driver was already grumbling, and saying we would be too late for the train, and no more time could be spared to wait for my truant husband. My trunk and box were therefore loaded into the wagon, I clambered up to a seat beside the driver, and before Wallace got out of sight he saw us trundling away to the Central Depot. Arrived there, we found the prediction of the expressman true; the train was just moving out as we entered the inclosure, and there was nothing for me to do but to wait for the next train.

Before it was time forthe next train to leave, Nelles

came, gave me fifteen dollars, accompanied me on board
the cars and found me a seat, bade me a cold adieu, left
me alone, and, in a short time, I was on my way to push
my fortune among entire strangers as best I might.

CHAPTER XVIII.

As the train slowly moved out from the depot into the darkness of the night (for it was nearly eight o'clock, of a dreary, stormy night, on which I left Chicago), I felt that I was really alone and desolate in the wide world; and my heart sunk within me as I thought of my prospects for the future. I was going to a place of which I knew nothing, and where there was not a single soul whom I knew, to enter upon the duties of a life of which I had had no experience, and my purse contained just fifteen dollars—all my fortune—and even a part of that I must pay for my ride to my destination. And then, what if my experiment at Niles should prove a failure—what would become of me in that event? Heaven only knew.

These thoughts occupied my mind during the entire of my ride from Chicago to Niles, and most effectually prevented me from sleeping any of the time; and, when we reached my stopping place, I knew not what to do or where to go. I had never stopped there before, did not know a single soul in the place, and had no idea where my employer lived or where to make inquiries for him. I inquired of several persons, and was finally directed to an aristocratic looking (for that place) mansion, where I found what was expected to be my future home, and first met with the woman whom, for the first time since my childhood, I was to call mistress. That first interview satisfied me that my stay at her house would be short. There was an air of haughty disdain about her, a sort of reckless contempt for the feelings of others, which, though

regarded by some of the shoddy aristocracy of the present day as evidence of good breeding, is, in my judgment,
the very reverse, and stamps its possessor as at once
devoid of all the finer feelings which mark the true gentleman or lady.

What, though the necessities of society demand that
there should be gradations and distinct classifications
among its members; what, though some are born to
wealth and fortune and others to poverty and toil: is that
any reason why the first is any better, or has any finer
feelings, than the last? If one is born to an heritage of
poverty, and compelled to labor, from day to day, in order
to obtain the bread which sustains their existence, and
another is born to wealth, and thus enabled to employ the
paid labor of the less fortunate class: does that, by any
means, demonstrate that the latter class is possessed of *all*
the finer feelings and sensibilities of our common humanity; or does it give them a right to trample upon and disre-
gard all the feelings of their less fortunate employés? Or,
suppose one to be born to wealth and station, and by some
reverse of fortune be swept from their high estate to mingle in the walks of poverty and want; and, suppose
another born in the circle of indigence, and, by some
stroke of fortune, be suddenly placed in the possession of
the most boundless wealth: can any advocate of the priv-
ilege of aristocracy tell me by what sort of alchemy the
first is at once debased into an animal destitute of all
feeling and sensibility, while the last is at once invested
with all those delicate nerves which, in the opinion of
some, make up the delicate lady of fashion? No, indeed.
Well has the poet said—

> "Honor and fame from no condition rise,
> Act well your part—there all the honor lies."

Before I had been with my new mistress two days I had made up my mind to leave her, and resort to some other means of earning my livelihood. The haughtiness and contempt for the feelings of her employés, which I had marked during our first interview, were displayed in the most offensive manner upon every possible occasion, and soon rendered my position there not only unpleasant but unendurable. I accordingly left there, and, having determined to try some other mode of earning a livelihood, left Niles for Detroit.

Arrived there, I rented a small house, already furnished, took two or three boarders, and also took some washing to do. Getting to Detroit had consumed my fifteen dollars, and I hardly knew what I should do to get along until my boarders began to pay up, which, of course, I did not expect them to do until the end of a week at any rate. My washing, however, brought me a little money, and I managed to get along, though compelled to go in debt at my grocer's and my butcher's. I wrote to Nelles, telling him of my situation and asking some assistance from him, but without eliciting any reply. Doubtless he was too much engaged to take any notice of letters from one who was no more to him than his wife. He had gotten me out of his way and did not intend to be troubled with me any more.

Still I struggled on, and tried to make a comfortable living, but the work was too hard for me, and I soon found that something else must be done. I could either have managed my boarding-house, or done what washing was on hand, but both together I could not do, and neither one alone would support me. I have already informed the reader that Captain Lake was dead—his wife had returned to her family in the South, and there was no one to whom

I could apply for advice or assistance; but one thing was manifest — it was impossible for me to stay there and live in this way. Accordingly I gave up my house, and, going to an employment office, applied for a situation. They sent me to the house of a Mr. Cones, an Express agent, and a most thorough and perfect gentleman.

Upon arriving at his house, I found the family to consist only of himself, his wife and her sister, and his father-in-law, one of the kindest and most agreeable old gentlemen I ever knew. They were all very kind to me, but this good old man was more than kind—he could not have treated me more affectionately had I been his daughter. I hired to them to do general house-work, at two dollars per week, and for a time everything passed off in the most pleasant and agreeable manner. The work was not beyond my strength, and the family could not have treated me better than they did. I passed for a young widow, and for some time no one of the many visitors at Mrs. Cones', or even the family, knew any better.

But, although my lot was outwardly as happy as could have been expected under the circumstances, inwardly my mind was borne down by a weight of sorrow almost too heavy to be borne. Nor is it strange that such should have been the case; for what was there in my past life to excite any but the most sorrowful feelings? My life had been one constant scene of clouds and darkness, with only here and there a ray of sunshine, which served but to make darkness, both preceding and following it, more dense, impenetrable and frightful. And in my present employment I had abundance of time and opportunity to think of these things. As I daily witnessed the happiness of the family around me, and compared it with my own wretched lot, it made my own fortune appear so dark by the contrast, that it well-nigh made me murmur against the justice of God who had meted out such different fortunes to us. Do not think I envied them their happiness. I did not, nor would I have detracted one single atom from their felicity to have purchased for myself a lifetime of unalloyed happiness—but I could not help making the contrast between their lot and mine.

Constant brooding over these things was not without its sad effects, not only upon my mind, but also upon my physical health. I became first moody and morose, and then, finally, really ill, and unable to perform my daily tasks. I was compelled to abstain altogether from work, and took to my bed, from which it was thought for some days, I would never rise. But the kind care and attention of Mrs. Cones and her sister, aided by my naturally strong constitution, triumphed over the disease, and in time I was restored to comparative health once more.

During my sickness I had been deranged a great part of the time, and had raved almost constantly about my family troubles, thus most effectually revealing the fact that I was other than I seemed. And when, as my convalescence approached, Mrs. Cones came to me one day and seating herself by my bedside, asked me to tell her all about my past life, and who Eugene Mason and Frank Nelles were, I expected to be severely blamed for having deceived her as to my being a widow. But not so. As I explained my situation to her, the tears of sympathy welled up from her warm, full heart, and gathering me to her bosom, she said:

" My poor child! how you have suffered. Why did you not tell me of this before?"

" Because, I was ashamed to reveal the story of my troubles. I preferred to suffer them in silence rather than inflict so uninteresting and unlovely a tale upon any one else."

"And this silent suffering is what has made you sick. If you had confided your secret to me, had shared it with me, it would have been safe, and you most likely spared this fit of sickness."

"I know I ought have trusted you, but I was afraid to. One is so uncertain of meeting any sympathy in this world."

"That is true, but no one ever appealed to me in vain. I must tell my husband, and we will then see what can be done for you."

Mr. Cones asked me some questions, after hearing my story from his wife, and then wrote a letter to Nelles in which he told him I was there sick, out of money and in debt, and that he ought to do something for me. No answer was ever received to this letter, and, as the weary days grew into a week, the anxiety which I constantly endured about my situation caused me to relapse, and again I lay at death's door, and again Mr. Cones communicated my condition to Mr. Nelles. He informed him by telegraph of my severe illness, and told him if he wanted to see me alive to come on without delay; but to this dispatch no answer was ever vouchsafed. I was at that time inclined to be charitable, and to think that Nelles had never received this letter and telegram, but he has since acknowledged to me that he did receive both! So much for the love he once professed for me. Had our situations been reversed, and had he sent for me, I would have gone to him, had I gone barefooted and begged my way from house to house. But I can not believe that all men are thus inconstant.

But it was not the will of Providence that I should die

at this time. Gradually I recovered—little by little health and strength came back to my wasted and enfeebled frame, until at last I was able to leave my bed, then my room, and, finally, the house. As soon as my health was sufficiently restored to enable me to go about, I began making arrangements to leave my kind friends; for I felt that more active life was what I needed—something in which there would be less of monotony, and in which the excitement of change would prevent my mind from brooding so constantly over the dark past. It was this which had caused my sickness, and I feared to encounter the same dread monster again. They urged me to remain with them; but, when I gave them my reasons for going, they acquiesced in their justice and propriety, and ceased to offer any further opposition. They asked me what I intended to do; but this was something I had not decided upon. Mr. Cones then suggested that I should engage in canvassing for some publishing-house—in short, should become a "Book Agent." I did not like this much at first, fearing I should fail; but, at any rate, it would possess the merit of constant change—would keep my thoughts employed—and I finally decided to adopt it.

This matter settled, the next question was, where, and from what house, I would endeavor to obtain employment. After debating the pros and cons of various places, for some time, I at last made up my mind that I would return to Chicago and seek employment there. The reader may think strange that I decided to go to a place where I had endured so much of sorrow, and where so many of my bitterest enemies were living; but I had an object in so doing, which will more fully appear in the sequel.

But, before going to Chicago, I wished to go to Indiana and locate my residence there. I had several objects in doing this: the first of which was this—I had determined to obtain a divorce from my unworthy husband, in case certain matters turned out as I thought they would, upon my visit to Chicago; and I had been informed that the laws of that State were such as to render the attainment of that object comparatively easy and inexpensive to a resident of the State; and, as I had no particular ties to bind me to one place more than another, I might as well live where I could easily accomplish this object as any place else. And, I may remark here, that I have never seen any occasion to regret having chosen that State for my residence. Some of my warmest friends are inhabitants of the noble State of Indiana; and, in all parts of the State, I have met with a kindliness of feeling, and a genuine heart-welcome, which convinces me that the Hoosiers are as generous in sentiment as their soldiers, in the late civil war, proved themselves to be brave and fearless in battle. But to return to my story.

As my funds had long since been exhausted, I had but one way of raising the means necessary to prosecute my plans, and that was by selling some of my clothing. Mr. Cones offered to loan me the money; but his kindness had already been severely taxed, and I was unwilling to test it any further; preferring to be independent, if it was in my power. I accordingly went out and sold my wedding-dress and some other clothing, from which I realized a very handsome sum of money, and started for Indianapolis. Upon arriving there I selected lodgings, left the greater part of my clothing there, taking with me only enough for a change or two, and started for Chicago, to see what could be done in the way of pushing my fortune. Another object, which I wished to accomplish, was to learn if Nelles was still living, what he was doing, whether he had received Mr. Cones' letter and dispatch, and why he had not answered them.

Upon reaching Chicago, I went at once to the railroad office, on State street, and called for Mr. Webb, the Superintendent. He and Nelles were well acquainted, and I felt confident he could tell me of his whereabouts if he was in the city, and my confidence was not, in this instance at least, at all misplaced. He told me at once that Nelles was in the city, was alive and well, and was working for a man by the name of Lake, on Randolph street, near Union. I knew the place very well—went there, and almost the first person I met was my step-son, Wallace. He seemed very much surprised to see me, they having considered me dead some time since, but he seemed pleased at the meeting, and when I asked if his father was there, promptly replied in the affirmative, and at once went to call him.

He came, but oh! how cold and constrained the meeting. He did not ask me where I was living, nor about my health, or manifest the least interest in my welfare, nor would he even take me to his boarding-house, or tell me where it was. I then asked him for some money to pay my expenses, but he refused, saying he had none that he could spare. He, however, promised to come to the Rock Island House, in the evening, to see me, and said he would then give me some money. But he only said this for the purpose of getting rid of me, for he never came near me. I must not omit to state that, in this interview, he admitted that he had received Mr. Cones' letter and telegram during my illness, but offered no excuse for not answering them in any way.

After this interview, I went back to the Rock Island House, fully resolved in my own mind, if he did not come

16

(and I had not much idea he would) that evening, according to his promise, never to call upon him for assistance again, or in any way to recognize him as my husband, save by going on with my proceeding for divorce just as early as the laws of the State, where my residence now was, would permit of my doing so. Evening came, but, according to my anticipations, he did not, and from that day to this I have never seen or communicated with him.

At the Rock Island House I got hold of the Chicago Tribune, and turning at once to the column of "Wants," found the following notice :

WANTED, Agents, both ladies and gentlemen, to canvass for "Tried and True, or Love and Loyalty," a new book destined to have an immense sale. Apply to W. J. Holland, 38 Lombard Block, Chicago.

The name of the work struck me favorably, and I determined to apply at once for a situation. But it was too late to do anything that evening, and beside, I was a little in hopes that Nelles would keep his promise, and call on me that evening. I therefore cut out the advertisement, resolving to call at the place indicated early the next morning.

The next morning at ten o'clock found me at No. 38 Lombard Block. The gentleman in attendance was very kind and pleasant, and, in answer to my inquiries, told me the work was just out; that he was the general agent for Illinois, and he thought an active, energetic agent could do well with the work. He gave me the terms upon which the work would be furnished to agents, and the price at which they would be allowed to sell it. I was at that time very green in relation to such matters, and thought the margin allowed was enormous, and that a fortune would in a short time crown my efforts. Though I have since learned by experience that the colors in which the business was then presented to my view were more roseate than the facts warranted, still I take occasion to say that the energetic, active book agent, who pursues the business with tact and judgment, need never fear such a thing as a failure. If properly doing their duty, they are certain of fair returns, in a pecuniary point of view, while the avocation presents the ever-recurring charm of novelty and change, and affords facilities for the study of human nature almost unequaled by any other pursuit. But to return to my interview with Mr. Holland.

He asked me where I wished to canvass, and suggested Peoria County, Illinois, as a good place; and having no objections to going there, I finally made arrangements with him to canvass exclusively that county, if I should decide to canvass for him at all. He then told me that my first book would cost two dollars and a half, which must be paid in advance, and that circulars, subscription books, and all other necessary documents would be furnished free of charge. I had not the money to pay him for my first book, but was too proud to tell him so, and therefore left, promising to call on Monday, and acquaint him with my determination.

I at once began to cast about to see where I could raise the money necessary to start in business. It would cost me between fourteen and fifteen dollars to pay my hotel bill, buy my book, pay my fare to Peoria, and meet such other expenses as I must necessarily incur before I could get to work. What could I dispose of to raise it? I had no clothing with me that I could spare, and I could think of nothing but my canary birds. And yet, how could I part with them? They had been my companions ever since that cold parting with my husband at the Central

Depot in Chicago; they were my only pets, and seemed almost as dear to me as though they had been children of my own flesh and blood. Then I thought of my watch. Perhaps something could be raised on that. I went to a pawnbroker, and, showing him my watch, asked him how much he would loan me on it. He replied, eight dollars was all he could afford. This would not meet my necessities, and now no resource was left but to sell my birds.

I took them and went upon Madison street, and was there told, by a gentleman, that I might leave them with him for a time, and let him hear them sing, and if they suited him he would buy them. They were, I think, the sweetest singers I ever heard in my life, and were certainly the most perfect pets I ever saw. One of them in particular, would come out of the cage and lie in my hand as if dead, while I would pretend to cry over it and mourn for it. But this time it was no pretense with me. As I displayed this little trick to the gentleman, I cried in reality as though my heart would break at the thought of parting with them.

When I came back, after an absence of about an hour, I told the gentleman I could not sell my birds, but if he would let me have seven dollars (the amount he proposed to give for them), I would leave them with him, with the understanding that if, at any time, I came back and paid him the seven dollars, with interest at the rate of twenty-five per cent., he should return them to me. To this he assented, and I then cried worse than ever. Had they been children it would not have been more painful to me to have parted with them, but it was finally done, and I went back to the hotel, where I took another crying spell. The landlady came in and asked me what was the matter.

I told her I had sold my birds—that I was going out canvassing, and, of course, could not take them with me, and hence had sold them. I was too proud to tell her that they had been sold to raise the money to start me in business, and hence put it upon the ground of my inability to care for them. She replied that I need not have sold them, for she would have taken care of them for me, but I answered it was now done and could not be helped.

I was now in possession of fifteen dollars, my sole and entire capital, and was about starting out with that sum (or rather what would be left of it after paying my hotel bill) to seek my fortune. This may seem like rather a slender foundation for such a fortune as I hoped to accumulate in time; but it is one of the beauties of our business that it requires little or no capital to start in it. If, like me, you can raise funds enough to buy your book and an old basket to carry it in, and can then pay your fare to the place where you are going to work, you are all right.

I waited until Monday, then went to Mr. Holland and paid him for a book, thus concluding the contract between us, and made my arrangements to proceed to my field of labor that very afternoon. Before going, however, I must purchase something or other in which to carry my book and papers. Time enough for that yet, however, and, as my business was finally settled and my mind relieved, I went to call upon an old friend for a short time before leaving the city, most likely forever.

This visit was productive of pleasure in more ways than one, aside from a little matter of business, by means of which my outfit was finally completed. In the first place, I had a very pleasant visit with the lady upon whom I called, told her all about my plans and prospects for the future, and received her congratulations and well wishes.

Then, just as I was about leaving, another old and valued friend came in—one who had been a friend to me in time of trouble—and my story had to be repeated to her, much to her astonishment. Mrs. Gregg, the last comer, was one of those kind, clever bodies, whom everybody loves and regards as a sister, and who can keep any article, be it clothing or anything else, forever and a day after. She had in her hand an old-fashioned basket, one, perhaps, that had been used to hold the fragments of fish we read of in the fifteenth chapter of Matthew, but which, owing to her wonderful tact in the art of preservation, was still sound and in good repair. As I looked at this basket, it suddenly occurred to me that this was the very thing to answer my purpose.

"Mrs. Gregg," said I, abruptly, "what will you take for your basket?"

"My basket," said the good lady, turning it over and looking at it on all sides; "do n't make fun of my basket. It has been my constant companion for a great many years."

"I am not making fun of it, I assure you. I am in sober earnest. It is just the thing to use in my canvassing, and I really want to buy it of you."

"Well, Annie, if you are in earnest, I may, perhaps, let you have it. But I supposed you were only making fun of it because it is old-fashioned."

"Indeed, I was not."

"Well," said the lady, again turning the basket around, and looking at it on all sides, "you may have it for one dollar."

"I will take it."

I paid her the dollar, she emptied the basket, and it was transferred to my possession, and has been my constant companion ever since. I have carried it wherever I went, and shall always keep it as a souvenir of one of the best friends I ever had; and she can keep a certain pitcher to remind her of me and a certain moving-day.

I then went to the hotel, paid my bill, went to the depot and bought a ticket to Peoria. This left just ten cents in my possession, and with this small fortune I took my seat on the cars, and was soon whirling out of the city to my new field of labor.

CHAPTER XIX.

As the cars bore me rapidly onward toward the place selected in which I was to begin my career as a "Book Agent," I had abundant time to review the situation and decide upon my course of action when I should finally arrive at the field. And the first point to determine was, how to get along with my ridiculously small fund and pay my way until returns from my labors began to come in, which would most likely be a week or more. Rather a difficult problem, say you, my dear reader? This may be so; and yet I found means to solve it to my entire satisfaction. Upon one thing I was determined—not to betray the low state of my finances to any one, for this could not be otherwise than disastrous to all my future plans. Such is the disposition of the world: let it be supposed that one has money; no matter whether he possesses honesty, merit, or anything else which should commend him to the confidence of the public, and every one is ready to stretch forth the helping hand; men will go out of their way, get down on their knees and crawl in the dirt, for the purpose of doing him a favor, whether they expect to receive any reward for it or not. But no matter what his merits may be, let it be understood (whether correctly or otherwise) that his purse is light, and none are ready to assist him, even though by so doing they were sure to immediately and pecuniarily benefit themselves; no faces are wreathed in smiles at his approach; no hand is stretched forth to relieve his most pressing necessities: but he is regarded with looks and frowns of ill-concealed contempt and aversion, while pockets are sternly buttoned up, and freezing coldness chills his very soul. Yes; if one wishes to cut himself off from all hope of success in this world, let him only cause it to be understood that he is poor. This I was resolved not to do. No one should know that I was without funds, and was dependent upon my daily labor for my support. I would stop at the best hotel in Peoria, leave my baggage (I had sent to Indianapolis and obtained a trunk full of my clothing) in the hands of the landlord as security for my bill, and go to work with energy and vigor, trusting in a kind Providence to crown my efforts with success. And I may add here, that the result has more than justified my expectations.

In due time we arrived at Peoria, and then, for the first time, my heart failed me in regard to the task before me. Entirely without experience in the work to which I had addressed myself—alone, in a large city, where there was not a single human being whom I had seen or of whom I knew anything—no one to whom I could apply for advice or assistance in case of emergency—is it strange that my heart should be somewhat cast down, and that my soul should shrink, somewhat, from the contest at hand; the bitter struggle with poverty and want, in which there were, at least, as many chances against me as there were in my favor? Add to these reflections the confusion created in my mind by the din and bustle ever attendant upon the arrival of a train: the hackmen, porters, omnibus-drivers, and all of that ilk, filling the air and torturing the ear with cries of all kinds; each one praising his own line, or his own house, or his own carriage, as superior to any and all others, and the reader (who doubtless has experienced, to his or her satisfaction, all these annoyances of travel) will not be surprised that, for a short time, our new-made book agent stood utterly bewildered, dumb-foundered, and at a loss what to do or where to go.

Notwithstanding the fact that I had so carefully laid and so fully digested all my plans of action during the passage of the train from Chicago, I fancy I was, for a time, as pitiable a spectacle of indecision and uncertainty as was ever seen upon this mundane sphere. It now affords me much amusement to recall the incidents of that first arrival in Peoria; but, then, believe me, dear reader, it was no laughing matter. I have no doubt the bystanders all thought that was the first time I had ever disembarked from a railway train; and, most certainly, my conduct was such as not to give the lie to such a supposi-tion. But relief at last came. As I stood, surrounded by a crowd of porters, hackmen, and the like, each one of whom was anxious to serve me (they did not know that ten cents was all my fortune), a gentleman and lady, whom I had noticed on the train, but with whom I had had no conversation, approached me, and the gentleman kindly asked me where I wished to go. I told him that I was a stranger in the city, having never been there be-fore, and that I wanted to go to a good hotel. He informed me that he lived in the city; that himself and wife were going up in town, and that if I would accom-pany them they would show me the way to the Peoria House, the best hotel in the place. I thanked him heart-ily for his kindness to a perfect stranger, and we at once set out, on foot, for our destination. After walking three or four blocks, we came in sight of a large brick house near the public square.

· "There, Miss," said my guide, pointing to a large brick building, " is the Peoria House."

Again I thanked him for his kindness, and, crossing the

street, went up a short flight of steps into the house, and
passed into the parlor.   My heart beat violently as I rung
the bell.   "What if I should fail, after all," I thought;
"what will become of me."

A boy came in answer to my summons, and stood awaiting my order.   I told him I wanted a room.   He retired,
and in a short time a gentleman came in with a key in
his hand, and, bowing politely, inquired if I wished a
room.

"If you please, sir."

"Have you any baggage, madam?"

"My trunk is at the depot," I replied, handing him my
check; "will you send for it?"

"Certainly, madam; will you have it sent to your
room?"

"Yes, sir.   Can I have supper?"

"Yes, I will show you to your room, and will then order supper.   What will you have?"

"Nothing but a cup of tea.   I am not well and can eat
but a mouthful."

He led the way up one flight of stairs into a small room
above the parlor, placed the light (for it was now quite
dark) on a small table in the room, bowed again and withdrew.   I was alone.   Yes, in that immense building, filled
with guests, in the very heart of a populous city, I was
alone.   There was not a soul among all the many thousands almost within sound of my voice upon whom I could
call for assistance of any kind, for comfort, or even sympathy.   I had fairly launched my frail bark upon the tempestuous ocean of life, and was about to undertake the
voyage with no comrade to cheer me, no chart or compass
to guide my wanderings, and no hope, save in the kindness of an overruling Providence, and my own courage

and energy. Ah! what if they should fail me at some critical moment? I looked around the room. It was furnished as hotel rooms usually are; a single bed, two chairs, a wash-stand and small table, while a hempen carpet covered the floor. There was nothing peculiar in the room, but it seemed to me that I could see the word "failure" written on every article it contained. Doubtless my nervous excitement tended to give the room a more gloomy look than it really possessed, for I afterward found it to be cne of the most pleasant rooms in the house. Such is the influence of the mind upon our outward senses.

At length there was a tap at the door, and the messenger boy came in to tell me my tea was ready and show me the way to the dining-room. I went down and found they had prepared a very fine lunch for me, for it was past the usual supper hour, but it was impossible for me to eat. Every morsel I tried to swallow seemed to choke me, and, after drinking part of a cup of tea, I rose from the table and returned to my room. I found the bit of candle with which it was supplied had entirely burned out, and my room was in total darkness. With some difficulty I found the bell-handle, and rang the bell, then waited patiently in darkness for the messenger, my heart beating so violently that I could hear its pulsations. I am not cowardly, but on this evening I was so much oppressed with my own feelings, hopes, doubts, and fears for the future, that I felt a degree of timidity entirely foreign to my nature. I was really and truly, in feeling and character, "a cat in a strange garret.

The boy finally came and brought me a lamp, and, as soon as he had gone, I undressed and went to bed, but not to sleep. Fears and apprehensions of failure still run riot through my brain, and most effectually banished slumber from my eyelids. But as I lay and tossed upon my sleepless couch, I resolved anew that no such word as failure should be found in my vocabulary; by my energy and industry I would deserve success, and if it did not crown my efforts, the fault, at least, should not be mine. No; I would yet show that I could live independent of Frank C. Nelles or any one else; that I could carve my own way in the world, in spite of the frowns of fortune, the inconstancy of friends, or the treachery of those from whom I had a right to expect better things. This was my resolve; how it has been carried out let the sequel show.

I rose early in the morning, made my toilet, and went down to the dining-room. Breakfast was just ready; the long hall was filled with guests and boarders, but, though I scanned each one closely, there was not a single face I knew. But my nervousness of the night before was all gone, and the fact that every one in the room was a stranger to me, did not annoy or disconcert me in the least. Nay, it was rather a matter of gratification to me that this was so than otherwise, for I had not then succeeded in ridding myself entirely of the idea, so sedulously inculcated by sundry newspapers, that there was something discreditable about the business I was about entering upon, and I rejoiced in the belief that my first attempt was to be made entirely among strangers. I have since learned to believe that the avocation of a book agent, though perhaps less elevated in the judgment of the world than some others, is still, if pursued in a proper and becoming manner, just as creditable as any other, and certain it is that, it is as useful and beneficial to society as many others which might be named. It is undeniable that a vast deal of useful, interesting and beneficial literature, which might otherwise remain for years, or perhaps

forever, in comparative obscurity, is brought prominently
before the public by means of the system of canvassing
now so much in vogue among publishers and wholesale and
retail book houses. And surely, no occupation which tends
so directly, and so powerfully to the dissemination of light
and knowledge among the masses, as does book agency,
can be called useless, degrading, or disreputable. Through
the efforts of the book agent, many a family, who otherwise would not purchase a book of any kind from one
year's end to another, is induced to subscribe for some
work of interest and benefit. A taste for reading is thereby
cultivated, for it is well known "the appetite grows upon
what it feeds upon," other books are purchased, periodi-
cals are subscribed for, and in time this family, first reached
by the judicious and persevering efforts of that much
abused class of individuals of whom the writer is proud
to be one, is elevated from the slough of ignorance in
which they formerly wallowed, to a position of respecta-
bility and credit among the intelligent ones of the land.
This is no picture of the imagination. The writer can
point to numerous instances in which a taste for reading
and literature has been first developed and called into
being by publications of which she was the fortunate
seller. But, says the querulous, objecting fault-finder, the
business is not followed for the purpose of doing good,
but only to put money into the purse of the agent. Very
well, my cynical friend, what avocation do you follow?
Do you pursue it for the purpose solely of being useful to
your fellow-men, or is not the hope of gain a slight—just
a very slight — incentive to your exertions? And yet,
you would be hardly willing to admit that your chosen
pursuit was on that account useless, and ought to be
frowned out of existence by community, or that it was de-

grading to you. And why judge us more harshly than you are willing to be judged? No, all occupations, not in themselves hurtful or immoral, are alike honorable and useful, and all are alike pursued by their respective votaries for the purpose of gain. The accumulation of money is the prime object with all, and no one is disgraced by following any laudable employment with all the energy God has given him, simply because that is the object. Human nature is by the Omniscence of the Almighty so constituted that all occupations and all professions are necessary to each other, and it does not become the follower of one occupation to sneer at another, and to say, "I am more respectable and more useful to community than thou art." But let us return from this digression.

My abstinence of the evening before, together with my long railroad ride, had given me a keen appetite; we had a good breakfast, and the reader may be assured I did ample justice to it. Then armed with the veritable old basket purchased of my friend Mrs. Gregg, and containing my subscription book, and specimen copy of the book, I sallied forth in quest of subscribers. It must be confessed that my heart palpitated a trifle quicker than usual, as I approached a gentleman and asked him to look at my book, and, if it pleased him, to subscribe for it. He was the proprietor of a large dry goods store, and he looked at the book with so much apparent interest, that I felt very confident my first attempt in the line of my new business was about to prove a success. But not so. After looking at it for some time, he finally handed it back to me, declining to subscribe; but his refusal was couched in such kind and gentlemanly terms, that so far from feeling disheartened by this first failure, I was rather encouraged than otherwise. Had I met with such an unkind and ill-

natured refusal as I have since frequently done, I am by
no means sure but my book agency would have terminated
then and there, for my spirits were not then strong enough
to endure a very severe rebuff.

But his kindly disposition encouraged me, and I turned
from that first interview more resolved than ever that success should finally crown my efforts. I left the old gentleman and went into another store where my utmost
efforts to obtain a single subscriber were doomed to disappointment. There were several clerks there, all of whom
looked at the book, but none were willing to invest any
amount in it. And the same result attended my application at several stores in the same vicinity; all declined to
subscribe. The reasons given for refusal were as various
and as numerous as the persons to whom application was
made. One said: "I would take the book, but have no
place to keep it;" another, "That is not my style of reading at all;" another, "I am not able to buy it;" while
still another, belonging to the class who believe everybody
dishonest, perhaps because they judge others by themselves, perhaps from some other cause, said: "I never subscribe for anything; if I want a book, I go and buy it, but
no book agents for me." I have often since heard the
same reason given, and I never heard it without thinking
to myself that the utterer would take the last crust of
bread from a widow and her starving children, provided he
could do so with safety; that nature designed him for a
knave and sharper, and that nothing but lack of opportunity, want of ability, or the fear of the law prevented him
from becoming one. No man ever charged all his fellow-
men with being dishonest unless he was conscious of some
want of principle himself, or, unless he was deficient in
good sound sense, and thought to acquire a reputation for

being sharp by suspecting the motives and intentions of everybody else. But those who belong to the latter class can rest assured that, so far from achieving such reputation, they are certain to be rated at their true value by those who listen to their silly pretensions.

And thus the time wore away. I visited place after place, and tried in vain to awaken sufficient interest in my book to induce somebody to buy it, until the forenoon was nearly spent; nothing had been done, and I was almost disheartened. It seemed almost impossible for me to go back to my hotel without at least one subscriber, and yet the prospect that I would be compelled to do so seemed very bright. Coming at length to a flight of stairs running up from the street, I mechanically ascended them, though, it must be confessed, with but little hope of effecting anything. Near the head of the stairs was a low office, occupied by a Mr. King, and I hesitated some time whether to venture in there or not, but finally decided to try it. Mr. King received me in a very gentlemanly manner, listened courteously to my request, examined the book, and, better than all, subscribed for it. Eureka! I had made a beginning at last. The ice was broken, and, with renewed confidence, I went in search of further patronage, for I now had a name to which I could refer those whom I solicited to subscribe.

The next room was occupied by a lawyer by the name of Brown. As soon as I showed him my book, and told him Mr. King had subscribed—"Well," said he, in an abrupt, but pleasant sort of way, "if King can stand it, I guess I can." And down went his name. Just across the hall was a sign informing the public that H. M. Harris dispensed law (and, I suppose, justice,) to those who were in need of his services, and I went in there. Upon

17

making my business known, Mr. Harris at once put his
name down. I went down that flight of stairs with a
much lighter heart than when I went up. Three subscribers had been secured, and they were names which would
be available to me as references in my future canvassing.
And in the very next room I found proof of this opinion.
It was a shoe-store, situated at the foot of the staircase I
had just descended. The gentleman in attendance received
me very politely, and when my book was presented for his
inspection, seemed very much pleased with it, and in answer to my remark that I had just commenced canvassing,
and had only taken three names, asked to see my list. I
handed it to him.

"H. M. Harris; good lawyer and good man. W. P.
Brown; I know him: he is a fine fellow. And King,
too—Madam, you have three of the best names in Peoria. How much did you say?"

"Two dollars and seventy-five cents."

"I will take one. When will you deliver?"

"I will bring the book in a few days. Good morning, sir."

"Good morning, madam. Success to you."

I went into the next store; but there my good names
availed me nothing. They wanted nothing of the kind—
would not even look at my book, or even hardly let me
tell them what it was. It is just barely possible, from
what I have since learned of the politics of that establishment, that the last word in the title of the book was
offensive to the proprietor, and hence his very abrupt
refusal to look at it. This did not, however, occur to me
at the time. I only thought he was decidedly mean in
refusing to look at the work at all. I thought, even if he
did not wish to subscribe, he might at least have treated

me kindly, and refused in a gentlemanly manner. But, never mind; I had already, in the first half day of my canvassing, sold four copies; and this was anything but discouraging.

It was now noon, and time for me to return to my hotel for dinner. But with how much more elation of spirits I entered that hotel than I had quitted it in the morning the reader may well imagine. My success, in the avocation I had chosen, seemed to me now assured, and the idea of failure was now forever banished from my cogitations. In proportion as my spirits had been depressed before fairly entering upon my work, they were now elated; and visions of wealth and ease arose before me. My mind was just as much in fault in one instance as in the other, and I had yet much to learn in regard to my new profession. I had yet to learn that, because one half day's labor had been attended with some degree of profit, I was not to regard my success as fully assured; but that in this, as in all other avocations, constant, energetic and judicious perseverance were necessary to attain one's object; that reverses of various kinds were to be anticipated, and that the book agent, who fancied his calling an easy as well as lucrative one, was doomed to the most certain and painful disappointment. That the business is profitable, if well and judiciously pursued, is undoubtedly true; but it is equally true, that it is profitable only when it is pursued with the most ceaseless and indefatigable energy.

After dinner was over—and, by the way, I ate much more heartily than at breakfast, from some cause or other—I went up into the parlor. There was a large number of ladies in the room, and the idea occurred to me that it would be a good time to exhibit a pleasing, as well as profitable combination of business and pleasure. Accordingly, I went and got my book, and asked the ladies to look at it; telling them I had arrived in the city only the night before; had been out that morning, and had sold four copies, and that I hoped to sell a large number in that very room before going out again. The book seemed to please them very well; for five of them put their names down at once, and others said they would subscribe as soon as they could see their husbands While we were still talking about the book, a young man came in to call on a young lady who was in the room, and she at once besought him to make her a present of the book. Of course he could not very well refuse, and down went the name of Miss Kate Freeman, the gentleman handing me two dollars and seventy-five cents, and telling me to deliver the book to her when it came.

I fancied I had now done a very good day's work, and, as I had some letters to write, decided not to go out that afternoon at all. I accordingly wrote to Mr. Holland to send me twenty copies of the book, the price to be collected on delivery by the express company, and then set about finding some place where my living would be less expensive than at the Peoria House. Although my business appeared to be prosperous, still two dollars a day was a heavy drain on my finances, and one that I was anxious to avoid if possible. I found a very pleasant place with a most estimable lady, and secured a room at six dollars a week, and then went to settle my bill at the hotel and move to my new home. At the Peoria House my bill was two dollars and a half, and a drayman took my trunk to my boarding house for twenty-five cents: so that I arrived there with just the same amount of money I had on arriving in the city, to wit: ten cents. But I

did not feel as much disheartened as then; for I now had
on the subscription book, which was then a blank, no less
than ten names, each one of which was worth a dollar to
me; that being the profit allowed me on each copy sold.
Even if I did not take another name for a week, I would
still be able to pay my board and have some money left;
and, of course, it was not to be expected that I would do
nothing in that time. I liked the business, and certainly
my prospects were all that could be desired.

After a good night's rest in my new place of abode, I
went to work again with vigor, and worked hard all the
next day, excepting only the time absolutely necessary to
go to my meals, and, when I came to count up the proceeds of the labor of the day, found that my list had been
increased by eleven names. I now had, in all, twenty-one
names, representing, as the net proceeds of two day's
canvassing, no less than twenty-one dollars in my purse.
True the money was not in my hands yet, but then I felt
sure of it all. Surely it would not be difficult for me to
live at that rate. Twenty-one dollars in two days, was
more than in the wildest dreams of my imagination I had
ever dared to hope. Who would not be a book agent
when such returns as this were received? But, on the
other hand, who would be a book agent when such scenes
as are described in my opening chapter are presented?
But in my experience the good has far outweighed the
evil since adopting my present calling.

The next day, I canvassed all day, and came home at
night with eight new names, and one of them, a gentleman boarding at the same house, had paid me in advance
for his copy, upon condition that he should be allowed to
read my copy at once. To this I agreed upon the further
condition that, inasmuch as I had never read the book

myself, he should read it aloud to me. I would then be
much better prepared to explain the character of the book,
and doubted not the effect upon my sales would be very
considerable. I found the book to be very interesting,
and well worth the price asked for it.

The next day my efforts were rewarded with the addition of six names to my already very respectable list. It
is true my sales to-day had not equaled those of either
of the other days, but still six dollars was no mean day's
work, and could I only be assured of that each day of my
labor, it would be very satisfactory. At any rate it would
afford me a very comfortable living, and enable me to
" lay up something for a rainy day," and for old age. And
this is all any one ought to ask in this world, for it is all
that is really worth having.

In the evening I went to the express office, and found
that my twenty copies had come, but there was no less
than thirty-five dollars to be paid on them, and my purse
contained, in treasury-note and postage currency, the sum
of two dollars and eighty-five cents, all told. I counted
it over and over again in the vain hope that more could be
made of it, but the result was just the same every time—
one two-dollar bill, one fifty-cent piece, one twenty-five
cent piece, and one ten cent-piece, all current money
of the United States, was everything I could find. The
agent observed my perplexity and kindly relieved me from
my difficulty, after asking some questions, by telling me
to take one book and deliver it ; then with the proceeds
of that sale get another, and so on until the whole were
taken.

How gladly I accepted his offer. I paid him one dollar
and three-quarters for one book, then got the money for
that and had enough to get two more ; then got three and

delivered them, paying in each time what money I received until the whole twenty were delivered, and I had twenty dollars in my purse. Twenty dollars did I say? Let me not forget the faithful ten cents which had stood by me so long. I had twenty dollars and ten cents, less, of course, the amount paid at the hotel, and the amount I paid the drayman for moving me to my present very comfortable quarters.

But why inflict upon my readers the details of each day's work? Why annoy them with the particulars of each refusal I met with, from purse-proud, haughty, self-sufficient individuals, who could see nothing meritorious in a woman struggling against adverse fate to earn an honest livelihood, or in the book which such a woman would sell— why mention the covert sneers, under the cloak of friendly advice, with which my applications were often met by those who claimed to be gentlemen, but whose gentility would never be recognized by the world, but for this claim—why recount the particulars of the kindly words, and friendly wishes, which with some noble natures even took away the pain of their refusal, and which were really strengthening to my soul—I say, why burden the pages of this record with all these? Suffice it to say that when my weekly report for the week ending on Saturday was sent to the general agent, I was able to report sales of no less than forty copies.

Forty subscribers in one week! Only think of that! Forty dollars earned fairly and honestly by my own honest toil! Why, Nelles only received fifty-five dollars *a month* from the railroad company, and I could earn nearly that amount in a week. Hurrah for the life of a book agent! No more hard work for me. No more washing for the miserable pittance of a few dollars a day—that was "played out," to use a slang phrase. No, indeed. I was far above that sort of labor. I would soon be rich. I would save all the money I earned, and, in a short time, would be able not only to redeem my watch; but my darling pets, my precious canary birds — they, too, were in pawn, and must be redeemed. Oh! yes, I had use for all the money I could earn, and it could not come too fast.

Such, dear reader, were the reflections caused by my first flush of success in the business of a book agent. How these reflections and these hopes have been realized will appear in the subsequent pages of this book.

CHAPTER XX.

I CLOSED my last chapter with an account of my first week's work as a book agent, and certainly the results of that week were sufficient to justify the most sanguine anticipations for the future. But, like everything else, the business has its ups and downs; its dark, as well as its light seasons; its rainy days, as well as its sunshine; and, having had a season of the latter, I was now about to take my turn at the former.

On Sunday it began to rain, and continued nearly the entire day: not a fierce, dashing rain, such as, by its very violence, gives the very best possible evidence of speedy cessation; but a dull, drizzling rain, which, while it is sufficiently violent to keep one within doors, not unfrequently lasts a week or more: just the kind of rain to dampen one's ardor in any enterprise, and most effectually depress the spirits. How I hoped it would not rain on Monday! With what eager anxiety, as evening approached, did I scan the horizon in hopes of detecting some indications of an abatement of the storm, which, if it continued, would be very likely to prevent me from doing anything the next day. Vain hope. The sun went down with his face entirely hidden in clouds; and, as the shades of night rapidly gathered around, the storm, instead of giving any indications of abatement, seemed to thicken and gather additional force, and I finally retired to rest with the conviction that the next day would be marked "lost" in my calendar.

And the morning did not give the lie to my anticipations of the evening before. It seemed to me, as I gazed at the dull, leaden sky, and listened to the dreary, monotonous patter of the falling rain, that a more gloomy or dismal day had never dawned upon my vision, and I knew not what to do. At one time I thought that, in spite of the elements and in defiance of the wrath of the storm-king, I would venture out and try to do something. It really seemed to me that the state of my finances would not admit of my losing the day; that I could not afford to be idle, but must go to work, rain or shine, at any and all hazards. But, then, no one would buy books on such a day as this. My efforts to do anything would be unavailing, and would, perhaps, only result in inducing a fit of sickness, which would not only cause me to lose much more time, but would ab·sorb all my little accumulation of the last week.

Accordingly I decided not to go out, but to put in that day at least in reading my book, make myself acquainted with it, and trust kind fortune for the morrow. But fortune, at least so far as the weather was concerned, refused to smile upon me. The next day the storm still continued and still I staid at home. On Wednesday it was the same, and my spirits sunk to the lowest possible ebb.

The next day I resolved to wait no longer, but to go to work in spite of the weather, and trust my own determined energy to accomplish something. Accordingly I borrowed an umbrella of one of the lady boarders, went out and bought one for myself; then, with my dress looped up to keep it out of the mud, and my faithful old basket on my arm, I set out upon my doubtful mission.

I went to a large building, the second story of which was filled with offices, for I had found that the men usually termed professional, were those who most liberally patronized me, and if anything at all could be done, it would most certainly be among that class. The first place I visited was the office of a celebrated physician of the city. He was sitting with his feet upon a table, his hands clasped behind his head, and gazing moodily out of the window. I accosted him and explained my business to him.

"The day is too dull and gloomy to buy or read books," said he, without changing his position in the least.

"But, Doctor, consider. A gentleman certainly ought to be willing to patronize a lady who has the hardihood to go out on such a day as this."

"Well, why don't you get married, and then you will not have to go out to work on such days as this?"

"Thank you, sir. I am not on the marriage list. I do not think I would be any better off married than I am unmarried. But will you subscribe for my book?"

"Did I not tell you I would not?"

"No, sir; you said no such thing. But even if you had said it, I am sure you would not allow my industry on such a day as this to go unrewarded."

"What is your industry to me? Why should I care whether you are industrious or not?"

"Because it is natural for every industrious man to like to see others as much so as himself."

"But how do you know that I am industrious?"

"Because, no man without the greatest amount of industry could attain to the eminence you have in your profession. Come, Doctor, give me your name."

"Well, you are certainly persevering, as well as industrious, and you deserve to succeed. It shall not be my fault if you do not."

With that he put his name down on my list. The little bit of flattery in which I indulged, though very barefaced, had evidently found the weak spot in his armor and settled the business for him. I thanked him, and went out from his presence smiling to myself at the ease with which I had penetrated his reserve.

My next stopping place was an insurance office. Sundry brass plates and signs gave information that the occupant was fully prepared to insure against fire, death, sickness, accident, and everything else, while the walls were covered with show cards of every description, setting forth the special merits of each particular company represented there. At the desk sat a gruff, cross-looking old man, and, at the first glance, my heart sunk at the prospect of making any impression on him. However, I would not go away without trying, and so I approached him.

"I have called this morning, sir, in hopes to sell you a book. It is just published, and is very interesting. Will you look at it?"

"No; I do n't want to buy any books. Go away. Do n't bother me. Do n't you see I am busy?"

"But, sir, I think if you would look at this, you would subscribe for it."

"I tell you, I do n't want it. I never subscribe for books."

"I have come out this dismal, rainy day, to try to earn an honest living. Please, sir, look at my book: I think your daughter would like it."

"Who told you I had a daughter?"

"No one, sir."

"How did you know it, then?"

"I only thought so. You look like the kind, indulgent father of a lovely daughter. Have you a daughter, sir?"

"Yes; I have as lovely a daughter as any parent need wish. Let me look at your book."

"Here it is, sir."

"It is very nicely bound, and appears to be readable. I guess my girl would like it. Let me see your list of names. You have a good many subscribers, but my daughter's name is not here; so I will put it down, and you can deliver the book here."

"Thank you, sir."

"There, you have got me to subscribe after I said I would not: now, take your traps and be off. You touched me in the right place when you spoke of my girl."

"Good day, sir."

And as I went down stairs I almost laughed aloud at the result of my little impromptu stratagem for circumventing old "Crusty," as I have named him. Should he see this book he will recognize the circumstance above related, and may not feel specially honored by the patronymic here given him. But he must learn to be more civil to callers, even if they do not come to have their lives or property insured, and thus put money in his purse.

I called at several other places that forenoon, but with uniform want of success. Not another name could I obtain, either by persuasion, entreaty or stratagem. Well, two names in half a day, and such a day as this, too, is better than nothing, and I will e'en go home to dinner, and hope for better luck next time. But in the afternoon the rain was even worse than in the morning, and go out I could not, though it seemed almost impossible for me to be idle. It had taken all I had made last week to pay my way thus far and redeem my watch and birds (which I had already done), except six dollars and a few cents. I could pay my board that week, but where was the means to come from to pay the next? Still, it would not help matters any to fret over it; and all that could be done was to wait, and hope, and pray for better weather.

It was well for me that I made hay while the sun shone, for it was utterly out of the question for me to do anything more that week. The rain poured down so unceasingly that it seemed to me it must stop from sheer exhaustion of the elements long before it did.

Saturday evening finally came, and my weekly report had to be sent forward to the general agent. The weather had not admitted of my doing anything more, and I had but the two names to report instead of the forty which had crowned my first week's labors in this place. The contrast was so great that I was almost tempted not to send any report, but, upon reflection, concluded that the matter could be so explained as to leave no unpleasant impressions on the mind of the general agent. Most certainly the horrid, rainy weather of the past week was a sufficient excuse for the small amount of work done. Accordingly, I sent off the document with such explanation as I could give, and in due time received a letter from the general agent to the effect that it was satisfactory, and wishing me better luck in the future.

Sunday was a clear day, and I thought that the storm-god had exhausted his forces, and that I would surely go to work on Monday with some prospect of success. But when the morning came I found that he had only been accumulating fresh strength for the next day, for it poured down harder than ever, and all hope of doing anything for that day was at an end. I had paid the landlady my board for the week just closed, and had but a few cents left in my pocket; and, unless the weather cleared up soon, I should have nothing when the next installment became due. But, be that as it might, it was now very clear that nothing could be done that day, and I therefore made no effort to go out at all.

Tuesday came, and it was still no better, and another day was lost, and I was getting almost discouraged. But I tried to do a little something. I went out in the afternoon and went to all the public offices, but all my efforts were in vain. No one would subscribe; and heart-sick and weary I wended my way home again in the evening, almost willing to surrender my agency and resort to some other means of earning a livelihood. Indeed, had I been able, at that time, to think of something else which promised sufficient returns to support me, it is very likely I should have embraced it; but all around me were strangers, and with no one to recommend or aid me, nothing could be done aside from the path already marked out, and all I could do was to take the bad weather with what patience I could muster; and, by this time, my small stock of that virtue so necessary to every book agent was well-nigh exhausted.

And so the week passed away, in rain and mud and idleness. It is true that, on Thursday, with a sort of reckless energy, I went out for a while, and tried to redeem a part of the lost past; but, after spending half an hour or more in inducing one man to subscribe, I gave up in despair, and went home again, fully resolved that even the prospect of starvation should not tempt me to go out again until the weather moderated and the storm ceased.

And thus, finally, Saturday came, and I had but one solitary subscriber to report. If I felt ashamed and mortified at sending in my report of the week before, what must have been my feelings now, that the amount of this week's sales was but half as large? But there was no help for it. The report must be sent, and the apparent failure must be explained as best I was able.

But there was a still more serious consideration than the smallness of my report to the general agent. My weekly board-bill was due to-day, and where was the money to come from to pay it? And not only this week, but others would come, and even if my indebtedness on this account were now paid, what provision could be made for the future? Such horrid weather as we had been having for the last two weeks would most effectually keep me from earning any money, but it would not prevent my weekly bills from becoming due, nor would it keep my landlady from demanding payment or sending me adrift, if I failed to comply with her very just demands.

This, dear reader, was the gloomy day referred to in my opening chapter. This was the day upon which, for the second time, I pawned my watch—not my watch, but Gussie's watch—a precious treasure, and which nothing but death, or the demand of him from whom I first received it, shall ever take from me. I hardly knew how to part with it a second time, so soon after redeeming it; but I could not starve, and I am sure, if Gussie should read these lines, he will not blame me for thus temporarily parting with it, to avoid that or a worse fate. Be assured that nothing shall induce me to part with it permanently so long as life and reason are spared to me.

But just now my situation was gloomy in the extreme. Six dollars must be paid weekly for my board or I must leave my present place of abode, and then what could be done? I had only made one dollar this week, and even that I had not received; for I could not order a solitary copy of the work, and must wait until the weather would enable me to resume my labors again. What could I do

but pawn the watch for means to provide me with food
and shelter?

I wanted something to do to pass away the time, and
keep my mind from dwelling upon the horrors of my situation. I felt like a guilty thing after my return from the
pawn-broker's, and something must be done. I went to
my room, in pursuance of the resolution mentioned in my
first chapter, and wrote for some time; but this only increased the gloom resting upon my spirits, and I finally
threw down the pen, and going to my landlady, asked for
work. Even if it paid me nothing, it would at least keep
my mind employed, and pass away the time. She had a
quilt on the frames, and told me I might work on that if
I liked, and she would pay me whatever it was worth.
Accordingly I went to work, and worked all the evening
for her, for the sole purpose of diverting my mind.

The next day was Sunday, and it cleared off once more.
The clouds dispersed, the sun came out beautifully, and
all nature appeared in gay and smiling colors once more.
My spirits rose; for I felt sure that on the morrow I
I would be able to resume my labors, and regain all and
more than I had lost.

And this time my predictions of fair weather were veri-
fied. The sun rose clear and beautiful on Monday morning, and so impatient was I to be at my work, that it was
with difficulty I waited for my breakfast. When that very
necessary affair was disposed of, I at once set out in search
of subscribers. Heretofore I had paid my respects to
stores, offices and the like, but to day my eyes and footsteps were turned in another direction, and private residences were my objective points. And my efforts were
crowned with very fair success, for when I turned my footsteps homeward, at nightfall, six names had been added to

18

my list. What mattered it that I was weary and well-nigh worn out with my incessant labors, or that food had not passed my lips since the matin meal—I had earned six dollars, enough to pay my board for a week, and my heart was light. What matter if Gussie's watch was in pawn for fifteen dollars—I had a month in which to redeem it, and that day had brought me nearly half enough for that purpose, and I was happy. I was in a good humor with myself and all the world, and began to think this earth was not such a bad place to inhabit, after all, and that the people of Peoria were not really the outcasts of creation. Nay, I even abated a very considerable amount of my hostility to the weather-god, and felt very much inclined to forgive him for the unfavorable character of the last two weeks. In fine, I was very much mollified.

The next day I went to that part of the city called "The Bluffs"—I know not why, unless because the people there are more inclined to "bluff" a stranger than elsewhere — and took, by the hardest of work, only three names. On my way home, however, I succeeded in getting a poor woman, whom I had asked for a drink of water, to put her name down, subject, however, to the consent of her husband. And, I may add, in this connection, that that consent was given, and the book taken with a hearty good-will, which was far more agreeable than that very often displayed by those who were rich in money, but poor in spirit, as compared with this loving and hard-working couple.

I had, therefore, obtained four subscribers this day, which gave me ground to hope for better success on the morrow. Ten subscribers this week thus far. Even if unsuccessful, or if the weather should again become bad, so as to prevent me from working at all, my report of this week would compare very favorably with those of the last two weeks, and my faith in future success was so strong as to induce me that night to write for twenty copies more.

My faith in the future was not disappointed by the result, for on the next day no less than eleven names were added to my list of subscribers. This was something like old times, and made me feel quite rich once more. I even began to consider in what bank it was best for me to deposit my earnings, so as to be sure that they would be safe, and I very seriously contemplated going to my old friend "Crusty," and asking his advice upon this important subject, or at least getting him to insure my fortune against loss by thieves, burglars, fire or flood, but finally concluded to wait until I had paid my debts, or at least received my money for the books I had sold to those eleven persons. The next day I only got one subscriber; but never mind — that was one dollar, and I would not starve if I only made that amount each day.

To illustrate the fact that book agents have all kinds of customers to deal with—a fact that has already to some extent appeared in these pages—let me here give the reader an account of my interview, on the next day, with a dentist by the name of G——, one of the first dentists in the city. I am sorry that I am unable at this time to give his name in full, for it is meet and proper that his name and business should be advertised in full in these pages without cost to him. And thus was the interview.

"Dr. G., I have a book to which I would like to call your attention for a few moments. I would like to add your name to my list of subscribers, and think you would be pleased with it."

"I do n't care about looking at it. Do n't know as I

want to buy any books. They generally cost more than they are worth."

"I called at your house and showed this to your wife. She was very anxious to get it, but did not like to put her name down without your consent, and referred me to you."

"Oh! yes, of course. My wife wants everything she sees any other woman have. Get two women together and they will ruin any man with their silly notions."

"Will you look at my book, sir?"

"Yes, I can look at it, but can't buy it."

"Can't you spend two dollars and seventy-five cents to please your wife? She wants the book."

"Of course, she wants it, but she don't need it. Beside money is very scarce. Don't you want your teeth fixed? If so, may be we can come to terms in that way."

"Yes, sir; I have two teeth I want extracted, and if you will subscribe for my book, I will have it done. If not, I will go elsewhere."

"Let me take out three teeth—enough to pay for the book, and I will subscribe."

"No, sir. Two is all I wish to lose."

"Well, sit down."

He took my subscription book, put down his name, and then proceeded to the extraction of my teeth, thus combining a fine stroke of business with the pleasure of making his wife a present of the value of two dollars and three-quarters! If that man does not succeed in accumulating a fortune, it will be only because meanness is not the surest road to wealth. I wanted the teeth extracted, but the idea of making that a condition of presenting his wife with a book which she wanted, and which she would have subscribed for, but for her wholesome fear of her lord and master! Perhaps the reader will think I would be in a hurry about delivering a book sold under such circumstances, but really I was not. When I had collected the money to redeem Gussie's watch, I rested very easy about it, and it was not until I had finished my canvassing in Peoria, and was ready to leave, that Mr. Dentist got his book. In taking leave of this subject, I beg to advise my fellow book agents to give Mr. G. a wide berth, unless they are ready to suffer the loss of teeth for the purpose of selling their publications. After leaving Mr. G. I went to several other places, and, by dint of hard and constant work, succeeded in getting eight more names that day, and this, too, without having to submit to any surgical operation of any kind. Indeed, in all my experience as a "Book Agent," Mr. G. is the only man whom I ever met who insisted upon paying his subscription by eliminating some of the members of the unfortunate canvasser. There may be others in the world, but it is extremely doubtful, and he should be preserved, in a glass case if need be, as a sort of curiosity for the edification and amusement of the rising generation.

The next day a hard and persistent canvass, from "early morn to dewy eve," only added one name to my list. I had got into a part of the city which was inhabited by the poorer classes, many of them Germans, just from "Faderland," and they had neither the means nor inclination to purchase anything in the way of English literature. I was not really surprised or disappointed at the result of my labors among that class, for but little could be anticipated, but still it would not do for me to pass them by. I was bound by my obligations and duties as an agent, to canvass the city thoroughly, and this I would do whether I obtained subscribers or not. And if I did this and failed to make sales, the fault, at least, would not be mine.

On Saturday I made my report to the general agent of sales of thirty copies that week. I felt very proud of the favorable contrast between this report and the one that had preceded it, and was still better satisfied when Mr. Holland wrote me saying he was " glad to learn from account of sales that the flood in Peoria had decayed and dried up, and that the waters were failing from off the ground."

The Sunday following was a lonely day, and as I contemplated the work of the past week (do n't think me, dear reader, irreverent or wicked for thinking of these matters on the Sabbath day; my mind was so full of the subject, and it was so necessary to my existence that I could not help it) my heart welled up with gratitude to Him by whose overruling providence the storm had been stayed, and I had been enabled to resume my toil with some prospect of success. To-day I attended church for the first time in Peoria. I had heretofore been so downhearted that I had not felt like going to church or anywhere else, but to-day, I, in part, made amends for lost time heretofore. I went to the Baptist church in the morning; to Sabbath-school in the afternoon, and to church again in the evening; heard good sermons, and passed the day very pleasantly, feeling better at night, both mentally and physically, than I had for some time.

The next week the weather was fair, and I worked all the week, with varying success. On Monday, I took six subscribers; on Tuesday, the utmost number possible to obtain by hard work was five; Wednesday my success was good, and ten names were added to my list before nightfall compelled me to desist; Thursday, only three names rewarded my exertions, and Friday I was compelled to content myself with barely one. And thus it went. I could compare my work to nothing in the world but fishing. On one day business would be good, and almost every one I asked would subscribe; on another day, under precisely the same circumstances, and, so far as it was possible for me to judge, with just as fair prospects of success, the utmost that could be done would be to take one, two, or three names. Every lover of piscatorial sports will recognize the similarity in this to his own experience. Nevertheless, my report this week turned out to be very respectable, being no less than twenty-five new subscribers, while I had delivered thirty copies previously taken.

About this time I had some difficulty with the agent of the express company relative to a lot of books shipped to me by Mr. Holland. It was during the rainy weather which had just closed, and while the books were in charge of the company, they had been exposed to the rain, and some of them had got wet and were very much damaged. I found that five of them were so much damaged as to be almost entirely unsaleable at any price, and I thought the company ought to take them and pay for them. Indeed, I was advised by my friends that they could be compelled to do so; but the agent declined to make any compensation, and the amount involved was so small that it did not seem to me worth while to make much fuss about it. Still it was a very heavy loss to me in the present condition of my finances; but I finally took them, and let my subscribers have them at cost, thus losing my profit of one dollar on each book, and getting nothing for that day's work. Up to this time the express agent had treated me very kindly and gentlemanly; but in this instance I regarded his conduct as anything else, and did not hesitate to tell him so.

He had not scrupled to take advantage of the unfortunate circumstances in which I, a woman without money and without friends, was placed, to repudiate an obligation which law and justice alike imposed on him, and had thus displayed a want of principle which, though perhaps not unusual with some men, should still be but a poor recommendation for the position he then occupied. It shall not be my fault if the world does not rate him at his true value.

Having by this time about completed my canvass of the city of Peoria, and believing that my difficulty with the express agent would render further transactions with that office unpleasant, I decided to change my locality, and canvass the little town of Elmwood, in the same county—leaving, for the present at least, so much of the city as I had not visited.

I must not omit, however, to bear testimony, in this place, to the kindness and generosity which were displayed toward me by a Mr. Tripp, residing in the city, before my departure. He was a merchant, and was one of my subscribers. I had a lot of books—thirty in number—to be delivered in order to supply all my customers. After the difficulty to which allusion has been made, the agent, contrary to his usual practice, and to vent his spite on me, refused to allow me to open the package in the office, and I had not money enough to pay the charges on them and take them away. In this emergency Mr. Tripp generously came to my assistance, advanced the money to pay the charges, and allowed me to take them away as I was able—paying him for them as I could raise the money. Some of my subscribers were not ready to take their books, and when I went away there were twelve copies still undelivered, which Mr. Tripp consented to retain and wait for his pay until the subscribers were ready to receive them. How different was his conduct from that of the express agent! For this kindness to a comparative stranger, he has her heartfelt thanks, and will assuredly some day receive his reward.

CHAPTER XXI.

I ARRIVED at Elmwood about two o'clock in the afternoon, and immediately set about finding a suitable boarding place.   In this I was extremely fortunate.   The place
selected for my head-quarters there, was the family of a
Mr. ——, a kind and considerate Christian gentleman,
while his wife was one of the most pleasant and agreeable
ladies it was ever my fortune to meet.   They were kind
and consistent followers of the meek and lowly Jesus,
and their treatment of me during my stay in their midst,
partook more of the character of that which might be
meted out to a dearly loved sister, than of that which
keepers of boarding-houses are wont to display toward
their guests.   There will ever be a green spot in my memory, to record the kindly deeds of this family toward the
lonely wanderer, who had come to them with no recom-
mendations, save those which appeal to the heart of
every true Christian.   "I was a stranger, and ye took
me in."

Indeed my heart holds grateful recollections of every
one in Elmwood, with whom it was my fortune to be
brought in contact during my stay in that place.   Never
has it been my lot to be treated with such uniform courtesy and kindness by every one.   Surely if good works,
and kind deeds toward the lone and unfortunate, are a
passport to future happiness, the people of that loveliest
of rural villages are on the high road to eternal bliss.
The reader must pardon my enthusiasm upon this subject,
for my situation there was so different from what had

been my usual experience, that it seems almost impossible to express my satisfaction at the contrast.

I have alluded particularly to the kindness of Mr. —— and his wife. The reader must pardon me for referring particularly to another instance of the unparalleled generosity with which the denizens of that place were wont to treat me, a perfect stranger. Among my earliest acquaintances was a young man by the name of J. Hopkins. He was a young man of the purest integrity and uprightness of character, and his heart overflowed with kindness to all with whom he was brought in contact. He had, too, one of those frank, noble natures which, suspecting no ill, regard every one as worthy of the same trust which his fine, manly countenance inspired in every one who met him. Altogether he was one of those men in whom, at first sight, you feel that it is safe to confide, and who never betray a trust reposed in them. He had been a soldier, and had lost an arm in the service of his country, but was now engaged in business which his goodness and universal popularity naturally rendered profitable.

Situated as I was, it was but natural that I should confide to him my situation and pecuniary embarrassments: with a nobleness and generosity which may sometimes be equaled but never excelled, he came to my relief, and freely tendered me any assistance I might desire. And during all the time that I remained in Elmwood, the same generosity was continued. Was money needed to take a package of books from the express office; his purse was at my command, and without security of any kind, he allowed me to take my books and pay for them as I chose. Nay, more, any business which I was at a loss how to transact, I had but to submit to him, and it was done in the most correct and expeditious manner, and that, too,

without fee or reward beyond my poor thanks and my
most fervent gratitude.   He took my pawn-ticket, and redeemed my watch from the grasp of the old skinflint,
in Peoria, with whom I had pawned it—I of course furnishing the money to do so—and when I offered to compensate him for his trouble, he positively refused to receive
anything.   I owed him frequently, during my stay in Elmwood, as high as thirty, forty or fifty dollars at a time, and
he never asked me for a cent of money at any time, but
just left the time of payment to my own convenience.   A
brother could not have done more for me, and his kindness will never be forgotten.

It took me but a few days to canvass Elmwood, when
I finally got at work.   There was a weekly paper published in the place, in which I had advertised the work
upon my first arrival, and everybody was ready to subscribe or refuse as soon as the work was submitted for
their inspection.   I have very often in small places derived great benefit in my canvassing, by advertising my
publications in the local papers.   The same results do not
follow advertisements in large cities, but in a small village
like Elmwood, destitute of anything which tends to excite
the public pulse, the local journals are read with an avid-
ity which the residents of the city never know, and when
anything is once advertised, it attracts the attention of
the entire community ; it is canvassed in every possible
aspect, and people have their minds made up one way or
the other as to its merits.   And when the agent finally
appears, every one is ready to give a decided answer.   I
did very well in Elmwood, having succeeded in selling no less
than forty copies of the work in a little town of not more,
I should think, than one thousand inhabitants.   And this,
as before stated, was accomplished in but a very few days.

WAITING FOR THE WAGON.

There are several little country towns, as Southport, Pittsville, etc, lying about equal distances from Elmwood, and off of any railroad or other public conveyance. Having finished my work in the latter place, I decided to go and canvass these little towns; but the puzzling question was, how to get there, and how to transfer my books and baggage there. After considerable cogitation upon this subject, I finally concluded not to move my headquarters from Elmwood; but, to retain my present boarding-place, and, taking a few books, go by some chance conveyance, which might present itself, to one of the little towns before mentioned. A single instance will illustrate my mode of doing this business.

Having, for several days, tried in vain to obtain a conveyance from Elmwood to Southport, I finally, on one bright Monday morning, took a large market-basket — it would hold just fifteen "Tried and Trues," and was so heavy that it was all I could do to lift it—filled it with books, and going out a little way on the Southport road, sat down under a tree to "wait for the wagon." I sat there for several hours before any conveyance came along going my way, though quite a number passed me going the other way. But, reflecting that the stream would by and by be flowing the other way, I maintained my seat with what patience I could. Noon came, and no team had made its appearance going my way. I took out a lunch I had brought with me, ate it, and still waited, hoping that my patience would finally be rewarded by the sight of an approaching wagon, and at last one made its appearance. As it drew near, I approached the roadside and signed the driver to stop, which he did.

"I give you good day, sir. Are you going to Southport?"

"I am, madam. Is there anything I can do for you?"

"I want to get there. Can I ride with you?"

"I have a tolerably good load; but if you do not mind riding on a load of shelled corn, guess I can accommodate you."

"Oh! sir, I can ride anywhere. If you will take me and my basket of butter, I shall be ever so much obliged."

"Very well, madam; I can take you. Just bring your basket here. Why! you can hardly lift it. How many pounds of butter have you there?"

"I do n't know just how many pounds I have."

By this time I was in the wagon; he started up his team; and, for some little time, we jogged on in silence. At length he spoke —

"Your butter is for sale, I suppose?"

"Yes, sir."

"How much do you ask for it?"

"It is put up in rolls, of the value of two dollars and seventy-five cents each."

"Two dollars and seventy-five cents! Why, they must be very large and heavy rolls."

"No, sir; not very large. Would you like to see one?"

"Why, yes; if you please."

"Here, sir," said I, raising the cover of the basket, and producing a copy of "Tried and True," "is one of my rolls of butter."

"Why, that is a book. Bless my heart, madam, is that basket full of books?"

"It is, sir. You can look for yourself," said I, raising the cover of the basket as I spoke, so that he could have a good view of its contents. "How do you like the looks of them?"

"But you said you had butter in the basket."

"Well, I sell these books, and, when I want any butter, I buy it with the proceeds of the books. It is the only way I have to get any butter, or bread either, for that matter; and, hence, there is nothing wrong in my saying they are my butter. They are; and my bread and clothing, too."

"Well," said he, laughing, "you make out a very good case."

"I think so, sir. Won't you help me to make out a still better one by buying one of my rolls of butter?"

"I can't see what it is."

"Well, let me take the lines and drive the team a little way while you examine it. I think you will buy one if you only look at it."

He laid down his whip, took the book, and handed the lines to me. He was soon absorbed in the book, and I drove on, while he took no note of anything at all. I could have driven the team to Chicago, and he would never have known the difference, so interested was he in the story he held in his hand. I finally grew impatient lest he should finish the book before we reached our destination, and, touching him on the shoulder with the whip, said:

"Had you not better buy the book, and read it when you get home? We shall soon be in Southport."

He started, looked a little ashamed of having so forgotten himself, but paid me for the book without a word. I thanked him, and resigned the lines to him, and in a short time we arrived at Southport, where I bid him "good day," while he passed on through the town. He lived at Princeville, a few miles farther on, and was then on his way home.

This, dear reader, was the manner in which I reached the village of Southport, and this may serve as a sample of the way in which I went about to canvass the several other little towns which are scattered throughout Peoria county. Of course, the reader will not understand that I always rode on a load of corn, or that I was always so fortunate as to sell a copy of my book to my impromptu coachman. But I visited all these little towns simply by watching by the roadside for a chance to ride. And I say, to the credit of the farmers of that county, that I never found one, no matter what the circumstances, who was unwilling to transport me and my "basket of butter," or who treated me in any but the most respectful and courteous manner.

It was about five o'clock in the evening when I dismissed my carriage in the streets of Southport. I had never been there before, but had by this time become pretty well accustomed to being among strangers, and it gave me no uneasiness. There was no hotel in the place, and I went to a private house, made known my name and business to them, and engaged lodgings for the night. I succeeded in interesting them in the merits of "Tried and True," and sold them a copy of the work.

The next morning I went to work with a will, and canvassed the entire town, selling all the books I had with me but five copies. With these I started on foot for Elmwood, intending to sell them out at the farm-houses along the road. I was several days in getting back, for I stopped at every house along the road, staying each night just where nightfall overtook me, and finding but few persons who were able or willing to buy. However, when I finally reached Elmwood, about two o'clock on Saturday afternoon, I had not a single book left, and had, beside, taken orders for three more, to be left in Mr. Hopkins' hands. He again displayed his generosity by advancing me the money upon them, and taking his chances of getting it back from my subscribers—and I am very happy to say they all paid him up in a very short time. Had they not done so, I should most certainly have refunded him the money before leaving that section of the country.

In this way I worked until I had canvassed the entire county, and the time came for me to leave Elmwood and its vicinity, perhaps forever. How I hated to leave! I had been so happy there, and had so many good friends, that I almost dreaded to leave them and go among entire strangers again. I had seen more real happiness there than I had at any time or place since the sad discovery, in Cincinnati, which led to the separation of Mason and myself. Would I ever see as much happiness again?

In one particular I had deceived my Elmwood friends; but, under the circumstances in which I was placed, I can not think they will blame me very sorely. I had not imparted to any one any portion of my past history, and had held myself out to them as a widow. It was not altogether right, but no one was injured thereby, and it seemed to me to be almost necessary to my self-preservation that my past life should not be known to them. If any of them should, by chance, read this story, they will understand my reasons for the deception; and, while once more thanking them, one and all, for their uniform kindness to me, I most humbly beg their pardon for the trifling deception I practiced upon them. Had I known them as well, when I went among them, as I now do, I should not have hesitated to tell them just how I was situated; but I did not, and when I came to know them well, it was then too late to correct the error: at least I feared that it was, and dreaded the loss of position which I feared would follow an exposition of my real situation. Once more I beg the pardon of each and every one for the deception.

19

During this time I had not heard one word from or of my truant husband. I knew not whether he was living or dead, or, if living, what he was doing, and it is not to be supposed that he was any better informed as to my movements. At times this gave me very little trouble, for though I had loved him with all the power of affection, had regarded him as almost more than mortal, and had, in my fancy, clothed him with attributes of nobleness which belong to none but the most perfect of God's creatures, still it was impossible for me to forget that he had insulted and abused me; had put upon me the foulest wrong which can be offered to a faithful and trusting wife; had violated every vow which he assumed in the presence of God and man; had betrayed the confidence and trust I had reposed in him, and, to crown his infamy, had driven me from the home and protection he had sworn to give me, to support myself or perish among strangers, while he gave no care or thought to the fate of her whom he had endowed with the sacred name of wife. When I reflected upon these things; when faithful memory presented the picture of the wrongs I had endured at his hands—oh! then was my once ardent love for him turned to hate, and while praying heaven's choicest vengeance upon him, I had wished that his hated name might never again be sounded in my ears. But there were other times, when the memory of my former love for that base and unworthy man would sweep, like a torrent, over my soul; my heart would soften toward him, and I would willingly have forgiven all my wrongs for the poor boon of one kindly word of remembrance from him; one single token to show that he cherished a pleasing memory of the past, now gone forever. But it never came.

Oh! there is no anguish like that endured by a faithful,

true-hearted woman who has loved with her whole soul; who has reveled in all the bright dreams of mutual and sanctified affection, and has been rudely and suddenly awakened from her bright dream of happiness, only to learn that she has been betrayed, deceived, and imposed upon; that all the priceless treasures of her soul have been given to an unworthy object, and have been remorselessly thrown aside, and trampled into the dust of the earth, by him whom she believed to be true and faithful as the needle to the pole. Happy then the heart that can break, and thus avoid the storm; the fierce conflict of passion, which, unless tempered by the kindness and mercy of Him whose handiwork we all are, will shatter to atoms the frail fabric upon which its violence is spent, and leave it, at the last, a shapeless and unsightly wreck. Happy the spirit which has power to transform its former love into hate, and avoid the dread conflict by thus filling the soul with an inhabitant which, though unpleasant and detestable, is still able to expel forever the love which there formerly reigned supreme.

Upon bidding adieu to my kind friends in Elmwood, I shipped all my baggage to Chillicothe, accompanying it myself as far as Rockhill, where I stopped off to canvass for a few days. I only did tolerably well there, selling not more than a dozen or fifteen in all, and not liking the place, and feeling but little encouraged by the prospect there, I shook off the dust from my feet against that town and returned to Peoria, where several little matters of business claimed my attention. The reader must know that, up to this time, I had not delivered any book to the man who pulls teeth to pay his subscription—my old friend Mr. Dr. Dentist G.—and this must be done; beside, I was still a little in debt to Mr. Tripp, and wanted to discharge the pecuniary obligation to him under which I was laboring, for my other obligations it was impossible that I ever should discharge.

Accordingly, I arranged these little matters in Peoria, and then took the cars for Chillicothe, where I arrived in due time, and, for a short season, worked with very fair success. I sold quite a number of books there, and business finally becoming dull, went in a wagon to Princeville. But my experience there was such as to induce me to warn all my fellow book agents, if any of them should, perchance, attempt to canvass that section of country, to avoid Princeville as they would the deserts of Arabia. The people there seem to have a most holy horror of all kinds of literature, and to regard traveling book agents as, in some sort, enemies of the country, aliens and outlaws. I labored three days, assiduously, to break through the crust of exclusiveness which surrounded them, but with such poor success that I only sold one book, and that through the aid of my old friend, the wagoner, upon whose load of corn I rode from Elmwood to Southport. It is barely possible that the seed thus sown may have fallen upon good ground, and that some other agent could do better there than I did, but it is extremely doubtful, and I think the language of Holy Writ might, with safety, be applied to Princeville, changing only names to suit the case. "Princeville is joined to her idols, let her alone."

From Princeville I started in a wagon for Lawn Ridge. Observing that the road was good, and the country well settled, by what appeared to be a class of well-to-do farmers, I took five copies, and directing the wagoner what disposition to make of the balance of my books, upon his arrival at Lawn Ridge, walked down a lane to a comfortable-looking farm-house, which stood but a short distance off the main road. An old woman was sitting on the porch knitting, while a large and fierce-looking dog came growling toward me, as I opened the gate. The old woman made no effort to check him, and I was really afraid of him.

"Good morning, madam. Will your dog bite me?"

"Oh! no. He never bites nobody. He does a mighty sight of growlin', but he haint never bit anybody yit. Come in."

"Madam, I have some books to sell, and am very much in need of money. Won't you take pity on me, and buy one?"

"Where you goin', miss?"

"I am going to Lawn Ridge."

"Why, you don't say. Are you goin' to walk to Lawn Ridge, and carry all them there books?"

"I am, indeed, unless I sell them before I get there."

"Well, really. Why, where did you come from?"

"I came from Princeville."

"Du tell. Well, now, mebby my boy Tom will buy one on 'em, jest to help you along. Tom! come here. Here's a book would jest suit you—come and buy one of this 'ere woman. She's come from Princeville, and is goin' to walk all the way to Lawn Ridge and carry 'em, if she don't sell 'em."

Her "boy Tom," a great, awkward lout, of twenty-five or six, who was working in a garden hard by, came up, and expressed almost as much sympathy for my hard lot as his mother, and, out of pure charity, bought a book. I thanked them for their kindness, but have very grave doubts whether that book has ever been read to this day. However, I had accomplished my mission, and, with a light heart, and my load lightened by one copy of "Tried and True," I returned to the road, and again bent my footsteps in the direction of Lawn Ridge. After walking a mile, I came to another house, where I called, and, exposing my wares, tried to make a sale, but here the same appeals to their charity were in vain. They expressed sympathy for my hard lot, but were unable to raise the money. Thanking them for their sympathy and good will, although I derived no pecuniary benefit from its expression, I rested a short time, and then pursued my journey.

The next house was half a mile distant, and it was now almost noon. When I arrived there I was weary and hungry, and asked the lady of the house for something to eat. She gave me a bowl of milk and some fresh bread and butter: saying they had been to dinner, and that was all she had at hand. I sat down to my frugal meal, and, while appeasing the cravings of my appetite, asked them to look at my books. The entire family gathered around, and were very much pleased with the appearance of the work,

"What is the price of your book?" said the lady at last.

"I am selling them at two dollars and seventy-five cents. I think the book is really worth three dollars; but I only ask two and three-quarters. Will you take one?"

"I think we will," said she, producing a purse and counting out the exact sum.

"Thank you, madam," said I, rising as I spoke; "and now what shall I pay you for my dinner; for it is time for me to go."

"Nothing at all. I charge nothing for such a dinner as that."

"But, madam, it was worth a good deal to me."

"Well, if it was worth anything to you, you are entirely welcome to it. It is worth nothing to me."

I thanked her heartily for her kindness, and resumed my journey. There are bright spots in this gloomy world of ours; and this kind lady, thus bestowing her simple refreshment, without reward, upon an entire stranger, whom she never expected to see again, demonstrated that she inhabited one of those bright spots, and that the true religion of Jesus Christ abode with her there.

At the next house I met one of those over-zealous people who attach all importance to the name, while they entirely lose sight of the substance. An account of my interview with the lady of the house will illustrate this fact.

"How do you do, madam? Can I rest a short time? I am walking to Lawn Ridge, and am very tired."

"Certainly; come in."

"Madam, I am a book agent, and would like to sell you a book. Will you look at them?"

"We have plenty of books; but I will look at yours."

"This is a new work, madam—has been published but a few weeks, and is one of the most interesting I ever read. I charge nothing for looking at them."

"Oh! this is a novel. I never read novels. I do not think it is right to waste one's time in that way."

"You do n't! Madam, what papers are those lying on the table?"

"That? Why, that is the New York Ledger."

"Do you take it?"

"Yes, ma'am; and have for a good many years."

"Who reads it—you or your family?"

"Oh! we all read it. We could not get along without that."

"And, yet, you never read novels!"

"Never."

"The New York Ledger, I suppose, is not a series of

novels from one year's end to another. It is only a newspaper. But is it any better to read a long tale of fiction in the Ledger than it would be to read the same story done up in book form. But, as you never read novels, it is not worth while to waste time in trying to sell you one. Good morning, madam."

And, gathering my shawl majestically about my person, I stalked from her presence, indignant at her hypocrisy, or pitying her ignorance. I was not certain which feeling predominated.

After passing and calling at one or two other houses, without effecting any sales, I arrived at a comfortable-looking place; and, as it was nearly night, and I was very weary, I decided to stay all night, if they would keep me. To my application for lodgings, the answer was:

"We never turn any body out of doors, and you can stay."

I rested very well that night, and the next morning prevailed on my landlady to take a book, and pay me two dollars in money, allowing my bill for supper, bed and breakfast, to settle the balance of the price. I finally reached Lawn Ridge, about four o'clock in the afternoon; having sold all the books with which I started. My long walk had made me very weary and footsore, but still I had done very well, and felt content.

Upon arriving at Lawn Ridge, my first care was to secure a good stopping-place for the night, after which I went to the store of Mr. Parsons, where my wagoner had informed me he would leave my package of books. I found them all right; and Mr. Parsons very much of a gentleman. He gave me the books, and before I left the store I succeeded in selling him one. This favorable beginning, I thought, augured well for my success in Lawn

Ridge, aud I was not disappointed, for, though the place contained only about twenty or twenty-five houses, I sold some five or six copies there, and was ready by the middle of the afternoon to take my seat in a wagon which I fortunately found going to Chillicothe. It was now absolutely necessary for me to return there to order more books, my present stock having become almost exhausted.

There was some delay about getting my books, and I had to wait several days for them. I very much hated to lose the time, for it was pleasant weather, and it was very uncertain what it would be when I was ready to go to work again, and, beside, I could not afford to remain idle. Finally, however, my books came to hand, and, without the delay of a single day, I set out for the country, having decided to try and introduce a little light among the benighted farmers of that region. Candor, however, compels me to admit that the dissemination of knowledge was not the only, nor, indeed, the principal, motive which induced me to take a basket of heavy books on my arm, and start on a pedestrian excursion for the rural districts. No; anxious as I am to do all the good I can in this world, it is very doubtful if this alone would have induced me to adopt the character of a missionary among that people. Nay, more: I will confess that the desire to replenish my purse had more to do with my resolution than the desire of being serviceable to my fellow men. But so long as the motive was not in itself evil, I am confident my readers will not withhold from me the credit of the good which my itinerancy in that region may have done.

One good effect resulting from my present trip, was, the discovery of some cases of destitution, at which humanity must shudder, and Christianity weep; and which demand the immediate attention of the overseers of the poor for

the county of Peoria—cases, too, which would never have
been known, but for my journey, because, from outward
indications, no one would have supposed them to exist.
Allow me to illustrate this by recounting a single incident.

On my first day out, I called at the house of a Mr.——,
but, no, I will not publish his name to the world, but will
furnish it to the overseers of the poor upon their address-
ing me at Indianapolis, Indiana, and sending a stamp for
return postage — so let the name pass for the present.
Suffice it to say that the poor wretch lived in a large two-
story frame house, while the yards, filled with stock, and
barns apparently bursting with plenty, seemed to indicate
the possession of many of the comforts of life, and even
some of the luxuries, by the proprietor—so deceptive are
appearances often found to be in this vain world of ours.

As soon as my soul fell upon this supposed abode of
plenty, I chuckled with glee, and my heart was glad.
"Now," said I to myself, "here will I sell large numbers,
to-wit: one copy of ' Tried and True,' and my purse shall
groan with the additional burden of two dollars and seventy-five cents, current money of the United States, while
the load upon my arm shall be proportionately lightened.
Alas! how vain are all human calculations — how deceptive all merely mortal appearances. I would not for a
moment have supposed that the place before me was the
abode of poverty and misery, sufficient to have drawn tears
from the eyes of a potato. But I was soon undeceived.

As I opened the gate, a large and fierce-looking dog
came forward, with much noise and many demonstrations
of anger at my intrusion. Now, if I have any pet horror,
it is big dogs, especially when they act as this one did;
and for a short time I stood trembling, and actually fearing I should be rent limb from limb, after the very unpleas-

ant manner in which the rulers of the world were wont to treat the early Christians. At length, however, the master of the canine brute before me made his appearance.

"Good morning, sir."

"Good morning, madam."

"I am afraid of your dog. Will he hurt me?"

"O no, madam; he won't hurt you. Go away, Beaver. Come in, madam. Go away, Beaver—do you hear me?"

"I am so much afraid of dogs, especially such large, savage ones as this, that I hardly know what to do."

"He is not savage. He makes a great deal of noise, but never bites, except at night."

By this time we had entered the house, where sat a lady sewing. The house was furnished in a very comfortable style, and even yet I had no idea of the wretched poverty which existed among its inmates, and which was soon to be revealed to my astonished vision. I resumed the conversation:

"I am a book agent, and have here, 'Tried and True,' a new work, just published, and would like to sell you a copy. Madam, I think you will like the book. It is so very interesting that I sat up all one night to read it. Will you look at it?" and I handed her a copy.

She hesitated, but finally took the book, looking, in a sort of scared, startled way, at her husband. He spoke:

"Well, really, madam, I should like to buy the book, but really times are too hard, and I am too poor to buy books now."

"What! with all that stock in the yard; with this fine house, furnished in the best of style; those barns, doubtless filled with grain—you are too poor to buy a book, the price of which is only two dollars and seventy-five cents!"

"Yes, madam, I am really too poor. Two dollars and

seventy-five cents, did you say? It is a large sum, and can not be picked up every day."

"Do you own this farm?"

"Yes, ma'am."

"And is it paid for? and this stock, those cattle and horses—are they yours, and paid for?"

"Yes, ma'am; I own it all, and do not owe any man a cent in the world."

"And yet you are not able to pay two dollars and seventy-five cents for a most interesting book?"

"Indeed, I am not."

"Have you any children?"

"Yes; we have four—two sons and two daughters; and I tell you, it costs a heap of money to feed and clothe them."

"Well, sir, if you have four children dependent upon you for support, and, owning all the property I see around me, you are still unable to invest two dollars and three-quarters in food for their minds, I pity them and you. I would not be as mean and miserly as that, for the wealth of Crœsus. Had you given any other reason than poverty for your refusal to subscribe, I should have accepted it, and gone my way without a word; but the idea of lack of ability, on your part, is too ridiculous. Rather say you are too miserly to afford your children that which they need to fit them to discharge their duties in life with due propriety and credit to themselves. Good day, sir."

With this exposition of my feelings upon this subject, I took my book from the lady and left the house. I earnestly commend those four children to the attention of the commissioners of Peoria county; for, if allowed to grow up under the kind and fostering care (?) of their unnatural and miserly father, they are sure to become fit candidates for the gallows or the State prison, and it may cost the county more to care for them in that way, than to see that they are properly cared for and educated in their youth. "An ounce of preventive is worth a pound of cure."

But such instances of meanness, I am happy to state, are, so far as my experience as a book agent goes, rare in the United States. I have canvassed in nearly all of the north-western States, and have generally found the people more ready to part with their money for the purpose of procuring the aliment necessary to the culture and development of their mental faculties, than for any other object. And it is this peculiarity of the American people which gives them their high standing, as an intelligent and enlightened nation, among the powers of the earth, and renders the overthrow of liberty among us a moral impossibility. It is no unusual thing to find the house of a poor man, who toils from day to day for his daily bread, furnished with a well-selected little library, in which works of history and the sciences are familiarly intermingled with those lighter works, which, while they serve to amuse and occupy a passing hour, are still not without their lessons of wisdom and instruction to the inquiring mind. What, though such a man wear patched clothes, or be even clad in tatters; what, though his wife's best dress be but a "calico," or a simple muslin; what, though his furniture be plain, and his table be furnished with no silverware or costly viands: still can I respect and admire such a man, for I know that, in him, goodness and honor abound, and that the liberty bequeathed to us by our forefathers, has there a sturdy and uncompromising defense. But, once more to my labors.

I canvassed all this week (or rather what was left of it, for I did not start out until Wednesday), sold out all my books, and finally found myself, on Saturday night, the inmate of a farm-house, about eight miles from Chillicothe, which place, the reader will please to remember, was now my headquarters. I had now canvassed, pretty thoroughly, all my county, except one little town, by the name of Loudon, and its vicinity; and I was so anxious to finish my work that I decided to go to Chillicothe the next day. Sunday morning came. It was a bright, pleasant day; and there being no conveyance at hand, and learning that the roads were good all the way, I set out, in the early morning, to walk there. It was quite an undertaking for me, considering that it was not my intention to stop by the way; but it must be remembered, that I had been practicing pedestrianism considerably of late, and I boldly essayed the march. I reached my boarding-house a little after noon, pretty thoroughly worn out, and entirely willing to rest the next day; thus gaining nothing whatever by my Sunday's tramp.

On Tuesday, however, feeling sufficiently refreshed, I set out for Loudon, and, going vigorously to work, canvassed the place in a short time, selling ten copies of the work there. Loudon I found to be a very pleasant little place; and the result of my labors there will demonstrate, to the satisfaction of every one, that it was inhabited by a class of people very different from those I had found at Princeville and one or two other places in the county. But it mattered very little to me now. I had finished my work among them, and was about to leave their midst, while it was extremely uncertain whether I would ever meet any of them again.

At that time I had but little idea of ever publishing this sketch of my life—much less that I should, in person, canvass Peoria county for subscribers, which I shall, in all probability do, if Heaven spares my life, and nothing occurs to prevent my doing so.

Upon leaving Loudon I returned at once to Chillicothe, from which place I intended to take my final departure to Chicago, there to perfect arrangements for more extensive work in my new line of duty; for I had no idea of giving up the business of selling books by subscription. It was reasonably profitable, and would afford me a comfortable living; I liked the sort of excitement and change attending it; and, beside, it kept my mind constantly employed, to the almost utter exclusion of contemplation of the hideous past. For these reasons, it was my intention to still pursue it; and, in order to render that pursuit even more successful, it was necessary that I should repair to Chicago to make some new and more extended arrangements.

CHAPTER XXII.

It had become absolutely necessary for me to visit Chicago in order to provide means for my future support. I was now out of work—had finished the task assigned me—and, without work it was impossible for me to live. And work I could not get except by going there. There was one consideration which rendered my contemplated visit somewhat distasteful to me. Frank C. Nelles still lived there, and I did not wish to meet him under any circumstances. Of course, it was not absolutely certain that we would meet—my stay there would be brief—but still we might, and a meeting would be in the last degree unpleasant to me. But I could not sit still and starve, and go I must.

Before going, however, I must get myself a few things which were necessary to render me presentable in the city. I needed a new bonnet, to replace the one I had worn last winter; my gloves were worn out; my shoes, though very suitable for canvassing, on foot, throughout the county of Peoria, were hardly the things to wear upon the streets of Chicago; in fact, I needed a full supply of those little articles which ladies buy when they go "shopping." But, dear me, I would rather canvass half a day, on foot, in the country, than to go out "shopping" for a single half hour. How ladies can admire these shopping expeditions is more than I can conceive. There is nothing in life that seems more annoying to me than to start out and go from place to place, looking for this article or that, and, finally, going home after having bought, perhaps, a dollar's worth of goods. But there are women who really enjoy this sort of thing; who will go from place to place for an entire day, for the sole purpose of looking at goods, and with no intention of buying anything, and who finally return home, after having annoyed, as much as was in their power, every shop-keeper and clerk on their route, without having bought a single thing. I said they were women—pardon me, they are not—they are mere puppets of fashion, the extent of whose ambition is only to appear in the latest fashion, and to serve as a sort of walking advertisement for certain fashionable milliners and dress-makers. But for them the latter class would starve.

But, however distasteful it might be, my shopping had to be done, and so I set about it energetically. I was now out of debt, and had fifty-five dollars in money, honestly and fairly earned by my own toil, and there was no reason why I should go to Chicago looking as shabbily as I now did. I therefore went out and bought what I needed, including a black bonnet; for, as I was passing for a widow, it was but proper for me to assume, to some extent, the appearance of one. Beside, if black is a symbol of sorrow, surely my past life had been such as to entitle me to wear black as long as I should live, even though I should attain to the age of Methuselah.

When I had completed my purchases, and fitted myself out to my entire satisfaction, I took the cars for Chicago, arriving there without any incidents worthy of note. I went at once to the Sherman House, and registered myself as Mrs. S. A. Nelles, of Chicago. I knew they published daily lists of their arrivals, and thought Frank would thus learn that I was in the city; for though I should take no pains to find him, still I was weak enough to indulge a little hope, in spite of my resolution not to see

20

him, or have any communication with him, that when he found that I was in Chicago, he would come to see me. What might have been the result if he had done so, is more than can now be told, for at times I still loved him, in spite of myself, but he never came, although I heard of him before leaving the city, as will presently appear. I now rejoice that he did not come.

After getting settled at the Sherman House, I went to call on Mr. Holland, at 38 Lombard Block. He was very glad to see me, and complimented me very highly on my success, saying my sales had exceeded those of any other of his agents during the same time, and that he hoped I would take another county. I told him I wished to go to Indiana, and would like to have two points there, Indianapolis and Michigan City. The reader is well aware of the reasons which induced me to seek the former place; and I had good, and, to myself, satisfactory reasons for wanting to go to the latter, though it is not necessary to tell what they were.

Mr. Holland replied that he could give me Michigan City, but that Indianapolis was not in his district, it was under the control of the Columbus, Ohio, general agency, but he thought he could get it for me, and would try and do so. I thanked him for his kindness, and, having no further business to transact with him, went at once to make arrangements for my departure to my new field of labor.

I went back to the Sherman House, eat my dinner and paid for it, and then went to call on Mr. Kennedy, the publisher of " The Home Circle," and largely interested in the sale of " The Memorial of President Lincoln," and applied to him for the agency of both those publications. Mr. Holland had given me some very flattering testimonials, and I had no difficulty in forming an engagement with Mr. Kennedy, not only to canvass Michigan City, but also Indianapolis. I then went back to the Sherman House, ordered my baggage to the depot, and checked my trunks to Indianapolis, intending to stop but a short time in Michigan City. It was still some hours until the train would start, and I again went up in town and bought a dozen photographs of distinguished Generals, for which I paid the sum of one dollar. I had to purchase copies of " The Home Circle," and of " The Memorial," and I now had but two dollars and some few cents left in my purse.

As I was walking down State street, on my way to the depot, a gentleman bowed to me from a street car which was passing, and stopping the car, got out and came toward me. At first I did not recognize him, but when he came up and offered me his hand I knew him. It was Robert Nelles, a brother of my husband. He told me Frank was somewhere in the city, and was doing much better than he had formerly done. I told him he might tell him when he saw him that I was living in Indiana, and was now on my way home; that I was doing well, and asked no help from him, and that I had called on him the last time for assistance. He asked me when I was going to leave the city; and I told him I should go on the first train over the Michigan Central Road. Would he come to the depot? I would like to have a talk with him. He asked me what time the cars left. I told him about seven o'clock; and he said he would be there before that time.

We then parted, and I began to reflect upon the probable results of the proposed interview, and decided that it had better not take place. I was afraid he would bring Frank with him, and that they would suspect my motive in removing to Indiana, and would take steps to prevent

the accomplishment of my purpose. And, to tell the truth,
I was afraid to meet my husband. In spite of all his
wrongs I still loved him, and I was afraid my treacherous
heart, in case he made any overtures to me, would betray
me into living with him again, which I had fully made up
my mind never to do. Accordingly I changed my plans,
and, instead of waiting until seven o'clock, went away on a
freight train which left at five. If Robert Nelles reads
these lines, he will understand why he did not find me
when he came to the depot that evening, if he came
at all.

I arrived in Michigan City with but fifteen or twenty
cents in my purse, but this gave me very little trouble. I
had been in just as bad a situation as this before, and by
putting a bold face on the matter, and going to work with
reasonable energy, had succeeded in getting through with
my troubles; and there was no reason why I should not
do so again.

I went to the hotel, and freely told the landlord my sit
uation—how I had come there to canvass the place for
subscribers for "Tried and True," and "The Life of Mr.
Lincoln;" that I also had some photographs for sale, and
that I had neither money nor baggage, having sent my
baggage to Indianapolis, whither I was going as soon as I
had canvassed that place. He heard me through, and then
asked to see my photographs. I showed them to him, and
told him the price at which I sold them—twenty-five cents
each. He took four in payment of my bill for supper, bed
and breakfast, and I started out to sell the balance, which
I did in a very few minutes, and could have sold three
times as many more if I had had them. The people of
Michigan City are very patriotic, and photographs of successful leaders of the Union army are good stock to sell

among them. I had further evidence of this patriotism the next day.

The next day I went to work, and, by vigorous exertions, succeeded in obtaining four subscribers, three of them being to the life of our late murdered President, and only one to "Tried and True." I returned to supper at night, almost tired out, and went to bed very early. It was plain to me that something must be done by which I could realize more money among these "sand hillers." They all admired Mr, Lincoln and would buy his life if they had time to read it, but the excitement about the construction of their harbor was just beginning to assume the form of an epidemic, and no one seemed able or willing to spend any time in reading, or even talking about anything but perches of stone, Government piers, dredge-boats, water lots, and eligible corners. One man, a prominent lawyer of the place, upon my asking him to buy "The Life of Lincoln," somewhat startled me by replying, "If the title is all right I will give you one hundred and twenty dollars a foot. Did you say it fronted on the creek?" I explained to him that it was a book and not a water lot, or sand-hill, I was trying to sell, whereat he became disgusted, and refused to hold any further communication with me. But, with all their hurry, they would take time to buy and look at photographs, for these took neither time nor mental labor to comprehend, and left them free to pursue their favorite speculations. It was plain, then, that this was my best line of investment. Accordingly, I ordered another lot of these from Chicago, and while waiting for them to come, made one more effort to break through the crust of speculation which seemed to enclose the entire people. My success was but limited, for a hard day's work only added two names to my list of subscribers for

the life of the President, and one to the list of "Tried and
True."   But when my photographs came, business revived
again; and I soon disposed of all I had, and ordered more.

But my day of usefulness in this place was evidently
on the wane, and I decided to go to La Porte and try my
fortune there for a short time.   I could not canvass there
for "Tried and True," but I could sell photographs and
take names for "The Memorial;" for, although Mr. Kennedy had only appointed me agent for Indianapolis and
Michigan City, he had told me, verbally, that the entire
State was open, and that I might sell anywhere I could.
But at La Porte I fared even worse than at Michigan City,
though from causes altogether different.   The people there
were not so madly engaged in absurd speculations upon
the value of inaccessible sand mountains; but their superior intelligence, and devotion to the memory of our mar-
tyred President, had already induced them to invest very
liberally in remembrances of his greatness; and, in nearly
every house I visited, I found a copy of some one of the
numerous "Lives" which had already found their way
into print.   At another time, and with another work, I
found La Porte to be a most excellent place for book
agents who pursue their labors legitimately and honestly;
but the community was already supplied with what I had
now to sell, and of course my labors were in vain.   But,
notwithstanding my poor success, I liked the place so
much that I almost decided to settle there permanently if
I ever should get money enough ahead to buy me a home
anywhere.   Some of my warmest friends reside in La
Porte; and, whether I ever settle there or not, I shall
always retain a most lively recollection of that most beautiful city of northern Indiana.

Returning to Michigan City, after an absence of three

days, I was fortunate enough to strike a vein which, by being vigorously worked, yielded some very substantial returns. The first thing I did, after my return, was to procure and sell two dozen photographs, which I did in one day. The next day I spent in canvassing, and with a degree of success which astonished even myself—taking no less than eight subscribers for "The Life of Lincoln," three for "Tried and True," and five for "The Home Circle." Such success, in view of my former experience there, was truly surprising, and inclined me to think more kindly of Michigan City and its inhabitants than had been my wont. Nay; I even forgave the lawyer before-mentioned for his absent-mindedness, and nearly resolved not to put him in my book; but, I finally compromised the matter, by deciding to publish the incident, but keep his name to myself; hence, none of my friends need ask me for it. I hope Mr. —— will thank me for even this degree of forbearance.

Having about finished my work in Michigan City, I ordered books for all my subscribers, forwarded Mr. Kennedy the names of subscribers to "The Home Circle," and, when my books came, proceeded to deliver them without delay, having done which I took an account of funds on hand, and found I had enough to pay my fare to Indianapolis and to pay a week's board after I got there. This was eminently satisfactory; for I felt sure that, before the week would expire, I could do enough to again replenish my purse.

Accordingly, I settled up all my bills in Michigan City, and, embarking upon the cars of that horror of all travelers, the Louisville, New Albany, and Chicago Railroad, in due time arrived at the capital city of the Hoosier State. Upon inquiry, and presenting my checks at the baggage-

room of the Union Depot, I found them all right, they
having been there, the baggage-man said, with an air as
if he were relating some wonderful circumstance, a full
week, if not more. I beg to remind the reader that my
trunks had been sent direct from Chicago, and that it had
not taken me a week or more to come from Michigan City
to this place. I make this explanation in order that no
injustice may be done to the rapidity with which the Louisville, New Albany, and Chicago Railroad transports its
passengers; and I take great pleasure in saying, that a
person might, even at that time, go by this route, from
Michigan City to Indianapolis, in less than a week; and,
since then, the management and speed of the cars upon
that road have been materially improved.

My first care was to look for a suitable boarding-place
—the man with whom I had left my trunk, when there before, having gone away; leaving my baggage, however, at
the house of a neighbor until I should call for it. I found
a good room at the house of a Mr. Joseph Aston, No 44
South Tennessee Street; paid him six dollars for a week's
board, in advance, and moved my things there, designing
to make it my home, at least until I had accomplished
one of the objects which first induced me to remove my
residence to Indiana.

CHAPTER XXIII.

Behold me, then, dear reader, fairly domiciled in the State which was to be my future residence. 'T is true, my home had been here for some time, but I had been so much away on business, that, up to this time, I hardly ventured to call myself a Hoosier, even by adoption; but now I felt that the title really belonged to me, and I could say, without any mental reservation, that I was an Indianian.

I did nothing more than to establish my quarters, upon the day of my arrival in the city, it being near nightfall, and I very much wearied when I arrived there; but the next day I went to work with a will, and, by hard and steady effort, succeeded in getting ten subscribers to the "Life of Lincoln," and two for "Tried and True." I ordered a lot of books, of both kinds, and went on with my canvassing, thinking the prospects were very favorable for my doing a good business there. But, alas! how deceptive are all human appearances. I soon found that the flattering prospects, under which I had started out, were but for a day; that they were even more ephemeral than the butterfly; and that, with the works I had, it was impossible to succeed there. The citizens of Indianapolis were too well supplied with literature of the class I was selling, and it was necessary for me to have something else—something which had not been already sold there; and at the same time I was sufficiently aware of the state of the public mind, to know that something con-

nected with the late rebellion would sell better than anything else.

Accordingly, after having labored over a week, and
taken about twenty-one names for all my publications
together, I wrote to a Mr. Lillie, of Chicago, for the agency
of "The Lost Cause," a Southern history of the war, by
Mr. Pollard, late editor of the "Richmond Examiner."
Mr. Lillie referred me to Mr. George B. Fessenden, of Cincinnati, and I at once addressed him on the subject,
receiving by express, in return, the agency of the work,
accompanied with a prospectus, subscription book, and
some instructions. As for the last, however, I fancied
that I knew about as much about the business of a book
agent as Mr. Fessenden did.

I immediately went to work with my new book, and
found that, if I only knew what parties to approach, a very
good business could be done; but I was too much of a
stranger in the city, and knew not where to apply. I
thought if I could get an agent, who was well acquainted
in the city, and have that agent take orders, while I would
deliver the books, we could make the arrangement mutu-
ally profitable. Accordingly I inserted, in the "Herald,"
the following notice:

WANTED—A person, well acquainted in the city, to canvass for the "Southern History of the War, by E. A. Pollard." Call at No. 44 South Tennessee Street. No one
need apply unless they are well acquainted in the city,
and can bring good references.

In a few hours after this notice made its appearance, I
had several callers, and soon succeeded in making an arrangement with a gentleman to canvass on my own terms.
It is not necessary to give these terms to the reader, suffice it to say, that it worked well, and I soon found I could

pay my agent all that I had agreed to, and still make more money than when I was alone. While he canvassed, I delivered the books, and also continued my trade in photographs, of which I sold a great many; and the profits upon them being enormous, I was doing a very fine business. In about two weeks we had sold no less than fifty copies of "The Lost Cause," and my profits from that source alone were about fifty dollars. Add to this the fact that I made about as much more from the sale of photographs, and the reader will have no difficulty in comprehending the fact that my business was in a flourishing condition.

About this time I learned that the property left by my brother Frank, when he went into the rebel army, had been confiscated by order of the authorities at Washington, and made application for its restitution; alleging my own loyalty as the ground of my claim. I received a favorable reply to my application, and was fully satisfied that if I had the money to go South, and hunt up the necessary proofs, and submit them to the consideration of the proper officers, there would be no difficulty in my succeeding; but there was the rub. The one hundred dollars in my possession would go but a little way in the prosecution of a claim of so much magnitude as this, and whatever was to be done must be done quickly, and the only thing I could do was to work the harder, and raise all that I possibly could for this purpose.

The holidays were close at hand, and it occurred to me that if I had a book suitable for a Christmas or New-Year's gift, I might do well with that for the next two or three weeks, and having noticed in the Journal the advertisement of such a book, published by a Mr. Newell, in Vinton's Block, I called upon him, and secured the agency for the sale of it.   It was called The Republican Court, and was a most beautifully gotten-up book—just the thing for a young man to use in softening the obdurate heart of his mistress.   Armed with this document, in addition to those I had on hand already, I went to work with a vigor which produced the most happy results, and, in a short time, felt myself able, pecuniarily, to undertake my contemplated journey to the South.

Before starting, however, I shipped, by express, to a dear friend in San Francisco, California, a copy of The Republican Court, The Lost Cause, and a finely-bound copy of Robinson Crusoe, as a holiday gift.   I trust he received them in due time, and that they served to assure him that there was one in the world who will never, never forget his kindness to her in her hour of trouble.

I then arranged my affairs so as to leave all my business in the city in the hands of the agent before referred to, and started out, intending to go to the South before I came back to Indianapolis again, which must be by the first of April next ensuing.   I had commenced proceedings for a divorce from my husband, and as the case would be tried in April, I felt that it was necessary for me to be in the city at that time.

I went as far as Shelbyville, in company with another lady; stepped off there, and staid a few days, selling several books, and then went on to Cincinnati, where I wished to have an interview with Mr. Fessenden, relative to affairs in Indianapolis, and some other business matters. In due time I arrived in Cincinnati and at once called on Mr. Fessenden, who was not a little surprised to see me, and earnestly asked me why I had left Indianapolis.   I replied by giving him the address of my agent there, and telling him that I had left everything in his hands, and that I thought he would find no cause of complaint against him.

"But, Mrs. Nelles," said he, "we cannot give you up as an agent. You are altogether too valuable to us."

"But I have worked a long time for you," said I, "and now I must work for myself a little."

"Have you not been working for yourself, at the same time you were working for me? Has not the sale of my publications been profitable to you, as well as to me?"

"Yes; but there are other matters which claim my attention."

"What are these other matters? Are you going to marry and give up selling books?"

"No," I replied, laughing; "I am not going to marry. I am going to return to my old home in the South."

And then I told him about my application for the restitution of the confiscated property of my brother, and that I was going South to find the evidence relative to it.

"Just the thing," said he. "Take some of my publications along with you to sell, and thus help to defray your expenses. I have no agents in the South, and you can sell wherever you see proper."

"But times are so hard down there, that I am afraid nothing can be done."

"I do not suppose you can sell as many books there as you can in the North, but still I believe you can do something, and every little helps, you know."

"What have you that I can sell there?"

"Take 'The Lost Cause.'"

"I would prefer something else."

"Well, I have a new book, just out, with which I am sure you can do well there. I will appoint you a roving agent anywhere in the Southern States."

" What is it?"

"The General History of Freemasonry in Europe; translated from the French of Emanuel Rebold, by J. F. Brennan, Esq."

The title of the book struck me favorably. I had long been an ardent admirer of Freemasonry; my father, and brother Frank, had both been Masons, as also my step-father, Captain Lake; and I felt that these facts gave me some claims upon the fraternity, and that, aside from the intrinsic merits of the work, they would aid me in effecting sales of it among the craft. I knew, too, that Freemasonry had very many followers in the South, and that they were generally very ardently attached to the order, and would be more likely to buy a book upon that subject than any other. I had my father's diploma in my possession, and the exhibition of this would help to prove my claims upon the Masonic brotherhood; and, even if I failed in the attempt to sell, it would involve but very little expense—only the cost of the outfit—while, if I succeeded, the result could not be otherwise than good, in more senses than one. These reflections decided me in favor of taking the appointment he offered me; and I told him I would accept his proposition, paid him for a book, bid him good-bye, and returned to my hotel.

Upon examining the book, I found the names of some of my ancestors honorably mentioned in its pages, and was more than ever satisfied that I had accepted Mr. Fessenden's proposition. I now felt that I had a direct personal interest in the work; for, while I was carrying on my accustomed avocation, I was also spreading a knowledge of the virtues and usefulness of my revered grand-father; and this afforded me no small satisfaction. And this is one reason, among others, why I have continued in the sale of this work until the present time, and why I regard it with more affection than any work I have ever sold.

The same evening that I left Mr. Fessenden, I took passage, on board a river packet, for Memphis; and, about five o'clock in the evening, she cast off her moorings, and quietly dropped down the stream. It was dark, and there was nothing to be seen, and nothing to detain me on deck; so I went to my state-room, and, at an early hour, retired to rest.

In due time, and without any incidents worthy of note, I arrived at Memphis. My trip, down the river, had been very pleasant, and I had enjoyed it very much; but a period was now to be put to my enjoyment: for, when we rounded to at the landing at Memphis, it was raining with violence, and the mud lay, in the streets, apparently of an interminable depth. In view of this state of facts, I decided to make my stay in Memphis of very brief duration. I had intended trying to sell some books there; but the weather was such as evidently to render hopeless any attempt at canvassing, and, of course, I must forego it for the present, and hope for better weather on my return.

There were two or three men in Memphis whom it was necessary for me to see, in connection with the business which had originally brought me to the South, and the labor of wading through the mud and rain to hunt them up, was all I cared about attempting; but from that it would not do to shrink. Beside, I had encountered these adversaries before, and had learned the very important fact that I was neither sugar nor salt, and that there was not the least danger of my melting away. Accordingly, armed with a formidable cotton umbrella, and a pair of stout brogans, I plunged into the apparently endless and bottom-

less sea of mud before me, and, bravely breasting its waves,
in due time found the parties of whom I was in search.
My interviews with every one of them were in the highest
degree satisfactory; and it was with no little elation of
spirits that I announced to myself that my business was
completed, and took the cars for Atlanta, the next step in
my journey, and where I hoped to complete the evidence
which was to put me in possession of my deceased brother's
estates.

As we rolled onward toward Atlanta, through a region
of country every foot of which had been the scene of the
desolating operations of hostile armies, how did my heart
throb with anguish as I gazed upon the almost entire destruction of that once lovely land! For miles upon miles
the country was destitute of fences, and, in many instances,
of houses, while the very humblest forms of vegetation
seemed trodden out of existence, and even out of sight,
under the hoofs of animals and the feet of thousands of
armed men; acres upon acres of ground, which had once
borne magnificent crops of corn, and cotton, and tobacco,
and wheat, now wearied and pained the eye by their broad
stretch of lifeless brown, unrelieved by the least display
of green; the long lines of trenches and rifle-pits told elo-
quent stories of hours of toil expended for the sole purpose
of more effectually destroying our fellow-men; the little
mounds of earth, which here and there marked the landscape in every direction, spoke eloquently of some brave
soul who, clad either in the blue or the gray, had offered
up his life upon the altar of a cause which, to him, was holy
and just; while, occasionally, a thicker and more numerous collection of these tell-tale heaps of earth would speak
of the mortal and breathless struggle in which those who
now rested there so quietly, had once manfully and bravely

borne their part. What mattered it to me, as I gazed upon these speaking monuments of brave men's prowess, whether they held the corses of our own brave soldier boys, or whether those lonely resting-places were filled with the remains of the misguided, but no less brave, soldiers of the confederacy? They were alike the resting-places of brave and true men, each one of whom had some friends in some far-off land, perchance, to mourn their loss, and shed the silent tear of sorrow o'er their untimely decease; and, though I had no sympathy with the cause which had called these brave men to arms, still I could respect their manhood, their devotion to their convictions of right, and could drop the sympathetic tear over their violent and bloody decease. I could not but think that, somewhere in the broad, sunny lands of which those around us were a part, I had an only and dearly loved brother, whose head was pillowed, until the last great day, upon just such a lowly bed as these; who had fallen in the same cause, which I believed to be unjust and unholy; who had fallen, as the brave men around us had fallen, in the discharge of what he deemed to be his duty; and my heart was incapable of entertaining any feeling of bitterness toward any of the fallen braves amid whose tombs our train was wending its way.

From these reflections, my mind naturally wandered away to the fate of the unfortunate people who had inhabited this country before the breaking out of the rebellion. Although a long time had elapsed since the close of hostilities, the country, in this particular, as well as in all others, still bore traces of the fearful struggle through which it had passed, and in the plainest manner indicated the fearful character of the punishment which their folly and madness had brought upon this miserable people. It was true, it was the fruit of their own crime and folly, and

21

for which they ought to suffer; but surely their punishment had been equal to the magnitude of their offense, and ought to fully satisfy the most clamorous demands of vengeance. Surely their ruined, desolated farms; their property destroyed, or taken for military purposes, without the possibility of their receiving any compensation; their once happy homes, from which they had been compelled to flee to avoid the deadly hail-storm of bullets which swept over them, and which were too often mere masses of blackened and shapeless ruins; the accumulations of years of toil and privation swept away forever; and, above all, the sable weeds of mourning, which enveloped every Southern face, were most powerful evidences of the severity of the punishment meted out to them, and ought, as far as human vengeance can go, to fully compensate for the wrong they had done. It is true, that the suffering, caused by the war, had not fallen upon this section alone; it is true, that by the firesides of the North, places had been made vacant, and many a brave son, noble brother, and kind, indulgent husband and father had gone forth from loving friends never to return; that woe and misery had there, too, as well as in the South, been sown broadcast to gratify the most gigantic and criminal ambition of the age; but all the other sad results of the conflict had been visited upon the South alone. I am no apologist for the crime which the leaders of the rebellion inaugurated against the most beneficent and the freest government upon which the sun ever shone, and upon them I would willingly see visited the most direful punishment which the human imagination could devise; but for their poor, deluded, misguided followers, the evidences of suffering which I saw on all sides awakened in my breast naught but feelings of the most intense pity.

There was another reflection which occurred to my mind, in connection with this subject, and which seems to me to have no little bearing on the determination of the policy with which the two sections ought to be regarded in contemplating the results of the contest. While both sections alike mourn the loss of thousands of fallen braves, the sorrow of the loyalists is tempered with their well-earned and well-merited thought of glorious victory won, and they can exult in the proud consciousness that the friends whom they mourn fell in defense of a holy and noble cause, and by their deaths aided in the achievement of the grand triumph of right and justice. But to the South none of the consolations flowing from this reflection are vouchsafed. Their cup of sorrow is unmixed by any pleasing thoughts, save the recollection of the personal bravery of the fallen, while its bitterness is enhanced by the deep humiliation of utter defeat, and the fact that the valuable lives, so lost, were sacrificed in an unjust and iniquitous cause. If anything can add poignancy to the sorrows they must endure, it must be this very reflection.

But while my mind was thus dwelling upon the results of the war, the cars were bearing me onward to Atlanta, and at last the Gate City of the South burst upon our view; but, alas! it was no longer the lovely, flourishing city it was when I last beheld it. Then long rows of magnificent structures lined all its principal streets, while its suburbs were filled with magnificent private residences, adorned with all that wealth could purchase, or that taste of man could devise to gratify the senses, or enhance the peace and happiness which there reigned supreme. Now, the entire business part of the city was a mass of shapeless and unsighty ruins. Whole blocks, which had once stood erect, tall and stately, and were the pride, not only of their owners, but of every denizen of the city, were now mere heaps of rubbish, bricks and mortar; while, in many instances, the palatial residences and magnificent grounds of the suburbs had, by their occupancy as quarters for troops, been shorn of all their original beauty, and reduced to a state of chaos and confusion, from which it would take years to resuscitate them, even if they could ever be restored to anything like their former condition. I had read, in the public journals, the accounts of the hard fate which befell the city of Atlanta when, at the end of a campaign almost unparalleled in history, she fell into the hands of Sherman and his victorious legions; but I was utterly unprepared for the sad scene of desolation which was presented to my view. Although I knew that such was the fate of war, and that the curse had been brought upon the city by her own people and friends, still I could not but feel saddened in my inmost heart when I came to fully realize the ruin that had been wrought; and I covered my eyes to shut out the hateful sight, while the hot, scalding tears of agony bedewed my cheeks.

CHAPTER XXIV.

SUCH was my return to Atlanta, after an absence of nearly five years. What a blight had fallen upon the place during that time! And yet it was no worse than the blight which had fallen upon my own life during the same time. The contrast between Atlanta, as it was then, and as I now beheld it, was no greater than the contrast between my situation then, and what it now was. Then I fondly believed myself the wife of a noble and honorable man, and with every prospect of a long and happy life before me, in the enjoyment of which I should cease to remember the sorrows of my childhood. Since then I had learned that I was not his wife; had separated from him, and united my fortunes with those of a man who had proved to be only less base than he—had finally parted with him forever, and was now alone in the world, with no one upon whom I could lean for support under any circumstances. Then I had a dearly loved brother, on whom, in times of sorest distress, I could rely for relief and assistance—now my brother was gone, and I stood alone, the last of my family, and comparatively helpless. Is it strange that, as this terrible view of my situation rushed across my mind, my heart sunk within me, and I again almost wished that I might lie down, too, and die, and be at rest forever? But why indulge these gloomy reflections? I had work to do, and would strive in the midst of my labors to forget all my sorrows. But this was easier said than done, for at every step I took there was

something to remind me of the past, and of my bitter loneliness.

I went out to the Lake mansion. It was like all the
rest, in ruins. Some portions of the walls were standing,
but that was all—the grounds, the shrubbery, the fences,
the grove which had once been the pride and admiration
of the surrounding country—all were gone, and only sufficient traces remained to indicate what had once been
there and remind me of their former beauty. At the
negro-quarters I found some of the old servants of the
plantation, who were living there and cultivating some of
the ground, under the protection of the Freedman's Bureau. Tom and Silvie were both dead, they told me, while
Caroline had married, and was living at some distance
from there, with a little family of children growing up
around her.

Sick at heart, I turned away, and went in search of the
graves of my loved ones. There they lay, side by side,
but so neglected and overgrown with weeds that it was
with difficulty I could find them. There were the graves
of mother, Henry, Kate, baby May, and my own little
darling, and another had been added since I was there
last. A plain board stood at its head, with simply the
words Frank Hamilton on it. This, then, was the last
resting-place of the last survivor of my family. As I
stood thus alone by the graves of my departed friends,
my mind wandered back to the time when I stood thus
by the side of my father's tomb, in the far off city of Philadelphia, and a sense of my utter loneliness so overcame
me that I burst into tears, and, offering up a prayer to my
Heavenly Father for protection, I turned and left the
ground. As I wandered back to the city, I thought how
much pleasure I had anticipated in the early days of my

marriage with Frank Nelles, in paying the visit I had just made. I had then contemplated this visit with him at my side, while his tears would mingle with mine in silent respect to the memory of my departed kinsmen. There, too, by the side of those graves, I would put him in possession of all the facts in my past history, of which he had hitherto been kept in ignorance, and would implore his pardon for the partial deception I had practiced upon him; but, like all my other castles of air, this had now fallen about my ears, and was lying in ruins at my feet. Such had ever been my life—one constant scene of disappointments and sorrows.

I returned to the city and put up at the only hotel there was in the place, where I passed the night almost in tears, for sleep I could not. My mind was too much occupied with gloomy reminiscences of the past, and dark forebodings of the future, to allow me to rest, and with the first flush of the dawn I arose from my uneasy couch to attempt the work which had brought me there, intending to transact it as speedily as possible, and bid adieu forever to a place so fraught with sorrowful memories as was now the city of Atlanta. How I fretted until the arrival of business hours would enable me to visit the public offices, and attend to the matter which I hoped would put me in possession of wealth, and enable me to give up the life of a book agent forever. I may now whisper in the ear of my reader, however, that were I in possession of the most boundless wealth, I do not think I would give up the avocation of buying and selling books as an agent. I would still follow the business, not as a means of making money simply, though, as has already appeared in these pages, it is very profitable, but from pure love of it. This is in confidence, and is the result of my present views—

then everything was distasteful to me, and my only
thought was to get the means which my brother had provided for my support; get my divorce from Nelles; then
finish this history of my life; and, after placing a copy of
it in his hands, retire from the public gaze forever. Yes, I
would recover my property; would get Carrie, and adopt
some little orphan boy for a playmate for her; would let
Frank Nelles know what he had lost by his cruelty and
treachery to me; and would then, in seclusion, and in the
society alone of my dear children, find consolation for all
the sorrows I had endured. These were, then, my plans;
but I am bound to confess that, to a great extent, they
have thus far failed of being realized.

The mystic hour of nine—standard hour with men who
are elected to serve the will of the people—having at
length arrived, I sallied forth to see what could be done
toward the fulfillment of my mission. My first call was
at the office of the Register of Deeds, which I found occupied by a very polite and accommodating gentleman.
The records had, fortunately, escaped the storm of general destruction which had swept over the devoted city;
and we were soon immersed in a profound examination of
their pages. We soon found where Frank had made over
all his property to me, in the event of his decease. This
was the first step gained in the investigation; but now
the question arose, what was the present condition of the
property thus conveyed? Was it in such a condition that
it could be identified, and a tangible claim for its restitution be presented to the General Government? Further
investigation revealed the fact that, much of it had been
sold for taxes, under the authority of the Confederate
Government—all had been confiscated, upon the suppression of the rebellion, and there seemed little prospect of

recovering anything, except at the end of a long course of expensive litigation, which I was but illy prepared to undertake. My heart was not a little dismayed at the prospect before me; but, nevertheless, I had already gone too far, and expended too much money, to think of shrinking from the contest at the present stage. Accordingly, I procured, from the recorder, duly certified copies of all the deeds in any way bearing upon my property (or that which I claimed), and went to the office of an attorney, whom he recommended as the best in the city, designing to place all the papers in his hands, and leave him to pursue his own judgment as to the best course of proceeding, while I returned to my home in Indiana, obtained my divorce, and supported myself at my business, until the final issue of my application at Washington.

I was fortunate in securing the services of an attorney of the highest degree of talent, and whose eminence in his profession was a sure guarantee that my affairs would receive the most prompt and careful attention at his hands—none other than the Hon. F. M. Goodman. He at once undertook my case, and assured me that no pains or trouble should be spared to bring it to an early and successful issue. Satisfied that I had done all that could be done to insure success, I decided not to remain any longer in Atlanta, but to return, at once, to Indiana. I hated to leave the place without making any efforts whatever for the sale of my book; but, the truth was, that everything was in such a depressed condition there, that I felt sure any effort of mine would be vain. There was no money in the country, and without that "root of all evil," it was but little use for me to take any names for the book, even if the people would, under such circumstances, be likely to look with favor upon a proposition to subscribe. Beside, there was too many unpleasant memories clustering around that section of country for me to remain there any longer than stern necessity demanded.

Accordingly, as soon as my arrangements with Mr. Goodman were completed to my satisfaction, I settled my bill at the hotel and took the first train for Chattanooga, having been in Atlanta just four days, instead of four weeks, at least, as I had intended when leaving Cincinnati.

I omitted to say, in its proper place, that I had written from Memphis, on my way down, to a son of my husband in Chicago; to which letter, however, I never received any answer; thus proving that I was not only cast off by my husband, but also by the whole family; no doubt through the influence of him from whom I had a right to expect different treatment. But the only effect of this neglect was to strengthen and confirm me in the resolution to sever my connection with them forever, by means of the decree of divorce for which I was about applying.

From Chattanooga I pursued my way through Nashville to Louisville, whence I went by mail-packet to Cincinnati, only stopping at each place so long as was necessary on account of the delay in connection of trains and the like. I reached Cincinnati in four days from the time of leaving Atlanta—having only been absent about three weeks.

I called at once upon Mr. Fessenden, who expressed no little astonishment at seeing me back so soon, and still more when I informed him that I had not sold a single copy of the History of Freemasonry. I did not tell him that the book had not been once offered for sale, but told him that times were so hard there that nothing could be done, and that I had, therefore, decided to return to a more promising field. He asked me something about the business which had taken me there, but I evaded any direct information relative to it, and only told him that, in the present confused state of affairs there, it was impossible to accomplish any thing in any line of business.

I then returned to the subject of "The General History of Freemasonry," and told him that, as I had done so poorly in my trip to the South, I thought he ought to give me a chance to make myself whole by giving me an opportunity to sell the book where there could be something made of it. He asked me where I would like to work. I told him I would like the entire State of Indiana, and the counties of Southern Michigan along the line of the Michigan Southern & Northern Indiana Railroad. He replied, with a smile, that my desires were very moderate, and that he thought he could gratify them, adding, with a slight dash of flattery, that he knew of no one to whom he would rather intrust this district than to myself. I also made arrangements with him to canvass the same territory for "The History of Morgan's Cavalry," which last, however, I kept but a short time.

My business in Cincinnati being ended, I left that city the next morning, for Indianapolis, to devote myself once more to my chosen avocation, and, at the same time, attend to getting my divorce, after which I would be free to change my location, or do anything else, at my own pleasure. I had not said anything to any one about the motive which induced my visit to the South, nor, indeed, did anybody in Indianapolis know that my journey had been extended beyond Memphis; and I decided not to enlighten anybody at the present, either as to where I had been, or as to my prospects in the South. Certainly, it was nobody's business, and I would only leave them to suppose that my absence had been caused by some matter in connection with my agency.

In due time I arrived in Indianapolis, and went at once to my old boarding-house, at No. 44 South Tennessee street, where I was very gladly welcomed by all the family. In pursuance of my resolution, I said nothing about my Southern journey, merely going about my business as usual, and occasionally dropping a remark about the condition of affairs in Memphis, in order to convey the impression that that city had been my stopping-place during my absence from home.

In the mean time, my attorneys had commenced proceedings for my divorce, and, Mr. Nelles being a non-resident of the State, it was necessary to advertise the pendency of the suit in some newspaper published in the city. This was rather unpleasant, as giving too much publicity to a matter about which I, very naturally, desired as much secresy as possible; but there was no help for it, and, accordingly, the necessary affidavit was filed, and the cause duly published in the Weekly Indiana State Journal. After this expose of one of my objects in locating at Indianapolis, it was with fear and trembling that I attempted to do anything in the way of canvassing. It seemed to me that every one must have read it, that they would know who I was, and would make unpleasant comments about it whenever I applied for a subscriber. Doubtless my fears were entirely unfounded, and that not one person in every thousand of the inhabitants of Indianapolis had ever seen the notice, or would know to whom it referred; but still they existed, and they finally made so much impression on my mind as to induce me to withdraw almost entirely from active canvassing myself.

But as I had not yet succeeded in getting an agent to

my satisfaction, I had to keep on at work myself, and with my Masonic work I was doing very well. In three days' time I took no less than twenty-five subscribers for this work, the mayor of the city being the first one; and to his kindness I am indebted for much of my success there. I was but little acquainted with the Masonic fraternity there, but, having been informed that Mayor Cavin was one, I had asked him to give me the names of men whom he thought would be likely to take the book. He very kindly gave me a long list of names, and in no one instance did I fail to sell a copy of the work to one whose name he had given me. I sold, altogether, about one hundred copies of this work in Indianapolis; many of them to members of the Legislature, which happened to be in session at the time I was canvassing there.

During the same time I had sold only five or six copies of the "History of Morgan's Cavalry," and feeling that I could not devote sufficient time to this work, without interfering with the other, I gave it up entirely, and returned to Mr. Fessenden several copies already ordered. In fact, I was so much interested in the sale of the Masonic history, and was succeeding so well with it, that I really felt but little inclination to work for anything else.

Having, however, learned by accident that all the subscribers to "The Lost Cause" had not been supplied, and that there was some dissatisfaction among them in consequence, I called upon Mr. Barbour, the gentleman in whose hands I had left the agency for that work upon my starting South, took from him his list of subscribers, revoked his agency, and took charge of the sales of the work in person. I delivered books to all whose names he had taken, and took two or three new subscribers; then, finding it an up-hill business, I declined to work for it any

more, and finally gave up canvassing for everything ex·
cept the Masonic history, devoting all my time and attention to that.

With this work I was doing very well, indeed. I had
now been at work for it only about a month, and, as the
reader is already informed, had sold about one hundred
copies; but Indianapolis had been pretty thoroughly canvassed, and sales were getting very dull. I, therefore,
decided to leave there, for a time, and try my fortune a
little farther north—at Lafayette, and some of the other
towns along the line of the Wabash Valley Railroad. I
also decided that I would not try to get subscribers for
anything but the Masonic history, believing that it would
only be a waste of time to do so. My experience had
taught me that the agent who attempted to canvass, at the
same time, for five or six different works, was not likely to
do well with any of them. The best way, in my judgment, is to select some good work, and give all one's
efforts to that, to the utter exclusion of everything else.
Of course, a reasonable degree of sagacity must be exercised in the selection of a suitable work with which to
travel; but if one attempts to work for several publications at the same time, they are likely, by a division of
their exertions, to succeed in making a failure with all.

Having decided to visit Lafayette, I called upon a prominent Mason of Indianapolis, and asked him to give me a
letter of introduction to somebody, in that place, who
would be likely to extend to me some aid in introducing
the work. He very readily and cheerfully complied with
my request, and gave me letters to several parties there.
Perhaps there is no more suitable opportunity than this,
to acknowledge the obligations I am under to the Masonic
fraternity, as a body, for the kindness and assistance they

have invariably rendered me in selling this work. It has
been my usual custom, upon visiting any place for the
first time, to call upon some prominent member, or members, of the fraternity, for lists of names to guide me in my
canvassing; and again, upon leaving for another place, to
ask for letters of introduction to some leading member of
the Order in the place whither I was going; and in no
solitary instance has compliance with these requests been
refused; and the assistance, thus rendered, has been invaluable to me, and will be ever most gratefully remembered;
and I desire here to return my heartfelt thanks, not only
to each and every one of the members of that ancient and
honorable Order, for the uniform kindness and courtesy
with which they have treated me, but especially to those
who have assisted me in the manner above indicated.
May their kindness be returned to them a thousand fold.

In due time I arrived in La Fayette, and at once called
upon one of the gentlemen to whom I had received a letter of introduction. He treated me with the kindness
which has always marked the conduct of the fraternity
toward me, bought a book, and introduced me to several
other gentlemen, all of whom purchased books. I sold
five or six copies there, and having thus sown seed
which I hoped would, in time, bear abundant fruit, I decided to leave La Fayette, a short time, go up to Delphi
and Logansport, see what could be done there, and return
to La Fayette again on my way to Indianapolis. This
trip was the poorest which ever occurred in all my experience as a book agent. I was absent some three days
from La Fayette, and did not sell a single copy of the
work during the whole time. The Masons, in all the
places visited by me, seemed more dead than alive—more
intent on making money than acquainting themselves with

the history and origin of their order—more devoted to the worship of Mammon, than to the cultivation of a knowledge of the science of which this fraternity claims to be one of the principal exponents. There was among them a state of coldness and indifference to the good of the Order, which I have very rarely found. May they arouse from their lethargy in time to prevent their everlasting dissolution as an order.

The same feeling prevailed to a considerable extent, though in not quite so great a degree, at La Fayette; and I became convinced that, for the present, at least, I could not do enough there to pay expenses. My trip had already cost me much more than the profits realized from it, and, under such circumstances, it was worse than folly to extend my stay in the place. I therefore packed up my "traps" and returned home, fully resolved never to canvass along the line of the Wabash Valley Railroad, or, at least, until there was some evidence of more vitality among the Masons there.

CHAPTER XXV.

Upon my return to Indianapolis, I decided to change my plan of operations, for a time. I had been traveling constantly since entering upon the duties of a book agent, was weary and somewhat worn down, and needed some rest. The plan adopted, for a time, was this—to advertise for agents to canvass in my field, while I would supply them with the work, as a sort of general agent, and would take a class in my old occupation—that of teaching painting. Accordingly, I resumed the agency of two or three works, which I had discarded; obtained one or two others, so as to be able to supply my agents with any thing they might desire; obtained a suitable room in which to receive my pupils, and advertised in several of the leading papers, throughout the State, for agents. I also inserted advertisements for pupils, in all the papers of the city, and commenced reviewing and furbishing up my artistic qualities.

Applications for employment, as agents, were soon very numerous, and in a few weeks I had no less than a dozen agents at work for me, in different parts of the State. The works with which they were furnished were all that I had ever canvassed for, with the addition of a most beautiful little book for the juvenile portion of the community, entitled "The Children's Album." I do not think I have ever known a work more interesting, or more beneficial, to be put in the hands of the rising generation. I charge the publishers nothing for this notice of their work, for it

merits all and more than can be said in its favor by so
poor a pen as mine.

While making and perfecting these arrangements, the
other branch of business marked out for myself had not
been neglected. Applications for admission to my school
of painting had poured in upon me, and my class was
soon as large as my rooms would allow me to accommodate, and several applicants had been refused admission
for want of room. And so assiduously had I practiced
my art that I found myself qualified to impart instruction,
not only to their entire satisfaction, but, what was much
better, to my own. And thus matters went on swimmingly, and, for a time, I succeeded better, pecuniarily,
than I had at any time since starting as a book agent.
But my expenses were very heavy, and I did not lay up
money very fast. Aside from my ordinary expenses of
every-day life, the extensive litigation I was conducting,
both at Indianapolis and Atlanta, was a constant drain
on my finances, and kept me at rather a low ebb. There
were constant applications from my counsel for money
for some purpose or other—now, five dollars to pay for
a certified copy of some old deed or other; then ten or
fifteen dollars to pay for taking depositions; again ten dollars would be wanted for searching some record at Washington, and so it went on. I was making money fast, and,
had it not been for these constant demands upon my
purse, could have accumulated some property, but it would
take a princely income to stand these prodigious drains
upon it. But I looked forward with hope to the time
when it would all be at an end, and the money I was now
forced to expend for these objects would be saved to me,
when better times must certainly ensue.

About this time I had an operation performed on my

left eye, which had been affected from my birth. It turned outwardly, and, aside from its disfiguring effect upon my countenance, it was, at times, a source of considerable annoyance to me, and not a little interfered with my sight. There was a professional oculist in the city, by the name of Dr. Charles Wall, who sustained a very high name in his profession, and who had published some certificates of very remarkable cures performed under his treatment; and I had myself known of several very bad cases of "cross eyes" which he had treated with the utmost success. I made up my mind to apply to him for relief from my affliction, and, accordingly, called at his office and asked him if he could straighten my eye. He examined it, asked me some questions about it, and said he could cure it by performing a surgical operation upon it. I told him, if it was to be operated upon, I would like to have some friend present at the time, and he replied that he would like to have some medical gentleman witness the operation, and that, if it suited me, he would perform it at ten o'clock the next day. I told him that Dr. Athon and Dr. Barnes were friends of mine, and that, if he had no objections, I would bring them with me at that time; to which he very readily assented, saying it was just what he would have desired.

At the appointed time the next morning, Dr. Athon, Dr. Barnes and myself, went to Dr. Wall's office, No. 21 West Maryland street, and I took my seat in the operating chair. The doctors wanted me to take chloroform, or some other anæsthetic agent; but this I refused to do, feeling assured that my courage and nerve were sufficient to endure the operation, and wishing to see all that was done, especially as I was myself to be the victim. Well, I had my own way, and the operation was performed while I was in my natural state; nor would I even suffer any one to hold my hands or head. The operation was short, and much less painful than I had anticipated, but still very unpleasant.

I immediately returned to my boarding-house, and, for half an hour or so, experienced no uneasiness from the cutting of my eye: then suddenly began a sharp pain in the eye-ball, which continued all day and all night, and gave me no little alarm, lest it should involve the loss of sight in that eye. When I arose the next morning, and looked in the glass, I found that quite a large lump had grown up on my eye where he had cut it; and, still more alarmed than ever, I hastened as early as I could to Dr. Wall's office. He smiled at my fears, and told me the lump would all disappear in a short time; that it was but the natural result of the operation, and need give me no uneasiness. He gave me some eye-water, and a small brush to apply it with, and I went away, feeling very much relieved; for I had the utmost confidence in his skill and ability.

As I shall not recur to this subject again, I may remark here that my expectations of benefit from this operation have been but partially realized, and that, though I paid Dr. Wall a very liberal fee for performing the operation, my eye has really received but very little benefit from it. It is better than when I went to him, but still far from perfect, as will be apparent to any one who will examine the portrait which forms the frontispiece of the work. Still, I do not condemn the doctor, for, I doubt not, he is well-skilled in diseases of the eye; though, in my own case, his success was not so decided as I hoped, and had been led by him to expect.

Finding that the condition of my eye interfered somewhat with my convenience and success as a teacher of painting, I concluded to give up my class for a time, and resume my travels, at least until my eye should be fully recovered from the effects of the recent operation. Before setting out, however, I wanted to learn the art of cutting dresses by a new method, and connect that with my book agency, believing it would be a source of considerable profit to me. I accordingly went to a Mrs. S. C. Ewing, and applied for instruction in the coveted art. She charged twelve dollars for giving lessons, which was more money than I really knew how to spare; but I had a painting, worth fifteen dollars, which I proposed to give her for my course of instruction, and she accepted my offer. The art was very easy to acquire, and in one day I could cut and fit dresses, by this mode, as well as Mrs. Ewing herself.

With my books and some charts, I then started out, not doubting I should do well; but, as I soon found, and as the reader will soon see, the result did not equal my anticipations; and I found, upon this trip, another illustration of the truth of the proposition I advanced some time since: that the book agent whose exertions are divided among several things, is not likely to succeed well with anything.

Upon leaving Indianapolis I went at once to Lebanon, the county seat of Boone county. It was just about dark when I arrived there, and, of course, nothing could be done that night. I went to the Andrews' House for the night, wading through mud nearly a foot deep to get there, for it had been raining several days, and the streets were almost impassable. The next morning I went to a printing office and engaged one hundred small circulars to be printed and distributed, setting forth the value of my new system of cutting dresses, and went out to canvass for "The History of Freemasonry" while they were being circulated, for I had brought ten copies of the work with me. I visited all the business places in Lebanon, during the forenoon, and succeeded in selling three copies of the book, which, I think, was doing very well, considering the size of the town.

By this time my advertisements had been distributed, and, after eating a hearty dinner, I set out to see what could be done with my charts. Of course, my calls were now made upon the ladies, at their houses, instead of at the business places. At the first house at which I called, the following conversation ensued:

"Good morning, madam. I am selling charts for a new mode of cutting dresses—the most perfect thing of the kind I ever saw—and teaching the use of them. Would you like to learn?"

"Well, I don't know whether it would be of much benefit to me or not. I generally have my dresses cut by a dressmaker."

"But, by the use of this, you can cut and fit your own dresses, and thus save trouble and expense."

"There are so many humbugs, now-a-days, that one hardly knows what or whom to trust; and I believe I will not have anything to do with it."

"But, madam, you can see for yourself that this is no humbug. It is so simple and plain that any one can understand it, and so certain in its results that it is almost impossible to make a mistake, or have an ill-fitting dress. I am very sure you would like it."

"Well," said she, after examining it some time, "I do like its appearance, and would like to learn; but, to tell the truth, I have not got the money."

"Well, madam, I shall be in town for several days—it may be for a week—and if you will board me while I stay here, I will teach you the art, and furnish you with a chart."

"How long will you be here?"

"I can not tell exactly. Until I have canvassed the whole of the town. It may be two or three days, or it may be a week; though probably not so long."

"Upon those terms I will take lessons. You can come here at any time you choose."

I at once sat down, gave her a lesson, and explained the use of the chart to her; then sent to the Andrews' House for my baggage, and again set out upon my canvassing. I felt very well, for I had made a beginning; the lady, whose name I had obtained, was one of the leaders in the little social circle of the place, and I felt no doubt her influence would aid me in the prosecution of my work; and the result showed that I was not mistaken.

At the next house, the lady was very cold and distant; did not care about looking at my charts, or hearing my explanations; but as soon as I told her that Mrs. Dr. M'Cloud (the lady with whom I was stopping) was learning, as was also Mrs. Andrews, at the hotel, her whole manner changed, and she at once manifested the utmost interest in it. She finally concluded she very much wanted to learn, but would not subscribe until she consulted with her husband, who would not be at home until tea-time. Could I call again, in the evening, or the next morning? Certainly; I would call the next morning, and hoped to be honored with her patronàge. With this assurance I left her, receiving from her a parting injunction to call the next day; and I may remark here, that this injunction was cheerfully and faithfully obeyed, and that I added her name to my list of subscribers. Such is the result and power of rank and fashion! Had not Mrs. Dr. M'Cloud become a subscriber, this lady would not; and, doubtless, the same remark will apply to every lady whose name I procured in Lebanon. Fashionable society, in Lebanon, as elsewhere, is very much like a flock of sheep; they will stand huddled together, uncertain what to do, until some one, with more decision than the others, makes a break in some particular direction, when, pell-mell, away go the whole herd, following closely in the tracks of their leader, without the least regard for consequences. This gregarious disposition of the human race has been of immense service to me in many instances besides the one above mentioned.

I canvassed the remainder of the day, and at night had four ladies' engaged to learn dress-cutting, beside several others who, like my friend above mentioned, wanted to consult their husbands about the matter before incurring any expense; and I found that, in every instance of the kind, the promise to consult "husband" was equivalent to a promise to subscribe; thus proving to my mind either that the ladies in Lebanon have very kind and indulgent husbands, or that they have the art of governing their liege lords more skillfully and successfully than their sisters in some other parts of the world of which I have some knowledge.

I remained in Lebanon about a week, and finding that my work there was practically done, and that no more money was to be made there, I went to Thorntown, in the same county. I had done very well in Lebanon, but was destined to fare still better in the place to which I had now come, owing, in part, to the spirit of rivalry existing between the two towns, in which the ladies of each bore their full share; for no sooner did I exhibit to the ladies of Thorntown the list of names I had obtained at Lebanon, than they, at once, said Lebanon should not go ahead of them in anything pertaining to the world of fashion, and I soon had all I could do. This rivalry seemed very foolish to me, but as long as I was reaping the benefits of it, I was not disposed to utter any complaints, or attempt to quell it.

I remained in Thorntown three days, sold five copies of Masonic history, disposed of a large number of charts, and instructed several ladies in the art of cutting their own dresses, when I left there and went to Attica. Here I fared the poorest, for some time, that I had any where on my present trip. For two days I labored faithfully; but could not get any one either to buy a book or to patronize the new mode of cutting dresses. Meantime my bill at the Revere House, where I stopped, was accumulating, at the rate of three dollars a day, while I was earning nothing at all; and I was fast becoming disheartened. The people all seemed as poor as Job's turkey, or as stingy as a miser, I could not tell which, and I was almost tempted to give up in despair and leave the place, though it was very much against both inclination and principle to give up without doing anything. After reflecting some time upon the matter, I concluded to stay one day longer, visit some of the places I had visited already, and make one more effort to penetrate the crust in which they had intrenched themselves. There was a Mrs. Rodgers, who lived in a fine stone house, and seemed to be a sort of leader among the *ton*, and, though I had already called upon her once, I determined to go there again, and try to make the same arrangement with her that I had with Mrs. M'Cloud, upon going to Lebanon. I could not afford to stay there any longer, and pay three dollars a day for my board, while doing nothing; but if I could get to stay a week with Mrs. Rodgers, and pay my way by giving her instruction and selling her a chart, I could afford that.   Beside, I would then be able to say I had made one sale in the great city of Attica.

Accordingly, the next day I called, for the second time, upon Mrs. Rodgers, at the stone mansion.   She received me quite coolly, and seemed, for a time, very much disinclined to even talk about receiving instruction; but I persevered, and finally made her the same proposition which had succeeded so well with Mrs. M'Cloud.   At this she seemed to relent a little, and we finally made the same arrangement—I was to board with her during my stay there, be it longer or shorter, and, in return, was to teach her the art, and furnish her with a chart.   In pursuance of this arrangement, my baggage was removed to her house that very morning; and I went to work, with renewed zeal, feeling that the crust was now penetrated, and that I might hope for some degree of success.

And I was not disappointed.   The gregarious nature of fashionable society, as at Lebanon, was my very good friend. I told every lady upon whom I called that Mrs. Rodgers was learning of me—a *furore* was created upon the subject, and in two days I had all the applicants for instruction that could possibly be attended to by working early and late.   I was more than gratified—I was delighted at the result of my tactics; and had learned that, to succeed anywhere, it was only necessary to get some leader of fashion interested in my work.   Such is the influence and importance which attaches to a single name; and I determined that, hereafter, wherever I might go to work, I would adopt the same plan, which had succeeded so well here.   If, by its use, I could make sales in the town of Attica, surely I need have no misgivings about trying it any where else.   Anything which would break through the crust there, would penetrate any shell, however old or firmly formed.

I remained in Attica a little over a week, and, upon leaving the place, found that I had made more money than at Lebanon and Thorntown both, notwithstanding the discouraging prospects of the first two days. So much for society being like a flock of sheep.

From Attica I went to Danville, Illinois, and at once entered upon a very good course of business, having had much less trouble in effecting a start there than at any other place visited on my present journey—the people there seeming much more inclined to patronize a traveling agent, than in Indiana. They seemed less inclined to suspect the honesty and motives of a stranger than the Hoosiers, and to realize more readily the value of the articles I was offering for sale.

But my stay there was destined to be of short duration. Just in the midst of my career of prosperity, a letter arrived from my attorneys, informing me that my presence was very urgently and imperatively necessary in Indianapolis, in connection with my suit for a divorce. Of course, it was very unpleasant to leave my present location while business was so flourishing; but the affair at Indianapolis was of paramount importance, and such a summons must not be neglected; and, accordingly, I packed up my things, left my business there in the hands of an agent who had been appointed and fully instructed by me, and hastened homeward by the most direct and expeditious route. Upon reaching Indianapolis, I found, however, that my presence might just as well have been dispensed with as not, had it only been known in time; for, owing to an unexpected decision of the Court, we would be compelled to postpone the case until another term.

My counsel were not to blame for this delay, for it was a matter which they could not foresee, but it was none the less a most bitter disappointment to me, for I had counted upon closing up that affair at the present time, and then I would be free to return to the South, and attend closely to the prosecution of my claim for the restitution of my brother's property. This I did not wish to do so long as affairs were in such a shape that Frank Nelles could claim any part of the property which I might recover; and hence the delay was very annoying to me, beside involving considerable expense, which I was but illy able to afford. But there was no help for it, and nothing for me to do save to go to work again to raise the funds necessary to meet these demands upon my purse.

And these demands had recently been increased by my own action. The reader will remember that Carrie was with a relative of Captain Lake's, in New Orleans, whither he had sent her to be raised and educated. I had not seen her for a long time, and my heart yearned to clasp the little darling to my bosom once more. She was all I had to live for, or to love; and my business had prospered so as to enable me to support her by my own exertions, and, accordingly, I sent for her. The friends with whom she was staying, were very much opposed to her coming, but my claim upon her was stronger than theirs. She wanted to come to "mamma," and they finally yielded, and sent her to me. She arrived in safety, and the fond mother who has been for a long time separated from a dearly-loved child, can imagine the pleasure with which I once more held in my arms the darling little one who, though no relative to me, had still become as dear to me as though of my own flesh and blood.

Besides Carrie, I had another little, helpless being dependent upon me for support. I have already mentioned my intention to adopt a little boy as a playmate for Carrie. Some time had elapsed since that resolution was formed, and I had met with no opportunity to obtain a child whose appearance pleased me. But, visiting one day the county asylum for the poor, I saw just the boy I wanted. He was an orphan, with no friends to care for him; his father had been a brave soldier in defense of his country, in the hour of peril, and had died in the battle of Five Forks, just as final victory was perching upon the National Banner; his mother, a frail, delicate woman, had survived the shock of her husband's violent death but a few weeks, and he was thus left alone in this cold, wide, unfriendly world. He was just about Carrie's age, about five years; while his light, curly hair, deep, earnest, blue eyes, and finely molded features, sufficiently resembled hers to warrant me in calling them brother and sister. I accordingly took him from the asylum, and by order of the Court of Common Pleas of Marion County, formally adopted him as my own child, and presented him to Carrie as her little brother. She had still some recollection of the brothers she had lost, and her little heart was delighted beyond measure at the restoration of one of them to her. They are as happy together as it is possible for children to be, and my heart throbs with all a mother's pride, as I gaze upon my beauties; for though they are really no relation to me, they are as dear to me as they could possibly be, were they of my own flesh and blood.

But, of course, I could not support them in idleness, and I must at once go to work to provide the means for their sustenance and education. My first care was to find a good boarding-school for children, at which I could be certain they would be properly cared for, and receive such attention and education as was necessary and suitable for children of that age.   After some trouble, I found a location which I thought possessed all the requirements which my jealous care of their mental and moral necessities demanded, and arrangements were soon made for their reception by the matron of the establishment.   And it affords me pleasure to say here that it would have been simply impossible that my selection of a location for my darlings could have been more fortunate; for the lady, in whose charge they still remain, combines within herself all the elements necessary to render their stay with her both pleasant and profitable to them.   Of large and extended experience in the management of children; tender and kind, but firm and prudent in her government; she brings to the discharge of the important duties of her position, a Christian consciousness of the weighty responsibilities devolving upon her, and a devout, prayerful determination to discharge those responsibilities in the wisest and most beneficial manner for the interest of the little ones under her care.   Under these circumstances, how could they be otherwise than happy and properly cared for, or how could they be better situated, so long as it is necessary for them to be deprived of a mother's care?   And, indeed, I am not sure but they are better off with Mrs. —— than they would be with me.

Having concluded this arrangement to my satisfaction, I decided to visit northern Indiana, and, perhaps, some parts of Illinois, and canvass for my Masonic history.   I had had sufficient experience in trying to work for two or three publications, or other articles, at one time, and my mind was fully made up never to be guilty of that folly again. So long as I continued to travel and canvass as an agent, my attention should not be divided between a half dozen different objects, and I be thus prevented from doing justice to any of them or to myself.

CHAPTER XXVI.

My present destination was La Porte, Indiana, where I had been informed the Masonic fraternity were quite numerous, and very active, and where I hoped to sell a large number of books. Before starting, however, I called upon William Hacker, Esq., Secretary of the grand lodge of the State, and he very kindly gave me a letter commending the work in very flattering terms, and also gave me letters of introduction to several prominent members of the fraternity there. Armed with these documents, and provided with a policy of insurance against the accidents of travel, I once more committed myself to the tender mercies of the Louisville, New Albany & Chicago Railroad Company, and in due time, without any incidents worthy of especial note, reached the very pleasant town for which I had set out.

Upon reaching La Porte, my first care was to secure a good and suitable boarding-place during my stay there. I was fortunate enough to find a good room, and the best of accommodations, in a house kept Mr. C. D. Church, (lately a lieutenant in the Union army), at the corner of Jackson and Prairie streets, but a short distance from the main business part of the city, and at once made arrangements with the gentlemanly proprietor for remaining there so long as I was in La Porte.

I next called upon Mr. E. G. Hamilton, to whom I had a letter of introduction, and had a long conversation with him about the Masonic fraternity, and the prospects of success there. I found Mr. Hamilton a fine, portly gentleman, rather below the medium hight, somewhat bald, very affable and polite, but with a peculiar nasal twang or whine in his voice, to listen to which tried my risibilities sorely, and tempted me several times to overstep the bounds of the politeness which he was so continually exemplifying before me—not from any want of respect for him, but because his manner was simply amusing to me. No one could be kinder to me than he was, and, from the bottom of my heart, I thank him therefor. Indeed, the fraternity in and about La Porte are all entitled to and receive my heartiest thanks for favors received at their hands.

Mr. Hamilton informed me that there were two lodges in the city, with an aggregate membership of about one hundred and forty; that both lodges were in a flourishing condition, and rapidly increasing in numbers; and that the interest in the welfare of the Order had never before been as high, in La Porte, as at the present time. Through his instrumentality I formed the acquaintance of several Masans of great prominence, and whose virtues and devotion to the craft have already given them high positions in the Masonic world; among whom may be mentioned P. D. G. M. John B. Fravel; Dr. G. M. Dakin, W. M., of Excelsior Lodge; P. G. Winn, W. M., of La Porte Lodge; E. G. McCollum, Esq., R. A. Hews, Esq., and many others whose names it were useless to enumerate. Mr. Hamilton himself is one of the most ardent disciples of Masonry I have ever met, and, though of but little more than two years standing in the Order, has already penetrated deeper into its arena than many a man who has spent a long life in connection with the mystic brotherhood.

He gave me quite a list of names of men who he thought would be likely to subscribe for the work, and I set out upon my labors, meeting, in almost every instance, with the most gratifying success. Very few, indeed, were
23

the Masons in La Porte, whom I asked in vain to purchase
a work which so well portrayed the origin and principles
of their order. They are live Masons there, and everything which tends to elucidate the benefits of their institution, and its claim to the confidence of the world, they
gladly welcome.

Of course, here, as elsewhere, there are exceptions to
this general rule, one of which I must be permitted to
mention. In the office of a friend, who was furnishing me
a more extended list of names than Mr. Hamilton had
done, I, one day, met and was introduced to a Mr. Walker
—"Elder Walker," I think my friend called him. This
prefix, at any rate, he was entitled to, having been, at one
time, engaged in the work of the ministry, though now, I
believe, not laboring in that field. He was a stout, wiry
old man, with white hair, and a complexion of such florid-
ity that, but for his well-known character of sterling morality, and his intense hatred of drunkenness in all its
forms, he might be almost suspected of having, at some
time or other, tampered too much with "the worm of the
still." His portly, rotund person, indicative of good living,
terminated in a pair of pedal extremities of extraordinary
size, which were inclosed in most hideously-squeaking
cowhide boots; while a massive, square head was connected to the upper extremity of the trunk by a short,
thick neck, which looked as though it might safely bid
defiance to the hangman's rope, even if the Elder should
ever be brought to test its qualities—an event which seems
exceedingly improbable. His form was very erect, his
movements quick and nervous, and an air of the most supreme satisfaction, with himself and the rest of the world,
pervaded every feature. He was one of those men who
constantly annoy you by assenting, in the most gracious

manner, to everything you say, and, at the same time, remove all pretext for anger by their ready compliance, and against whom the shafts of argument or sarcasm are as harmless, and glide off as easily, as water poured from a tin dipper upon the well-mailed back of a duck; and, to crown all, he enjoys among his large circle of acquaintances, by whom he is sincerely respected, the reputation of being just the least bit of a "bore."

"There," said my friend, after the ceremony of introduction had been performed, and the requisite bows had been made, "is a subject for your art."

"Y-e-e-s," chimed in *the Elder*, "I am a very proper subject for the machinations of your art. What is it?"

"I am canvassing for 'The General History of Freemasonry in Europe,' and would like to sell you a copy."

"'The General History of Freemasonry!' Well, really, that must be a very fine thing, and a work which ought to be in the hands of every Mason in the country, especially of those who are just beginning to tread the thorny road which leads to the flowery repose of Masonic peace and happiness."

I was quite startled by this somewhat extraordinary poetical display, but my friend seemed to take it as a matter of course, and I returned to the charge.

"The work is highly recommended by prominent Masons in all parts of the country, and, among others, by William Hacker, Grand Secretary of the Grand Lodge of the State."

"It is? Why, it must be a splendid work! Brother Hacker is a good man, and would recommend none but a work of sterling merit to the confidence of the brotherhood, to whose service he has earnestly and consistently devoted the best portion of a long and well-spent life. And he really recommends the book, does he?"

"Yes, sir, I have a letter in his own hand-writing, recommending it in the highest terms."

"I want to know! So you know Brother Hacker? He is a splendid man."

"Yes, sir, I am acquainted with him."

"You are? And he has recommended this work in a letter composed by his own mighty mind, and indited by his own hand?"

"I have said so, sir."

"Yes, yes; I know you have. Have you the letter with you?"

"It is in my trunk, at my boarding-house. I can show it if necessary."

"Yes. Hum. Where do you board?"

"At Mr. Church's."

"What! Lieutenant Church."

"Yes, sir."

"Why! he is a good man. I guess he keeps a good boarding-house, and ministers to the necessities of the weary, hungry, and way-worn traveler in the most approved manner. I never stopped at his house; but have always heard that character ascribed to him, by his patrons and admirers, whose name is legion."

"Yes, he keeps a very good house. But let us talk about the book."

"Certainly. Such a work as that; from the pen, doubtless, of one of the most eminent authors and philologists the world has ever produced, and recommended by a man of such gigantic intellect, such sterling integrity, and such unquestioned devotion to the good of Freemasonry, as Brother William Hacker, Grand Secretary of the Grand Lodge of the State of Indiana, is worthy of being the theme of conversation wherever civilized language prevails, as long as the sun shall roll his ceaseless rounds. Why, Brother ——," turning to my friend, "you ought to purchase a copy of this most invaluable work, and place it among the most cherished volumes of your family library, there to remain, and be read and admired by your children and your children's children, down to the seventieth generation."

"But," said I, laughing in spite of myself, at this rhapsody, "he has already bought a copy, and now I want to sell you one."

"He has! Well, he has done just right. No man, in his situation, can afford to be without it."

"Then, sir, I hope you will take one."

"I must take time to consider of the subject, madam. Men very often get themselves into almost inextricable difficulties by acting from impulse and without proper reflection. But, in the first place, I must premise that my situation and that of my friend here is vastly different. It is unnecessary that I should enlarge upon the points of difference between our respective positions—they are apparent at a glance. But, I will consider of the subject, and advise you of my conclusions."

I saw that it was useless to urge the subject further, and made him no answer, and he soon after withdrew. I was not a little amused, as well as somewhat disgusted, at the result of this interview; but my friend laughed heartily at my discomfiture, saying it was no more than he anticipated; that he was very sure "the Elder" could not be induced to subscribe; and that he had introduced him merely for the purpose of getting a good joke on me. I thanked him for his kindness (?), and promised him I would be even with him some day; and thus the matter ended.

I canvassed in La Porte about a week, and sold some sixty copies of the work there, being the best week's work I had yet done since I became a book agent. I also visited several little towns, throughout the county, and sold quite a number of works there. My trip, thus far, had been very profitable, and I was, in consequence, very much elated in spirits. Surely, at the rate at which I was making money, I should have no difficulty in providing for my two little ones; and they were all I had to care for in the world. If God would mercifully spare my life, and protect me in health and strength, I had no fears but I could raise them comfortably, and in a manner that would render them a credit, not only to me, but to themselves.

But my work in La Porte was done, and it was necessary for me to seek other fields. I very much hated to leave this place, for I had made some warm friends there —friends who will dwell in my memory, and whose kindness will not be forgotten, so long as my life is spared and reason remains an inmate of my soul—but necessity demanded it, and it is an old adage that "necessity knows no law." Accordingly, I procured, from my friends, letters of introduction to several of the prominent Masons of South Bend, and started for that point, where I arrived about seven o'clock in the evening, and retired to rest for the night, without learning much about the town.

The next morning I arose early, and took a walk before breakfast, in order "to spy out the land," and decide upon my chances for success there. At first sight I did not like the appearance of the place much, and was almost tempted to go on without trying to do anything there.

There were scarcely any side-walks in the town, and what there were, were in a sad state of dilapidation; the weather had been rainy for some time, and the streets were in anything but a pleasant condition for pedestrian feats; many of the business houses had an old, tumble-down appearance, and altogether the place was not, at first view, calculated to inspire any great love in the mind of a stranger. But I remembered that I had done very well in places of no more promising appearance than this, and I decided to try to do something; but, at the same time, made up my mind to recommend to the Mayor and Council that they do something to improve the condition of their streets and side-walks, and to suggest, at the same time, that their place would appear much more attractive in the eyes of strangers if this recommendation were complied with.

Having decided to remain and try my fortune here for a short time, I called upon several of the parties to whom I had letters of introduction, delivered my letters, and introduced my work. All seemed much pleased with it, and my success was such as not to cause the least regret that I had decided to remain there. The Order seemed to be in a very healthy, flourishing condition there, and to be composed of men who had its real good at heart, and were more interested in perfecting themselves in a knowledge of its mysteries, than in merely increasing the numbers of its membership. Among such men my success could not be other than most gratifying, and I am happy to record the fact that, in the four days which I spent there, I sold no less than thirty-one copies of my favorite work. Surely, a most auspicious result in a town of such unpromising appearance as, at first view, to almost discourage even me, in spite of my extensive experience.

From South Bend I went to Mishawaka, only four miles further east, and found it a very pleasant place—indeed, to my notion, a more pleasant place than South Bend, though the latter is the larger town, and is the county seat of the county. There seemed to me to be much more life and animation in Mishawaka, and more business done, than in South Bend, considering the size of the two places; but it might be that it was owing in part to the more favorable auspices under which I saw Mishawaka. The weather was magnificent while I was there, and the whole town was clad in its holiday attire, while South Bend was in mud and sorrow when I saw her last.

I canvassed Mishawaka in three days, selling something over a score of books, but, although they had been ordered sometime before, they had not yet come, and, of course, until they arrived, they could not be delivered; so there was nothing for it but to wait with what patience I could command under the circumstances. For a week I remained there idle, and my anxiety to be at work mounted to almost fever heat. But there was no good in fretting. The books would not come any sooner for it, and the only thing in my power was to amuse myself in the best manner possible, and thus pass away the time while waiting. I was boarding in the family of a Mr. Taylor, a very nice, pleasant place, and both Mr. Taylor and his wife were very fond of fishing. They had often invited me to join them in their piscatorial expeditions along the banks of the silvery St. Joseph, but I had as often declined.

But at length time grew so heavy on my hands that, one "bright day in the morning," I decided to accept their oft-repeated invitation, and accompany them. Armed with proper tackle, rods, lines, hooks, bait, etc., and an immense basket, in which to deposit the finny spoils of the deep (river), we wended our way to a pleasant nook, where Mr. Taylor assured us we should find plenty of fish. I could not bait my hook myself, but Mr. Taylor affixed the tempting morsel, while Mrs. Taylor performed the same feat for herself, and we cast in our lines, nothing doubting (at least I did not) that we should soon be blest with as great an abundance of fish as were the Apostles, when, at the command of our Savior, they cast their net upon the right side of the ship. Soon after casting in her line, Mrs. Taylor drew it again to the surface, and, with a flourish and a "whish," landed a fine large sunfish upon the bank just back of where we sat. Again she put in her hook, and again drew it forth, and this time a noble perch was dangling at the end of her line. Again and again was this scene repeated—now sunfish, now perch, now something else—until she had caught five or six fine fellows, and her husband nearly as many more; but I had not had a solitary nibble. I was getting out of all manner of patience, when, suddenly, I felt the short, quick jerk which indicated that a fish was after my bait. Trembling with eager anxiety, I drew it to the surface, when, lo! a gigantic water-dog made his appearance, securely hooked to my line; but how to get him off was the question. It is no trouble for me to eat fish when they are nicely prepared for the table, but the idea of taking hold of a live one—ugh! it makes me shudder even to this day. Several times I tried to muster sufficient courage to accomplish this feat, but each time his flopping and floundering drove me away demoralized, until at last I was fain to give it up. Mr. Taylor then came to my assistance, and removed the monster, baited my hook again, and again I committed my line to the pearly deep. Another season of anxious waiting and watching, another nibble at my line, another sharp pull,

and, this time, I brought out a large catfish. I tried to
take him off, but he looked so much worse than the other,
with his huge goggle eyes, immense mouth, and wicked-
looking horns, that he frightened me more than the other;
and again Mr. Taylor was compelled to come to my assistance. Once more I tried my luck, and, this time, another water-dog was the result of some half hour's patient
watching.

By this time the sun was getting high in the heavens,
and it was time for us to return home; so we proceeded to
enumerate the results of the morning's sport, or rather
labor, for such it was to me. Mr. and Mrs. Taylor had
caught some twenty-three fish, every one of which was fit
for use; while I had succeeded in landing three, not one
of which was of the least possible value for any purpose.
I was not a little disgusted at my luck, or, rather, at my
want of it, and made up my mind that nature never designed me for a fisherman, and that I could succeed much
better as a book agent. As I said before, I can do something in the way of eating fish, when they are properly
prepared and on the table, but this is the only part of a
fisherman's life I am fit for.

But I had already wasted too much time in this place,
and decided to stay here no longer, but would go and canvass Elkhart and Goshen, and then return here and deliver my books. I had ordered books to be sent to Goshen
at the same time that I had ordered those at Mishawaka,
and, doubtless, they would be there by the time I had finished canvassing, and I could then deliver all at once, and
thus close up my business in this part of the country. I,
therefore, packed up my "traps," bade adieu to the kind
friends who had tried so hard to initiate me into the mysteries of the sport of fishing, but with such poor success,

and took the cars for Elkhart, where I arrived in due time without incident.

Upon reaching this place, I went to work with a vigor which was intended to make up for all the time lost by the neglect of my publisher, with whom I was already quite out of patience for his dilatoriness; but my patience was yet to be more sorely tried from this source.

My efforts here were very successful, and in a week no less than forty names of subscribers had been added to my already magnificent list of subscribers for the Masonic history. I felt proud of my week's work, and thought that what had been done was deserving of compliment. Surely the sale of forty copies of a single work, in a little town like Elkhart, was something to be proud of, and I venture the assertion, that not five canvassing agents in the United States can show a better report for the same time and under the same circumstances; but it shows what energy and determination, when properly applied, can accomplish, even under unfavorable circumstances.

From Elkhart I went to Goshen, nothing doubting that I should find my books there, as more than two weeks had now elapsed since they had been ordered; but again I was doomed to disappointment, for, to my inquiry for books, the express agent politely replied, "There is nothing here for Mrs. S. A. Nelles." What could it mean? Surely my orders had been received by the publisher, and why there should be so much want of promptness in filling them, was entirely beyond my comprehension. I would write to Mr. Fessenden, give him a piece of my mind, and learn what he meant by thus keeping me idle through his neglect, and, in the meantime, would canvass Goshen and the surrounding country, and by that time my answer, as well as the books, would most likely arrive. Accordingly

I indited a letter, "short, sharp, and decisive" in its terms, mailed it, and went to work.

For about a week I labored faithfully, and with very fair success, having sold some twenty-eight or twenty-nine copies to the citizens of Goshen. I had called almost daily, during the time, at the express office, and each day, "Still not arrived," had been the answer of the agent to my look of inquiry. I was becoming disheartened, and, to add to my annoyance, was still without any reply to my letter of inquiry, written one week ago. But what could I do? Manifestly nothing more than to wait, with what patience I could command, until such time as his majesty, Mr. George B. Fessenden, should see fit to honor me with his notice once more.

I wrote him another letter, and then went to canvass in the country, for a few days, until he should have time to answer this. I worked energetically among the farmers of that region, and succeeded in selling books enough to pay my expenses and something more, at the end of which time I returned to Goshen, and again presented myself at the Express office. "Nothing has come for you, Miss," said the agent.

I turned away without any reply, almost sick at heart, and bent my steps to the Post-office.

"What name?" said the delivery clerk.

"Mrs. S. A. Nelles."

"Yes, here is one," and he handed me a letter.

It bore the Cincinnati post-mark, and I broke the seal with eager anxiety. It ran thus:

"Mrs. S. A. Nelles—I am sorry to say we are out of the General History of Freemasonry, and will not be able to fill your orders for some time to come. In about two weeks we hope to be able to supply all your calls. Regretting this delay, but hoping it may prove no serious inconvenience to you, I remain, etc.,

GEO. B. FESSENDEN."

Out of books, indeed! No serious inconvenience, forsooth! This letter capped the climax—this was the last feather that broke the camel's back. What business had he to get out of books? He knew I was selling a great many—he knew that I was at work all the time, and that, in the last three months, I had sold over three hundred copies. I reported my sales to him weekly, and he knew, or ought to have known, about how many I would require; and why did he allow his stock to become exhausted? It was easy for him to say he hoped it would put me to no serious inconvenience; and it was a small matter to him that I had to lie idle, or almost so, for weeks at a time, on account of his neglect; but to me it was not a small matter. It was my meat and drink: upon the sales of the book he was "out of," depended my support and that of my two little babes, at Indianapolis; and to me it was a very "serious inconvenience." But I would see that the same thing did not happen again while I worked for him. I would order books for a month or more before I expected to visit a place, and would report that place canvassed, and thus I might possibly get them when I wanted them.

Such were my reflections as I read this letter, but, for the present, I could do nothing. I would have to wait the two weeks any how, and what should I do during that time? I had heard that there was a very superior school for little children, at Springfield, Illinois, and I decided, while waiting Mr. Fessenden's "inconvenience," to go there and see if it was desirable to send my children there, inasmuch as the lady in whose charge they now were, had intimated to me that she might possibly break up her establishment and remove from the city. By the time I could make that journey, his two weeks would likely be up, and then I might hope to have my order filled, and be ablo to supply my subscribers in this part of the country. So it was determined.

CHAPTER XXVII.

In pursuance of the determination mentioned at the close of the last chapter, I settled up my affairs at Goshen, so far as it was possible for me to do; called upon the express agent, and informed him of my intended absence for about two weeks, and requested him to retain in his office any packages coming for me until my return, which he promised to do; took leave of my friends there, and embarked on the cars for La Porte; for it was my intention to stop there a short time, and visit some of my many friends in that city. Arriving there in due time, I found my friends all well, and passed a day or two as pleasantly as I ever did anywhere in my life. I had taken the degrees of the Eastern Star during my stay in Goshen, and as the friend who had introduced me to Elder Walker was very proficient in these degrees, I availed myself of his kindness to become more acquainted with them than I had hitherto been.

And just here I desire to bear my testimony to the value of these degrees, and to express my surprise that they are not more generally worked and understood among the Masonic fraternity and their wives and daughters. Nothing, within my knowledge, will secure that protection and assistance which every wife and daughter of a Mason has a right to demand at the hands of the entire fraternity, so readily and certainly, as a knowledge of these degrees; and certainly there is nothing which brings us, who are debarred by the rules of the Order from full admission to its secrets, into such close fellowship and affiliation, so to speak, with this ancient and honorable Order, as a thorough acquaintance therewith. The only difficulty in the way is the fact, that Master Masons, who are thoroughly posted in the secret work and ritual of the Order, do not, as a general thing, take the pains to acquire a thorough knowledge of these degrees, and that ladies upon whom they have been conferred, do not take sufficient interest in them, from the very fact just cited, to retain enough of them to make them useful. To remedy this evil, I would have every Master Mason, as much required to perfect himself in these degrees, as he is in the three symbolical degrees of the blue lodge, and would have ladies, upon whom they have been conferred, organize lodges, schools of instruction, etc., as do our husbands and brothers, and render themselves as perfect in their mysteries as do Master Masons in the rituals of their institution. In this way the Order of The Eastern Star can be made really and permanently useful, and the beneficient design of its founder be carried out to a full and practical realization.

That the "Eastern Star" lodges here alluded to, can be made really useful and beneficial, as well as permanent, is proven by the fact that they are already in successful operation in some parts of the United States, though by no means generally organized throughout the land. There is one at Goshen, one at New Albany, and probably in other parts of the State, and also in the State of Michigan, and probably other States of the Union. Let the number of these organizations be extended until they become as universally known and recognized as are Masonic Lodges, and then woman will really derive some benefit from that which was invented by an eminent and worthy brother for her sole good. But to return to myself and my visit.

Among other things, I had a good, hearty laugh with my friend about my attempt to "canvass" Elder Walker. I was still a little sore over the matter, and could hardly believe the assertion of my friend, that the "Elder" had not put on a little extra style for the occasion, and that this was his natural style of conversation whenever he wanted to be very impressive; but he insisted so strongly that this was the case that I was forced to yield my own opinions, though insisting that it was certainly a very extraordinary style, and the "Elder" a very remarkable man. Doubtless he got into this high-flown style while laboring in the pulpit, and has seen no particular reason for dropping it. I remained in LaPorte some two or three days, visited all my friends, and then pursued my journey to the capitol of Illinois.

I did not visit Springfield for the purpose of canvassing for the Masonic history, it being beyond my jurisdiction, but I was still nominally agent for one or two other works which I had a right to sell in that field, and I took them along, thinking I might, perhaps, sell enough to pay my expenses there and back. I also took my specimen copy of the Masonic history, merely because it was in my trunk, and I did not care to leave it, lest it should be lost.

Upon arriving in Springfield I learned that there was no agent in that territory for the Masonic history, and concluded that, as I had a sort of "roving commission," authorizing me to sell anywhere except in territory occupied by other agents, I would try that a while, and, accordingly, went to work for it. I also offered for sale, at the same time, the other publications brought with me, and for nearly a week I did a very good business, taking something over fifty names for the various works. I then made arrangements with a gentleman there, to deliver the books

24

when they should be sent to him, and collect the pay for them, allowing him to retain a certain per cent. for his trouble. I ordered the books sent to me at La Porte, and intended shipping them from there to him myself. I had an object in this which the reader will not fail to perceive.

While pursuing my labors, I had not neglected the object which originally induced me to come to Springfield, and my inquiries had almost satisfied me that, although the school there was a very good one, still nothing would be gained by sending my children there, especially so long as the present arrangement could be maintained at Indianapolis. The reader will bear in mind, that there was no positive certainty that the school there would be discontinued at the present, and even should it be, I thought I knew of places where, without intending any disparagement to the institution at Springfield, my little ones could be sent with much more satisfaction to me than there. Still, I had come to investigate the merits of the institution, and would not do it injustice, or depart without making that investigation as thorough as my abilities and circumstances would admit.

I therefore visited the establishment, and had a long interview with the lady who officiates as principal. She was a very lady-like and matronly personage, somewhat past the middle age, and evidently desirous of doing justice to the mental, moral, and physical qualities of the little ones intrusted to her care. The school was well and pleasantly located, the children seemed to enjoy themselves very well, and my impressions of the school, from this examination, were just the same as those formed from my inquiries—that while there was no doubt of its genuine merit, still there were places where my little ones could be established more to my satisfaction than there. Others might differ with me, might be better qualified to judge than myself—it is the right and the duty of every one having the care of children, to decide these matters for themselves—but I could not see this school in a light which would induce me to give it the preference over several others within my knowledge.

My work in Springfield was done, and still I was not ready to leave. In and about Springfield are several places which the events of the last six years have rendered of historic value to every American whose heart thrills with true devotion to his country, and reveres all that is great and good in her history, and I could not leave the place without visiting the tomb, and the former home, of Abraham Lincoln. Securing the companionship of a friend, who was well acquainted with the locality, we set out the next day, while the morning was yet in its infancy, and the air was cool and fresh, for the cemetery where lie the mortal remains of a man who occupies a place in the great American heart second to none of the elevated and noble characters who have adorned the pages of her history.

The cemetery at Springfield is, I think, the finest, in its arrangement and ornamentation, I ever saw. Other cities and other communities have taken pains to ornament and render attractive the last resting-places of their loved and honored dead, but to Springfield must be awarded the palm of having more nearly attained perfection, in this respect, than any other place within my knowledge. The smooth, green, and closely-shaven lawn, cut hither and thither with finely graveled walks; the regular and beautiful arrangement of lots and burial places; the pleasant arbors, scattered here and there, throughout

the grounds, give the place more the appearance of a
finely-arranged garden than of a charnel-house; while the
splendid firs and other evergreens, which rise on every
hand, and through which are peeping forth, in every direction, tall and stately obelisks, more simple monuments
and plain white marble slabs, are suggestive of a sense of
coolness and peace, which at once brings to the mind, in
all their loveliness and sweetness and power, those beautiful lines in which Montgomery has described the calm
rest of the grave.   And as we passed within the gate, and
I stood enchanted with the beauties of the scene before
me, I found myself almost unconsciously repeating:

> "There is a calm for those who weep,
> A rest for weary pilgrims found,
> They softly lie and sweetly sleep
> Low in the ground."

I was completely lost in admiration, and, for a time,
could do nothing but stand and gaze upon the beauties of
the scene; but we passed onward, and at last stood by the
tomb of the noble man, who, with a singular unselfishness,
and the most noble devotion to the good of his country,
had stood unmoved at the helm of the ship of state, and
by his own mighty genius had guided her safely through
the storm which threatened to ingulf her, and had finally,
when she was just entering the harbor of peace and everlasting security, and when he could see the approaching
end of all his toils and labors, fallen by the hand of an
assassin, whose name and memory will be execrated by
every lover of liberty and free government down to the
latest fragment of recorded time.

Ah! what emotions thrilled my soul, as I stood by the
tomb of this man, who, born in the humblest walks of life,
and in his youth devoted to the most menial avocati ns,

had, by the force of his own unaided genius, and the native goodness of his character, risen to the highest position in the gift of a proud and powerful people; and had achieved for himself a crown of glory, by the side of which the brightest and most costly diadem of an European monarch sinks into the most utter insignificance. The mighty struggle, through which the nation had just passed, and the burdens of which she was still bearing, from the firing of the first hostile gun at the unarmed steamer Star of the West, to the last closing drama in the wilderness of Georgia, passed in review before my mind's eye, as I stood, with bowed head and reverent demeanor, beside the tomb of him who, under Heaven, had directed the armies of the Union to final victory. In fancy's eye, I beheld the the marshaling of squadrons, and the setting in array of hostile forces; I heard the clang of arms, the trampling of armed hosts, the roar of cannon, and the crash of musketry; I witnessed the ever-varying and shifting scenes of the battle-field, as victory now hung in the balance, now inclined to this side, now to that; I beheld the gory aspect of the field of conflict when the strife was ended, and heard the low moans of the wounded and the dying, as the thirsty earth eagerly drank up the life-blood which was fast oozing from their contracting veins; I saw a mighty procession of mangled, armless, legless men closely filing by, and exhibiting their wounds as claims to the memory and gratitude of the country which their valor and their sacrifices had helped to preserve; I looked upon a long line of gaunt, haggard forms, clad in tatters, and with reason half dethroned by the horrors of Andersonville, and Salisbury, and Belle Isle, while closely following in their train, came half a million of spectral phantom figures, who had bidden adieu to home and friends, and gone forth to lay down their lives in this unnatural, unholy, and need-less war; and among this last procession I recognized the tall and stately form of an only and dearly-loved brother; and, as I reflected that he had fallen, not in defense of his country, but in the mistaken and misguided effort to destroy it, my heart throbbed with anguish, and I turned away my head, and wept in the bitterness of sorrow.

But I looked yet again, and, lo! the brighter side of the picture appeared. I beheld the nations of the earth in mighty conclave assembled, and among them towered one tall and stately, upon whose escutcheon no blot was to be seen, whose banner gleamed in all parts of the habitable globe, whose government, founded upon the rock of eternal truth and justice, bade defiance to the assaults of the mad waves of passion and prejudice; I listened to the glad songs of four millions of beings elevated by this struggle from the condition of mere chattels to the glad estate of men and women; I saw the shackles stricken from their limbs, and cast into the sea which is bottomless, and whence they shall never be resurrected; I witnessed the eyes of the struggling poor among every kindred, nation, tongue, and people under the whole heaven turned toward our own beloved land, as the beacon of all their hopes, and the aim of all their desires, and I said within myself, "Surely this result is well worth all it cost to obtain it."

I looked yet again, and the future was unfolded, as a scroll, to my view; and I saw the starry banner—emblem of our nation's sovereignty—waving, in calm and peaceful triumph, over the whole of the habitable globe. I beheld liberty, free government, law, and order everywhere prevailing, and dispensing their rich blessings to the entire human race; I heard the rejoicings of countless millions, because of their release from the bondage and oppression which had so long bowed them to the very dust; I witnessed the sword beaten into the plowshare, and the spear into the pruning hook, the nations of earth refusing to learn war any more, and the whole human family devoting themselves to the arts of peace; I saw love, and fellowship, and good will, prevailing among all ranks and classes of mankind, and every man seeking his neighbor's welfare before his own; and I said, "Surely this man was an instrument in the hand of God, and this Rebellion one of His appointed means to work out the high and noble destiny which He has appointed for the children of men "—and the vision was gone.

I bowed my head in reverent devotion beside this shrine of the pilgrimage of a nation, plucked a rose from a vine planted there by the hand of affection, turned away with my friend, and, casting one last, long, lingering glance at the magnificent beauties of this silent house of the dead, we left the cemetery, and returned to the city, where we had still another pilgrimage to make—another visit to pay.

Our destination was now the house which had been the home of Mr. Lincoln before he had been called by the voice of the nation to assume the mighty responsibilities which had eventuated in his death; and thither, without delay, we bent our steps. It is a large, old-fashioned, two-story structure of wood; and its situation bears testimony to the true and correct taste of him who had formerly occupied it.

We found the house in charge of a kind, elderly lady, by the name of Mrs. ——, who, as soon as we expressed our desire to visit the house and grounds, kindly offered to accompany us on our tour of exploration. She first took us to the family sitting-room, where Mr. Lincoln used to unbend from the cares of the world, and, in the bosom of his family, showed himself the kind husband and father, the tender-hearted man of affectionate feeling, the faithful monitor and profound instructor which he really was. It is in the bosom of his family alone, in the quiet of the home circle, whence all deception is banished, and where trust and confidence alone abound, that man can throw off, entirely, the mask which contact with the world compels him to wear, and appear, in truth, himself; and Mr. Lincoln is said never to have appeared to more advantage than in those moments of ease and happy confidence. And the affectionate veneration, amounting almost to idolatry, in which his memory is held by all who ever had an opportunity of enjoying these seasons with him, prove how fully he was qualified to act his part there.

We next visited the large old-fashioned parlor, and stood in the room where Mr. Lincoln had received his friends in the pleasant moments of conviviality; where he had entertained and amused his guests with his quaint humor, solid sense, and inexhaustible fund of anecdote, and, where it was said to be impossible for any one to spend an hour in his society without going away sensibly improved and made happier. In the social circle he was conspicuous. His fine conversational powers, his genial humor—which had not the least tinge of unkindness or sarcasm, except when called forth by some covert or direct attack upon himself, or upon some of his ideas of right, when he could make it act like a two-edged sword, and invariably turned the laugh against his antagonist—and his well-known goodness of heart, made him a universal favorite in society, and the center of every circle, and gave him a power and an influence, in community, which is seldom equaled, and which was always exercised for good.

From the parlor, we went to the room which had been used by Mr. Lincoln as his library, and where, by constant study and patient reflection, he had trained his naturally great mind to habits of discernment and patient steadiness under trial, which so admirably fitted him for the high and mighty destiny which he was to fulfill—that of being the chosen leader of a mighty nation in a dreadful struggle, involving its very life, and the issue of which was, for a time, at least, doubtful, but which, under the direction of Divine Providence, had at last reached such a glorious termination.

But why particularize further? Suffice it to say, that we visited every room in the house, and that each recalled some pleasing recollection of the great and good man who had once inhabited it, but who now, by the instrumentality of a murderer, slept the sleep which shall know no waking, until the last great day when the dead of all nations shall be gathered together, and the murderer and his victim shall meet before the Eternal Throne, to receive the reward of their deeds in this life.

We then went to the garden, and our kind hostess gathered me a bouquet of flowers which had been planted and cultivated by the hands of Mrs. Lincoln, and which were, from this association, more precious to me than any gift of jewels could possibly be. They have long since faded and withered, but still I keep them, and shall until they molder into their original dust.

With heartfelt thanks for her kindness, for she steadily refused any other compensation, we bade our kind entertainer farewell, and I returned with my friend to her

home, musing upon the end of all human greatness, which
I had that day seen exemplified by so striking an illustration.   Abraham Lincoln had occupied the most exalted
station which any man can attain in this world; he had
achieved for himself a reputation second to none of the
illustrious personages who have adorned and illuminated
the pages of the world's history; a nation loved and revered his name; an entire race hailed him as their de-
liverer and benefactor; but all this could not shield him
from the assassin's hand, and he now slept in the silent
tomb—honored, it is true, by all mankind, but alike un-
mindful of a nation's reverence and honor, the tears of
mourning friends, the blessings of those whom he had delivered from bondage, or the regrets of the world.

The next day I left Springfield and returned to La
Porte, where I found awaiting me the books ordered there
for my subscribers in the place just left.   Of course, they
were at once shipped to my agent there, and, it may be
remarked here, that they reached him in safety, were
promptly delivered, and the proceeds as promptly and
faithfully accounted for; for which he is hereby tendered
my warmest thanks.   I remained a day or two in La
Porte, visiting my friends and transacting some business
relative to matters aside from my agency; then went to
Mishawaka, where my books had already arrived, and
supplied all my subscribers; did the same at Elkhart and
Goshen, and the surrounding country, and my work in
northern Indiana was ended, for the present, at least.   In
all probability, however, I shall revisit that locality at
some future period; for my heart holds a sincere affection
for it, and some of my most cherished friends reside there.

But I had been a long time absent from my little
adopted darlings, and was naturally getting impatient to

clasp them once more to my bosom, gaze upon their beautiful features, all beaming with affection and love for me; and to witness the improvement and development which they had made since my departure. Accordingly, my course was turned thitherward, and in due time I arrived at my home in the capital city of Indiana. I found my darlings well and happy, under the care of their kind instructress, and was proud and happy to note the manifest improvement in each, which had resulted from her judicious and faithful labors. They, on their part, were as glad to see me as I was to see them, and though it is possible the world contained at that time three happier beings than we were, I must be allowed to say that I regard it exceedingly improbable.

———

CONCLUSION.

LET the reader imagine that some time has elapsed since the close of the last chapter, and has brought with it corresponding changes in my situation. I no longer reside in Indianapolis, nor do I pursue the avocation of a book agent. I have abandoned it, not from choice, for I still, at times, long for the pleasant scenes and incidents which marked the days of my canvassing, and which, in spite of some unpleasant events, invested it with a charm which can never fade from my memory; but because it was no longer necessary for me to pursue it, and I felt that duty to my adopted children demanded that I should cease from my wanderings, and devote my time and attention to their care and education; and if the reader will call at a pleasant mansion in the midst of a beautiful grove, two and a half miles from the city of Lexington, Kentucky, he will

there find Annie Nelles, happy in the society of her two
children, Carrie and Willie, both of whom have steadily
improved in beauty and intelligence.

You may inquire why I selected this place for my home;
and my answer is, simply because it more nearly resem-
bles the home of my childhood than any other place within
my knowledge. The house stands upon the same gentle
elevation, and is surrounded by the same lovely grove;
while in the rear a lovely spring bubbles up from the
ground, and lends the same air of delicious coolness to the
appearance of the whole. My old servant, Caroline, together with her husband and family, occupy a house on '
the farm, and, under his careful and thrifty tillage, mine
is the model farm of the surrounding country.

But whence came the means necessary to purchase this
beautiful home? A portion of it I earned at my chosen
avocation, and the balance I realized from the sale of some
of my property in Georgia, my application for the restitution of which was, after some delay, granted by the general government, and my independence and comfort for
life was thus secured.

My divorce was granted by the court in Indianapolis,
and, from that time to this, I have had no communication
of any kind with Frank Nelles, nor do I know where he
is, or, indeed, whether he is living or dead. For some
time I feared he would, upon learning of my pecuniary
succeses, seek me out and annoy me with entreaties to
resume the relation which I once bore to him—he is sufficiently mercenary and selfish to do this—but all fears of
this kind have ceased, and I now entertain no apprehensions of any trouble or annoyance from him. I shall
never marry again; but will devote all my time and energies to the care and cultivation of the two adopted dar-

lings who are the pride and joy of my heart; and, if God wills that they shall be spared to me, and go on in the course they are already pursuing, I shall find in their society ample recompense for all the toils and sorrows I have endured in the past.

That I am happy in my present situation, it is needless to say. My life has abounded in sorrow and misery; it has been a stormy and tempestuous sea; of almost every species of wretchedness I have endured my full share, but through the goodness and mercy of Him who overruleth all things, my lot of bitterness and woe has been turned into joy and gladness. Through His care and protecting kindness I have surmounted all my troubles, and have at last gained the haven of peace and earthly happiness, and my heart daily and hourly goes out in praise and thanksgiving toward Him for all his care and watchfulness over me.

A word or two in relation to certain characters who have appeared in this history, and I take my leave of you.

Long after my final separation from Eugene Giles Mason, I learned that the child who is so dear to my heart, and whom I have taught to call me by the name of "mother"—my own little Carrie—was the child of him whom I then supposed to be my husband, by the only daughter of a wealthy Georgia planter. Her mother died in giving her birth, and was thus spared the long life of shame and sorrow which would otherwise have been her portion. It was Mason himself who brought her to the door in the basket on that night of lonely watching. He had resorted to this means to conceal from me the knowledge of his crime, as well against morality as against myself, and, after ringing the door-bell, had concealed himself in the shrubbery until Silvie took the basket within the door, when he sneaked away until it was time for him to come home. It matters not how I learned these facts —their authenticity is entirely unquestionable—and this was my Carrie's birth.

As for Mason himself, his life was wicked and his death was sudden and violent. He was descending the Mississippi river in a steamboat, and having engaged in a violent altercation with a fellow-passenger, he was suddenly struck overboard, and, in spite of the utmost efforts to save him, he was finally drowned, and his lifeless body was not recovered for some days. In the confusion attending his disappearance, his murderer leaped overboard, swam ashore, and finally made his escape. And so died Eugene Giles Mason, a man whose talents and business qualifications, if properly directed and controlled by virtuous and upright sentiments, would have rendered him an ornament to any society, but who, by his moral deformity, had rendered himself only a curse to the world and to humanity. And thus he was hurried into the presence of his Maker, unwarned and unannounced, with all of his sins upon his head unexpiated and unrepented of. May we indulge the hope that He who is all goodness and kindness, and who wills that none of His creatures shall perish, judged his soul, not in anger, but in mercy and tenderness. His body lies buried in a lonely neglected and unknown grave, on the bank of the Mississippi river, but a short distance from the city of Memphis.

And now, dear reader, my task is ended, and it only remains for us to part, perhaps forever, perhaps not. Whether the public will ever hear from me again or not, is not now for me to say, and depends upon future events entirely— perhaps somewhat upon the manner in which this first effort shall be received by a descriminating, but generous public. Should life and health and strength be spared me, and my children grow up to maturity, as I fondly hope and anticipate they will, and should the world judge kindly of this very imperfect attempt to relate some of the principal events of my life, I may, perhaps, at some time in the future, again claim its attention.

I have already mentioned the motives which have induced me to unvail the sorrowful past, and expose to the public gaze the errors and imperfections of my past life, as well as the wrongs and sorrows which I have endured: that it was done from a sense of duty alone, and in the hope that it might serve as a warning to others to avoid the rock on which I made shipwreck of my own happiness and peace of mind; and I have only to add, that I have constantly endeavored to discharge that duty in the same sense, and with the same motives, which first prompted me to undertake it. If, by exposing the secrets of my life, I shall have added, in the most trifling degree, to the motives which exist for pursuing the right and avoiding the wrong, the object which prompted me to undertake the publication of this work will have been accomplished, and I shall be amply repaid for all the labor expended upon it.

Finally, dear reader, thanking you for the kind attention which has induced you to accompany me thus far, and repeating my prayer, that you will judge leniently of the many faults and imperfections with which this work abounds, I bid you a kind and affectionate farewell.

TO FRANK C. NELLES.

SELECTED AND ADDRESSED BY ANNIE NELLES.

" Be it so ; we part forever ;
  Let the past as nothing be—
If I had not loved thee, never
  Hadst thou been thus dear to me.

" Had I not loved thee and been slighted,
  That I better could have borne—
Love is quelled when unrequited,
  By the rising pulse of scorn.

" Pride may cool what passion heated,
  Time may tame the wayward will,
But the heart in friendship cheated,
  Throbs with woe's most mad'ning thrill.

" Oh ! there is a silent sorrow
  Which can find no vent in speech—
Which disdains relief to borrow
  From the hights that song can reach.

" Like the clankless chain enthralling—
  Like the sleepless dreams that mock—
Like the frigid ice-drops falling
  From the surf-surrounded rock ;

" Such the cold and sickening feeling,
  Thou hast caused this heart to know—
Stabbed the deeper by concealing
  From the world its bitter woe.

" Once it fondly, proudly deemed thee
  All that fancy's self could paint—
Once it honored and esteemed thee
  As its idol and its saint.

" More thou wert to me than mortal,
  Not as man I looked on thee—
Then, why, like all the rest deceive me ;
  Why heap man's worst curse on me ?

" Wert thou but a friend assuming
　　Friendship's smile and husband's art,
And, in borrowed beauty blooming,
　　Trifling with a trusting heart?

" By that eye which once could glisten
　　With appealing glance to me—
By that ear which once could listen
　　To each tale I told to thee;

" By that lip its smile bestowing,
　　Which could soften sorrow's gush—
By that cheek, once brightly glowing
　　With pure friendship's well-feigned blush—

" By all those charms united,
　　Thou hast wrought thy wanton will,
And, without compunction, blighted
　　What thou would'st not kindly kill.

" Yet I curse thee not in sadness—
　　Still, I feel how dear thou wert—
Oh! I could not, e'en in madness,
　　Doom thee to thy just desert.

" Live, and when my life is over,
　　Should thine be lengthened long,
Thou may'st then, too late, discover
　　By thy feelings, all my wrong.

" Ere that hour, false one—hear me—
　　Thou shalt feel what I do now,
While my spirit, hovering near thee,
　　Still recalls thy broken vow.

" But 't is useless to upbraid thee
　　With thy past or present state—
What thou wert, my fancy made thee—
　　What thou art, I know too late."

THE END.

25